THE DEAD GATE

J.J. Eliyas

THE DEAD GATE

Prologue

"And your findings?" asked the Preceptor from the pulpit. He was a severe man in robes of creme and gold thread.

The acolyte looked to his master and waited deferentially for him to respond. It would not be proper to speak out of turn to the Preceptor. There were protocols here that even someone with his background could not transgress.

The priest cleared his throat and nervous sweat welled on his balding pate. The Assembly of Inquiry was quiet, several hundred waiting to hear what evidence the two had found.

"It appears that we were mistaken, young Adon and I," the priest said tentatively. Adon shot him a startled glance but kept his mouth shut.

"The acolytes in question, all three, appear to have been decapitated as a result of the cave in. It was an accident."

"Untrue!" Adon blurted out, his green eyes darting to the Preceptor. A murmur began to spread through the assembly.

"What is this?" the Preceptor asked in a gravel-filled voice. He lowered his gaze to Adon.

"It is not your place, Adon," his master warned, but it was half-hearted.

"That is not what we found. A falling pillar does not decapitate three acolytes. It does not line up their bodies, face down and naked, or place their heads, sans eyes, upon the back of a different body. Disasters do not treat corpses this way!"

The Preceptor frowned grimly as the Assembly erupted in dismay, several acolytes filtered in from the alcove to listen in and the Preceptor of the Temple of Tarn had to strike the podium with his mace to get order.

"Elaborate," he said sonorously.

"These three were from Ord. They came after it fell, fleeing what happened there. We never thought they were suspect but when we questioned their fellows, little was known about them. They kept to themselves.

"How does that affect anything?" came one shout from the assembly. "After all they went through in Ord."

"In and of itself it does not," Adon retorted. "In Ord, Myella and Duran corrupted the Temple, and brought forth the minions of Oran, leaving a dead city, much like Narn-toc. Here we found the beginning of similar necromancing. The remnants of what they were doing were left in the catacombs.

"There is blood not theirs, and a strange black fluid. It lies near dark runes burned in the wall. And there is a sense of deep darkness there, I cannot fathom. It is foul and corrupt."

"My young Acolyte has a vivid imagination," the priest stammered. He himself had not felt the darkness his acolyte talked of, and it galled him as much as it frightened him that he was not as adept in the Arts as his pupil. "Workers who found the bodies may have placed them such. And the runes could easily predate this Temple."

A murmur of assent rumbled through the Assembly.

"Are you all blind?" asked Adon in frustration. "Before you is evidence of Oran's involvement.

They were trying to open a *Gate*, or did. I pray to Tarn they did not succeed.

"We all have seen the signs of Power in the Dead City, faintly perceived through the *aether*. The Cult of Oran did gain acceptance in the courts of the Conclaveum, and I suspect among these three from Ord, as well."

A silence fell over the hall, deathly still. The only sound was that of rain pattering on the crystal dome above them. Adon plowed on.

"We turn a blind eye because we believe we are infallible but we can no longer deny the truth. The runes were of a form used by Iss. The three were meant as sacrifice and the placement of the heads to thwart Salvation."

"Supposition!" his mentor countered, frowning. It was interjected, clearly, to break his junior's stride. Adon looked at him in wonder, not comprehending why the man would want so desperately to hide what was clearly the truth.

"Are you all fools?!" Adon shouted and leveled a pointed finger at the assembly. The group as a whole suddenly erupted in angry argument and protest. Gesticulating and red-faced, the crowd was obviously incensed at his words. Adon shook his head in bafflement, finally turning toward the dais as the low voice of the Preceptor commanded his attention.

"Silence," he said softly. Then louder: "SILENCE!"

The cacophony of the assembly died down to hurried whispers, echoing through the vaulted space.

7

"I have heard enough," the Preceptor stood and smoothed his robe. He clasped his hands behind his back and looked toward the crystal dome of the temple. Rain now drummed upon the interlaced panes and covered the restless voices with its soft susurration. A peal of thunder broke his momentary pause and he surveyed the assembly, a grim smile upon his face.

"You see the danger don't you?" He started, and Adon felt a momentary relief that was soon dispelled. "I agree that Oran is involved here... insofar as he can create flights of fancy in a young mind."

Adon was about to retort but the Preceptor held up a silencing hand. "No, Adon. You have gone too far. Your mentor should have reined you in long ago. You forget your place: it is no longer of the Clave, but of the Temple. You know very little of these things, and this knowledge only comes with time. Perhaps in ten or so years you will see the folly of your ways --"

"Folly! How can you speak of folly, when you yourself see not the peril? The Temple itself is in jeopardy and you, in your blindness, do not see these signs." Adon looked imploringly into the crowd of the assembled, but they all stared blankly, some in shock, some waiting for further confrontation like spectators at theatre.

The Preceptor shook his head sadly. He looked to the priests and acolytes and then skyward to the dome as lightening flashed above. "I pray to Tarn that wisdom will fall upon you. I --"

A sudden clap of thunder exploded so loudly above them that it drowned out the rest of his words. As the booming echoes faded, there was a resounding pop and a sharp crack. All eyes turned upward to the crystalline dome. The air was thick with ozone and suddenly a dark fissure appeared in the dome, spreading quickly as rain pelted down on it, and then through it. Instinctively, Adon backed away from the center of the room, toward the entrance in the rear of the chamber. A few acolytes did the same, but the majority of the assemblage stared upward, as if frozen in mindless anticipation. It was though they were in a state of rapture; even Adon's eyes seemed riveted above. The Preceptor's quizzical gaze locked on the dome.

Adon shook his head to clear it. It was if some spell had tried to take hold of him, clouding his mind. He quickly motioned the acolytes out through the doors. He looked over his shoulder into the forum just as a tinkling cacophony of sound shattered the air behind him.

Sword-sized shards of broken crystal rained down upon the upward-gazing assembly. Adon could only stare in shock as the shrapnel speared down, impaling the majority of those standing motionless below. The room filled with a fine red mist of arterial blood, returning the hapless survivors to their senses. They cried out in despair, but soon their voices were overwhelmed by a hellish screeching that rose in pitch until Adon doubled over in agony. He felt a tugging on his arm as one of the acolytes sought to pull him further out of the forum, and it took all the strength he could muster to struggle the few feet over the threshold and not vomit. He began to close the doors behind him when he saw *the creature* descend on leathery

9

wing in a coalescence of malignancy; it drifted down to where the Preceptor stood frozen amid the slowly-settling bloody mist.

Adon, watched in horror as the creature of Oran descended into the Sanctuary in front of the preceptor. Hellish Frost of Oran emanated outward, the mist of blood freezing and falling like garnet snow, then was buried by a white rime that enveloped everything. As he closed the door and ran to escape with the other acolytes, the slaughter began in earnest.

They ran, their breath misting in the newly entered cold. Adon led them down the winding stair and into a side chamber; he knew of only one possible way to escape. At the end of the hallway there was a small door that led to the back of the winery; behind the large casks of wine.

The creature's bestial scream howled through the catacombs of the Sequestery. Darkness engulfed them, as they felt their way past storage casks. That noise of scraping and oblivion, the sound of the water crackling into ice followed them. Adon shuddered; he knew there was an even chance that he led the four novices to their deaths as much as away.

He scraped his head on the low ceiling, sweat chilled by the cool dryness of the chamber. There was a grate here, rusted and loose from the chamber wall. He grabbed the novices one by one and shoved them toward it. Steel scraped on stone as they wrenched the grate from its rotting bolts, and there was a dull ring of metal as it fell to the floor. The sound of slithering and scales and gnashing of bones grew louder in the distance, but at last, the fourth novice was through, and Adon soon followed.

Adon knew the peril they were in, not just for their lives, but for their immortal souls. Now he prayed silently to Tarn as he pulled himself through the duct and along the mold-encrusted stones. He heard the shallow breathing ahead of him and knew that his charges were very close to panic. Still, in low tones, he urged them on. Somewhere behind, the sound of pursuit by what could only be a *Deathwing* had ceased. He shook his head and felt the sweat fall again from his skin. He pushed hard to keep the dark thoughts at bay, especially images of the winged death in the Temple and the Preceptor eviscerated, or worse, in the Sanctuary.

He had warned them, he had warned them. He reflected, sadly, that even in the end the Preceptor had been unbelieving, even as the *Deathwing* had sundered the man's flesh. *Not so holy as to stop a Daemon* came the bitter thought, *and your much-vaunted "years" gave you no wisdom to foresee this*. Adon's luck, or was it Tarn's gift, had been with him long enough to allow him escape from the massacre. And here they were, crawling through the tunnels beneath the winery.

Ahead, the novices had stopped and he saw a faint glow of red. *What was this?* He now could make out the faces of the four. Marella, she was the first. Then Jiyn, gods but he looked scared in the crimson light. Tabit and Frey stood silently shivering, they were the youngest, just boys really.

Adon squeezed ahead of them and looked out through the grate, feeling Marella's fear as he pressed against her. She touched his hand a

11

moment, seeking comfort, and he turned his green eyes to her, somehow trying to convey a bit of strength. She smiled weakly and he was glad for that. Even through the dirt and sweat, she was a beautiful woman, and her attempt at bravery gave him a moment's courage. He looked through the grate and up at the Temple. They were at the tunnel's end, just outside the courtyard of the Sequestery.

He shoved hard at the grate and it came loose, even more easily than the other one had. Carefully he lowered it to the earth, and as he was about to squeeze through to the ground he heard Tabit and Frey scream. He looked down sharply, urging the *aether* to enhance his vision. He saw a snakelike tentacle wrap around the boys; then just as quickly they were pulled from his Vision.

"*Daemon!*" he hissed. Jiyn's scream fell short, strangled in mid-cry. Adon flung himself out of the tunnel, pulling Marella through as something, *it*, grabbed her ankles. He pulled her arms, anchoring his feet against the wall. Marella gasped in pain, her face turning red with the effort. Somewhere in the distance, Adon heard the rustling wings.

His muscles strained and he gasped; the air was breathtakingly cold and heavy with the fetid stench of Oran. He saw the skin on Marella's calves turn white. He looked into her eyes and saw a look of profound loss...and then she let go.

"No!" he shouted as she was pulled from his sight, and a low rumble of laughter more evil than he could imagine threatened to edge out all sanity. For a moment, he too was frozen, then he ran, blindly for a time, somehow managing to free

12

himself at last from the Sequestery grounds and from what had become of Tarn Hold.

He ran, and a dark mocking cry followed him.

Chapter 1

Tom Smiling Wolf scrambled over some disintegrating rock, not wanting to get too close to the edge of the path. It was a long nasty fall to his left.

The horses were far behind in a hidden arroyo, and he led his small group on a narrow path above the main road - if you could call it that - that led to the citadel of Helm and the Great Wall. He paused on the rock outcropping looking over his shoulder; he could not help but have that feeling of being watched. Creeping over a rock shelf, he looked north and there it was: the Great Wall. It loomed in the distance, rising nearly to the clouds. Mist now cloaked the base of the edifice along the river hiding most of Helm.

He pushed his hair out of his eyes, his lithe corded frame pressed low to minimize his silhouette. Light drenched everything red, like some monochromatic painting of the old West, yet somehow the Wall was untouched by the bloody tint. It stood as a black gash stretching from horizon to horizon, unsettling him to his very core.

Even though evening was well upon them, they did not dare light a fire or torch. Not here, not anywhere, at least until they were well into the Plains of Straw, about two days on foot. Even then, they risked exposure.

He had come to the Wall with three of Torec's men, crossing the Plains from Paravel, all within two weeks. Getting close to the Wall was not the problem; they had made their way easily through the narrow gorge that was the only pass to the south from the city of Helm. The large column of soldiers was marching south; they had paralleled the road to avoid detection. Where were they going? He was not privy to that information. Why were they going? Frowning cynically, he knew that Myella was behind this sudden movement of the troops. Soldiers in the livery of the Temple of Oran led the column of the Black Guard of the Wall. After watching the column of troops pass by, he and Torec's men had retreated away from the gorge and now camped on the approach to the long curve of the bridge that spanned the river. Two stout towers stood on the south side of the wide span; there would be no sneaking over the causeway without coming under the scrutiny of the military contingent that protected it. There would be no fording the river either; here it rushed a deep, turbulent green.

He eyed The Great Wall, still a good mile away despite its seeming nearness, trying to make sense of the thing, for it surely was not man-made. Tom had never seen anything like it; its base cut with striations of granite, but above the flood line, the wall went from dark gray to black. Within its wet surface, were embedded huge, fossilized bones, grotesquely twisted together as if ready to spring out in some horrific attack. In the dreary early evening light, the surface had taken on a fine, wet sheen, as if the fluid seeped from its core. To the west and almost out of vision, the gloom the Wall finally merged with the tall cliffs that eventually became the Doran Range.

Before them was the only point of entrance to the Conclaveum west of Qwen. Here the wall split open, nearly a thousand feet wide: the Breach.

Black in depth, and guarded by an island set in the middle of the river. Tom raised the spyglass Donon had handed him. The breach revealed the course of a river; flowing through it from the north. Intricate scaffolding spider webbed all the way to the summit of the Wall and huge braziers dotted the summit. Tom wondered if the Conclaveum had built a road up there, if that were even possible.

Below, and guarding the river, Kipris, Donon had called it, was the citadel of Helm, which sat on a small island. One tall tower marked the center, otherwise it was a low and imposing village, circled by walls that reached out into the water and enclosed the docks. If one wanted to gain entrance to the Conclaveum, one must first pass through Helm.

He sighed and lowered himself below the ridgeline. His four compatriots had already set about placing canvas windbreak over the dark niches to protect them, not from prying eyes, but rather the howling gale that usually sprung up and careened through the rock deformations. He gladly accepted water from Tyrhel, and slid into the narrow cave where Gayden was already putting down bedrolls. One of the things Tom had observed was that Torec's men did not talk much, even among themselves; they communicated mostly with their eyes and gestures. He wondered if this were a regional affectation, or a habit born of a mercenary's need for silence.

He leaned his bow quiver near his bedroll and sat down cross-legged, rubbing his one good eye. He squinted. His vision had been bothering him of late, for the past three months to be exact, since just before the Battle of the Seat. It could be anything, and it concerned him a little. Having been born three months prematurely, he had lost his right eye to infection. His left eye was okay, but not as sharp as he would like. Yet now, his vision would blur occasionally, finally taking on new clarity, then it would return as if nothing at all had happened.

It was not a good time for his vision to worsen, for sure. He shook his head and leaned it back against the cool stone. The men were readying to bed down, the quiet sounds of their toilet, a shallow cough, a whisper of conversation drifted over him. It was easy to forget he and his friends were in an alien world. Not so long ago, they came into this world through some dark sorcery, for some purpose they could not glean. Only a few short months, or an eternity, take your pick, he thought ruefully. It was definitely a shock, brought to a world where technology was non-existent and men commanded magic or wielded swords; all in a landscape riddled by oddities. Not too long ago, he was just another medical student hanging out with his friends at a Medieval Society Convention. Next thing you know he and his five friends were plucked out of the air and planted in a strange world where faction of the Conclaveum was trying to kill all who opposed them.

Not so different from their world that the finality of death was always present, he thought. Moreover, he and his friend had certainly dealt out their share. From almost the first moment they were brought here, Myella, daughter of the ruler of the Conclaveum, who sought to seize control for herself, had been hunted them tirelessly. She had

17

stopped a nothing to gain control over them; from ensorceling Joe, to killing Chill, and capturing John. In the end they had prevailed, but barely, thanks to some well found allies; overcoming Myella in Paravel only now to find themselves awaiting an attack from her allies within the Conclaveum who wished to propel her to the Seat of Power. Tom feared that when it came, it would rush over them like a wave.

He felt a tugging at his arm and looked down to find Kiera, his ferret, pulling at his sleeve; she was hungry. He petted her absently and opened up a pocket to reveal a mix of dried meat and nuts. She looked at it, curiously for a moment, and began to forage for the morsels she liked best. *Good ole Kiera,* he thought. *She never forgets the basics.*

He heard Gayden laugh, and looked up. Donon was backing out of the cave, tugging his britches. Gayden thumbed after him.

"Apparently the beans he had disagreed with him!" Tyhrel joined in the laughter and Tom smirked. Tom Smiling Wolf, a son of the Sioux Nation went about rolling out his bedding. He put his long bowie knife next to the head of it and sat down to brush his teeth with linen gauze and a stick. There was a loud groan from just outside the windbreak and the sound of a wet splat. Donon's two friends laughed loudly.

"Perhaps he picked up something else?" Tom asked but was not too concerned as he had been the victim of similar circumstances for two days of the ride north.

Tyhrel shrugged and looked toward the break, now illuminated by the setting sun. All cast in

18

russet. A dark pool of fluid began to seep under the canvas at the entrance.

"Oh, for Tarn's sake, Donon," scowled Gayden. "If you're gonna run, do it away from the cave." Tom looked up just as Kiera jumped into the fold of his over shirt, scared from the outburst.

Gayden twisted away, expecting the foul odor of excrement and instead caught the metallic tang of blood. "What?"

Tom dived for his knife. His quick reflexes sparing him from a grisly death as the windbreak disintegrated in a fusillade of steel spikes, several catching Gayden full on and nearly tearing his head off. Tom missing grabbing the hilt of his knife as he rolled right, behind an outcropping of stone, watching helplessly as Tyhrel made for the back of the cave, also catching spikes to his back, one impaling him to the cave wall.

Smiling Wolf hunched low against the stone, pushing deeper into the cave. He looked to Tyhrel, and in the dim light of the cavern could see he was still alive, if only barely. The man began to moan in pain and it slowly began to build. Tom noticed the projectile that had him pinned to the wall was vibrating and cooling from red-hot to black. Another gaping would sealed itself, but it looked as if the spike was writhing inside the man's body. His shrieking continued in waves now, reaching a crescendo until finally his eyes glazed over -- finally dead but only after interminable agony.

Tom did a swift self-inventory and noticed his arrows lay halfway to Tyrel's body and his bow was on the opposite wall. *Okay, is the attack over? Surely they will be doing a head count,* he thought.

Reaching out, he tried to touch the quiver with his fingers. Just as he got a grasp onto it shrapnel followed another series of low thuds as spikes imbedded in the back wall, tearing to pieces the remains of Tyhrel. One painfully grazed his ribs as he had leaned over, tearing his shirt and leaving a scrape. He ignored the pain and shrank further back into the cave, flinching as a cool breeze touched his neck. A quick glance upward showed him a narrow chimney and the first glimmering of stars outside. But was it too narrow?

He began to shrug out of anything that might catch on the stone and trap him. His satchel and Bowie he tied to a thin piece of rope. Next came Kiera; not wanting to crush her, he put her in the satchel and tied it closed. He would pull everything up after he got out, if he got out.

It was a hard squeeze for the first three feet, and he thought at the last point he would not get past. Leading with his right arm and scraping the left side of his face and body along the rough stone, with one final heave, he twisted through the narrow chimney and into a wider opening less than six feet from his starting point. Now the opening above was wide enough for two men.

He quickly pulled up the satchel and the knife and strapped them on. There were enough little ledges and grooves here that he could easily pull himself up the rest of the way. In a moment, he was ready to look.

Carefully he pulled himself out, watching for any attack, but none came. There were large outcroppings of malformed granite all around him. He lay flat and pulled himself in the opposite direction from the attack. He had to get as far away as possible. Behind him, he heard the sound of movement. Whoever it was, they were not concerned about stealth. He recognized the clinking of armor and heavy steps.

Finally he came to a narrow passage with high walls of rock on either side. He slid in and waited.

Tyhrel, Donon, Gayden, all dead in a manner of seconds, and only luck had spared him.

They were slaughtered, Tom thought angrily as he looked around the dark gorge. Night had fully fallen now. He had to get back to the horses, head southward to the Plains. This place was a maze of pitfalls, sinkholes and switchbacks; according to Tyrhel: warped by the sorcery used to raise the Great Wall.

Who were their assailants? he wondered. He had only heard them. It would probably serve him well if he spied them out; they would not expect that, maybe they did not even know they had missed one of their intended victims.

He slid past the rock formation and into another gulch, it was narrow but he could squeeze through. He splashed into the cold runoff and stopped abruptly, listening. Nothing.

He would follow the flow of the runoff for a time, even though he knew it would lead toward the river at the base of the Wall rather than in the direction he needed to go. The rock formations that thrust their way, finger-like to the sky, were jagged and treacherous.

Kiera crawled up around his neck, licking salt from his face. She smelled the blood on him and knew it was his, though luckily, a small one that

21

would not hinder him for the time being. He looked down, barely able to see in the pale moonlight. The spike had narrowly missed him, scraping along his ribs and giving him what looked like a third degree burn; in the time he had left the cave it had become a whitened blister surrounded by black and red char.

Nice, he thought. *Moreover, very unnatural.*

He scratched the ferret absently behind the ear, and then set her back into the pouch she had managed worm from. The sooner he got out of this rocky maze the better.

A short time later, he stopped and sank to his haunches, needing a moment of rest. It was funny how suddenly the stars above could give him enough light to see by, even in what seemed the blackest of gorges. Wondering if he would get out of this one alive, he leaned back against the cool rock and winced at the sound of his knife's hilt grating on stone.

Shit! He swore to himself. Such stupid mistake could get him killed.

Not a sound, except the wind whistling through the rocks. Nothing.

Then, a shadow, further down the gorge. He rolled to the side, hearing the low thump, and the ringing, as he saw a spike bury itself in the sandstone. Looking toward its source, he saw a figure outlined by a backdrop of constellations. The man's helmet obscured his face, but the weapon was memorable: a long, black staff, about two inches in diameter -- almost like a gun barrel -- that made a thumping sound as it spewed a spike. His assailant moved off to the right, trailing a hellish red glow.

Where did he go? Knife in hand, Tom looked for the form in the gloom.

Again, Tom was certain he could make out the dark figure near the end of the gorge, but then it was gone. *Wait...* other sounds, of scrabbling rocks and falling pebbles. Someone suddenly stood before him, not fifty feet away.

"So Smiling Wolf," he heard a raspy voice. It reminded him of something or someone he could not place. "My friend has come to Helm. You must not be happy with what you achieved in Paravel." His stalker walked slowly up the gorge towards him, using the staff as a walking stick. Tom could make out the symbol on the man's tabard; it was a hand, palm outward: The Hand of Keth.

"Well I'm in some deep shit now," he whispered. He had heard of the Hands of Keth. Then louder: "I'm surprised you haven't killed me yet."

"We don't want to kill *you*, Tom.*"

Smiling Wolf stepped back. He knew where he had heard the voice before and the familiar shape of the man's shadow, but that was impossible. He shook his head. He was no match for that staff. He sheathed his knife and relaxed, seemingly awaiting his fate.

"Is it that easy, *Tom*? Will you surrender? Guyle knew you were here so he sent us to find you. The others were of no consequence. But, *you* are another matter." The stout man was almost upon the Sioux. He lowered the staff, the point leveled at Tom's chest.

Tom dodged to the side at the last second, the thump almost knocking his breath away. He seemed

23

to scale the side of the rock wall. The Hand of Keth turned and Smiling Wolf cast his last three *shuriken* at him. Two bounced harmlessly off the mail, the third lodged in the helmet, just above the visor.

Great! he thought somewhat cynically, as he took off down the narrow gorge. He looked back just as he was about to round the bend. The Hand of Keth, on one knee, hastily pulled the helm from his head. Even in the starlight, Tom could see the stout features, the black hair, and the scar at the temple.

He sprinted as fast as he could, hardly hampered by the close quarters of the passage. He stopped abruptly, the sound of others around him. Looking ahead, all he could perceive was blackness; the rock formations merged and formed a tunnel.

Something slammed into his wounded side and a groan escaped his lips. He rolled forward to avoid the slash of the bladed weapon. Blood flowed freely down his side. Instinctively his own knife snapped out and he slashed back, over his shoulder. Turning he saw that he had pierced through the visor of one of the Hands. It lay there...dead?

"Tom...there is no escape. Not even death is an escape." He shuddered at the sound of the voice behind him. He dove into the shadow of the tunnel and, too late, realized that his pouch, and Kiera, lay on the ground at the Hand's feet; the strap severed by the creature's sword. He stopped and turned to go back, but his feet slipped on the loose gravel and he fell to his knees.

The Hand of Keth stepped over his dead comrade and walked to the pouch that lay at the foot of the tunnel. It squirmed on the rocky floor. He stooped and picked up the satchel. Pulling his gauntlet off, he grabbed the ferret from the bag, holding her aloft. The ferret looked at him and saw the blankness staring back. She bit furiously at the man's hand, between thumb and forefinger, and drew a dark bead of blood. The man grimaced, then a sneer twisted his lips and he squeezed.

The high-pitched squeal of the animal split the night, shattering the night. Finally, there came a sharp snap and the animal went limp. The Hand of Keth cast the limp carcass to the side.

"NO! You sonofabitch!" Tom hefted his knife ready to charge forward when the ground fell out below him.

...Slip, drop, rush and he was falling into a sinkhole, his stomach in his throat. The sinkhole had led to a tunnel that had flowed into another crevasse. It was a chute more like, then a cascade of water and rock. He slid along the steep grade in about three inches of water. For one mad moment, it crossed his mind that this was like a water-park ride, but then a jutting rock nearly cost him his good eye and he returned to the reality of the danger.

Bruised and battered, he tumbled along the winding way of the chute.

Just as he was starting to wonder if this roller-coaster ride would go on forever, Tom Smiling Wolf felt that stomach churning feeling of weightlessness, then a rush of air in his ears that almost deafened him. The Sioux shot out of the water slide and into open space, fifty feet above the river that ran along the base of the Great Wall.

What next? came the fleeting thought as he plunged into the icy water. Grazing his backside on the rocks, he fought for the surface. The current was strong and the turbulence fierce, but his head finally broke the surface. As he gulped for air, he began frantic strokes toward the south side of the river. At first his efforts were to no avail, he was dragged toward a dark crack in the base of the Wall. *A spillway?* He fought even harder and his strokes brought him nearer the south bank. He went with the current now, just keeping afloat. It seemed forever in the icy water, but he knew it was only moments as he passed beneath the bridge to Helm and floated by the docks. Once the current took him past Helm, he struck out for the south bank with renewed vigor. As he approached the shallows, he no longer felt the tug of the water's course. Bobbing in the choppy river, he tried to wipe the water from his good eye, but it blurred, and then doubled... how.

Of all times for this to happen! He reached out for a rock outcropping but missed. He tried again. He had no depth perception with one eye, but...his vision blurred, doubled, and then resolved into a clarity that was almost painful. The two images fused and became one.

He grabbed the rock and pulled himself to shore. Leaning against a boulder, he gazed at the black water that rushed past him into the night. Everything gone but his knife, he stared at his hands, torn and bruised by the sharp rocks. His wounded side was now only a dull, painful throb, numbed by the cold water.

He smiled grimly. Now he knew why his vision had been bothering him.

The Hand peered over the rim of the sinkhole that had engulfed the Outlander. No expression

26

came from him; rather he just hefted the staff, his *kris-voulge,* and began his trek back to the Great Wall and Guyle, his master.

Chapter 2

The sullen sky looked as if it were ready to heave a smothering layer of snow upon the earth. The wind ripped across scrub and stone, all that remained of the once verdant fields of autumn, carrying aloft the dark shadow in the sky. High amid the currents of air, the courier beast wheeled as the thermals warred with each other, almost strong enough to rip through the thin film of skin that spanned its pinions. Suddenly, the shiny black creature plunged downward at dizzying speed, extending its wings and sweeping just low enough to swirl the dead leaves from the cold ground, then pushing aloft again and onward to the west.

Mrick pushed his braid back and stepped over a pile of stones that had been cleared away from the keep. All that remained of Trevor's hold was two-thirds of the battlement and part of the main hall, very little had survived above the first floor, and the towers and spires were nothing more than a faint memory. Mrick sat down on a cask and watched the courier beast become a speck against the red smear of the setting sun.

That was just one of many. Over the past months, they had watched a score of the beasts fly west. None cared now for the ruined heap of rock and burnt-out buildings that were the remains of the village of Galfeon Yor. Nor had the columns of soldiers Mrick's men had encountered bothered with the former town. After what Duran and the Outlanders had wrought here, he doubted that any foe much cared to do any more damage; it was so far gone to disrepair.

A few fleeing villagers and farmers had brought Word: that Ord had fallen in much the same manner as Galfeon Yor. The devastation had been less fierce; the Lord of Ord, only in power for a couple of months, had been cowardly and had offered no resistance to the troops of the Conclaveum. Word also came that the Black Guard, having secured the Ghisik Pass, now had an open supply line from Helm to the West. They had easily occupied Tarn Hold, a city of good size that sat in the cradle of the Tarn Mountain Range, and Albien, a port city along the southern coast had been marked for conquest.

Mrick shook his head and spat, looking over his shoulder at the collapsed section of the battlement. Of course, they would be no closer to repairing the wall by the time true winter set in, yet he and his men kept busy - what else had they to do? Some of the refugees from Ord and a few farmers had passed through Galfeon Yor, but none stayed. The town that was Galfeon Yor held too many ghosts and too little promise; it was only a shadow of its former self. Many of the buildings that surrounded the square were naught more than charred timbers and crossbeams. Months before, Mrick and his men had searched all the houses and businesses and only found a handful of families huddled in their cellars, fearing for their lives. These soon left for villages and fishing communities to the south, or had gone east to Paravel and the towns that lie along that route. The rest of the inhabitants of the village lay at the bottom of the Deep, victims of Duran's slaughter and, no doubt, that Outlander Surik's treachery.

Treachery. He pulled forth his sword and looked down its sharp length. *Baxel's Bane,* he had named it. It was Sir Chill's; one of the six outlanders whose arrival in Galfeon Yor had spelled its doom. The sword; he had recovered it from the rubble of the main hall. He blamed it in part for his Captain's death, hence the designation. Now he took it up as a reminder of the hate that burned in his heart; a hate that had flamed to life when the Outlanders had caused the ruin of Galfeon Yor and the loss of Lord Trevor, his daughter Gabrielle, and Baxel, the finest Captain Mrick had ever served.

He looked along its steel length and beyond, to the ruined village below, and wondered if he could ever begin to rebuild what was lost. He shivered in the cool afternoon air and sheathed his blade. He sat and thought, and watched as a lone horseman approached the village. *Another refugee?*

He waited, hoping deep down inside it was one of the six Outlanders. That it was the bastard Bard William or perhaps Sir John. But, he knew it was neither. Now and then, the ruin of a building, or an odd remaining tree would obscure his view of the rider. This was an uncommon event, a refugee on horseback, possibly a lord seeking sanctuary in one of the free-states of the West. Mrick spat derisively. *We have had enough Lords of late.*

His men had gathered about him, twenty-four left, which was all. But it was enough. The horseman hauled his gelding to a skidding stop just a stone's throw away, then threw back his hood and nudged his horse forward cautiously. His cloak flared out behind him and Mrick could tell by the cut and quality of the cloth that if he was not a Lord at least he was a rich merchant. *No, a Lord*, Mrick thought as he saw the narrow blade at the man's side.

The man nodded at them from atop his mount, a wise position if he had to flee quickly. He was interesting in appearance. His hair was dark as a raven's feathers and long in back; yet he was clean-shaven. His eyes were deep green and sharp; his face bearing a resemblance Mrick could not place. He had an athletic build, obviously not tending toward laziness like many a nobleman. His clothing was rich blue, trimmed in silver thread. He did not come from any fishing village that was for certain, but he could have come from the North, from the Conclaveum.

"Are you *cavas*?" Mrick asked. It was slang for Conclaveum folk. He asked it in the Common Tongue, not Middle or High. The man's accent in Common, if any, could tell one from whence he came.

"Not *cavas*," he replied in a deep resonant voice, more for speech making or dialogue. The man quickly dismounted and Mrick's men edged back nervously.

"You flee the West and what the Conclaveum has wrought?"

"Yes," the man replied slowly. "The city of Tarn Hold. I was a student there." No accent that Mrick could tell, but he sounded educated.

"I have heard that it is a large city, but I have never been there."

"Not so large it could stand against Oran's Guard," the stranger continued. "And, since the past season crawling with *his* minions." He spat.

31

"Aye, I heard that from a merchant not two days gone," Mrick said.

"It fell a month ago. I have heard that Albien is under siege."

He eyed the stranger a moment more, and then stepped from the cask, offering the man his hand. "Mrick, once a vassal of Trevor Galfeon. Now the guard of this broken down keep."

"Trevor...Well met, Mrick, I am Adon."

"Adon, would you share bread with us this night? We don't have the fare that you are no doubt used to, but we have plenty of game hen and rabbit, and the fields were not so bare as to forbid us some potatoes and onions."

"It would be a fine fare indeed, Mrick. There are not many inns between Tarn and here, and I wanted to stay clear of Ord. I have heard that there is a dark pall that hangs over that city."

"I have not heard that. But come, you will tell us. As you can see, the castle did not fare well in an attack by Gelion's forces, but we have repaired some of the hall, and it will do for these cold nights. Barj, take his horse to the stable."

Adon bit into the heel of dark bread and only paused long enough to cut a wedge of cheese. Mrick looked on and smiled.

"I had not realized how famished I was, all that riding."

"Yes, well the hen did not last long, or the potatoes. But tell us, what is this news of Ord? You spoke of some evil?" Mrick played with the food on his plate.

"Evil, in truth," Adon frowned and set the knife and bread carefully on his plate. His voice was tight and controlled. "Night is not the best time to talk of it, and who would have thought... Not since the days of Iss... but I rattle on." He sighed and sat back in his chair, surveying the hall as his voice trailed away. Indeed, it was not much of a hall. Pillars still rose to support the vaulted ceiling, but the stress from the raging inferno of battle had cracked and scorched them. A fire blazed in the hearth, spilling light to one wall that was a jigsaw of raw timber and rock, hastily thrown together. The once-white flagstones now were covered with straw and dirt. Yet, it held not the sorcerous stench of Ord, and that made it a palace indeed.

"I do not follow you Adon," Mrick's words called him back to the present.

"My friend, I hesitate to tell, though it needs to be done. So: in Tarn Hold I was studying to become one of the Sequestered. Have you heard of such?"

"Tarn is a long way off; I fear that I am ignorant of such things."

"Yes, well, sometimes I think I would be grateful for a little more ignorance. The Sequestered are those who dedicate their lives to the seeking of knowledge and truth, to give up all worldly things and to follow a path few take, the path to be a Priest of Tarn. No more though; this path is closed to me." He frowned and sipped at the lukewarm karo. "It started about eight months ago. Strange things were happening in the city. Nobles dying mysteriously, some said from poison. The cult of Oran was gaining power as well as followers. Worse. A dark sorcerous presence roamed the night. It demanded a sacrifice within the halls of the Temple. And soon I found myself fleeing nameless horror. I fear that

Myella is playing with things that she knows nothing of, and Duran has brought force - "

"Hah!" Mrick shouted and his men looked up sharply. "That name again, it haunts me!"

"What? Duran?"

"Yes, those Outlanders are no doubt a part of that evil web."

Adon leaned forward on the table, his interest piqued. "Why does that name bother you so? And who are these Outlanders?" Mrick looked around nervously. A cold draft had found its way into the hall, causing the sconces to waver and dim.

"It all began with Duran, Lord Duran of Qwen. He came to Galfeon Yor, almost a year ago. What followed is what you see. On the heels of Duran came six Outlanders and the wrath of Gelion, the Regent of the Conclaveum in the Southern States. They claimed to have been shipwrecked on the southern coast and accosted by Gelion, but they escaped. Then, during the festival of the spring Duran poisoned the Lord of Ord and one of the Outlanders, Surik by name, disappeared.

"The Outlanders assumed that Gelion was behind it. Duran had eluded capture so they hired some mercenaries and took thirty of Lord Trevor's men, I among them, to raid the Regent's Seat; the one named Lord Michael suggested Surik would be there. Therefore, we did. Lord Michael killed Gelion, but we met almost no resistance. We learned later that at the same time we marched on the Regent's Seat, Duran had led a sizable force against Galfeon Yor. With the aid of sorcery, he wrought the destruction you see before you, and destroyed our people. My Captain, Baxel was

34

butchered like an animal, left to hang from the portcullis. Trevor and his daughter Gabrielle could not be found. And one of the Outlanders, Sir Chill, was killed.

"The remaining Outlanders left after that, with the mercenaries, for Paravel."

"This Outlander, dead you say?"

"Yes, left to die; he gave up his ghost soon after we arrived, and there was sorcery about him as he lay in the courtyard. His fellows buried him up on Hiiram's Hill, amid a stand of oak."

"Dead." Adon frowned. "I would very much like to see his grave."

"We will go in daylight if you wish, but not at night. The wolves have been getting brave of late, even coming into the town. Winter will bring worse."

"Yes it will."

"What now for you, Adon, where do you go? Obviously you cannot return to Tarn Hold, at least not until the Conclaveum has put order to their conquests."

"I can never go back to Tarn Hold. I had planned to go to Paravel, that is, if they have not also fallen to Myella."

"I have heard that they ousted her."

"What?" Adon let shock show on his features.

"Yes. A courier recently had the misfortune of flying too close to our arrows. We questioned him most thoroughly before he died. He said that the City Council, with the aid of the City Guard, removed her and her soldiers from the city. Apparently, this Myella had the poor judgment to kill their governor. In the wake of Gelion's death, she assumed control as Regent and removed the Seat to the port city of Paravel. The lords of the city did not take kindly to this and there was a fight, pitched at first, but she was finally removed from the city."

"How long?"

"Several months."

"By the gods of Carn, where have I been?"

"No doubt fearing for your life."

"No doubt."

"I must think, Mrick. Is there someplace I can rest?"

"Aye. There are a few rooms near the hall. Servants quarters, but all others are in disrepair."

"It will do."

The corridor was dark, but Adon knew that most of Mrick's men now slept, only two kept guard and he would not go near them. He carefully found his way along the soot-covered walls until he stood in what had been the kitchen. He lit a small taper, carefully hiding it in his palm. On the far wall, a door, canted to one side, gave entrance to the cellar. The power to break the keep had been strong, even from afar the tracing had brought him here. He had sensed it soon after leaving Ord; the aether carried heavy traces of it. But some even more powerful sorcery had been wrought down there, in the depths.

He carefully pushed the door aside, wincing as the melted hinges creaked. Adon moved down the steep and narrow steps, through the cellar, onward into the stores and the sub-basement. He had found the place that called to him. The tunnels spread off in several different directions from this point, but here, where there was a rent in the foundation and the clay spilled up like the blood of the earth, the trace was strongest. He knelt and surveyed the ground where once a protective ward had been traced onto the floor. In the distance, he could hear the steady drip of a cistern.

He traced a pattern in the air with his hand and the image of the past made him pale. The resonance in the *aether* was the same as that which he and his mentor had found in Tarn Hold. He quickly dispelled the trace, not bringing the remnant of the dark power back, or even the memory of it; it was too dangerous as it may recall the casting. *Whoever did this knew not what they were doing. Every time it is brought here, it gets stronger, and Oran's evil influence grows.* He sighed; he knew what he must do. He had to go to Narn-toc and find the text, then to his father and brother. *That fool necromancer Guyle must be behind this; always did he find the teaching of Iss most alluring.*

Lost in thought, he barely remembered finding his way through the cellar maze to the chambers above. He sat on the lumpy tick and thought. He would have to bring down what was left of this keep, or the evil might spread and become another gate. Like Ord. Like Narn-toc.

Chapter 3

John awoke in a cold sweat, his heart racing. Visions of the nightmare still lingered and his St. Christopher medal tingled just as it had the last time; the dream, the *shades*, and the city. He knew not what city. It sat on a peninsula amidst cold water, ancient and cold. Dead. No life walked in its streets and its buildings were covered with vines. The docks were bereft of any vessel, but there were the shadows and the creatures; evil, sinister and dark. *Daemon* came to John's mind. In the dream it was closing on night, the sun had set and the sky was a deep lavender, reflected in the mirrored calm of the waters.

The *Daemons* rose from the ruins, hundreds filling the sky, the rustle of wings and the smell of death. They blackened the evening sky, screaming with unholy glee. It was all around him and he was bound by the shadow, just as Chill had been. They came.

Then he awoke; he always awoke before they got to him. *Lest the Saint's Soul Die,* came the fleeting thought and then it was gone. He threw the covers off the bed and flinched as his feet struck the cold stones. Shaking off the dream he gazed out the arrow slit that made for a window. A cool breeze chilled the sweat from his skin. That dream had plagued him at least seven times in the past couple months. *God, has it been that long?* He thought as he shivered and looked over the roofs of Paravel. It had rained last night and runnels of water marked the tiled roofs all the way to the harbor and the distant sea. Autumn had swept through the city and the air had turned brisk, the sea was raw steel, rough and untamed. Thoughts of the Unseating of Myella crept into his awareness, crowding out the memory of the dream. Four months and now the leaves were turning and the days were getting shorter. After the fight at the Seat, Kelvin and the City Council had most thoroughly cast out any overt force of Myella from the city. The Guard of Oran was gone; the few Black Guard, gone; even the City Guard that were turned to Myella, gone or worse. The weeks that followed had scores of civilians leaving the city, to head toward Helm or Qwen. And afterward the air seemed lighter in the city and the people less troubled by fear of the Seat and the Surrogate of the South.

Still, there had been some trouble. Fires in the warehouse district sending several ships aflame, riots incited by sympathizers of the Conclaveum, and trouble with the poor. There seemed to be more people on the streets of late, coming to seek refuge from the West, on the heels of news about Ord and Tarn Hold.

What had they done? *They sat around and had done nothing.* No, that wasn't exactly true. Gabrielle had wanted desperately to search for her father, and knowing that he was destined to go to a place called the Tower of Pain, it fueled the desperation all the more. In an effort to learn more of Helm and the Conclaveum, Tom had volunteered to scout the Great Wall. He had gone with three of Torec's men, all hand-picked, but after six weeks there had been no word from Smiling Wolf, none.

Here they were, residents of the Protector's Keep, Lords without any money. They stayed in quarters reserved for nobles and guests of the Lord Protector and lived off the courtesy of Kelvin. He hated it and he hated the way Alaric looked at him whenever he visited. *Why are you still here?* It implied.

He jabbed the poker into the dying embers of his fireplace. It had been six months since Chill's death and Mike was no closer to finding a way back home. The self-made sorcerer insisted that the answer to the riddle lay with the one that brought them here: Guyle. *Great.* That one man lay behind the Great Wall and the amassed armies of the Conclaveum.

He spied his reflection in the mirror and winced. His hair was kept short, but he had not shaved in days. He ran his hand through his hair and began his morning routine. Soon he was dressed and heading down the hall.

It was a very Spartan and utilitarian keep that was Kelvin's. White stone walls, bereft of any decoration save an occasional suit of armor or coat of arms. No tapestry, no paintings, no arras. Once John had seen the man's personal chambers and was surprised they were not like the rest of the keep. They were decorated with taste and style, and filled with what Kelvin had called Narnist antiques. Even a clock was among his collection, though instead of numbers it reflected phases of the moon and even accounted for the change of the season. John looked down at his Omega Seamaster Automatic and smiled. Some things did not change.

He passed the bedchambers of his friends and comrades. It looked like Joe and Mike were out. Bill had left weeks ago with Torec and Tar'elah for the island state of Clef; trying to gain support for the inevitable. Gabrielle and Trianna shared two adjoining chambers in another wing, as was proper according to Gabrielle. The two guards at the end of the hall nodded as he walked by and then down the narrow stair. Soon he was in the courtyard and through the iron portcullis that separated the keep from the streets of Paravel.

The sky was a dreary gray, low clouds threatened to drench him even as he walked to the walls of the city. Yellow light pierced shuttered windows and water filled the gutters and cobbles, carrying at least some of the dirt and grime away. Now he was just another citizen of the city. Paravel was not noted for its functions of the court, especially with Myella and her lackeys gone. Only his dress told others that he was not a commoner and only because they had spared enough money - which they stole from the Seat just before it was looted by the citizenry - to keep them in decent clothes.

He rounded a corner. Several merchants were pulling their carts into the square. Even with the news of the war in the West the prices had not risen significantly, and food was not as scarce as it might become once Myella brought her war to the walls of Paravel; autumn had brought a rich harvest. He nodded his head to the merchants as they went about setting up canopies to cover their goods in the event of rain. Rain rarely prevented people from going to market, at least in a city this size.

Tom should be returning soon. Bearing what bad news he did not know. The chaos in the first month after the Unseating had led to three months

41

of increasing boredom. They had been building towers in the interim; towers with long ramps and a wide crest to support Mike's secret weapon. They were to be spaced about fifty yards apart along the city wall. The City Council had more than agreed to help with the construction. They also knew what was coming.

Masons would be working this morning, they had wanted to finish before the onset of winter, but it did not look good. He could almost feel the fetid breath of Myella at the nape of his neck, like a rabid dog.

***

Surik Shadowlord, Master of Shades, Rider of the Black Dragon and Bearer of the Sword Entius, looked to the north and to the Great Wall of the Conclaveum. He stood atop the battlements of the northern gate wall, watching as men labored to lay stone atop stout square towers that rose about six feet above the wall proper. Down below the workers were readying winches that would pull the great blocks into place.

Light brown hair blowing across steel gray eyes was absently brushed aside. His thin beard was meticulously trimmed and he carried himself in learned nobility if not born. He felt the first few drops of rain and scowled, this would surely slow the work if it were heavy; it had been of late. Kelvin said it was the rainy season, and hinted at a harsh autumn and a worse winter. Adjusting his cloak he hailed the foreman and turned, almost knocking John from the catwalk.

"Shouldn't sneak around like that," Joe muttered as he stepped back and looked at his friend.

"Should watch where you're going."

Joe scowled and cracked his knuckles through his leather gauntlets. "This waiting is driving me nuts." John nodded and leaned over the parapet, watching another day of work get under way. He looked up, taking in the breathtaking panorama. Before them spread the pastoral farmlands to the west and north of the city dotted occasionally by a few copses and beyond those the Plains of Straw. Low walls split up the land, marking an occasional homestead or farm, all now rich with the colors of the harvest season. Trees burnished copper and ruddy red, vivid even in the overcast as the early morning sunlight slanted beneath the clouds and across the fields.

...so what about you?"

"Huh?" said the Shadowlord as he was brought out of his daydream.

"I said that I was heading back to the foundry, what about you?"

"Yeah, sure," the artist replied, wondering if it would be that easy to head back.

***

Mike gazed into the forge fire and twisted his Manchu-style mustache, trying to figure out what had gone wrong: three castings and all bad. The prototype had been good...at least until the fifth round, and then the barrel had cracked, almost killing three foundry-men. They had used an alloy that would strengthen the barrel, but at this rate there was no way that they would be finished in time. He watched as Pelles ladled some low carbon ore into the kiln. *Maybe that will help.* But something was wrong, desperately wrong. The castings should have held and they should have at least eight cannons by now.

He turned away from the hellfire glow and yawned. He had been up all night, his sleep cycle reversed out of necessity. The foundry during the summer was like standing in the middle of a volcano, most of the work had to be done with the cool night. Looking to the rear of the foundry he could see that morning had come.

He knew he was neglecting his practice of sorcery. What had the riddle of the *Daemon* meant?

His relative grand is same to brother's hand.

Companions' ties, among choices,
But beware if the Saint's Soul dies.
What is wanted is that which you possess,
And what you possess is unknown.
You must create that of death.
It wields not death, but its wielder.
Fire and steel bound, it is mundane
Yet profound.

Of all the texts and grimoires he had poured over in the past four months only one had hinted at what the *Daemon* had said; the *Ih'dia* text that Joe had salvaged from the looting of the Seat. Joe felt it was valuable, though he didn't know why. It was very valuable, Mike knew; written by a sorcerer named Iss, in the age of Narn-toc, at about the time of the Raising of the Great Wall, nearly five centuries gone. Unfortunately the language was vague, almost a riddle itself, fraught with traps.

No matter, they knew who was behind them being brought here. He shied away from a spray of sparks as the ladle was tipped and the metal ran a white yellow into the casting. It had been Guyle, Mage Guyle, and Counselor to the Conclavator, Myella's uncle. *Was Trevor locked tight in the Tower of Pain?* There was a curious history to that Tower as well. One book had referred to it as the Tower of Im and then after Korman Iss had moved to Narn-toc it was referred to as the Tower of Iss. Apparently, the Conclave had wanted to tear it down, but it would have cost too much. Now it was Mage Guyle's, and he called it the Tower of Pain. Nice.

He did not care for the intrigues of the Conclaveum though there was much to learn in its history, but he had gotten a taste for it in Paravel, especially with the council and Chair Nathal. He stepped out into the cool morning, letting the heat wash his back. Pulling out his pipe, he stuffed some tobacco into the bowl and pulled deeply, touching a taper to it. Cool smoke rolled over the back of his throat. Fumbling in his pocket, he pulled out the orb; amber and translucent. He had created that when he had first gotten to this realm, and with it and his *Book of Shadows* he had managed to summon the *Daemon* and garner valuable information.

He grunted, hearing Pelles swear loudly. Pelles, the man who was probably the best blacksmith in Paravel, had made his flintlock. He now swore at the top of his lungs. Another casting gone badly and it should not have. Mike would gladly introduce gunpowder into this realm, but they also needed the cannons. He had no doubt in Pelles' ability, but why had not the forgings set? It was definitely putting him in a dark mood.

Leaning against the wooden timbers of the building and watching the crowd mill about in the early morning he soon spotted Joe and John meandering through the morning din. *Great, now they'll stick their noses in it.*

"Hey, Blotto!" shouted the Shadowlord. Mike growled low in his throat as the bearded man approached. John grinned, almost slipped in a puddle and followed the Shadowlord. Mike just shook his head.

"Yes, Surik Shadowbutte, Master of the Left Hand?" Mike's crystal blue eyes peered intently at the two. John burst into laughter.

"Nice, your Immenseness, what's up? Any cannons this morning?"

Mike scowled and looked over his shoulder. Pelles and his men had started to drag aside the casting as scrap. "Something is not right. We should have eight, now nine, cannons. What do we have? Nothing."

Joe's nostrils flared with the sharp smell of sulfur. Hammers rang loud and men wearing leather aprons sweated in the heat of the foundry. Joe watched Pelles walk toward them, anger and brooding on his brow like storm clouds.

"Again we try, and we fail!" he shouted over the din. "Milord Michael, I know that the steel is right. If you are not happy with my work-"

"Oh shut up, Pelles, you're the best and you know it. No, it must be something small, but where in the process? It's almost like the metal is experiencing too much fatigue, but I know that the carbon content is low enough for it not to get too brittle."

"Well, how then?"

"If I knew that Surik, I wouldn't be standing around like a turkey at Thanksgiving," Mike retorted.

"This really sets us back," John muttered.

"Tell me about it." Mike shook his head as they left Pelles to his work. Mike could not fathom what went wrong.

"Is it Pelles' fault?" John asked as they walked outside. It had started to rain heavily. They stood under the eaves, watching the water cascade over the tiles; much of it drained into a large barrel.

"Pelles? No, he's the best we got. I just can't figure this one out."

"Then Myella has us. We cannot stand a long siege, and we don't have the forces for a battle," Joe said it more to himself as he looked at the merchants running to escape the downpour.

"I'm going to talk to Kelvin. Maybe he has some ideas." John trotted off across the street, the rain making him indistinct after twenty yards. Joe and Mike watched him disappear then turned back to the forge. It had to be something.

John jogged the couple of blocks, finally giving up on staying dry. He passed the two guards at the portcullis and ran through the courtyard, ignoring the wain that sat near the kitchens. Once in the open hall he caught sight of Alaric Dirkajian,

Guildmaster Merchant. And there it was again. *Why are you still here?* His eyes held many implications. John frowned and approached the man.

He was slightly taller than John, with chiseled features. His hair was black and curly. And he was as deadly as a panther from what John had seen during the Unseating.

"Good morning, Alaric," John sighed as he shook out his cloak and draped it onto a chair. The great hall of the Keep was just as simple as the rest of the hold; large hearth, long table and chair for Justice Day. Normally open and airy, today there was a pall cast over the chamber.

"Lord Knight." The man nodded. He was waiting for Kelvin, no doubt. *Would he see him here or in his chambers?* John did not like the man, nor did he trust him. He reminded John of someone who could take Machiavelli to task. More assassin than merchant, the man looked like he would sooner prey on you than trade with you. He shook his head and smiled his most ingratiating smile. The man was abrupt.

"No word from the tracker," his voice was soft.

"Tom? No, but he has been gone only six weeks."

"Yes, but it is dangerous."

"He can handle himself."

"I could have garnered just as much information from the merchant trains that go to Qwen, and in shorter time."

"Nothing is better than first hand reports. Tom knows what he is doing."

"Yes, but I fear that things are worse now, especially with news of Duran's conquests in the

48

west." He paused and looked away, and then a thin-lipped smile lit upon his face. "And now my men tell me that your magical weapon is useless?"

"What?" John arched his brow and frowned at Alaric. He fingered the hilt of his sword and smiled at John's outburst.

"I know about the castings. The metal is bad. You endanger this whole city by being here. I would urge you to leave. Go anywhere, go to the south, or go across the sea from whence you came. I know not, for it must be beyond the land of the Krim. Your plans for meeting the forces of the Conclaveum are now nothing more than dreams, foolish dreams at best.

"Tell me, Lord Knight," he paused only a moment as some servants began mopping the floor some twenty feet away. "Have you thought of this? You and your friends are at peril. I will not have this city at peril. It is a free city now, but Myella knows you are here. Look at what her forces are doing in the West: capturing Ord, occupying Tarn Hold. I hear that Albien will be next. When will she come to reclaim you and your friends? Or attempt to take Paravel? I fear that when we Unseated Myella we upended the pot of boiling oil. I fear that soon she may even rule the Conclaveum, and then there will be no stopping her. I may have erred in helping you Outlanders."

John had no retort for the man; he knew that there was truth in what he said. He also knew that it was not only them that Myella wanted. She wanted the city. *Hell, she wants the entire South; she wants to reclaim what was lost.*

"Alaric, do you honestly believe that if we leave Myella will not lay siege to this city?"

"I will not be naive enough to say yes, Lord Knight. But, knowing that you are not here may stay her hand."

"She will rape this city like she raped Ord, and God knows what happened there *or* in Tarn Hold."

The Guildmaster sighed and leaned against the table. "I will not argue with you, Sir John. I will say this though: leave the city. If you do not you may doom us all."

"We were doomed from the moment Myella was born, Alaric Dirkajian." They both turned at the deep voice. Lord Kelvin, Castellan of the City stood near the banister at the summit of the stairway. He was a man of late middle years, with graying hair and a face lined and weathered. His stride was economic as he stepped briskly down the steps. Formerly a servant of the Conclaveum he now served the City. "The day she was spawned I was fighting the Krim in the far north. The day she came of age and attempted to seduce her brother I was appointed Protector of Helm; and the day she came to the South as Surrogate I was putting down a riot in the wharf district, here in Paravel. Trouble all the way, Alaric, and even if these young men leave the city, she will surely sweep through it with her Guard and destroy everything we hold dear."

John nodded, grateful that the man echoed his own thoughts.

"Now, Alaric, what can I do for you?" Alaric frowned and looked to the Lord Knight, then to the table.

"It seems that we have need of more City Guard in the warehouse district. Several fires were set last night and one of *my* ships was burnt to the water line."

"I am sorry to hear that Alaric, but I cannot spare the men. You know how it goes. I pull men from the north quarter and send them to the docks and there is a riot among the refugees. I pull men from the south quarter and all the rich merchants yell about being pilfered. My men are spread too thin."

"Then hire more men."

"More men? The city coffers are low enough with a thousand extra mouths to feed. No, I cannot even muster a militia because the men have families to care for and not enough hours in the day for them to work. It will have to do."

"Have to do? Not when I have traders with their cargo aflame. No!" Alaric turned and began to leave the hall. "I will hire my own men. Dock men who care not as much for the letter of the law."

With a sweep of his cloak, he was gone; the wooden doors slammed shut behind him.

"I cannot stomach that man," Kelvin muttered and sat down heavily in his chair. He seemed to notice John as an afterthought. "What can I do for you, Sir John?"

"I have bad news."

"Go ahead."

"No cannons, the latest castings were bad."

"By the gods of Carn, I did not need to hear that." He leaned forward on the table and rubbed his temples. "I fear I am getting too old for all this."

"We will have to plan for a long siege, but-"

"But, with the sorcery that Myella has it will not be a long one," Kelvin finished. "I would not blame you if you and your friends left."

"We cannot. The only place to go would be to Teshwa, to find Trevor."

"Young man in the coming months that might be the safest place for you."

Chapter 4

The rain had stopped for the moment and the copse they approached looked brown and dead in the dim morning light. Adon nearly jumped from his steed when he saw the trees. Mrick just sat on his roan, eyes narrowing. The trees were all bare, twisted and gray; they were dead, not dormant but dead. The stranger walked amid the trees and looked around. Here the copse faced to the west and to the setting sun and this was where they had buried the Outlander beneath a spreading oak. Adon looked down and saw the brown dirt, where no grass would grow. He saw the taint in the soil as it spread to the trees. He had no need to *trace*.

"It is corrupt," he stated simply.

"The grave has been there many months, but never have I seen such."

"No," Adon replied as he knelt before the grave. "That is not what I meant. Why do you think that the trees are dead? Why do you think no refugees have settled in your town?"

"The fall, some trees die. As for the people, they move on."

"Not here, this is the evil I spoke of last night, from Ord. When Gelion's sorcerers brought down the walls of Galfeon Yor, it tainted everything. There was no magick used here that was good, it wasa foul casting; it is that of Korman Iss and it defiles everything it touches."

"What of the Outlander."

"He was taken from here."

Mrick looked to the ground then eyed the stranger suspiciously. His horse shied nervously. "What you are saying is not possible."

"You are correct. At least it has not been possible in the last four hundred years. But, then there are the Hands of Keth, and I fear this casting has much to do with them."

"Galfeon Yor, it will become like this?" He gestured to the trees of the copse.

"Yes, Mrick."

The man-at-arms shook his head sadly. Then a fire filled his eyes when he linked it all to the Outlanders. He pounded his fist into the palm of his hand. "They will pay, these Outlanders."

"Mrick, I have a need."

"What mean you?"

Adon went to his horse and grabbed the saddle horn, pulling himself up. "I must go to Narn-toc, Mrick, and I have need of protection. For that protection I can pay gold."

"Narn-toc? What is there? Is that not the dead-city?"

"I must find something. Do I have your aid?"

"There is nothing for us here."

"There is not."

"Then you will have our aid."

Adon nodded grimly as he turned his horse back to the village. That was good, he would need them, but not for the worst. That he must do alone.

The steaming water was luxuriously pleasant against her soft skin. It dripped from the sponge, around the nape of her neck and down her chest. She sunk to her chin and drank in the humid air. It was quite a treat to have a hot bath as the days grew colder, and she languished in it. She put her legs up on the rim of the tub, massaging the soreness from her thighs. It was amazing what hot water could do for the pains of riding. Her long, lean legs stretched and her toes curled with pleasure. She sighed and pulled her hair back, braiding it quickly into a ponytail.

Suddenly her head was pulled back, her neck fully exposed, her chest rising out of the water. Pain shot through the back of her neck and water splashed over the rim as her legs thrashed back into the tub.

"That was careless, my dear," came a low menacing voice. She twisted to see her attacker, but he only pulled harder. Then she relaxed as she felt his hand move over her wet breasts to caress her. The man let go of her braid and sat on the edge of the tub, smiling. She laughed deep in her throat as his hand came to rest on the inside of her thigh.

"I know you are dangerous," Bale said as she looked to her superior with a smile.

"And you," Alaric replied as he traced a scar on her cheek, gotten from one of Ythrain's guards. His other hand left her flesh and plunged into the bath water between her legs. She moved sinuously back, leveled her eyes at his and licked her lips. His hand came out of the water with a stiletto.

"A nice bathing companion that," he said as he traced the point up the flat of her stomach and between the curves of her breasts. It came to rest at the base of her neck.

"You seem tense, Alaric. What is wrong?" For a casual question she made it sound seductive. He flipped the blade into the wall across the room effortlessly. Her hand found its way to his leg and rested there.

"Our profits are at risk because of the trouble that those Outlanders brought. I should have foreseen this, but I did not think Myella gave such import to them to bring war south of the Great Wall. If I had known they were valuable to her I would have turned them over personally. Now their very presence puts us in peril."

Bale smiled knowingly. She moved just enough to allow her hip to rise out of the water. He glanced down. "What do you plan to do?" she asked.

"You have known that from the beginning." He smiled cunningly, baring his teeth like a predator. "We use them for the moment. If Myella comes to take Paravel, we give her what she most wants and sue for peace. I would sooner kill those five than risk *my* city." He stood and pulled off his tunic, revealing a crisscross of dueling scars and old wounds. Bale gasped and rose out of the water, her hand reaching for the laces on his hose. The cool air flushed her, aroused her. His sword belt fell to the floor with a clatter and they embraced. Sharp nails left a trail of red along his shoulders.

***

John spent most of his mornings practicing forms, or *waza*, in the courtyard. Even without Tom to coach him, he found himself improving and even correcting his faults. Lately though, there were precious few City Guard in the keep to practice with and this morning, with Alaric's complaints, Kelvin had dispatched all but four of the guard from the

56

Hold to investigate the situation at the docks. The matter of not having enough men troubled him. With the impending siege and with more and more refugees in the city a solution had to be found. He did have an idea but it would require some thought. For the moment he put the thought aside and concentrated on what he was doing.

He stood in sweat soaked shirt, Japanese sword poised, and moved across the flagstones of the inner courtyard. The forms he had learned years ago had now become so ingrained that he moved through them almost without bidding, without thought, with utter fluidity. The newer forms came, but slowly and after many hours of practice. Much of his martial skills with the sword now seemed natural.

He paused after an hour's worth of a good practice. Now he practiced first with the Headsman's sword and then with the Japanese Katana. He used the heading sword because his blade would in no way hold up to the hack and slash techniques that most of the Legions of the Conclaveum used. During a siege he would require a heavy blade to block many of these blows and penetrate heavy plate armor and the broadsword was definitely a good weapon to fall back upon when the fighting grew intense. He looked at the heavy blade that lay atop a bench in the courtyard: the Sword of Justice that he had used at the Unseating. It was awkward and useless to him then, its balance odd and shifting. Now he used it masterfully, almost with equal skill to the Japanese blade. However, the forms were much different.

He went to the rain barrel and ladled out some water, the icy fluid quenching his thirst. He shivered, having forgotten how cool it had become of late; autumn was definitely here . Once more, he picked up the Japanese sword and paused as he caught the blur of his reflection in the gray satin metal of the katana, the folded steel fogged in the cooler air. The hamon, the line of martinsite crystals where the more ductile metal met the harder steel, was quite clear in the pearly morning light. He slid the katana back into the lacquered scabbard and strapped the weapon to his side. He had been getting in the habit of not wearing it, for some reason he knew that would have to stop.

Striding purposefully into the hall, he cradled the headsman's sword in the crook of his left arm. The wagon still stood by the kitchen; the horse, sleeping in its harness, was so still it looked to be frozen. A frown touched his features; it had grown quiet in the keep, not even the servants were about, nor the sergeant of the grounds. *Is Gabrielle around?* He wondered as he strode into the main hall. He set the heavy weapon on the long table. *Or have they all gone on a picnic?* It was dark inside the large chamber; the tapers and sconces had guttered out some time ago.

Apprehension edged into his thoughts as he walked the halls of Kelvin's keep. *This is odd*, the servants usually kept all the sconces lit and the fire in the main hall at a good blaze. He tentatively touched his St. Christopher medal through the fold in his tunic. It felt warm on his skin, tingling...

...A strangled scream, distant and faint, came from the east wing. *Gabrielle!* He was up the stairs and halfway down the hall when he realized his

58

error. He smiled grimly and rolled forward, it was his only chance.

Mike noticed immediately that there were not the usual guards at the gate. Joe pointed out offhandedly that the wagon had been sitting in the same place all morning. It was a delivery day, Mike knew, but usually that was done in the early morning hours. He drew his flintlock and checked the primer. *Why today of all days?* He thought.

Joe looked askance at the big man, and then decided to be prudent. Upon entering the hall he drew his bastard sword and gripped it with both hands. Mike noticed the ephemeral silver-blue glow in the dimly lit hall.

"Nice," he commented. Joe just responded with a wink. Mike skirted the hall and headed toward the doors that led deeper into the keep. Joe stayed back, covering the rear and wondering what was going on. Here he was with a magical sword - forged by a smith from Minnesota - acting as paranoid as Mike. There did not appear to be anyone in the keep and as Mike disappeared through the doors, the hall grew chill; the shadows deepened. Shivering involuntarily, Surik Shadowlord, Master of the Shades, concentrated on the ephemeral blue glow of his sword and to his surprise it brightened.

Mike cracked the heavy door at the other end of the hallwhich led to the kitchen and the servant areas. Here there was a darker, more pervasive pall. With his left hand he drew his short sword. He rounded the corner into the kitchen and froze.

Visually the first thing that assaulted his senses was the frost that covered everything. The hearth was dead and black, the logs thick with rime. The pots and pans all whitened. He almost slipped when crossing the threshold. And the air...the air was dead, like a freezer without ventilation: cold and dry. It was then that he saw the bodies of the servants and guards, twisted into a rictus laid out on the floor. Some gripped ladles others gripped their swords, but all of them had that horrible look in their eyes.

Whatever had happened, he knew that it was not natural and he knew that it was sorcery more powerful than he could wield. He tucked his gun into his belt and touched the butcher block. The ice was painful to the touch.

He was about to back out of the kitchen when the hair on the back of his neck rose. It felt as though someone with cold, icy breath was breathing down his back. When he heard the slither of scales he spun, his short blade flashing.

There was a hard impact and Mike's feet almost slid out from under him. *Daemon* was his immediate thought. Then: *No*. It was smaller and more tangible, a cousin of that creature perhaps, perhaps just as powerful. It swayed before him, grinning hellishly. He took it all in with a glance: skin, black or dark green, textured like sandpaper and rippling with power. Cold radiated from the being as well as a stench like a freshly opened septic tank. It had membranous wings that scraped the walls and ceiling as it swayed and slithered on a plated and scaled lower body. Yet the most unsettling thing about if was itsd head which had no eyes, just two twisted gashes that flared as if sniffing the air, A narrow row of small spikes ran from the brow ridge and spread out over the crest of its skull like a crown. It grinned, revealing sharp, dagger-like teeth.

He took it all in on the downward arc of his sword. The grin on the creature grew as the blade struck its hand, and for Mike it seemed the blade impacted a wall. He watched, almost trance-like as frost traveled up the length of the blade. As he tried to twist the sword away it shattered. He tried to use what was left of the blade by stabbing inward, but was again met by the hard plating of the creatures torso. He struck at the creature again, and this time the thing slithered forward and snatched the broken weapon from his hand. It disintegrated in a shower of frost.

"Shit!" Mike yelled as the thing backhanded him. He took the blow on the shoulder, and was flung against the wall. He collapsed on the floor.

"Outlander, Oran's reach is far and His minion's many." The voice grated on his nerves and it was like he was hearing the *Daemon's*, hellish voice all over again. He wanted to clasp his hands over his ears and shout the beast away.

"Cast in like, Outlander. The Saint's Soul will die! And you!" The creature talons clicked as it reached toward him.

A shout pierced from behind the unholy denizen of Oran and then there was a flash of black. The creature screamed and the beveled glass windows that lined the wall of the kitchen blew out. Surik Shadowlord's bastard sword had sheared through the creature's left wing and it tore off, shattering as it impacted on the floor. Mike rolled to the side just as Joe stepped back. The alchemist

61

drew his pistol and fired directly into the creatures face.

It lurched back; its tail whipped around and knocked Joe down the hall. Both talons went to its face as it screamed in agony, contorting as a silver light pierced its eyes and mouth, and shooting out of its ears and nostrils. Then the silver light spread as cracks appeared in the creatures body as its very fabric was torn apart. The whole creature shattered and fell to the floor in clumps of black, tainted ice.

In the distant wing of the Keep a long axe missed John as he rolled under it; the loud report of a pistol distracted the assailant long enough for John to square off against his enemy. Before him stood two in black armor. Their faces were effectively hidden by the strangely ornate helms they wore; both were armed, one with a morning star and the other with an axe.

Cornered, John stood at the bend of the corridor, looking down the hall into the wing where Gabrielle's chambers were. The man with the morning star lunged and swung. As the Lord Knight of Erie parried the blow, he caught the blur of the axe out of the corner of his eye. He threw himself at the first assailant and the axe cut the air behind him. The one who wielded the morning star stepped back as he was caught off guard. As the axeman adjusted his swing, John fell to the floor and rolled to the side. The axeman struck his cohort square in the chest; the blow lifted the man off his feet and sent him crashing into a displayed suit of armor. The axeman paused just long enough for John to sit up and shove the point of his katana beneath the man's surcoat and under his ribs, sending him to join his friend.

John got to his feet and flicked the tip of his blade, letting the blood splash the cloak of the dead man. He quickly ran down the length of the hall and came to Gabriella's chamber. At the door he listened but he heard nothing.

Wood exploded outward sending him tumbling back onto the body of the Hand. He lay there, chest heaving as he tried to catch his breath. A wave of cold power passed over him and he heard the crack of leather and the splintering of wood. The air that washed over him was cold, rank and fetid. Blackness crossed his vision as a scaled tail slapped onto the floor where he had been lying; wood splintered up from the sundered boards.

John looked up and gasped at the presence that loomed above him. All wings and tail, with the torso of a man and the skull of a demon, the creature reared back and laughed. It was the creature in his nightmare.

"Sooo, the White Knight. Thy Silver Light is Brightest! The Daemon will reward me!" Its voice was like ice and nails on a chalkboard. Arm snaking out, John could feel the cold radiate from it; he readied his sword but the need to use it never came. There was an earsplitting report and the creature reared back, almost falling in upon itself. Silver light spread from the gaping wound in its chest; silver light seemed to crack and split open the creature. With the sound of glass shattering the creature fell to the floor, naught more than a pile of black, sizzling ice.

John looked up to see Mike staring over the barrel of his flintlock. Joe, gaped at the sight, but soon slid past the big man and made his way toward the women's chambers. John was up on his feet and with him in a heartbeat.

He stopped.

Gabrielle sat huddled near the fireplace, a hot poker in her hand; she shuddered and gasped back tears. A black armored and helmeted man lay at her feet, the poker end stuck through the visor. Trianna lay on the floor, agony etching her frozen and dead features.

"She threw herself in front of it, and it did *that* to her!" Gabrielle cried out. The poker fell to the floor and she rushed to the safety of John's arms. He held her as she wept, and the scope of what had happened washed over him. Knees buckling, he took her from the room and passed his companions who now stood at the threshold; he saw his dismay mirrored in their eyes.

If their enemies had this power, they did not stand a chance.

Mike tore through his chambers, searching for his *Book of Shadows*. He had been making some notes on the text he had salvaged from Myella's Seat, the *Ih'dia*. The author's name was Korman Iss and much of the sorcery paralleled his own first steps in manipulation of the aether. Now with the minions of the *Daemon* in Kelvin's keep he did not know what to think. He did know that his first summoning of the Daemon had been a dreadful mistake.

He flung his clothes into the air, hoping to find his book buried beneath the detritus.

64

"Dammit!" he shouted as he ripped the heavy quilt from his bed, inadvertently knocking his jar of tobacco from the bed stand. It fell, spilling the cherry flavored tobacco onto the dingy leather cover of the *Ih'dia.* He grabbed it up in haste, noticing the black bound Book of Shadows beneath it.

He brought the hurricane lamp close; the light of the fireplace lacked the lumens needed to make out the fine writing in the book. There was light enough by far to read his own sprawling script, but the author of this ancient text had a fine, almost spidery writing style, that at times seemed to fade away.

He thumbed through the book. Written in the High Tongue of the Conclave, an ancient dialect, whose cadence was very formal and logical, it had taken him quite some time to plod through it. Much of the book seemed to be a preface, an introduction to the arts of sorcery and tapping the aether. He carefully looked over the various colored feathers used as reference markers.

He stopped and stared at the marker just short of the last page. Then he flipped to the last page, then he flipped to the front of the book, staring dumbfounded.

"Another text? A companion text? Volume Two? Why didn't I see this before?" He sat hard on the bed, looking at the open book before him. "Shit."

He closed his eyes and sighed. *If I had known...damn it*, but he did know better. The author of this text had assumed that the companion volume would be known. Mike had not guessed that was the case, until too late. He had been tapping the *aether* without complete knowledge. If he had known there was another step then he would not have tried half the things he had in the past three months.

He looked suddenly at the black book that sat on the floor. It stared back ominously and the hurricane lamp guttered. What had the old man at the Event said? *From the estate of Crowley? My ass!* He felt that prickling along the back of his neck and suddenly the *Book of Shadows* flipped open to a sigil toward the back of the book, beyond where he had written the last of his notes. *He* had not put it there. Somehow, he doubted that the book originated in his world.

The wall in front of him tore away stone by stone and Mike hastily drew a ward about himself with a wave of his hand. He clutched at the orb in his pocket feeling its heat radiating in his palm and realizing that it was glowing through the material of his tunic.

Mike stood on a ledge that had once been his quarters. Now before him lay a vista that was surreal in the twilight. Jagged rocks jutted like teeth into the sky; dark granite, rising high and only surmounted by the sea birds that drifted to the lofty summits. Below, the ocean was dusky lavender, reflecting the wash left by the setting sun. Dimly he was aware of a malign presence, something evil that stirred in the dim twilight below. There was a city on the water's edge, highlighted by an occasional gilt dome or spindly tower wrapped in ivy. It stretched out before him, once a vibrant metropolis; it was now a rotting dead thing. It had a malignant presence that seemed to be waiting, but for what? He noted that the high walls that encircled it from

66

the landside were unbroken and without a gate and the calm waters were split by a breakwater and a few jetties.

Looking at his own feet, he saw that he no longer stood on the flagstone floor of his room, but on a jagged outcropping of one of the finger-like mounts. Night fell as he stood there startled (clutching the orb so tight that his hand glowed red), he gazed out over the city and watched a speck rise out of the rent in the gilt dome. At first he thought it was a large bird, or even a courier beast, but then he felt a sinking feeling as it grew more defined. Despair gripped him in a physical vice.

Watching it approach, he felt both fascination and fear. Very similar to the creatures that had attacked them at Kelvin's Keep; it held an ominous power that the former did not. Blacker than night or the deepest abyss of hell, the creature still managed to reflect a slimy green and blue. Four taloned arms spread from an almost too human torso hidden occassionaly by the heavy thrust of its wings. Even at this distance and in the cool clean air of his lofty perch, Mike could smell the cold fetid odor of the demonic presence.

Its fiery eyes lit upon Mike and the *Daemon* winged toward the outlander. A grin spread across the obsidian skinned continence and Mike knew he had been recognized. A prickling told him his ward was probed, and the power that pulsed through the orb made it obvious that the Daemon could tear it away and rip Mike's soul from his corporeal body with ease.

Here, Mike was the summoned; he was in the *Daemon's* realm. He did not know how, or why. He did know, though, that his situation was dire.

The lavender sky deepened to cobalt and the Daemon alighted on a neighboring finger of rock, its snake-like lower body languidly wrapped around the pinnacle. Its thought, diseased and foul, found its way into Mike's mind.

Sooo, outlander, I have summoned thee. Hail thee the realm of Oran. It laughed and Mike heard it in his mind. It waved its arm at the city below. *Behold outlander; you are in the land between: that which was and now is. Here is where those of Oran thrived, where Korman Iss brought the aether to the world and where Oran walked for a time.*

"Why have you brought me here?"

Why, mortal? You have brought me! Thou did dare to summon me from my rest for mere knowledge of your inconsequential companions. You delve into that of Iss without thought and without reason. Now I have summoned thee. Here in Narn-toc I rule.

"I am not to be trifled with, Daemon. Remember I know your true Name!"

Do you, puny creature? And do you know the Souldeath, for which some within Oran would lovingly embrace, and which yet eludes? No, I thought not. But ere your journey in this realm is over the Saint's soul will find that respite, and the power shall not be Guyle's, but mine and Oran's.

"And Myella, does she fit into this?" The creature chuckled and Mike had the overwhelming urge to fall to his knees and vomit. The creature of

Oran looked at him, a darting tongue passing fang-like teeth, and eyes a blazing inferno.

Matter does it? Her designs are more material than her Master's. Her efforts are what you have recently faced. Her design falls within my Master's. But, for thou, none matters. Now your time is at an end mortal! Once you escaped me, not again. I give to Guyle what Guyle cannot take, and in the giving I shall taste your soul!

The creature of Oran sprang from its mount with heavy thrusts of its wings and with outstretched arms it speared toward Mike. The young man stood there, almost frozen with fear, but in that last instant, when the Daemon was upon him, Mike cast the orb directly into the creatures face.

An explosion of silver light blinded Mike to anything more than the image of the Daemon falling back to the city, to Narn-toc. And as quick as that it was over, Mike sat once more in his own chamber, staring at the *Ih'dia* and watching blood flow freely from his hand; cut by the sharp shards of the orb, now shattered and useless. He looked at the *Book of Shadows* debating on whether he ought to destroy it. Then he shook his head and gathered up his books. He reached up and felt the blood that dripped from the red weal that had been branded on his forehead during his encounter with Myella. He smiled grimly.

Narn-toc. The answer would lie there.

Chapter 5

Fire raged within the walls of Albien and the man who sat astride the gray warhorse thought about what lay before him. He was not a stone's throw from the city walls and the smoke that was billowing from the gate wall and its garrison just inside obscured the light of the moon. The commander smiled and nudged his mount to the side, out of the way of the battering ram that his men brought up the muddy and rutted road.

The rider grimaced as one of his men slipped and fell underneath the feet of his compatriots. *Fool, another man lost means more time getting within the walls.*

Boom! The ram met the huge wooden door, but no crack yet showed; Albien was made for siege. He cocked his head to the side, listening intently for the first crack, yet it was long in coming. He knew that his lieutenants would hear the break ere he did; his ear was ruined by a sword strike. His grip tightened on the saddle horn at the thought of the encounter; the stiffness in his shoulder reminded him all the more of the man who was responsible.

He shrugged his cloak over the rump of his mount and revealed a golden dagger encircled by a ring of fire emblazoned on his tunic; the symbol of the Guard of Oran and of the Regent of the Southern Seat. Lord Duran of Qwen felt no pride in wearing it, just duty.

First Ord had fallen with ease, already poisoned from within by the agents of Oran. The loss of two of its Lords within as many fortnights made that city ripe for the picking. Then Tarn Hold. That had been

70

long in the making; intrigue that had roots many years deep. Now Albien, but Albien had held; now a month they lay under siege. Duran's small army surrounded the city and attacked from all sides but the bay. On the waterside sat four triremes, ramming ships, ready to prevent passage of any vessel.

Albien would not be a complete corruption like Tarn Hold. Slowly, insidiously they had wormed their way into its heart, Myella releasing the spirit of the Keth into the night and slowly enveloping their souls in shades of darkness. Albien had been resistant, its people simple hardworking folk led by a man, noble and strong. Duran spat. He would soon feel that man quiver at the edge of his steel, just as he had the leaders in the other cities. He would imagine the Lord Knight of Erie dying before him. He had broken the council of Tarn Hold; killing four of the seven, and then taking the matriarch. She had been a beauty; he had shown her to the subjugated citizenry after his men had finished with her. She had moaned and sobbed, begging him for mercy, so he had cut her throat.

Yet, amid all this, thoughts of Gabrielle and a stolen kiss intruded.

Myella had watched at each victory and at each rape and sack. Flitting back and forth to Helm where the Black Guard amassed under her control, and where she slowly shifted the power from the White and Black Guard to that of the Cult of Oran. She plotted against the Conclave and no doubt plotted against her own uncle: Guyle.

Bastion would fall next. The capitals of the Western Provinces would all capitulate one by one

71

and he would be the master of the conquest. He laughed aloud and his men looked up startled. No matter, before this night was over Albien would fall. Within the next year, all of the South would be under his Regency. Could Surik Shadowlord, even under the control of Myella, have led these men to such victories? He did not think so. His nostrils flared at the stench of pitch and tar and burning flesh. Then, with a great crash the gate burst inward. What was this? He spotted one lone man astride a white stallion; no doubt the Duke. Duran unsheathed his sword and saluted the man and then with a wave of his saber Duran's horsemen swept toward the breach. Duran was astonished at the man's bravery, or was it stupidity, as he watched the Duke fend off the Guard of Oran with but a few footmen. Duran smiled as he saw the man's horse stagger then fall back, in toward the city. His smile faded as he realized what was happening.

"Fall back, you fools!" he shouted over the din of battle. On the walls, the arbalest and cross bowmen had taken up position and, as Duran's men moved within, a wave of arrows rained down on the Guard of Oran from both sides. Men on horse, wreaking confusion on the Guard and spelling doom for the besiegers, struck the men within the wall.

"Damn fools, pull back!" He nearly jerked his lieutenant from the saddle as he leaned over and shouted in the man's face. "Go in there and pull them back, Kiuf, or I'll send them to the Keth!"

The man went pale and nodded, then spurred his steed toward the middle of the fray. Soon even Duran lost him in the thick of the melee, smoke and night made the players indistinct. He sat back in his saddle; the hillock sloped low before him all the way to the city walls. Ever wary of the threat of projectiles he eased his mount back to the pavilion that sat out of harms range. The city militia had a penchant for wearing black also and at this distance it was hard to tell who fought whom. He had thought his men were among the best trained; obviously, he would have to reevaluate them if they did not end up dead.

The Duke was a good tactician, drawing his men in by flaunting himself as a prize, a pincer movement designed to fell the cavalry and demoralize the Guard of Oran. He looked over his shoulder to the tent and wondered if he should stoop so low to use the Sorcery of Oran. Minor sorcery ate Galfeon Yor, but then speed was of the essence and they needed to get the Outlander. Here he would rather have a clean victory, without the taint.

He closed his eyes, ignoring his men who protected him and let the sounds of battle, the clash of steel, the shouts of men, and the screams of the dying wash over him. There was the gong of a temple bell in the distance and the sound of wood burning, yet it was faint to his right ear, long since numbed.

Another six months of this and he would govern the South. Then he would march on Paravel and he would raze it, maybe sooner and, if the winter proved mild, late spring. Yes, he would split his force, which now numbered about fifteen thousand. In the Spring he would meet up with the rest of Oran's Guard who by then would be on the march to Narn-toc and they would lay siege to Paravel. He knew the siege would not last long;

they would blockade the harbor with ships from Clef and the city would be bursting at the seams with refugees from the West.

It consoled him that he would burn that city to the ground. It would be a cleansing to be rid of that black mark on his past, that failure. He would hang the White Knight by his entrails, Myella and Guyle be damned.

He heard soft laughter and looked over his shoulder. Myella.

"Duran, must I always come to your rescue? Your men founder at the breach even as their Duke rallies his people. Should the Keth fly and destroy at my behest?" She crossed her arms. Myella, High Priestess of Oran and Surrogate of the South stood in dark cloak and battle harness, her tawny figure intimidating. Long brown hair pulled back by a gold circlet, already announcing her as Conclavetrix. She looked at Duran, her dark eyes hooded and secretive.

"It is but a distraction. I will lose thirty or forty men and they will fall back. The Duke will repair the gate and the siege will last another fortnight. It is a game called war, my liege."

"Your attack is failing, dear Duran. If you want to reach Bastion by late fall then we must take Albien this week. Is it not a wonderful port by which to supply Narn-toc?"

"You are obsessed with Narn-toc," he muttered as he turned his eyes back to the battle. He noticed that his men pulled back sharply, more at the sight of several score horsemen than at the behest of his lieutenant.

"And you, my dear Regent, you are obsessed with Gabrielle. Why, when you could have her cousin?" Myella tilted her head to the side, letting her tongue caress her lips.

"It is in the wanting, my liege. Besides, I have had you, many a night." He laughed at the look of disdain that crossed her face. "No doubt I would tire of Gabrielle in time." His voice trailed off as he watched the Guard begin to fall back. She wanted to unleash the Keth he knew *that*. But this time he would not allow her that dark joy. He wanted this to be clean, with the fight of men and the contest of arms. *Gods, if those things were to be free they would corrupt all of Carn*. He shivered at the thought of the Keth. Remembering Ord and Tarn chilled him and made him despise himself for participating in those battles. Almost all the people of Ord dead, and they were surely better off than the few left broken or mad. The city was now as foul as any pit of Oran. Tarn Hold had been only a little better. There the people were subjugated, and Myella now had more than a few to serve her and Guyle. One quarter of the city despoiled by the Keth.

"One word and so falls Albien, Lord Duran, and as the West falls so shall the Outlanders. Just give me the word." Myella looked at him, her face expectant. He suddenly realized it was like the *kifu* drugs that the Krim used; addiction begets oblivion. The thought of it somehow made him furious and he twisted in his saddle to look down on her.

"I do not need your creatures of Oran to win this city! I need it as a port, not as a cesspool. The Keth will despoil this as they did Ord and Tarn

Hold. That I will not have! It will fall within the fortnight!" Duran watched her grow livid and storm back to the tent.

"Some day that too will be your undoing, Duran," he heard her growl.

"As it will with the White Knight, I am sure," Duran echoed as he motioned his steed toward his demoralized men. Maybe he would forget in the heat of battle.

Chapter 6

"Tell me about your sword, Mrick." Adon said it as subtly as he could while riding his steed over a narrow streambed. Mrick rode next to him, about a yard away, and looked up sharply.

"My sword?"

"Yes, I have not seen its likeness before. It looks to be made of a strange metal."

"Yes, well, twas formerly Sir Chill's, the outlander that we buried on Hiiram's hill. He told my master Baxel that it was made of some strange steel. I call it Baxel's Bane."

"Aptly named I am sure." Adon looked at the straight cross hilt for a moment and then let his gaze drift back to the road, no, path more like. The Southern Treadway had long since grown over with brush and weed, obscuring almost all of the mileposts that once marked the way through the Great Forest and the Teeth of Narn to the city of Narn-toc; the fabled capital of the older Conclaveum.

Here the trees rose to mammoth height and girth, dwarfing the younger woods in elevation and age. Ferns graced the path that now deer and other game took, telling of the age that had passed since the last man or woman had made the sojourn to the Dead City. It had been days since they began their passage beneath the boughs of the Great Forest, which now rained leaves of brilliant orange and burnt umber, bright yellow and dusky red. With every breeze, a wash of color would obscure the party of twenty-four led by Barj, Mrick's second. Autumn was upon them as rays of golden sunlight speared through the canopy of leaf and wood to glint off mail and lance point.

"I have never traveled this far east. I was born in a small fishing village and there recruited by Baxel. I had thought Galfeon Yor a big city until I had visited Ord in my eighteenth year. Have you traveled this way?"

"Once before, with my father, when I was a child."

"Is your father a noble?"

Adon smiled cynically and nodded. "Aye, yet I care not for the intrigues of the court."

"We did not have that at Trevor's Keep."

"Then I envy your Lord Trevor for that sensibility."

There was a long pause as both men became lost in their thoughts. The sounds of the horse's hooves on rock, the rustling of dried leaves and the creak of the limbs in gentle wind, it could lull a man to sleep. Adon's last journey to the city had not been quite so idyllic.

"I must have been about five," Adon continued, "when my father and a few of his trusted retainers brought my brother and me to Narn-toc. It had been to teach us a lesson, he said. I don't think it was this exact route, I think we came the Paravel way. It was in the fall, like now, and we came upon the city in the early evening. It was quiet, almost serene and you would not think anything odd except that there should have been thousands of people; there were none. You could feel an underlying unease. There were secrets within that city, but there was no want for them. We stood beneath the Teeth of Narn and looked upon the seamless wall. My father explained that what had become of Narn-toc could become of anyone who had greed in his or her heart and abused power.

"He would not let my brother or I go into the city, but he and Suren, his Elder, went within the sealed walls. My brother and I begged to go also. *No*, he said. It was too dangerous. Why? We asked. 'Because what lies within tempts a man and the darkness would devour such a fragile soul as yours over the years to come.'"

"And you take us to this evil place?" Mrick was shocked. He reined in his horse sharply, letting Barj and the rest of the party round a bend. He looked at Adon a long minute before feeling a chill at the man's steady gaze.

"I would not jeopardize you or your men, Mrick. *I* go to the Dead City. You are my escort there, and I have paid you for such. I do not, however, expect you to accompany me within the walls."

"Why?"

"Then I shall finish my story?"

"Go on," replied Mrick as he urged the horse forward.

"We camped outside those walls, my father's men at arms staying with us to assure our safety. My father and a few others went into Narn-toc. They returned later that same day, their faces were ashen and they would not speak. Later that night we heard the thunder of wings. It was like bats fleeing a cave, those sounds. Suren looked to my father, saying that *it* was still there in the city. My father hushed him and forbade him to speak of *it*. Suren

79

went mad later that year and died. They were not bats, not winged animals in the night"

"Courier beast?"

"I think not, friend Mrick. It was something more malevolent. Something confined within the walls of Narn-toc, something that had awakened after a long slumber. It was maddening to any but those with the strongest of wills. Alas, Suren, even though he was knowledgeable, must had been weak of will.

"The next morning my father turned toward the road and left Narn-toc behind. He never spoke of it in the days of travel that followed. Not until we were in the safety of our home."

"Why do you go there?"

"I think you know why. What happened in Ord and threatens Albien. What has passed in Tarn Hold and what has destroyed Galfeon Yor threatens to destroy you and others. While I was sequestered, I warned my brothers of it. They would not listen. They thought I was young and impetuous and prone to fancy. Well, it destroyed the Sequestiary just as surely as an assassin in the night and sent many of us into hiding. Only because of my faith in Tarn and clear wits did I escape the city before it fell to the Keth and Oran.

"What I saw at Galfeon Yor frightens me. It tells me that one of your Outlanders is delving into something that he should not. There is only one way to prevent it. To find the *Ih'dia Om* of Korman Iss and forever bind the Keth to Narn-toc."

"You confuse me with riddles, friend Adon. What is this *Ih'dia Om*, and who is Korman Iss, and what are the Keth?"

"There are dark things in this world, things that should not even be discussed in the light of day; especially not this near Narn-toc. Nevertheless, I feel that it is my responsibility to take you there informed.

"At one time Narn-toc was the Summer Seat of the Conclaveum, til its ruler Untheran, engaged a Sorcerer to make him immortal. This Sorcerer was Korman Iss, and he was opposed by his own apprentice Ghin-jo, and the two great Captains of the Guard, Ythrinny and Exten Rhinn.

"Ythrinny commanded the Black Guard who held the Summer Seat, and Exten Rhinn Commanded the White guard of the Winter Seat. Suffice to say, that when they tried to oust Untheran and his mage, war broke out. And in this horrific war such forces were let loose that the Great Wall was brought forth and a terrible evil was unleashed in Narn-toc."

"Did Untheran get his immortality?"

"Oh, yes. He achieved eternity with Oran." He smiled wryly.

"Some would say it nothing more than Myth, friend Mrick. I know not, it could be."

"That is why Narn-toc is called the Dead City, because they perished from the evil?"

"In a way, but definitely not in one battle. In the cloak of night the Daemon and his Keth descended into the city and beneath it. That is where the evil lies, for that is the path to the underworld. For some reason, there is a *Gate* deep below the city, which offers a way by which these creatures may travel. Over the years, the power of Oran devoured the souls of the people of Narn-toc. It maligned them, turning them inward upon themselves. It made them paranoid and fearful. Those strong enough fled to the West, the others remained within the walls. The Conclave fell back behind the security of the Great Wall. The city dwindled and became stagnant. Finally, the only inhabitants were the corrupted souls of the damned. Or so it is said. The walls were sealed, but some looters go in now and then. Fools all, they risk their mortal souls for material wealth."

"But these Keth are free now?"

"I believe so and other creatures. Iss was very adept at the dark arts."

"And what of Tarn, what force has he to fight these dark things?"

"Tarn is truth and light. Tarn reveals what lies in the dark."

"That does not console me."

"No, but look the sun is low on the horizon and soon the Southern Treadway will descend to the Teeth of Narn. Let us hail Barj, who I see is well ahead, and make camp."

"Aye, no more talk of the dark." He paused. "Is there a defense against Oran?"

"Do not fear Oran this night, just his minions. And good friend Mrick, I think that blade of yours may ward even the Keth away." Adon chuckled and it heartened the man-at-arms. Mrick spurred his horse onward to Barj and the rest of the men. Adon frowned and looked over the lengthening shadows on the forest floor. It was not good to talk of such in the night. He would ward the camp, especially this close to Narn-toc.

Night came fast to the Great Forest. Lengthening rays of golden light were soon obscured by the wide girth of the trunks and left the group of travelers in the dim twilight. Barj was quick to build a fire in a small glade that had once been home to a vintner and his vines. Now nothing more than a stone foundation remained and wild grapes twined about the stone columns that once supported wooden beams. Most of the men gathered about the fire, warming their hands in the chill night air and laughing around mouthfuls of sweet grapes.

Hours before, they had passed dark igneous rock formations that cut through the trees like wading giants, it told Adon that they were closer to the Teeth of Narn than he had thought. Now as Adon watched Mrick skin and dress two fat rabbits, he wondered if it was wise to have brought Mrick and his men to Narn-toc. He knew that there could have been no other way, already the dark sorcery of Galfeon Yor and what happened there had begun to eat at them. Soon they would have succumbed to a dark bitterness and eventually the evil that was brought on by using the sorcery of Iss. In closing the *gate* at Galfeon Yor he had destroyed what remained of the keep, making the tunnels and catacombs beneath the castle fall in upon themselves. Thus, Tarn's Magic had sealed the path and any hope remaining for that village becoming more than a ghost town was lost.

Leaning against a broken column, he rested his chin on his fist and watched Mrick. The man laughed as he spit the rabbit, joking about how it was barely enough for himself let alone his men. Soon the scent of cooking meat lent itself to that of pine and mulch, fat soon hissed on the burning coals. Adon passed up his portion, stating he was not that hungry. As the men eventually bedded down, a lone guard whittled at a piece of wood. Adon slipped into the shadows and the darkness of the forest.

In the darkness, he felt more than saw the density of the trees thin and the darker, more solid shapes began to take form. Here, more than anywhere else in this world, the raw bones of the earth were prominent. Heavy rock, black and jagged thrust up from the fertile soil, pushing like fingers toward the sky. Soon the woods of the Great Forest gave way to pine and other fir trees. The Teeth of Narn became dark silhouettes against the starry backdrop of the night sky. The air took on a more chill and damp atmosphere. Adon felt the same change that he had felt all those years ago; it was unmistakable.

It could have been a lapse for him to come out into the night this close to the Dead City. Some of the teachers in Tarn Hold had said that the evil had grown, that even the land around the city became maligned and touched by the presence of Oran and his minions. Even as he came to the pass that led through the Teeth, he knew, he felt, that his teachers were right, even though precious few had believed his foretelling of danger to the city of Tarn Hold.

Forest soon gave way to the harsh rocky substrate and pine needle and leaf no longer softened the course of the path. Like black fingers, pushing from hell the Teeth of Narn thrust towards the sky, hundreds of feet, blocking out Shaj'il Cziffer and the stars. As the Teeth rose like a wall on either side of him, they also parted down the center allowing the faint light of the moon to show

84

the way to the once proud capital of the Conclaveum. Knowing he should wait until the morning, yet drawn like a loadstone, he approached the edge of the Teeth and looked over the descent and down to the ocean and the city of Narn-toc.

His breath hissed between his teeth as he looked upon the Dead City. There were lights in Narn-toc, dead no longer.

Chapter 7

It was in the early afternoon when Tom Smiling Wolf spotted the hawk circling in the distance. He had been paralleling the Great Wall for almost a week now; the Crevasse, Kiera, and the Hand of Keth were far behind.

Kiera, his poor Kiera. He knew what her fate had been; the tie between them was gone.

Then there was Chill.

He thought of the Hand of Keth. The voice of the Hand had been so familiar. It was the voice of Chill; he knew he was not mistaken. *But how?* Chill had been killed. He had helped bury his friend and now he had faced a simulacrum of the stout man. *How?* The question kept blocking out all other thought in his mind. *I have to tell the guys about this.*

He moved through the thicket, overstepping a rock, slipped and almost fell into a deep streambed. His vision kept fading in and out in his right eye. *My eye is made out of glass and I can see out of the damn thing!* It was impossible for any type of biological regeneration to have taken place. *What then? Magical?* He shook his head as his vision became binocular. He spotted what the hawk had been wheeling over; there was a small, almost smokeless campfire in a dense wood, not in the open fields between the thickets.

Daylight was quickly fading as he trundled down the slope of the hill and into the stand of trees. He clutched at his side where the Hand of Keth's staff nicked him. A week passing by had not healed it nearly as quickly as was his wont. By now, there should have been a dark scab and tender skin beneath, but instead there was a scabrous wound seeping white fluid. He had treated it the best he could with clotting herbs and a mixture of clay and root, and it had slowly begun to heal. Even now, though, he knew that he was fighting an infection. His skin was dry and feverish and nausea had prevented him from keeping anything but crude tea down.

It would have been in his best interests to avoid the copse and the person, or people, or *things* that had built the fire. Prudence, however, was not always the course that Tom Smiling Wolf took, he being a descendant of the Lakota. Consoled by the fact that he at least retained his knife, he stole through the copse amid oak and maple touched by the colors of fall.

He paused and listened carefully for any hint that his progress might have been detected. He had taken the same precautions in the Crevasse at Helm; there all his men had ended up dead and Kiera as well. *Had it been Chill?* He peered over a moss-covered boulder and to the small clearing below. There was the fire and a spitted rabbit, but no one was tending the small blaze.

It was strange, Tom noted, a feeling that was somewhat distant as he licked dry lips and rested his cheek on the cool comfort of the rock, kneeling in the waist high ferns. He could almost taste the roasting meat; smell the juices, hot and savory, dripping from the lean haunches. His mouth was watering at the sight of this small game. Maybe it was the fever or his hunger, he did not know. He threw all caution to the wind and stepped down into the clearing, his steps were heavy and awkward. Up blew the fallen leaves, obscuring his vision, biting with the hiss of bark and branch. He cast his arm in front of his face to ward off the glancing blows. Sharp silence followed as the whirlwind ceased.

He stood staring at the tip of his own knife, not a centimeter from his left eye, the one of flesh.

"I heard you coming for quite some time," said a voice and Tom looked to the man at the other end of his own knife. Weakness almost buckled his legs and it was an effort to focus on he who now held Tom's life in peril.

The man stood in tattered white cloak, now dingy with dirt and mud, sleeveless tunic baring arms just as filthy as the rest of his clothes, and boots, more suited for the court than the wild. The man wore a makeshift kilt, not the traditional breeches that were common to the more southerly. It may have been more functional than cultural, given the condition of the rest of the man's clothing.

Tom's gaze wandered haphazardly up to the man's face. Narrow, with eyes like a hawk, steely and with a hint of wildness, and maybe even admiration for this man who stood with effort barely an inch from his own knife. His hair was lighter than Tom's, bleached across the brow, and he wore a beard unkempt and not very long. His skin was dark, yet that was fading even as the fall faded into winter.

Kiera is dead. Now his mind was spinning away, like one of those leaves caught up by the wind. Another man had his knife. *I am without weapon, friends gone, time gone, and place gone.* He squeezed his eyes shut and opened them. *I can see with both my eyes. This will take some rethinking.* Even with fever, Smiling Wolf managed to knock aside the knife and lunge precariously for the man. But the man, healthy and without the taint of the poison that the Hand of Keth's staff had left in Tom, casually stepped to the side as Tom stumbled and fell flat on his face; unconscious, the wound taking its toll.

Smiling Wolf was loping over the land, his brothers next to him, and his sisters behind. Frost lay on the ground and the hunt brought nothing. Those with two legs had driven their kind to the setting sun and had left little for those of the land. Now, as he stopped and lapped some water from a stream, he watched through the thicket as a black line of the two-legged ran the ridge a short span away. They looked to the other side, what was the other side?

Ah, the place where caves rose above the ground. Now the two-legged let it *loose. First the smell came. His hackles rose. Then came the sounds, the discord and shattering, that of antlers on the rock. A low growl rose in his brothers throats and he joined them in a howl as the* Deathwing *leapt from the* Gate *and over the ridge.*

Soon the place of the two-legged was with the bright fire and the stench of death and more. White Beard looked at him, a smile grew, and lips revealed sharp canines, wishing to tear at Deathwing. *This was for the two-legged, not his kind. Yet, was it? He sensed distress in his other half, that which was not mentioned because it crossed the space of aether into the Great Rolling Land. He knew he must go to himself.*

Ache gave way eventually to warmth. The pain in his side was gone and no more did he feel numbed by the fever. He looked about. Night had fallen and he lay wrapped in a tattered white cloak, a fire blazed not two feet away, sending sparks and embers into the night sky. His side was wrapped tightly in cloth and he noted that the edge of a broad leaf was tucked between it and his flesh. The wound did not seep any longer and only the dark stain that was blood, not infection, soiled the bandage. He sat up and noticed that he was quite hungry, and this became even more evident when he saw that not one, but two rabbits cooked over the fire.

Slowly he looked around finding his knife thrust into the ground a few feet away. He eyed it suspiciously and stayed where he was. *Where was the steely-eyed man?*

He breathed deeply, not really remembering how long he had lain here, surely several hours for his wound to have a new dressing.

He reached out and pinched a piece of the rabbit from the spit. It was hot, but it tasted good as the juice caressed his palate; he was famished.

"Chien et ien, kir et tuin giremn." Tom looked over his shoulder at the man who had so mysteriously disarmed him. Clad in the same clothes save the cloak, now cleaner and hair slicked back with wetness. He threw two fish at Tom's feet.

"Chien et si?" the man said, as he looked down at Tom, then he shook his head and squatted down by the fire. "I must remember that you Southerners speak little of the Higher tongues." His accent was strange to Tom's ears, and it reminded him faintly of Myella's.

90

"Do you eat your fish raw or cooked?"

"It doesn't matter," Tom muttered, looking somewhat dazedly at the two silver-scaled fish on the ground near the fire.

"I'll cook them. I don't want you weakened if these fish carry a sickness."

Tom nodded as the man leaned over and began to scale the fish on the edge of Tom's blade. "How long?" he asked as he let the cloak fall away and leaned closer to the fire. "Several hours, I take it?"

"Several days, Southerner."

"What?" Tom was incredulous. Had his fever been that bad to confuse his time sense? He scanned the sky above the thicket quickly and looked for the moon. Sure enough the ringed satellite was now waxing gibbous where before it had been a half moon.

"You were in the midst of, how do you say? A fever sleep, from the wound of the *kris-voulge*. They are hard to heal, and even a glancing blow has caused a strong man to die." He wrapped the scaled and gutted fish in a wet leaf and pushed it under the glowing coals. "I recognized it; I have seen it a few times on the battlefield. Not many men or women will use a *kris-voulge* because it is unpredictable and there is certain manipulation of the *aether* that the user finds...distressing. It is not a wholesome weapon, and I have seen the thing backfire more than once. I recognized the wound though, and the way it festers. I have dressed you in the common whitesap leaf. It draws out the poison and leaves a restorative. Two more days and you will be fine."

"I don't have two days."

91

"You will have less if you push yourself." Tom grunted and sat back against the bole of a fallen tree. Instinctively his body told him that this man was right. Silence slowly took the minutes, and soon the voices of the night took over, the cicada and the cricket, an owl somewhere, and in the distance the echo of wolves. *Wolves, what is it about wolves?*

Tom found himself startled from dozing and looking at a piece of bark in his lap. It held one cooked and blackened fish, two haunches of rabbit, and what looked like wild onion.

"Go ahead, Southerner, it will give you strength."

"Tom, my name is Tom Smiling Wolf. I am a tracker and a guide." He looked up at his host's unsmiling blue eyes.

"Marad," the man said and looked down. "And for the moment, I am nothing."

Chapter 8

"People lose sight of the past, they don't remember. In their failure to remember they often miss the greater schemes and resolve only that which is in the present.

"I was but a child when my grandfather told me of Narn-toc, the evil there, and what men do in greed. He had seen it from his felucca - lost at sea in a storm - when he was as a child, and when he told me he was ancient and near death. Now I am nearing his age. The cycle follows, but few remember beyond those historians and sorcerers who deem it important. Very few do.

"There is little written of the Shadowed Lands: The realm of Oran. I prattle on like an old man that I am, and forget my guests. How is the karo?"

Bill nodded between a sip of the hot drink, realized how stupid he must look and said, "It is good, friend Farok."

Farok nodded in silent acknowledgment. Wisps of sparse white hair tangled over a shiny leathern pate. His face had the craggy weathered features of a man who had spent years at sea or in the desert. Lined and tough, very little fat still remained on this man; now he was mostly sinew and bone, a remnant of his youth; a shadow himself.

He leaned over the hearth pot and stirred the contents, then cocked his head to the side and paused. "Your friends return." The door slammed open.

Two hooded and cloaked figures hurried in, the wind whipped into the room, carrying leaves and sleet. As soon as the door shut the first threw back his hood to reveal sharp aquiline features, trimmed beard and a face crossed with two scars; one ran along the bridge of his nose and beneath his eyes and the other ran from his temple to his jaw line. Torec el'Kirien, former merchant of Clef and now mercenary, cast a weary eye on the small stead. Then he casually shrugged off his cloak and nodded to Bill. His companion followed suit, letting her mass of wavy hair fall from the hood. She looked with those piercing eyes that Bill had come to respect and love. Tar'elah clad in leather hunting clothes sat down on the floor and began to unlace her boots.

"My young friend Torec," began their host. He now carefully ladled the stew into shallow wooden bowls, being careful not to overflow the vessels by placing his fingers at their edge. "I was just explaining to the Bard here what people forget."

"Come Farok, Bard William will come to think that we are an island of historians."

"And well he should. *What are the sword and the pike but weapons of war, by which honest men become savages and the innocent, suffer? What after innocence but art?* Thus I quote from the Qin el'Aba."

"Is that a religious book?" Bill asked, never one to stray from learning more of these people.

"A religious book? No, more poetry. I wrote it. Qin el'Aba in the Middle Tongue means: Thoughts on Sunset."

"Farok was one of the most noted poets of Clef, before the Guard of Oran came."

"Torec practices more in sophistry than flattery, friend Bard. Those agents of the Conclaveum

94

tolerated my diatribes as much as they tolerate the withholding of taxes. My poetry earned me this." He pointed to his face and smiled, Bill's gaze was drawn not to the old man's smile, rather to the eyeless sockets.

"You see my friend, just before Torec had to flee Clef, I was put to task for my writings and my outspoken beliefs. The Regent was not very tolerant."

Bill shook his head, Tar'elah looked quizzically at his disgust as she whisked off her tunic and quickly pulled a wool blanket about her; Bill sensed it was more from the cold than from modesty.

"So they blinded you."

"They took my sight, thinking that if I could not read I could not speak or write. Of course, they were wrong. I have a scribe, and occasionally I will speak, in private to a select few. No more at the Steps of the Mount."

"You were foolish to go there that day," Torec interjected. He sat at the rickety table and spooned some of the broth.

"Do not berate an old man for the tradition of his family." He turned to Bill, his eyes like pits in the dark cabin. "You see Bard, twas the tradition of my grandfather, my father, and me to speak on the seventh day of Jaffe, every year, to address all people in social commentary, and regail the previous year.

"It was one of those brilliantly clear days, where the sky is the richest blue, the water a deep emerald green, and the clouds are like cushions placed sparingly amid the cobalt. The garrison of the Guard of Oran had occupied the island since

Optun. Yes, there were many of them there, but of them, I thought nothing. My only thoughts were of the tradition in my family and the oratory that I had prepared.

"Oh, it was a fine speech, denouncing the evil of complacency and dominance. The Conclaveum was the predator state, devouring the smaller, weaker, but often creatively brilliant city-states. It was to be my finest speech, but I was then blind even more so than now. My arrogance overbore my reason. I found myself before a crowd of citizens, but in their midst was the rot that had infested my fair Clef. The Guard of Oran!"

Torec nodded; the crackling of the hearth fire, the wind whistling through the eaves, left them enraptured by Farok's tale. The man sat back in his chair, blackened sockets now only shadows, and Bill could see the man's former stately self. The aristocratic lines and penetrating brows were not lost, just disguised by the years. He heaved a heavy sigh and his fingers kneaded a woolen cloak nervously.

"They took me then, and not another of my fellows attempted to stop them, even though they outnumbered the guard at least twenty to one. I think that was more of a hint of the rot that had taken Clef than anything.

"They did this to me," he said as he gestured to his face. "Only after they ransacked and burned my villa and killed my wife and the servants. That was the most difficult thing that I had ever watched, and I believe that they sensed it. One of the Guards, an officer by name of Ectel took a hot brand to my eyes.

"'No more will you have to watch!' he said. And here I am." He motioned about the hovel. "My legacy."

***

Torec watched the emerald waves lap against the rock-strewn shore, wetting the rich green mosses and grass that separated Farok's hut and the sea by naught more than a stone's throw. This was the leeward side of the isle, once the site of estates of the wealthier merchants and families of Clef, now only dotted with ruins and burnt out villas. Torec could make out the blackened white-stone wall of his former estate in the distance, overgrown and crumbling. As his thoughts wandered over his past he sensed someone approach from the hut.

"I am an exile, and only now did I realize this."

"We are all exiles in our own fashion," the Bard's replied. Torec did not glance back but felt the younger man at his shoulder.

"I suppose we create our own prisons. What of you Bard, do you build walls?"

"We all do, but it is what they are designed for that guides our actions."

"How so?"

"Do we build them to keep something out, or something in? And what is worse?"

"You are wise beyond your years Bard."

"Me? No, I just point out the obvious." Bill rested his hand on Torec's shoulder. The merchant tensed for a moment, then accepted the token of friendship.

"That was once my home, Bard. Now all that remains is the wall and part of the aqueduct. You know, I imported the tile from Qwen, from the kilns there; nothing quite like that color, not quite blue, not quite green, lost in between. I had a garden, and a gardener. There was a pond with fish. At one time, we of Clef were very proud of our gardens and ponds. We did not expect what happened."

"Where we come from we also tend to take things for granted," Bill said, noting how this spot reminded him of Marblehead. "We were free."

"You are wrong my young friend. Freedom is just another form of tyranny, bound by illusion. We were ever looking outward; we did not expect the rot from within. Fed no doubt by Myella and the Guard of Oran, we destroyed ourselves. It is the eye that looks always away for evil, that rarely casts its glance inward. We did this to ourselves."

"Then how can it be undone, Torec."

"If the rot is in the limb you must cut it off."

"What if the rot is here?" Bill asked, tapping his forehead.

"There are always new beginnings, Bard." Torec turned and smiled at the young musician. He really had not answered the question.

Clef was a large island, several days east and north of Paravel by *felucca*, one of the faster ships available to the merchant class. Rough limestone and high promontories cut its shoreline. It seemed that autumn only brought out the richer greens of the shore and the amber and dusky reds in the orchards that ringed the Mount; rising like a pinnacle to dominate northern shore of the island; overshadowing the cities and villages.

Once marked by shipping activity Clef now seemed frozen under the watchful eye of the Guard of Oran. Ghostly fishing villages dotted the shore, peopled by folk who were reluctantly subservient else they might find themselves in burned out estates like those who had dissented. No more, as the Guard's thoroughness made sure that no one of influence would speak out against the righteous Conclaveum.

The Mount surveyed the whole of the island-state. Orchards dotted the lower slopes of the Mount that thrust upward on the northern quarter of the isle; itself slanted like a sundial, casting a shadow to either side of the island in the morning and then the afternoon. Below the western face of the Mount sat Avard Clef, capital of the island-state. Yet, this city, once a teaming and thriving center of trade, fed by a canal that cut its way from the western port village of Icam, was now haunted by the economics of tyranny. There was an old adage that the Guard of Oran was remiss in studying: *Once the coffers are empty, you cannot feed the children with the wood and the leather of which it is made.*

Slowly, over the past several years merchants realizing that troops of the Conclaveum occupied Clef were reluctant to put in port and pay the high tariffs that the Regent was imposing. The season passed without Obright the One-eyed or Gambril of the Silk Mongers gracing the halls of the merchant's guild. It seemed as though the golden age of Clef had passed and now dominance by an outside force was to govern the destiny of the island-state.

So it seemed, at least to Rhianne ar'Liaiyne, governor of Clef. Still the merchant halls were graced by courtiers and traders, though now tension was apparent and the laughter strained. The few that came to meet the governor and offer their wares were asking higher and higher prices for their goods.

Rhianne ar'Liaiyne sat pensively on the high chair of her station looking over what should have been a hall crowded with merchants awaiting her audience, instead she looked at the hollow eyes of the lower nobility; the young rich, now poor. They stood at a distance aware of her mood. With one raised eyebrow she looked over her two guard dogs romping in the middle of the floor, often sliding on the shiny marble tiles. Ikn, the red maned female, and Teg the cream colored male, tangled with one another in amusement, aloof of the courtiers and servants. Ar'Liaiyne was not amused; today was the second of sales and already she was paying outrageous amounts to compensate for the high taxes. Pursing her lips she sat back, crossed her arms, and her foot began tapping out a deadly stiletto rhythm that the aids and attendants knew all too well. Bad weather was brewing on the mount. Blue eyes flashed and golden hair was tossed back by a slender, but bejeweled hand. One would say she was attractive, nay beautiful, if not for the anger that dwelt beneath the surface of that alabaster face; possibly it was held in check only by the strength inherit in the strong lines of her nose and jaw.

One would say that a person of her scant years, only just past one third of a century, had little or no business as governor of Clef, except possibly as a puppet for the Conclaveum. Ar'Liaiyne was far from that. Schooled in all the laws and politics of the island-state from an early age, she had acquired the position through wit and the simple mathematics of attrition. The former governor had been very stupid in his dealings with the Guard of Oran, and soon very few qualified individuals had wanted the lofty position, or for that matter to be associated with anyone who aspired to it. She had to agree that now it was barely a position worth having.

She sighed, smoothed her magenta silk gown and adjusted the golden chain that bound it to her slim waist. Ectel, that bastard, had entered the hall and was walking with purpose toward her. She watched as the courtiers and staff backed into the shadows. Some even left hurriedly, not wanting to be seen. She gazed a moment at her perfectly manicured nails; *that* always took them off guard, at least until she sliced them with her razor tongue and fed them to the sharks.

Ikn and Teg noticed the intrusion; immediately their hackles rose and they crouched down, ready to leap at their master's command. A low, menacing growl issued from between sharp clenched teeth. Ectel stopped, frowned and then looked to ar'Liaiyne, who returned an icy smile.

"Ikn, Teg, let the Commander through. You're scaring him." The two guard dogs looked back, wondering if they should heed her or just pounce on the man. Soon they came bounding back to ar'Liaiyne, their black tongues licking at her palm. Teg stationed herself on the right, Ikn on the left. Ectel approached to within ten feet of the governor then stopped as once more the hounds issued a low growl.

"What brings you to the Hall of Merchants on what used to be a profitable trading day?" More than a bit of sarcasm laced her words.

"You know very well," Ectel said in a voice that crackled like sap in a fire. "Taxes were due three days ago. You are late."

Ar'Liaiyne gazed with intense dislike at the man. He wore the uniform of the Guard of Oran; black tabard with dagger encircled by fire, all in silver thread. He stood there, one of those dangerous little men, with the heart of a zealot and the means to enforce his beliefs. Shorter by half a head than her, he had thinning hair and a round face with hollows for eyes. Thin lips betrayed crooked teeth and a false smile. He was stout to be sure, but ar'Liaiyne noticed that he would look better strung up by the neck. *Just a few inches taller. It would do wonders for his attitude.*

"Look around, Ectel. Do you see brisk business and the coffers full? I think not. Thanks to, and I am sure of this, the well intentions of the Conclaveum in their effort to bring this no doubt unruly state to utter submission, we have very few visitors to the Hall of Merchants who are not gouging us to compensate for the tariffs. Unless you count that poor fool out of Qwen selling wool. I think he may have garnered say...three gold shenk for a few dozen bushels. Your tax of that would be, oh..." she tapped the side of her head, annoying the Guardsman. "That would be three silver shenk. Just about one tenth."

"Don't belabor the subject, or you may find yourself in the precarious position of all those other radicals on the leeward side of the island."

102

"Oh, do tell, Ectel. Maybe if you hadn't been rash and killed half of the guildmasters and nobles, and burned their estates to the ground there might have been someone who could barter more tactfully with these extortionists."

"We all have quotas, Rhianne-"

"Don't be so familiar with me, Ectel. My suitors, even dear Brunwurst, are not allowed to use such a familiar tone in public. Gods above, Ikn and Teg would castrate them. What a shame that would be."

"What is the point of this? You know your responsibilities. You and your council tread on dangerous ground. My Regent will-"

"The Regent, Ectel? Not since the first month you occupied this island have I seen the Regent. Is he too busy that he sends us his lackeys?"

"You know very little, Rhianne ar'Liaiyne. Here the ice is thin." He took a step forward and Ikn was immediately on her feet and uttering a low growl. He looked at the dog and scowled. Ar'Liaiyne rubbed her hand through its thick mane but it stayed its post. "One word from me, *Governor*, and all this come crashing down."

"So what, Ectel. You bore me. If all this comes crashing down," she said as she gestured to the Hall of Merchants about her. "You will have nothing. And you can only get nothing from nothing."

The Guardsman threw his head back and laughed aloud. She swore he looked about to faint from the red cast that took over his otherwise pale face. Then he abruptly stopped, placed hand on hilt and turned on his heel. He began his stride toward the doors, looking over his shoulder only once.

"One week," he said in what could be almost a merry tone. "You have one week, ar'Liaiyne. Then you will learn that indeed something can be gotten from nothing. The Hand will assure you of that."

He was gone in a moment and the governor felt a chill settle over the Hall. She slumped back on her seat and looked over the high chamber, now seemingly overtaken by gloom. Those that remained shuffled their feet and murmured nervously. She motioned with her hand and Ikn and Teg followed the steps of the little man the length of the chamber to the oaken doors.

Ar'Liaiyne thanked the gods that few of the servants or courtiers had been near enough to hear that last exchange, the worst in a series of four and now this threat of the Keth. Thoughtfully tilting her head to rest on her hand, she wondered where she would be in one week. She knew very little of Oran and his minions beyond the bedtime stories that her Nana had told her; stories told to frighten a little child. Would her head grace one of the pikes in front of the Regent's Keep, or would she somehow suffer a fate worse than death? She knew that her own personal funds fell short of what was required to pay the tax, not that she would surrender them knowing she might have to flee the Isle of Clef or do something just as equally rash.

She sighed as Ikn and Teg sniffed and growled dangerously at the door. Realizing her allies were very few within the Council, her thoughts turned to other options. She knew of the ships at Icam, but few people would openly oppose the Guard of Oran even when it was obvious they were being leeched of their lifeblood, they all seemed fools not seeing what was happening to them. Complacency was eating away at the once proud and cultured citizens of Clef. She pounded her fist on the armrest; the two hounds looked up sharply in her direction then sprinted quickly to her chair, sensing her distress. They circled for a moment then collapsed at her feet, their fur warming her.

Ikn and Teg, named after the goddess and god of the sea traders. She wondered if they were her only friends.

"Soon, my precious ones. Ectel may regret his insults yet."

They looked up to her with expectant eyes, and then they both sighed and in unison rested their heads on forelegs, ever watchful of their mistress.

Chapter 9

Bill looked to the Mount and the setting sun; orange and yellow shimmered about the peak and left the remainder in silhouette. The city of Avard Clef lay at its base wrapped in twilight, its lights hinting of warmth on this chill autumnal night.

He hefted his walking stick and nodded to a peasant that was laboring to get a bushel of wheat loaded into his cart. The man looked at the minstrel with a weary eye, and then looked away. Even as the remaining daylight faded, Bill saw the man ward himself superstitiously and hunch over his load. Bill shook his head and continued up the road; it now began to wind through orchard and vineyard, gradually increasing in grade until it came to the whitewashed walls of Avard Clef.

Some distance off the road Bill could make out estates. Some dark and vacated, others lit and full of end of the day activities. He scratched at his head and wondered what it would be like to be warm and comfortable in one of those houses, not a worry in the world about strife and conflict, oppression and poverty.

"They know me," Torec had said. "It would be a foolish risk. My face was well known." And Tar'elah. Her heavy accent and demeanor would give her away easily. It was up to Bill, or rather Bard William D'Asturien. He may be the least known of the six, now five, but that did not make him a coward. After the Battle for the Seat in Paravel something had changed. Life had become a little more precious. *And not to be wasted on the likes of Myella and Duran,* he thought bitterly, the vision of Chill's death overshadowing all else.

So it was that he walked to Avard Clef, no sword or shield to protect him, only a walking stick from Farok and his own wits. He supposed he came into this world with about the same. Dressed as a traveling minstrel, carrying an *Ighuire* over his back - thanks to Farok again - he strode to the gate wall.

Lights sprang out from the shuttered windows of the gatehouse. Torec had said the captain of the gate was a citizen and would hardly care who went within the city. But, he must watch out for the Guard of Oran, and so he cautiously approached, wary of any man who might wear the livery of that evil cohort.

Like I could see them in the dark anyway, came a fleeting thought. There were several men milling about in the lamplight, their faces and clothing obscured by shadow. Bill paused and then walked on through. They were unmindful of him, playing dice or some such thing and drinking. What *he* would not do for a cold beer.

Time enough for that later. He looked carefully about. It was much like Paravel, though the flavor of the city seemed brighter with its whitewashed buildings trimmed in bright blue or gay red. The signs on the shops were all brightly painted, the boulevard lined with trees; all this was made clear by closely spaced lamps lit early in the evening. He could tell that even while occupied the city was kept well, no doubt the pride of the people showing through.

He followed the stately avenue that was before him, keeping to the sidewalk and ever mindful to nod at the passing people as Torec reminded him was the custom. Of course he would not look too out of place.

There it was: Bobel's, a restaurant of some repute. One did not come to the Island of Clef without stopping there. A little dissent was good as long as it was kept in check. It was said that Bobel's was a haven for the dissidents. Torec had said that a few of his former livery now worked there and so it was that Bard D'Asturien came with a message.

The sound of the people within heartened him and so did the aromas. He patted the coinage that Farok had given him; at least he would eat well this night.

He entered and was greeted by a hostess. She was attractive in a simple way, more than likely it was her disposition. He was soon seated at a table near the pool in the center of the room. Torec was right, those of Clef did pride themselves on their gardens and ponds, and Bobel's had both. Amid the sweet aroma of flowers, the splashing of water and fish, the low hum of conversation and the smell of excellent food his senses were almost overwhelmed. He felt wonderfully relieved that no one noticed him, or thought him out of place. He was soon sipping a red wine that Farok had assertively recommended earlier that day. It was delicious.

His waiter returned bearing a dish of smoked fish and some type of pepper. He profusely apologized for the exorbitant price of the catch, but with the Guard on the island and all.

Bill smiled knowingly and paused as if in thought. "The Chef...is it one Tilva ar'Jimra?"

The man looked at Bill oddly for a moment, and then nodded, not sure if he should place the two tined fork on the plate or into Bill's eye.

"I am acquainted with a merchant that is all; one of the family el'Kirien."

The waiter flushed, dropping the fork against the wine glass. A few patrons looked up at the disruption but then all returned to normal.

"I shall express your compliments on the chef's meal." Soon the man was gone, through the kitchen entrance.

It was amazing, Bill thought, how some things seemed so normal. This restaurant for instance could have been a fine, if exotic, dining establishment in any city back home. He took a bite of the smoked fish and was surprised to find it delicately seasoned with what tasted like dill and lemon. Bill soon found himself satisfied and relishing the slightly tannic taste of the wine. He sat back. If only Tar'elah was here.

When they had first arrived, skipping ashore in a dingy from a passing merchant ship, they had found a few moments in the ruins of Torec's estate. She had melted into his arms and they had made passionate love under Shaj'il Cziffer.

The waiter brought him from his thoughts of Tar'elah. The young man had returned with a small plate.

"Your compliment to the chef was well received; he baked this *fresh* for you as thanks. Be aware, it is hot."

He set it before the Bard as he cleared the empty dishes. Bill watched him go and wondered what he had meant. It was a confection of some

109

sorts, steaming and with honey dripping over it. He carefully split it with his fork and as he was savoring the sweet dessert, he noticed a tiny piece of parchment amid the dough. Luckily, none of the dripping honey had gotten to it.

As he was surreptitiously tucking the note into his napkin, he looked up to see two dogs trotting past his table. Stunned, he watched as this parade was followed by an attractive rear-end clad in a very shear silken gown. Looking up he noticed the owner of the fine derriere was staring back at him, noting his wandering eyes. Red suffused his cheeks and he hurriedly looked away. She frowned but was soon seated at a table with a very heavily muscled man. "Sir Brunwurst," she had said and all else was obscured by the noise of the dining room. She pulled back a wavy strand of golden hair, and then opened her napkin and once more Bill caught her flashing blue eyes. She stared at him with open disapproval for a moment and then her two dogs stood at alert. She whispered something and they were soon at Bill's table, growling at him. Brunwurst and several other patrons were now looking at him.

The first thing on his mind was not the dogs growling, but rather why would anyone bring them to a restaurant? He wasn't afraid though, but he probably should have been. He clucked low in his throat and lowered his hand palm up, so that it rested just below the dog's mouths. They stopped growling instantly and looked at him curiously, not quite sure what to make of this two legged beast. In their confusion, they did not notice Bill get up and

110

leave. They only realized when they did not get any scraps, that he was gone.

"So, Tilva ar'Jimra is still a chef, good. He was the best damn one that I had."

"He was your chef?"

"I and another merchant owned Bobel's. When I left Clef Bobel el'Lorin became full owner. I take it the food was excellent?"

"Yes, but pricey."

"The Occupation no doubt. What is this?" He looked at the note, trying to make out the tiny script crammed onto the parchment. "It seems that we came at a fortunate time. There is a meeting of peoples opposed to the Occupation three nights from now at Crag Place, in the Mount."

"Crag Place?"

Torec nodded as he tossed the note into Farok's hearth. Tar'elah was sharpening her short sword and talking to the blind man in hushed tones on the other side of the room. Bill looked at her for a moment and then to Torec.

"Who will be there? I thought all those that opposed the Guard of Oran were either dead or driven off."

"True, but in the time between the initial occupation and now people have grown weary. Realizing that the yoke fits better on the ox than on people, tiny groups have sprouted in the villages and towns, and even in Avard Clef. There will be a meeting with the leaders and a new ally, one who has monetary resources that the resistance lacks. Tilva will be there three nights hence."

"On the Mount?"

"Yes."

"And you got all this from that tiny note."

Torec grinned. "When one has to convey much, one writes very small."

Torec and Tar'elah had remained in the back of the wagon as Bill drove it along the Circuit to the north side of the Mount. Torec leaned out over the seat and Tar'elah sat silently in the rear, gazing into twilight as they trundled along the rutted road.

"This Crag Place, what is it?" Bill asked as he snapped the reins to get a bit more speed from the old beast.

"It is from before Avard Clef. A long time ago there were only villages along the coast, not much else along the rivers except vineyards and a few estates. Only with the merchant trade did Avard Clef spring up.

"Crag Place was a quarry and, in the time of the old Conclaveum, a defendable retreat for the people of the villages during raids by the Krim. It is high up in the Mount and one must first traverse through a pass. When one gets through," and he gestured with his hands in a sweeping motion, "one finds a broad plateau with a sheer rock face rising on three sides all the way to the summit. My people quarried the stone that is in most of our buildings. There are many caves there, and also a clear cold lake."

"So there will be some of your friends up there?"

"If I still have any. No doubt many thought I was dead. After I left Clef, Garis and a few of my retainers met up with me in Qwen. It was then that we went to raid with Lirel's mercenary group on some Conclaveum plantations near Baed and Helm. That's where I got this." He pointed to the

112

horizontal scar that ran beneath his eyes on over the bridge of his nose.

Bill nodded and reined in the horse at the hostel. There was nothing around for miles except this small building, a barn, and a wood of old oak. Torec had told him this place was little known to even the citizens of Clef. In later years, the more affluent merchants used it for a hunting lodge and Bill gathered from the exchange that Torec must have been *very* affluent.

Torec hopped out of the wagon and Tar'elah followed suit. He hitched the beast to a post and adjusted his cloak. His sword and helm he left in the wagon and even Tar'elah left her weapons behind. Bill grabbed his jacket and walking stick and followed them down. A boy greeted Torec and soon his palm held a shenk; the boy eagerly promised to feed and clean the draft horse.

They went inside and found the great-room empty. A fire crackled in the hearth and the floor covered with fresh rushes, but there was not a soul about. Torec sat heavily on a bench and Bill followed suit. Tar'elah just stood, looking around like a wary cat. Eventually, an old man came from what must have been the cellar. He carried a cask in his arms and was having a difficult time, wheezing and puffing, he looked about to collapse. Bill quickly went over and took the cask from him. It was heavy but his thickly corded arms accepted the weight with ease. The old man smiled gratefully and Bill took it to the bar that stood to one side of the room.

"Thank yee, young sir. I fear that I am getten on in years." He wiped sweat from his brow and looked to his guests. "Rooms for the night?" He asked it with some expectancy in his voice.

"Of course," Torec said quickly and smiled.

"Wonderful!" replied the proprietor. "Aye, many have passed through these past days, but nary a one to stay. Sometin about fishin up at Crag Place. Eh, I don't know what, cept flatfish.

"Glen!" he shouted and startled Tar'elah. He smiled apologetically and called out again. "Glen el'Ropa, where in damnation-"

"Here, Gran-Ta," came a tiny voice. The stable boy stuck his head in. True to his word he had a basket of oats and a brush.

"After you tend their horse arrange for several rooms and see to the stew!"

"Yessir!"

Bill smiled and Tar'elah frowned. Torec just handed the owner several pieces of silver.

"My Lord! This is too much. How long will you stay?"

"Just one night and most of the day tomorrow. Come sunset tomorrow we go fishing."

The old man shook his head and shuffled off to see to their rooms.

Torec had been gone to the common room to speak at length to the proprietor. Tar'elah, enigmatic Tar'elah, sat sharpening her sword. The room was small but very well kept.

"It didn't get dull in two days," he stated from where he sat by the window. He watched as the leaves sparkled with the dropping rain. A few feet beyond the window it was pitch black interrupted only by occasional lightening.

She looked up at him and said nothing. He sighed and rested his head against the windowpane.

"You could loosen up a bit."

"I am quite loose. I stretch every morning. What is wrong, Bill?" It was asked in that strangely lilting accent she had.

"I dunno."

"You do not know?"

"Just meloncholy."

She set her short sword at the foot of the bed and began to unlace her bodice. Her hair tangled at the base of her neck. Her bright eyes flashed. A smile grew on Bill's face as she leaned forward and began to unbutton his worn oxford.

"Meloncholy?"

"No."

The journey to Crag Place from the hostel took a good six hours. Torec knew that at least some of the dissidents had been through the hostel over the past several days. He just hoped that his informant had not been wrong about the time of the meeting and they would show up late.

Night had long since fallen and for Bill it seemed that his memory of Clef would be mostly of sunsets and cool nights, wrapped in the arms of Tar'elah. About him rose the bulk of the Mount. The eastern slope cut a jagged and rough gash up the island; often the locus of quarries and mines. They meandered through a pass illuminated by only their torches.

Torec and Tar'elah seemed unflagging in their hike upward; Bill on the other hand was winded and his hands were bruised and scraped from the hurried handholds he had taken. Just as he was about to call

115

a halt to their progress the narrow defile opened up to a moonlit basin, surrounded by several hundred feet of sheer rock whose black lip obscured the sky. Before them was a well-trod path amid slabs of limestone and chipped rock. About one hundred spans ahead was the small lake that Torec had mentioned. It seemed to glow an iridescent blue with the light of Shaj'il Cziffer. Bill noticed that much of the quarry was now below the surface; it must have filled after a spring or aquifer had been struck. The combination of steep rock face, dotted with caves and the small lake, gave Crag Place a surreal cast in the light of the moon. In a flat clearing, on the opposite side of the lake, there were small fires; people milling about their camps occasionally obscured them.

Torec quickly gutted his own torch and moved cautiously into the basin. Bill knew eyes were raking him like hot coals, but from whence they came, he did not know. Several times, he caught himself looking over his shoulder. It was reassuring to hear the thrum of a cricket, but why had not a sentry accosted them?

"Torec-"

"Hush...There, to the left among the rocks, a guard."

He was right. Bill could see a man huddled against the moonlit stone. He could make out the gleam of a sword or spear, he wasn't sure. Then the man faded into the shadows with naught more than a whisper.

"I have been recognized."

"How do you know?" asked the Bard.

"The men on the cliffs would have killed us long since," Tar'elah replied for the merchant.

"Oh."

In the clearing they were greeted by Tilva ar'Jimra, a short, uncompromising man who smiled with sincere warmth as he hugged Torec el'Kirien. Bill did not think he really looked like a chef; it was Bobel who actually looked the part. He was a corpulent man whose face was hidden in a thick layer of fat and who looked like he enjoyed dining at his restaurant to the point of gluttony. He seemed nice enough though.

Soon the night found them sitting around a fire, Torec recounting some of his journeys and his role in the Unseating of Myella in Paravel. Tilva and Bobel el'Lorin listened intently and at the conclusion, they both frowned.

"So," rumbled Bobel. "You leave Clef in the hands of the Guard to make your fortune, and now you return seeking aid for your friends in Paravel." He shook his head. "Have you changed that much Citizen?"

"You know me, Bobel," and Torec's voice was low. "I could not stay. What happened here was long in the making. If I could have chosen otherwise my mistress would not be dead and my house anything more than a pile of stones. I spoke out, Bobel, you did not. We all make our choices and we live with them."

"So we do. Tilva, here, says that your companion sampled the fare." He turned to Bill, his eyes probing. "What did you think of Bobel's?"

"Excellent. Though I was surprised to see you allowed dogs in the dining room."

117

Bobel tilted his head back and roared with laughter. "Oh, minstrel, do tell. We normally don't."

Torec looked to the Bard for an explanation.

"There was a woman at the restaurant, and she came with two large dogs."

Torec looked back to Bobel. "Yes, my friend, it was she. Rhianne. She is governor now."

"Governor?"

"Yes, and the other day she earned Ectel's wrath and hence the Regent's, that dog of Oran."

"I did not know she was still on the island." Torec leaned back into the darkness, letting the night obscure what passed over his face.

"She was at Bobel's for my *Olec ghrik*."

"Yours?"

"Well you were off the island. I added a touch of *cinril*."

"It will taste like Karo."

"She was with Sir Brunwurst."

"Brunwurst?" Bill could almost hear the wince in Torec's voice. "He's a big oaf."

"Yes, but he does pay attention-"

"Enough, Bobel. We move from the path. What are our chances of getting aid?"

"Aid? You must have the mind sickness. Look around. Here are the delegates from forty villages and towns to discuss what they can do about the Guard of Oran that sit in their own back-yard, and you want to know if we can support Paravel."

"It does sound outlandish doesn't it?" Tilva chuckled and Bobel turned red with laughter.

"You were ever the optimist. No, I am afraid that for the moment it won't be possible. The Regent is bleeding us dry. He taxes the merchants, the

118

merchants raise their prices, and we are caught in between. Ectel gave Rhianne an ultimatum on Second Day, and it is rumored he threatened with a Hand of Keth."

"He is bluffing," echoed Tilva.

"Is he?" Bobel asked of his chef. "Even Torec, here, tells of strange things passing in Paravel."

"It was rumored that you have found someone who could finance the effort?"

"Ah, you get ahead of me. At this moment there are three triremes and eight feluccas in the harbor at Icam. What are they loaded with, you ask? Arms and men, mercenaries from Qwen on their way to Albien. Poor Albien, for I have convinced the captain of those mercenaries that Albien has already fallen to the Black Guard of the Wall, and that his interests lay in Clef. We require only the gold."

"Surely, with the merchants and nobles here you have enough," Torec echoed.

"Aye, normally we would, but this Regent keeps us poor enough to worry about where the meals for the people are coming from, and how harsh the winter will be. The coffers are low."

"Who is this financier, then?" Bill intoned.

"Rhianne ar'Liaiyne."

Bill frowned and Torec sputtered.

"That's my gold!"

"What?"

"Before I fled she held chair of the House where my money was. She was the head of the largest banking House on the island. She saw the dire straits I was in and Sealed all my funds. To her benefit no doubt. It looked to the Guard that I was living beyond my means, but-"

"Well, you had no need of it once you left Clef, now did you?"

"You will never know. Will she be here soon?"

"She already is. That tent near the lake."

Dawn broke, light creeping over the edge of the rock walls. The basin was still cast in deep shadow, but with consideration for the need for secrecy the fires were put out long ago.

Torec had not slept much the night before. He sat up and watched the sun break over the horizon from the entrance of the defile. He was too preoccupied to notice the sunrise, or anything else for that matter, and so he wandered back to Bobel's campfire. He made karo as Bill stirred from his bedding

So, it came back to Rhianne. Had it not always? He asked himself. Not since he had left Clef had his feelings been so mixed. *And why is she with that fool of a man, Brunwurst?* Being involved with her had been a mistake from the very beginning. Farok and his father had been right in telling him to stay clear of that ambitious young woman. He shook his head and burned his lips on the steaming karo, almost causing the remainder to land in his lap.

"Nerves?" Bill asked with some concern. He stood there without a shirt, letting the cold waken him. Steam rose off his shoulders and his skin had taken on the texture of gooseflesh. Torec just grunted. Bill hurriedly pulled on his sweater and squatted near the man.

"It is Rhianne, I am quite...how do you say...nervous about the meeting."

"I know how you feel, trust me."

"I do friend Bard."

120

It was not until the first rays of sunlight speared down from the rock lip of the basin that the group of would-be conspirators met. Slowly as camp was broken, and the delegates from the various villages and towns of Clef began to talk more freely, did they converge on Rhianne ar'Liaiyne's tent.

"She is a notoriously late sleeper," Torec commented to Bill, as he and Tar'elah followed the lithe man through the thick of the crowd to the colorful tent. Bobel and Tilva were already waiting for them at the head of the crowd. Word that ar'Liaiyne may fund their revolt brought anticipation and what Bill perceived as a certain amount of angst.

Bill found himself and Tar'elah waiting expectantly behind Torec el'Kirien as he stood among his former associates. After a few moments, the Governor's two hounds bounded down from the tangle of rocks that guarded the mouth of the defile. Bill was amazed at the intelligence that he saw in those eyes. Both hounds had heavy manes, one red and one cream; each one placed itself on either side of the tent flap, their black tongues lolling.

"I've known those two since they were pups," Torec remarked. "Ikn and Teg. She named them after the gods of the sea traders."

"Dog is god spelled backward, you know," Bill quipped.

Torec smiled wryly. Abruptly the tent flap was thrown back by a bulk of a man. Bill recognized him as the man he had seen at Bobel's. Sir Brunwurst.

He was certainly thick. Bill noticed that even Tar'elah was peering curiously around Torec's shoulder, to get a better glimpse of the heavily built man.

His head swiveled around, lantern like jaws and heavy brow seeming a second behind. His hair was cut short, and he wore a kilt and baldric. He used a nasty looking broad sword to hold open the flap as Rhianne ar'Liaiyne ducked her head and exited. She looked upon the expectant faces, her gaze finally falling on Torec. A flush touched her cheeks, but that was the only form of recognition she would allow.

She was dressed a little more appropriately than the night at the restaurant, Bill noticed. Now she wore a split skirt, good for riding, and a short jacket. It was made of a fine weave of wool and accented by a riding hat and a dagger off each hip, one was silver and one gold.

"So, you want *my* gold," she said, emphasizing as she looked at Torec. "You think you can throw the Guard of Oran off this island?"

Muttered words met her steely blue gaze. She raised an eyebrow and that squelched even those. "What makes you think you are able? And why did you not do this from the very beginning? Instead of sitting by idly to watch half the guildmasters of the island burn with their estates - or flee on the fastest felucca?

"You have mercenaries sitting in the harbor at Icam. Do you think that the Regent of Oran is not aware of this? My people tell me that yesterday morn he blockaded the harbor with his warships. That means no mercenaries, or weapons, or any hope for this forsaken island. The Guard is too strong and I do not know why I am here." She turned to retreat back into her tent. Bill surprised himself by speaking up.

"We did it in Paravel, it can be done here."

She stopped and looked over her shoulder, past Torec and to the young man that she recognized from Bobel's.

"You. I do not know you."

Bill stepped forward and Brunwurst stepped in front of ar'Liaiyne. He crossed his massive arms; he looked about to pop a vein.

"Bard William D'Asturien, minstrel, outlander, and Troubadour of the Legion of the Black Skull." Everyone else in the group exaggerated their titles so why couldn't he.

"I remember you from the restaurant. What have you to do with this?"

"I am companion to Torec el'Kirien and Tar'elah of the Si'hi'dar. I believe that Torec is of some former acquaintance?"

"I know of him." Brunwurst frowned as there was some open laughter at this, but Rhianne brushed it off. "What is this of the Southern Seat?"

"*Id'hala!* Woman, you know what happened in Paravel. If not then your informants are unworthy of the silver you pay them." Torec stepped forward, ignorant of the angry glare he got from the massive Sir Brunwurst; the man leveled an evil gaze at the merchant and his knuckles whitened.

"What was your part in Paravel?"

"That story is too long and complicated to retell here. Now we must discuss Clef and the Guard of Oran and what has become of our island."

"Our *island*," she repeated bitterly. "I recall that *you*, Torec el'Kirien, were on the fastest felucca off the isle. This is no longer your matter. Bobel has already told me that you seek our aid. The Conclaveum's wrath is not something to await lightly, eh Torec?

"And as for you, minstrel, you can go back to Paravel. We have our own problems."

"Aye," interjected Torec. "One must tend their own garden before they help another. Are your taxes due soon?"

Her eyes flashed and Brunwurst took a step forward; Ikn and Tag both snapped alert, but it was not Torec to whom they paid attention. There was a low thump, a streak of red and a loud hiss sent them barking loudly and circling about the governor. Bobel pitched forward clutching at his chest. A black spike had entered between his shoulder blade and spine. As he lay on the ground, he writhed in pain and the fat flesh of his back surreally rippled outward from the point of entry; it seemed as though the projectile was still ricocheting within his body.

Chaos reigned as the fifty or so dissidents scrambled from the immediate area. Bill saw a blur as Brunwurst drew his sword and scowled. Ar'Liaiyne stood stunned and then was pushed to cover by Tilva ar'Jimra. Bill heard a horn blow and watched as the rim of the bowl began to change definition in the form of men in black tabard. Looking back into the defile he could see a host of armored and helmeted soldiers. One carried a banner of the Guard of Oran and another sported a hand, palm outward on his tabard. He carried a black staff that smoked like the barrel of a rifle.

124

Bill was tugged by the sleeve of his sweater toward the rock face of the quarry. Tar'elah clutched her short sword in her right hand as she pulled him to some sort of cover. Out of the corner of his eye, he saw Torec facing the defile and Brunwurst by his side with sword raised. It all seemed to collapse into slow motion.

"It is an ambush, Bard." He heard it distantly even though it came from Tar'elah.

Chapter 10

The Tower of Iss was over a thousand years old. It was a tall narrow tower, many spans at its base, which spiraled into the sky and was topped by jagged horns of steel that often attracted lightening. The stone was black-green, slick even on the driest summer day, and it was the Mage Guyle's, his by the XIX Dictum of the Conclave, the Counselor's property no matter how foul or demented the man had become.

It was its depths, though, that few had seen and returned to the daylight to talk about. Entrance to the tower was barred to most, and only a few of the Clave even stepped onto the walled grounds that were nestled in the north quarter of the city. Few came to the gates, few wanted to, and most supplies came via a canal that ran from the Kipris River to the dock at the east wall.

Down and down and down, into the roots of the Tower of Iss, into the depths that known as the old city. Into the darkness that the light of day never touched except in the dim memory of those that had passed this way before and not returned. It was not enough that the oppressive weight of the tower pushed down into the depths. The weight of years and years of construction and reconstruction, razing and building; it was all here. One passed by the relatively new stone foundation of the Tower of Iss, then to older flags. Finally, the roots of the old city began to show and at every landing tunnels and corridors split off into the stygian blackness that had seen neither torch nor lamp in decades. It was not into the heights of the Tower of Iss that prisoners were brought, to dwell upon their crimes and receive punishment; instead, they were taken into the depths.

As Ironeas Vien Crona, Conclavator of the CXXVI Clave, Inherit Ruler of the Noble Conclaveum, lay in State amid the Clave; Trevor Galfeon Crona was led down the wide and ill-lit stair of the Tower of Iss by his half-brother Mage Guyle Hyl Crona and two Hands of Keth.

It was obvious that captivity was wearing on the former Lord of Galfeon Yor. His hair and beard were filthy and his clothing was in tatters. Shackles tore at his wrists, leaving him bloody and raw. He was much thinner now than in his previous days residing in the South. He looked at the one Hand of Keth with pain and frustration. Sir Chill. He had taken to referring to the man as Sir Chill. He held a faint glimmer of hope that the stout man might remember him as a patron when he had sought asylum from Gelion. Some of the Hands had called him Sir Chill the Cold. *That may be closer to the mark,* thought Trevor. He had never before seen a Hand of Keth, though he had read much about the transformation and its permanence. He had seen Sir Chill given the mortal wound and left to die. How a soul in departure could stand the agony of returning was beyond him, but then, he could understand how it would lead to the Hand of Keth: a creature totally under the dominion of Oran.

Guyle's staff clicked on the steps, and the sound was followed by that of the Hand's kris-voulge. He stumbled and was caught by Sir Chill; the metal gauntleted hand gripped his upper arm until there was pain, then numbness. He was thankful that the

127

dull black metal of the voulge had not been used to hold him back as the other Hand had done. His earlier stumble had left a long red weal that burned, along his chest and shoulder.

"Soon, soon," cackled Guyle, his waxy pallor turning a parchment yellow in the torchlight. His sunken eyes looked back a moment, then a degenerate smile lit his face. "My Lord Ironeas is dead. The Conclavator's heir is dead. The Conclavator's second heir is not to found, nor could he take that Seat once having entered the Sequestiary. Long live the Conclavatrix!" He laughed again.

"Soon, dear half-brother. My task with you was not complete. Ironeas' death was not a painless one. No, that poison his doctors thought they arrested was long in the making. It took his blood and it took his life, and the agony that burned beneath his skin was unlike any that my Tower has ever vomited forth!"

"And is that what you have prepared for me?"

"No. Not so with you. You shall linger long." He stopped on a landing and swung around. His cloak flailed out about him and his blue veined hand pointed at Trevor's face. Energy danced from the signet ring across his knuckles but no further.

"Secrets you do not know. These are all mine. Memories expunged by the Sixteenth Dictum during the Seventy Fifth Conclave. Remember those dates? It was the time of the Great Wall and the Betrayal of Korman Iss." He continued down the steps waving his hand as if lecturing a child of something that was far beyond his ken.

"Untheran - I know that you recognize the name. Untheran had planned a great alliance, and had charged Korman Iss to bring it about. It was an alliance with Oran that would open the *Gates*. Korman Iss sought Oran's aid; he knew that he alone could not achieve this end. However, the cost was great. Only because of my greatness as a Mage and a Necromancer have I not succumbed to the utter damnation that eventually befell Untheran. It was unfortunate for Korman Iss that he had befriended the Krim, for when the Daemon returned to Narn-toc, Korman was ready to flee on one of their ships, but they abandoned him, as did Gin-jo." He stopped before a great door set into the wall and waved his staff; it swung open without a sound. The slow, steady drip of water could be heard within and Trevor had to suppress a gag as the cool fetid air of the place reached him. He was shoved within and Guyle followed.

"Behold, brother. I give you Bej-et of the Krim." Trevor looked up. Sitting at the far end of the chamber, upon a green jade seat, was a creature of alien beauty. She was Krim. Her hair was like quicksilver and passed straight down about her shoulders and her strange, delicately chiseled features. She was tall and thin, and wore armor that was chitinous in nature; it was so transparent that it seemed to be made of glass. Here skin was the color of bronze and her eyes were upturned and all black; no evident iris and no white, just pure blackness.

She sat there shackled to the chair and looked with hatred at Guyle.

"Now," Guyle said softly. "This will be the payment for the betrayal of the Krim. This will be

129

payment for your betrayal of me, Trevor. You two shall be linked. I will extinguish the line Galfeon. I will be given my due. My revenge exacted."

The door to the chamber slammed shut. Trevor looked up to see Bj-et's eyes boring into his.

Chapter 11

Albien fell within the two fortnights that Duran had predicted. Yet in its death it cost the Guard of Oran such losses it would be remembered for many years. Seeing their own mortality the people of the port city rallied with ferocity, sending waves of militia and city guard at the entrenched besiegers. The grounds about the city were soaked with the blood of defender and assailant. Three times the line was broken, only to have the rear guard come forth and drive the defending army back to the city.

The Duke was not foolish, he knew that the city could not stand a long siege with a harsh winter coming and all his supply lines cut. Duran knew this as well. Yet the Duke hoped.

The final blow came on a windy eve, when the clouds were thick off the ocean and the evening was nigh. Catapult and sling had steadily pounded the wall until nothing remained but a pile of rubble and stone several spans high and deep. Those who wore the tabards of the Conclaveum could make out the walls and roofs of shops and houses within; they knew the end was in sight. Duran's mounted cavalry had already made several assaults at the gate wall, only to be driven back by the Duke and his best men. The losses were great on both sides but it was fate that decided the day.

Duran watched it all from his pavilion set atop the hill. The Duke was mounted and shouting harsh orders over his men, who in turn were effectively holding at bay Duran's cavalry. As the horsemen fell back to regroup the militia rallied and drove even harder, scattering the mounted men in all directions. Even as Duran was swearing an oath to Oran, the Duke was raising his sword in defiance at the Army of the North. His banner man, excited, waved the pole with the standard next to the Duke. Unfortunately, this startled the Duke's horse. The mount jumped nervously to the side, and the Duke fought hard to regain his balance. The horse, however, was not so lucky; one leg twisted sharply at an angle, having encountered a large piece of stone long since fallen from the wall. Its leg snapped under the weight and the Duke pitched to the side, impaling himself on the sharp point of the standard.

It seemed to Duran that time stood still. Silence passed over the field and he could imagine hearing the gasp of the standard bearer. He could hear the breath whistle through the teeth of the Duke as his heart pumped one last time.

Without thought, Duran was on his horse and spurring it down the hill, waving his blade to urge his men on behind him. Some saw and understood immediately, a cheer spread through their ranks. Others missed the catastrophe that had befallen the Duke of Albien, but seeing their Commander charging into battle was enough to get them motivated.

The Duke's Militia fell like wheat to the scythe. The walls were swarmed by the Guard and all within soon felt the wrath of the frustrated and weary soldiers. Within hours the city was aflame, and Duran, who had prided himself on not allowing the Keth to descend upon the city as Myella had insisted, still felt somewhat hollow at the victory. Even as the melee had ceased near the gate and the militia had dispersed, the Duke remained. Duran reined his horse in by the man's screaming mount, its leg a bloody broken mass of tissue and bone. He silenced it quickly with his sword and then looked to the Duke.

Duran had been witness to many battles and to deaths gory beyond description, but the Duke's had unsettled him the most. There he stood, as if propping himself up on the standard. The spear tipped staff had entered under the arm of the breastplate, and had passed out behind his shoulder. The banner itself made a dingy cape that his right arm was tangled in. His legs were out stiff. Just as he had pushed himself away from the fallen horse so he stood there, a tripod, two legs natural and one of wood.

Yet, what would haunt Duran in his dreams was the look in the Duke's eyes, as he took that unnatural pose of death. Clear faced, the eyes held a hint of sorrow, surprise and dismay. His lips curled to form the word 'no,' maybe. Duran looked at the Defender of Albien, and in the days that would follow, that is how the people of the South would refer to the martyred Duke. Duran wondered if someday he would take such a pose.

He rode on into the city, leaving the Duke of Albien to welcome the Guard. The Duke stood there, like that, for several days. Then his body and the standard disappeared. Some said that he was doomed to wander the walls of Albien as a spirit.

Mist swirled in the late afternoon. Burned red by the setting sun, the harbor lay in an eerie twilight. Footfalls echoed hollowly on the wooden planking, soaked with water and blood. Duran

133

would have thought himself in Qwen if not for the smell of fire and rot from the city proper. He waited, drawing his cloak about his shoulders, moisture collecting on the fringe and his own beard. First, he noticed the creaking of wood, then the soft lap of seawater. Ever so slowly the dark ship came into view, parting the mist like the cobwebs of sleep. It was a large ship of the Guard, sitting in the harbor of Albien. He watched as the vessel reefed its sails and dropped ropes to the nearby dock. The ship, called *Edrin,* sported three masts, one central mast that splayed three booms, and two lesser masts, one fore and aft. It towered over him, the prow of this ship sporting the banner of the dagger encircled by a ring of flame. *What new orders did Myella have for him?*

Duran shuddered. In the bloody gloaming, ethereal figures moved along the deck. What plans and designs did his Conclavatrix have for him? Was it to be Paravel or Bastion? He waited for the Captain of the ship. With the new orders Duran's force would move on and be replaced by the occupants of this vessel; the Guard of Oran.

Behind him the low walls of Albien beckoned, comfort in their desolation, beyond, all floated free through the mist and the glass of the Southern Sea. He suddenly felt very alone.

They call me Regent, and all I wanted was you, Gabrielle. Many a night he had tried to sate his desire. Men brought him women from the streets and courts of Albien, dark haired and pretty, and afterward he still felt the emptiness and something else - the gnawing. He was being eaten up inside by his desires, desires that he could not quench.

He walked back toward Albien, his sword slapping out a rhythm. As the sight of the *Edrin* faded with the twilight, torches appeared upon the walls of the city. His men, the men of his army, of the Regent of the South, posted sentry and waited.

He passed within the walls and glanced askance at the contingent. Soon, Lord Duran of Qwen was lost in the deep shadows of his thoughts and those of the occupied city.

Chapter 12

Shale crashed from the ledge to the rock-strewn beach below and Barj looked over his shoulder nervously, hoping that it sounded natural, or at least be muffled by the slow ebb of the surf a stone's throw away. Finally, his steed, legs shaking and lungs heaving, found its way to the dark rocks at the base of the cliff. Shaj'il Cziffer lent a faint sheen to the wet stones, rounded and slick with wear. His gray mare snorted and mist shot from its nostrils. Barj pulled the reins, guiding the nervous mount over the last large rock and onto the relatively forgiving gravel.

The tide pulled the ocean back from the cliffs; a cloak of quicksilver exposing the rough skin of the earth. Above them, and along the shore, the Teeth of Narn rose skyward, blocking out the northern sky. Here the Teeth shot out of the water, Barj thought sardonically, *like the skipping stones of giants, caught in mud.*

Mrick and Adon had decided to make the descent to sea level. They had left the High Road that ran from the Great Forest through the Teeth some time ago. For some reason Adon had been worried about leaving themselves in the open when they took the descent directly down to Narn-toc. After some conferring with Mrick, Adon had led them down a narrow and treacherous grade. At first Barj had thought the path would lead to a precipitous fall, but it switched back often enough to allow a dangerous passage to the beach below. Barj believed the path would be much easier by day, but Adon had wanted to be away from the High Road that night.

Once off the shale, he let go the reins and watched his mare find her way to the other horses in one of the many deep grottoes that dotted the cliffs. Tucking his gloves into his sword belt, he then placed a leather thong in his mouth and pulled his straight brown hair back into a ponytail. He tied it off quickly and went to join Mrick by the tiny fire.

Thank Tarn for the small fire. He only noticed the cold now that the worry of coming down the cliff had passed. His toes were so grateful that he nearly pushed his boots into the coals. Kael, one of the men, put a wineskin into his hand and he took a deep drought. Now Mrick was deep in conversation with the nobleman; that was what Barj had deemed the raven-haired fellow from Tarn Hold. Barj watched as Mrick listened intently to what Adon was saying. He had only seen Baxel's man act so with Trevor or Gabrielle. *Had this man from Tarn Hold somehow managed to gain the loyalty of Mrick?* He watched Mrick nod, leaning on one knee as he stepped up onto a rock. His left hand draped over the pommel of his sword, *Baxel's Bane*, and his braid flung over his shoulder. Barj had to admire the man. He had taken up Baxel's place when all hope seemed lost and had kept the last two dozen of Trevor's men-at-arms together when there was little left to protect. He had given the men purpose and even as the purpose changed, he still brought loyalty.

"What think you?" Kael asked. There was a nervous tremor in his voice. "Does this man lead us to the undead, or to death's door?"

Barj looked at Kael sharply. Nervous Kael. His hair was tangled, combed back to hide a bald spot. He was tall and lank and looked around like a ferret, just the type to talk for the sake of filling the quiet. It did not matter that much of what he said was unimportant, only that he said it, and in doing so annoyed most of the other men.

"If it was to our deaths then Mrick would not follow him. No, he has a purpose, but 'it is not for me or you to say, just obey,' as the saying goes."

Kael grunted and cast his eyes to the fire, illuminating his sallow cheeks and weak chin, emphasizing his nervous glances. "I've met his type before, in Ord. Lords n' Ladies are akin. They order us around without a care for us."

"He's paying us Kael, not forcing our hand. You can leave any time."

"For what? That horse is Mrick's. You want me to walk out of here? The Great Forest is haunted and I wouldna last a night alone."

"Where we go may be worse," Adon spoke from the darkness. Kael jumped back and almost slipped on the slick shale. Several of the other men laughed and Kael just glared at them. Barj wrung his hands in the warmth of the fire and looked to the dark haired man.

"You pay we go, isn't that right, Mrick?"

"Aye," said the other man. They were of the same age, he and Mrick. Even though Baxel had made Mrick his second they were alike in many different ways.

"And if it be death's gate or Oran's hell then-" Kael stuttered.

Adon hissed sharply and cut the other man off. He stepped into the light, his green eyes defying the flames. "Do not speak that name this close to the city, else you will find right away if that hell exists."

Taken aback, Kael's eyes narrowed as he searched the other's face. "Forgive me, I didn't-"

Adon shook his head and looked to the water. "There is nothing to forgive. It is just that other men have scoffed and it earned them death or damnation. I want to spare you that. I-" and he paused, gazing out into the water, caught as if by a siren. Mrick and Barj followed his gaze to into the darkness.

The silent black monoliths of the Teeth were matte against the quicksilver surface of the ocean. Weaving its way west up the shore between the jagged rocks was a ghostly vessel. Sails reefed, slender oars dipped into to the water, a rhythm that matched by the slow beat of drum. Dirge-like the sound came, a slow and steady call to pace. Though no lights marked the vessel, an ephemeral glow seemed to chase the bow wave, illuminating the prow and draft of the huge ship. Slowly it passed them, and soon the Teeth obscured it from their view.

It happened in a moment and it left a shiver run up Barj's back. Kael was left speechless, and the rest of the men muttered nervously. Barj looked to Adon. His dark unreadable face still gazed out over the water. Mrick too was lost in his own thoughts. Barj began kicking the fire out and soon only the red coals gave enough light for them to spread canvas on the ground for their bedding. A dark pall had descended on the troupe.

Barj looked to Mrick, a frown on his otherwise impassive face. "Before middle-night Adon and I go to the dead-city, Barj. You have the men, if we do not return by middle-day, take the men and go up the coast to Paravel. Or, if you would rather, to Bastion Hold."

"But-"

"None of that. Adon wishes to go it alone. I told him he spends his gold as he pleases, but I go with him to make sure it gets to your hands.

"Now remember, not past middle-day." Mrick waited for Barj to nod, and then the darkness soon swallowed him as he moved deeper into the grotto where Adon stood by the horses.

"Aye," Barj whispered to no one but himself. "But you did not say whether middle-day on the morrow, or on the fortnight, Mrick."

Adon kept to the cliff wall as he moved ever closer to the city of Narn-toc. If he strained he could hear the tolling of a ships bell in the distance, *or was it a temple bell?* He was not sure. That tolling bell brought back memories of Tarn Hold and none of them good. Behind him, Mrick cursed under his breath as he slipped on a slick rock. He looked over his shoulder to see Mrick scowling as he readjusted his sword and slung it over his back. Adon waited until the younger man caught up, and then once more looked along the shoreline to the swollen moon that hung low on the horizon, somehow managing to wend its way through the Teeth.

There were more regular shapes in the moonlight. Straight and true, the towers of the city of Narn-toc at one time were beautiful in their multicolored hues. Not anymore. When last he was here, as a child, they were black with soot and filth; the mold and lichen of centuries without care.

They rounded a curve in the cliff and stopped. The surf licked at their boots as they surveyed what was before them.

A low plain began as the descent fell to sea level. This was where his father's entourage camped when they made their way into the dead-city. It was a grassy peninsula, without tree or bush, guarded by a dike on the north and south sides. Obviously, the peninsula fell below sea level. Adon noted with passing interest that if an army were to lay siege one could destroy a part of the dike adjoined by two towers. The sea would rush in, leaving only the higher roadway clear in a low tide.

What caught his attention now were the signs of life evident in the city. There were flickering torches on the walls and a beacon in the harbor for ships that sat in the protected port. From this angle he could see at least a dozen masts above the curtain wall.

"What now, friend Adon?"

The disciple of Tarn looked at the distant city. He could make out blackness in the wall where the road rose to meet it, a circular opening, as if there was once a round shield that was rolled to the side. Towers and the roofs of buildings were silhouetted, but he knew that at least some of them were now inhabited.

"What now? A good question indeed. It had been my original intention to come to the dead-city, go within to the ill reputed Keep of Iss, retrieve the *Ih'dia Om,* and leave. But, now I don't know if that is possible." He squatted down and looked at the

141

stout young man before him. "I cannot ask you to go any farther. Several nights ago, when I first learned that there were people in Narn-toc, I knew that I must go in, however, now I see there are greater forces in Narn-toc than I had anticipated. Whether pay or no, I have no right to ask you to go with me."

"You cannot do this along, friend Adon. I comprehend little of your quest. However, if what you say about the darker forces afoot in that city yonder is true, then you will fare poorly if you do not have a sword at your back. I know not of sorcery, but I have no small skill at arms. From the looks of you, a sword is no stranger, yet my father suckled me on the thing. In the village where I grew up you could be one of three things, a fisher, a trader, or a man-at-arms. Well, my father had no skill at bargaining, was far from a master fisher, but sure as Carn is old could use a sword. When Baxel and I left our village, Trevor tested us most thoroughly against bandits and thieves. I assure you, I can help."

Adon laughed. "Such a speech, Mrick, how could I not take you along. Nevertheless, I fear we must wait and watch. Tonight I doubt if we can gain entrance. As you see, the only way in is through that portal. Entering in the day is out of the question, as is this night. Tomorrow night, maybe, but by then your men may be gone."

"Gone? If I know Barj he'll be sitting there till the new moon. No, you are better off having my men at your beck. I'll go back and inform them of the new plan."

142

"Aye, but wait a bit. We have til noon on the morrow. Day is several hours away and we can scout out the dike and the wall."

"Then, to the dead-city it is." Adon was silently on his feet, his green eyes flashing and a tight smile on his face. Mrick could not help but feel a certain flush of excitement as he followed in the footsteps of the nobleman; an excitement he had rarely felt in the service of Trevor.

The shadows ruled this moonlit night in Narn-toc. The men of the Black Guard, five hundred strong, sealed their barracks doors with a steel reinforced timber and Captain Ghythel Boern attempted a cheery smile for his men; it seemed to fail miserably. Their garrison was in Ythrinny's Keep, away from the Field of Blood and the Gate of Untheran. They now occupied the only fortress in the city that did not carry the taint of darkness; it now housed five hundred men.

He unslung his sword and settled it against the large hearth of the great hall, absently noting that the leather scabbard was somewhat worn. Here, amid long tables of men eating their evening fare, there was a nervous quality to the chatter and the discourse. The first week his forces were in the city his men had run regular patrols, including duty at the wall. Now, with the arrival of the Guard of Oran, his men spent the nights within the barracks. Let the others haunt the streets of this strange city, with its twisty boulevards and strange buildings, with its towers that whistled like banshees when the wind sped off the sea.

The damnable Guards of Oran, it was an unspoken rule that they took the night watch, and left the day to his men. Only the Guard of Oran and the Hand of Keth wandered freely throughout the city. For all Boern cared they could keep this city of deep alleys and darkness.

His orders had been clear from the start. By default Myella had be nominated Conclavatrix by the Clave. Ironeas was dead and Adon was missing; Marad had supposedly committed suicide. He, his men and one hundred horses, had been ordered from Helm to sail up the Crevasse to the sea, garner supplies in Qwen and then follow the sea-lanes to Clef. There the Preceptor had accepted news of Myella's succession with a smile and had laden the ship with stores. Several more weeks along the coast found them looking at a very old navigational map which was good enough to guide them through the Teeth of Narn to the fabled and ancient Summer Seat of the Conclaveum.

Myella's orders had been very explicit. Occupy the city and await further instructions, and those instructions came with the Guard of Oran. He was to allow his men into only certain parts of the city. That was fine with him, for several of his men had disappeared already. Now the men knew the rule: stay in the barracks at night, within the boundaries set by day, and all would go smoothly.

Therefore, it was that the commander sat with his men for his evening fare, the tolling of a bell and a steady, distant beat, occasionally pierced the night. If he had any ideas about abandoning his post, he certainly entertained them now.

Chapter 13

"Why are you doing this?" John asked as he watched Mike cinch the strap on the saddle. The leather bags were packed thick and heavy with clothes and rations. Only Mike's mottled brown horse stood in the courtyard of Kelvin's Keep. He was alone in this.

"Look, Pelles can cover the foundry for me. He knows all the specifications. That is *if* we can figure out what is going wrong with the castings.

"Anyway, you and Joe can handle things here, wait for Tom and word from Bill. I'm going alone because Narn-toc is a veritable ghost town, and it would just be a waste of time for you. Besides, I'll travel faster alone."

"Oh, now you're the great explorer."

"Listen, Kelvin gave me a good map. It'll take me a couple weeks total. There are a few villages and towns along the way and I'll be able to stay at Inns. I can always send word back by courier if need be."

"All for this damned book?" John crossed his arms and scowled. He noticed that Mike had no weapon besides a knife.

"That 'damned book' may hold the key to getting us back home and might even give us a clue as to why we were brought here in the first place." He slapped the saddlebag shut and the horse stepped sharply to the side.

Mike pushed back sandy hair from his eyes and then rested his bare forearms over the saddle. John noticed the bandage wrapped around his friends hand, the same material as the headband he now

145

always wore. John knew it hid a strange scar, but he didn't know what had caused it. He looked at Mike for a long moment. The larger man continued. "I said once before that our strength lay with us as a group; I still believe that. However, I also believe I can gain a greater understanding of the machinations of Myella, and this Guyle fellow, if I retrieve the *Ih'dia Om*. I can handle myself. My knowledge of the aether, and the sorcery that manipulates it, has grown exponentially since we've come here. Trust me."

"Mike, if what you say is true, then how do you know this book isn't guarded?"

"I can handle it."

"Soon there is going to be an army laying siege to Paravel. Can you handle that? Kelvin and Alaric think it won't last very long, especially if Myella has those Keth creatures. The cannons don't work, and the militia is pitifully small."

"Joe said he would look into the cannons. If they don't work we switch to Plan B. Why don't you look into reinforcing the militia?"

"Plan B? What the hell is Plan B?"

"The Shadow knows." Mike grinned, somewhat psychotically at that, and swung up onto the saddle. The horse staggered, and then quickly adjusted to Mike's bulk. As he reined the steed around, Pelles strode through the main gate. There was a defiant look in his eyes as he passed the one guard who attempted to stop him. John waved the guardsman away.

"Sir John, Lord Michael, good morn to you both." John nodded to the older man and Mike just looked over the head of the horse; he was fingering

146

his mustache out of nervous habit. At Pelles' side was a long object wrapped in soft leather.

"'Tis a gift for Lord Michael, for his journey to the dead-city. It's an old commission, the man who wanted it was killed when he slipped on an icy dock and fell between his ship and the pier. This," he hefted the spear, "has been sitting in the back of my shop for six years, wrapped in oil cloth."

He hefted it up to Mike, who looked at it with appreciation. The spearhead was blackened from the forge, yet silvered along the edge, betraying razor sharpness. The shaft itself was a dark bluish-gray and fluted along its length. At two points along the shaft it was wrapped with leather; he could be confident of a sure grip.

"The man provided the shaft; he said it was a relic of some kind, from near Baed, just north of the Great Wall. It is said there was a battle there, so maybe it was a quarterstaff or part of a spear. I do know that I had a hellish time in welding the blade to the shaft. Good work I think."

"Pelles, I don't know what to say."

"How about thanks," John interjected.

"Thanks, Pelles."

"It is an honor, milord. I had it blessed at the Temple of Tarn. Narn-toc is an evil place and one should go with Tarn in such a quest." He nodded smartly, and before the two could say another word the smith was briskly walking back the way he came.

"It'll take some time to get used to it-"

"Not really," Mike cut in. "In Aikido you learn the way of the bo as well as the sword." He placed the spear across the saddle and, after fumbling in a pocket; he stuck his pipe between his teeth. "See ya."

"Be careful," John called and Mike just waved his hand as he nudged the horse out of the courtyard and into the city street.

Gabrielle looked through the leaded glass window and into the courtyard. She stared a long while after Lord Michael had left and Sir John had walked back to the inner keep. Somehow, she felt betrayed. Trianna, her servant and friend, was dead, and she had not shed a tear. She felt very cold and alone at this moment as she clutched her shawl about her shoulders. It had been a week since they had buried her friend just outside the city, away from the crowded public cemetery. *Trianna would have wanted it that way*, she thought.

She had watched her friend die a horrible death, frozen at the touch of the evil Keth. Only Sir John's intervention had spared her the same fate. She turned away from the leaded glass window, her hands clutched nervously at the fringe of her shawl. She looked over her chamber, now nearer Sir John and Surik's; yet, also farther away, it seemed. She looked at a tray of food one of the servants had brought in this morning; it lay there, untouched. She had lost her appetite long since.

She sat on the edge of her bed and stared for a long time into the crackling flames of the fireplace. It warmed her little. She could imagine at this moment that her father had no such luxury; the same for many of the people in this city.

There was a war in the West and people came to Paravel in droves. The streets were crowded and the larders were becoming bare. Had she been in

Galfeon Yor she could have done something; bartered for stores from Ord or Albien to keep the bellies of the poor children full. She could not do that in this city, where she was a Lady without claim.

Oh, she knew that Kelvin did his best, as did Chairman Nathal, but the peasants still came. She smoothed a crease in her woolen dress and sighed. Winter was coming and people would starve and die. Moreover, her father was lost to forces far in the North. *What had he hinted at? Am I really Myella's cousin?* She gazed at an old map that lay on her drawing table. It was a map of the Conclaveum; Lord Michael had found it in one of the libraries. It clearly showed the Great Wall, Helm City, and the route to Teshwa, the Seat of the Conclaveum. The city sat on the Kipris River, south of a large lake. A red mark on the map defined the Tower of Iss. Myella had said her father was to be sent to the Tower of Iss. It was a long journey to Teshwaand her father should be there by now, to meet whatever fate Myella and her uncle had in store for him.

There was a knock at her door and she started, no doubt one of the servants bringing her the midday meal. She called for the person to enter.

It was her Knight Protector, Sir John.

He must have just come up from the courtyard. It had been chilly outside and there was a flush to his face. Yet, he smiled crookedly and she felt her breath catch in her throat. She liked this man.

"I see you haven't touched your food," he commented as he closed the door behind him.

"You are very forward, Sir John."

149

"that is not considered forward where I come from."

"May I remind you that where you come from is far from here?"

"Touche."

She looked away from him and out the window; it seemed very dismal outside.

A frown lit upon his face as he moved to the hearth. He looked at the map and shook his head.

"We would go after him if we could. You know that-"

"Would you?" she bit back sharply. There was pain in her voice; she had experienced much loss. "Smiling Wolf has not returned and you have not heard word one from the Bard and Torec. Now, Lord Michael has gone off on some mad adventure leaving just Surik and yourself. Will there be anyone left when the walls are besieged?"

"They'll be back -"

"What makes you think so? Alaric says that Albien has fallen to the Armies of the North: the Black Guard and the Guard of Oran. Do you remember them, Sir John? They razed my home and now they raze the west. I am sure Duran leads them. He will return to Paravel when he feels strong enough. It might be in the spring, it could be in a fortnight."

"That's why Tom went to the Great Wall. He could learn something-"

She shook her head. "What? That there is an army marching this very instant to destroy Paravel? And what if this army killed him? What then?"

"I know Tom, he won't be killed."

150

"Did you know the same of Sir Chill?" He winced and she knew she had gone too far. Immediately his demeanor became more distant, even cold. He walked to the window, his back stiff.

"If I had an army, Gabrielle, I would lead it to Teshwa and to the Tower of Iss. I would free your father. God knows if it were my father I would have gone at it alone. As sure as we drove Myella from this city, we must strive to protect it.

"Believe me, Gabrielle, when this is over-"

"When we are prisoners or worse."

"I give you my word." He said it as he turned to her. It was then that he noticed the tears on her cheek. He went to her and knelt before her, taking her hands in his. His voice was low and soft.

"It is my vow, Gabrielle, that before this is over you will have your father at your side."

"You cannot promise me such-"

"It is a vow upon my Faith," he touched his medal and it felt warm, tingling, "and it is vow before my God!" He placed his head in her lap and she ran her fingers through his hair. He felt her tears on his neck as she silently cried.

Night came quickly to Paravel; the days had grown shorter with autumn. A cold wind blew off the sea, stripping the trees of their colorful leaves and bringing a chill draft through shutters and into the homes of the citizens of the Port City. They were the lucky ones, those with hearth and home. There were many more in the streets and in the alleys. The Preceptor of the Temple of Tarn had opened his doors and his church was now crowded with women and children. He had done his best to bless the ground that was once the Seat and Temple

151

of Oran. However, few refugees passed through the Gate of Osso to seek refuge in the buildings that remained.

Now, Preceptor Javin Skettes watched a lone figure wend his way between the mewling children and hungry mothers. Some grabbed at his trailing cloak, but pulled back when they saw the curved sword he wore at his side. Where the Preceptor always wore white vested robes, this young man wore strange clothes:blue britches and a blouse with a high neck and no buttons. Over these, yet under the cloak, he wore some kind of short coat made of leather. He recognized the young man as one of the Outlanders that helped drive Myella out of the city. Sir John.

"Welcome to Tarn's Home. I am the Preceptor here, Javin Skettes." He held out his hand to the young man.

"John, Sir John, Lord Knight of Erie."

"What brings you to the Temple? There is little room, but if you wish to pray I can find you some privacy..."

"I was walking by and I saw the Temple. I saw the refugees."

"That is not what brought you here."

John assessed the man. Skettes did not look like a fanatic. In fact, he reminded John of the Jesuit who had taught him civics in high school. He was clean cut and in his late forties; his hair was salt and peppered. His grip was firm.

John smiled, somewhat condescendingly, at the Preceptor's last remark and looked over the temple. Aside from the mass of people it was a beautiful building; thin columns, traced to the vaulted ceiling and at the top spread like lacey fingers. The temple was circular, constructed of white marble and in the dim lamplight glimmered like shell. From where John stood at the very center of the temple, the stained glass windows were spaced equidistant from the pillars; it was all very pleasing to look at. There was no altar, and the patterns in the stained glass windows were geometric; only one window, high up near the ceiling, contained the depiction of a hawk. The pews all faced inward, where the design in the mosaic floor was a starburst.

"Is that Tarn?" John asked as he gestured to the hawk.

"No, just a symbol."

John nodded his head and looked at the people. He was at a loss for words, but the Preceptor waited patiently.

"I hear that the Temple of Tarn is accepted throughout the Conclaveum."

"Yes," the man answered cautiously.

"Can we talk in private, Preceptor?"

"Follow me," Javin replied and turned. His vestment billowed out behind him as he strode quickly from the temple proper. He led John to an antechamber, which must have served as the man's office. He sat down on a comfortable chair and motioned John to sit on a wooden bench. The former parochial school student smiled wryly.

"What is troubling you?" Javin asked.

"Not two hours ago I made a vow to my God-"

"And you wish to be relieved of that vow?"

"No," John said, rather sharply. "I take vows very seriously. In my religion, which I haven't practiced very much lately, there is but One True

153

God. Now, I may not follow too closely the two thousand years of tradition that my religion espouses, but I do believe in Him as God, and as a guiding Hand in things."

"It sounds much like Tarn."

"It somehow wouldn't surprise me. In my land many different religions worship the same God."

"But, your vow troubles you?"

John looked around the office, noticing the plainness of the effects. "I vowed that someone who should be dead would be reunited with his daughter."

"Very disturbing." The priest steepled his fingers and gazed over them as he assessed the younger man. "And what if he is dead?"

"I don't believe that he is." He reached inside his turtleneck and pulled out his St. Christopher medal. "This is a symbol of my Faith. Don't make me explain it, it is a long story, but it helps me know things. Even though I don't understand everything that I see I do know that this person is still alive."

"There are similar talismans in Tarn's faith. I do believe you. I would very much like to learn of your God some day, but that is not the issue now. How may *I* help you?"

"You said earlier that the Temple of Tarn is accepted in the Conclaveum?"

"Most people within the Conclaveum worship Tarn; even though our Seat of Faith was in Tarn Hold in the west."

"Was?"

"It was destroyed months ago by Keth."

"What?"

"We have our sources."

"I am sorry."

"So am I. All the priests of Tarn were trained there, at the Sequestiary. Tarn works in mysterious ways."

"I need information from Teshwa."

The Preceptor looked at John for a long, hard moment. "This pertains to your vow?"

"The man I want to find may be in the Tower of Pain."

The man winced and put his fist to his forehead. "Trevor Galfeon Crona."

"You know of him?" John asked, though he didn't know what 'Crona' meant.

"We know much of what happens with regard to the Cult of Oran and its minions. Myella has spent much gold and time trying to purge the South of the Temple of Tarn. We had to go underground while her Seat was in Paravel. We owe you much, Sir John.

"Word has it that Trevor Galfeon Crona was taken to the Tower of Iss. That is all I know."

"I have never heard him referred to as 'Crona.' What is that?"

"A family name. Did you know that the Conclavator is dead?"

"The ruler of the Conclaveum? Kelvin may have said something." He wasn't really shocked. He had learned that Myella now proclaimed herself Conclavatrix.

"Did you know that the Conclavator was Ironeas?"

"Yes. Where is this all going?"

The Preceptor smiled and stood. Clasping his hands behind his back, he walked over to a bookshelf.

"Ironeas Vien Crona."

"What?" It took John a moment to realize where this may be going. "Are you telling me that Trevor and the Conclavator were related?"

"I am telling you that they were brothers." John just looked at the man, somewhat dumbfounded. *So, that was all the business about Myella calling Gabrielle her cousin. Myella was Ironeas' daughter.*

"Well, well, well. Isn't this causing all the pieces of the puzzle to fall in place?"

"Is it?"

"So this Counselor Guyle, he also is Trevor's brother?"

"Half-brother, I think. My sources in the Conclaveum tell me that there was some conflict in their youth. Guyle is in league with Oran and is pursuing his own form of vengeance."

"Thank you, Preceptor. You have been an incredible help." John looked at his watch and frowned. He had to be somewhere within the hour.

"Have I? On the other hand, have I muddied the waters? Does this help your vow at all?"

"Yes. Trevor would be valuable to Guyle. I don't think he would be killed right away."

"You are probably correct in that assumption. But, I am loathe to think of what Guyle is capable of."

"Preceptor, can you get any more information on Trevor? Specific information?"

156

"I can try. As I said, I owe you and your companions much for driving the evil from this city."

"Great, I would appreciate it. Now, I have to go." He stood and shook the older man's hand. "Thank you, Preceptor Javin."

"Come back to the Temple, my son."

"Count on it," John replied over his shoulder as he strode briskly out of the chamber.

"I will."

***

Dark clouds raced overhead obscuring the ringed moon, *Shaj'il Cziffer*. The shadows were deep in this quarter of the city - good for him, he thought. It seemed that lately the streets were teaming with people of all classes and races. Refugees from the west mixed with the citizens of Paravel leaving the alleys crowded and fetid.

The shadows deepened near a large building in the east quarter of the city. The 'Foundry' as the Outlanders called it. In reality, it was a large forge with a dozen furnaces and smelters. This was the structure wherein lay the secret weapon that they had hoped would defeat the Armies of the North: Mike's cannons. The heat spilled from the eaves, driving away the chill air and even though the anvils were silent this night, the warmth of the forge was still present.

A patrol of the city guard rounded the corner. There were not enough men in the Guard to assign to this building alone, no matter how important.

That was why he was here, to find out why the castings were all bad; what sorcery,.

He heard footsteps behind him and looked down at his watch. *Right on time.* He looked over his shoulder to see a figure in blue jeans and leather jacket. John.

"What's up, Joe," came a whisper. Joe/Surik grunted at the arrival of his friend and nodded to the foundry.

"Pelles left the sally port unlocked. It's not too late. I suggest we go in and wait."

"Right."

"You're dressed rather-"

"I know. I just felt like a change. I don't wear them that often."

"If it were day you would stand out like a sore thumb."

Faint firelight cast long shadows in the foundry. The heat of the fires kept the air warmon the casting room floor. Where Joe and John sat, it was close to sweltering. They sat atop a catwalk with the beamed ceiling just inches from their heads, , looking at the floor some twenty feet below. "My ass has fallen asleep."

"Yeah, well, I'm beginning to think Mike is full of shit."

"That could be. His going off alone is pretty weird."

"You mean beyond his usual weirdness?"

"What do you think?"

Joe winced as he too fidgeted. "Something scared Blotto. I don't know what, but he was downright desperate to get the other half of that book. Did you by chance see the mark on his forehead?"

"The scar?"

"Brand more like, looks like a rune or sigil, and God knows how he got that. I saw it one day when he was practicing his aikido. I don't think he knew I had. He is very conscious of it."

"Probably has to do with his dabbling in *whatever.*"

"Yeah, well I just wish he would have taken some men."

"He said we couldn't spare any men. I had to agree. Kelvin sure as hell wouldn't let any of his men go. Those left of Torec's people went with Tom. I just hope that he can take care of himself."

"Well, his little flintlock sure took care of that Keth. I really believe that if we get those cannons off the ground they could determine whether Paravel survives. If only we can get the castings to hold."

"He said there was a Plan B?"

"What? News to me, though I'm sure we could come up with something." Joe looked over the vast floor of the foundry. The flawed castings lay in a heap of scrap near the north wall, and near the furnace sat a small cauldron with still bubbling oil in it; it was on a low-wheeled wagon. He looked toward the main doors. *What the hell are we waiting here for?* He sighed and folded his arms. Johnwas lying prone along the catwalk, his sword in front of him.

"Well, I'll be a sonofabitch," John whispered.

"What?"

"Look near the ore bin, by the main furnace." Joe followed his friend's gaze to the bin and there, in hood and cloak, was a figure. The person was making hand gestures over the ore. There was a gleam of glass and what looked like a liquid being poured onto the ore, but they could not be sure.

"What's he doing?" John asked the Shadowlord.

"You got me, maybe sorcery, maybe something that will affect the casting. Your guess is as good as mine is. You want to take him?"

John thought for a moment. "Let's follow him."

They waited until the person was finished and watched as he went to a trap door in the floor of the foundry (they had not seen it before.) Only after the person had slipped through the trap door and closed it, did they leave the catwalk and approach the portal. There appeared to be no latch from this side. Joe looked around for a moment, trying to figure a way to open the door. His gaze lit upon a pry bar and soon he was lifting the hatch away from the floor.

Below was a ladder that descended to darkness. John looked at Joe, Joe looked back. A foul, rotten egg odor wafted up from below.

"How nice, a pit from hell." Joe wrinkled his nose and drew his sword, *Entius*. John stepped back as a faint, silver-blue flame flickered along the sword; it illuminated the two of them.

"You first, John," Joe said and cracked a wicked grin. John rolled his eyes and handed his sheathed katana to Joe. He dropped quickly down the ladder.

watched his friend descend into the blackness. He waited about thirty seconds before he heard a cough, then he dropped the Japanese blade down the shaft. John caught it deftly. He waited for Joe to join him, which took a little longer because the bearded man chose to carry his bastard sword, to illuminate his descent. Finally, the two men stood together in the gloom of the faintly lit tunnel. They both looked around. John did not notice any boot prints in the hard packed dirt.

"A little narrow for a sword fight," Joe commented as he brushed a cobweb from his hair. John nodded as if his friend would notice and saw immediately from where the rotten egg smell came. There was a small sack of some yellow, chalky stone - sulfur - it must have fallen from above some time ago. The sack had broken and some of the sulfur was laying in a puddle of dirty water, hence the smell. John picked up a dry piece.

"You said something about hell?" John queried. The self-styled Shadowlord just smiled and held out his sword. The silver-blue light illuminated the corridor for about fifteen feet all around.

"Which way, o' Necromancer of the Shades?"

"Hey, that's a good one. I'll have to remember it." Joe nodded ahead and they proceeded down the tunnel. He hoped that this little jaunt would at least solve the riddle of the castings.

The tunnel stretched on, occasionally paralleling another tunnel; a sewer that ran darkly with the wastewater of the city. Occasionally an arch would give way to the brick walled tunnel that ran deep with effluvia, and rats would scurry at their approach. They continued with caution, the air growing rank. John would occasionally mark the tunnel wall with the sulfurous chalk. Eventually the tunnel widened and opened to a circular chamber. Here the corridors split off like spokes from the hub of a wheel.

"Shit," Surik muttered. Sir John, Lord Knight of Erie, heaved a sigh; all the paths were alike.

"Now what?"

"You tell me, you're the one with the magical St. Christopher's medal."

"Me? You have a magic sword!"

"Uh...right." Joe looked down the length of the blade. "Well, *Entius*, which way?" He said it with some sarcasm, yet the sword tilted in his hands and angled to one of the corridors to the left.

"This is ludicrous," John commented. "It's like a bad fantasy movie. How do we know there isn't someone or *something* waiting to ambush us?"

"Orc's, demon's, troll's, we can handle them."

"You sound like Mike."

"I don't think any of those things are behind the sabotage of the cannons. I think there is a more mundane explanation."

John smiled to no one but himself. He motioned impatiently for Joe to follow the path that his sword had divined. The tunnel was level enough at first but then the grade changed and it began to noticeably slope down.

"We're going down," John remarked nervously.

"Yep."

"Maybe we should go back."

"What are you afraid of?"

"Dead things. Er, things that really aren't dead. I don't know." John's thoughts slid off on some tangent. *Why are we down here?* If someone was deliberately sabotaging the cannons, then they

162

intended for Myella to retake Paravel with ease. Who could do it without giving hint as to what caused the bad castings?

Slowly the tunnel leveled and they rounded a narrow corner. Joe held John back and motioned to the floor with his sword. The blade's glow flared at what appeared to be a shallow pool of water.

"Probably just a low spot."

"Yeah," Joe replied. "Or a trap."

"Ooh, paranoia."

Joe frowned and looked at the water. It was only about five feet across. He handed his glowing sword to John and immediately the hallway went pitch black. "Nice," the White Knight commented and Joe chuckled. He grabbed his friend by the shoulder and John placed the pommel back in his hands. The faint glow was back.

"This would make a great book," John said.

"Who would publish it?"

"Does it do that all the time?" John asked how the sword glowed silver blue while in Joe's hand.

"Only I can make it work. Now what?"

"You had the right idea." John leapt over the water. He cleared the other side by a foot. Joe leapt, with sword in hand, to join his friend.

"For all that trouble I hope it was a trap." Joe shook his head at his friend's remark then once more led the way down the tunnel.

"Do you think he went this way?"

"I certainly hope so. Otherwise I'm gonna melt this sword down and turn in my cape." John smirked. The tunnel widened slightly and all of a sudden, the light from Joe's sword faded out.

"Shit."

163

"What's the matter? Did you drop it?"

"No. It just went out."

"Battery gone dead?"

"Funny. Now how in the hell do we get back?"

"I..." John paused. It should have been completely dark in the tunnel. As it was, though, a faint yellow light emanated from the far end of the tunnel, from around a corner. Surik Shadowlord's eyes adjusted and they were soon creeping down the hall to get a look at the source of the light.

They found themselves looking into a cavernous chamber. Before them was one torch, lighting the doorway, and beyond the flagstones leveled out to encompass a long hall, the ceiling and opposite wall lost in darkness. Before them was a large pillar base that obscured their view of the center of the chamber. They heard voices coming from that vicinity.

"You know where we are?" Joe asked in a whisper.

"No. Do you?"

"Yeah. We're under the Temple of Oran. This is the sub-basement, I think."

"Great, just great. I gotta bad feeling about this."

"You always have a bad feeling. It's probably gas."

"Ha-ha. Let's get a look at what's on the other side of that pillar."

They edged their way around the dark pillar. Even here the opulence of Myella's Regency was evident. Upon closer inspection it was revealed that the pillars were not granite, but marble; a darkly mottled green and red marble that was polished mirror smooth. Here and there were a few cracks where the foundation had settled, but otherwise it was still in good shape.

Joe and John slid to their belly's, eyeing the knot of people that stood near a few crates, now used as tables, in the center of the chamber. Light emanated from a source above them, and it was not a natural source.

Twenty men stood in the center of the chamber. They were all dressed in normal street cloths; two that were locked in deep conversation. These were not Paravelian civilians. They carried themselves too proudly and they all carried the same type of sword.

"Guard of Oran?" Joe muttered over his shoulder.

"That or worse. Look at the one with the helmet."

Joe recognized the tabard from Kelvin's Keep. It had a hand emblazoned on the tunic, palm outward, a Hand of Keth. No one stood near this person and instead of a sword he carried a black staff with intricate runes upon its surface. The Hand talked to the sabateur and with another taller person, who had his back to them and was lost in shadow. The man rested his hand on a sword hilt.

*There's something familiar about that. But what?*John asked himself as he tried to inch a little closer. He could get a better look at the person if he had one more inch.

There was a loud thud as a piece of marble dislodged itself from the pillar; it tumbled and rolled along the floor into the chamber. Joe looked at John, whose eyes were wide in surprise. All the

165

guards and the Hand of Keth were looking right at them.

"So much for stealth."

"Let's get out of here!" John said and was on his feet in a flash. There was a loud thump from behind, and stone chips flew everywhere just as they ducked into the dark tunnel. The sounds of pursuit followed; the shouting of men and the sound of steel being drawn echoed down the tunnel.

John had grabbed the torch off the wall and it almost guttered as he ran. Joe was right behind him, urging him on.

"Follow the chalk marks," John called, panting, to his friend. Joe just grunted, almost getting caught up in his cloak and sheathed sword. Clearly, John had been more prudent in his selection of clothing.

The sounds of the guards behind were closer; obviously, they knew these tunnels and warrens better than the two outlanders did. John splashed through the water and Joe did the same. *So much for Joe's paranoia,* came the fleeting thought. He recognized the hub of corridors and stopped abruptly. There was no chalk here.

"That one," Joe said breathlessly.

"How do you know?"

"Smell the sewer?"

"Right." They ran down the opposite tunnel and, as Joe drew his sword, John tossed the flaming brand into the sewer water letting it gutter. Maybe that would slow the pursuit.

It did not. The guardsmen who followed shouted anew as their prey came into sight, thanks to Joe's glowing sword. John stopped abruptly, almost slamming into the ladder.

166

"Hurry, I've got a plan."

"Good, 'cus I don't." John rapidly climbed the ladder, almost missing a rung or two on the way up. He was through the hatch and pulling Joe up by the shoulders, almost impaling himself on *Entius*. Men working the first shift stared in surprise as they emerged from the hatchway.

"Don't you want to close that?" John asked, but his friend just shook his head and sheathed his blade. He shoved two men aside who were working with the cauldron of boiling oil and motioned John to help him.

"You're not going to-"

"Got any better ideas? Hurry, they were right on my ass. They'll be coming up the ladder any minute now." He tossed John a tamping rod, and then the two quickly shoved them through the rings on the vat and wagon. It took all they could muster to move the cauldron three feet to the trap door. Below, he heard the guardsmen on the ladder.

"This will give that Hand of Keth a second thought about sabotaging the cannons." They both heaved at the ladle, straining with all their might to tip the thing. Soon it was over, spilling its contents down through the trap door. There was a loud hiss and then the momentary muted screams of men as they were doused with the hot liquid. Steam and the stench of the burnt flesh and sulfur billowed up from below and Joe gasped aloud as they lowered the ladle down on the wagon. Staggering, he shut the trap door and jammed the tamping rod into the hinge. He leaned heavily on the bin and looked to see John bent over, hands on knees, gasping for air. The knight looked up and smiled.

"Think we could station a guard here?"

"Oh yeah," replied the Shadowlord. "We still have a saboteur and a Hand of Keth running around."

"Right, and I think I know where to get the men to do the guard duty."

"Where?"

"I saw plenty of young men in the streets. Men who, given the right tools, will be glad for a little adventure."

"You're going to recruit from the refugees. Now why didn't I think of that? What will you pay them?"

"Details."

"What will you call them?"

"The Swords. The Swords of the Legion of the Black Skull."

Chapter 14

Tom Smiling Wolf knew he smelled smoke long before he saw it; and see it he did, with the clarity of perfect binocular vision; it rose above the trees, casting a haze over the sun. He looked at Marad out of the corner of his eye and noticed that he too sensed that somewhere ahead there was a fire.

They had left the immediate vicinity of the crevasse. When Tom had first met Marad, he had been wandering for some time in a delusory fever-state. Now they traveled together, heading east to Qwen with the plan of catching a ship to Paravel.

The woods had thinned some time ago; they were making good time as they traversed the countryside. The pain in Tom's side had faded over the course of a week and he was sure that he would be one hundred percent in the next day or two.

It would not be long before he was back in Paravel, the fiasco at the Great Wall far behind. He would miss the plains though, and the woodlands. Out here, he was far away from the reality of this world. For all he knew this place could be in upstate New York. The trees were rich in the autumnal shades, their leaves burnished by the impendingwinter. Even though he walked amid the leaves he barely made a sound, and for that matter neither did Marad; Tom thought this was good.

He stopped and stood on a large boulder that thrust its way up through the underbrush. He looked out into a clearing and sniffed.

"Smoke?" queried Marad.

"Yes, but there is something else. It's not a normal wood fire, there are other things involved." He dropped from the boulder and adjusted his heavy knife. Marad followed him along the game path.

He watched this tracker, this man who he had saved from the poison of the *kris-voulge*. In the time that he had spent with him he learned a great deal, especially of his skills as a woodsman. However, he felt that this Smiling Wolf was holding something back. What was drawing him to Paravel? He had told the tracker that once they reached Qwen they would probably part ways. He definitely had plans on finding his sister and visiting a certain amount of justice on Kel.

This Southerner though, was not telling him everything. However, he did not tell the Southerner his secrets either. If the Southerner had business in Paravel, then it was just that, his business. He had his own vendetta. Paravel could wait for the moment.

His makeshift kilt caught on a bramble and he pulled it away. He would have to find a good pair of britches. He knew he must look like a wild man, with hair unkempt and gray eyes flaring. *Tarn, how I miss the cities,* he thought.Tom crouched at the edge of the tree line and Marad followed suit. Before them was the source of the smoke; a small town lay below. Black sooty smoke drifted up from the thatched roofs and out of the broken windows. From here they could see the carcasses of horses, a few sheep, and the twisted remains of a woman and her baby.

Tom frowned and looked over his shoulder to Marad.

"How long would you say."

"A day at the most." Marad's expertise on the battlefield made it an accurate estimate. Tom nodded and unslung his knife. He was up and moving across the open grass to the town. Marad followed, his walking stick casually slung over his shoulder.

The road ran through this town of homes built from river rock. Tom strode carefully, being cautious and ever wary of assailants. Marad noticed, right off, that there seemed to be no people about, not even a dog ran the streets. One would expect mourners and survivors. Here there were only burnt out houses, barns, and slaughtered livestock; the only bodies they had seen had been those of the woman and child and they had been charred beyond recognition.

Tom looked back at the man and motioned for him to check one of the barns. Marad did so and came back with nothing more than a shake of his head.

"Where is everybody? You don't just abandon your home." Marad did not say anything; he just waited for the tracker to decide their next move.

Tom looked up the road; there was a two-story building, maybe a hostel, which had fared the fires better than the other buildings. "You check that out," he pointed with his knife down the street. "I'll head up this way." Marad nodded to Smiling Wolf and went up the street.

Tom walked on, ignoring the acrid smoke. This whole thing reminded him of the sack of Galfeon Yor. There had been certain intensity to the fire; it scarred the buildings. Yet, at Galfeon Yor they had herded the townsfolk to a central spot, the Deep that surrounded Trevor's castle, and slaughtered them, sending them to a mass grave.

Lost in these thoughts he rounded the corner, looked down, and stopped dead. A wolf stood in the middle of the street...

...silver eyes stared at him as the wolf stood in the dirt road. Out of the corner of his new eye, Tom caught sight of another wolf. This one looked older and had a light beard marking along his neck. The first wolf gazed at the older one. Grey beard stared impassively at Tom a moment and then ran off towards the woods.

The other seemed to smile at Tom and turned, looked over its shoulder as if expecting the man to follow: itwalked toward the opposite edge of the village. Instinctively Tom followed the wolf, knowing that it meant for him to do so.

The burnt out buildings gave way to a small pasture and there the wolf sat. Tom stopped next to the wolf, flaring his nostrils at the stench of death. The wolf sat not a yard away but that was not what held his attention now. In the middle of the pasture was a standard. It was an iron post sporting a dagger, encircled by a ring of fire. It was the standard of the Guard of Oran.

Tied to the standard were three slaughtered hawks, each with a quarrel through its breast. The standard was placed as a marker in that field, for it was planted squarely in the middle of an uncovered mass grave. Tom,too shocked by the sight before him, just stand there, the wolf sitting at his side.

Some time later, Marad found Smiling Wolf still standing before the grave that must have held at least one hundred men, women, and children. He looked with surprise at the wolf that sat at the Southerner's side, but it just stared back, tongue lolling, and paid him no heed.

"The Guard of Oran has gotten brazen."

"What? You mean the grave?"

"That and the three hawks. Hawks are the symbol of Tarn, Oran's nemesis. It is blasphemy to kill them and display them thus. And to kill three is an ill omen."

Tom looked at Marad for a long time. It was as though he had forgotten the oddity of the wolf at his side. "This is something you are used to?"

Marad's eyes narrowed as he searched Tom's. "You never get used to this. I have seen much worse done to the Krim. Yet, that was war. For this," and he waved at the grave, "for this there is no excuse."

"What's going on?"

"I fear that there is much evil in this, and probably much more to come."

"Now is a good time that we both sat down and had a long talk about what we know."

"Aye, that would be best. But, let us get away from here."

"After we burn the bodies and destroy that standard." Marad nodded and they set about their business.

All the while, the wolf watched the two at work, building the pyre.

"We managed, with the help of the city guard to drive Myella from Paravel. After all, she was ultimately responsible for Chill's death. I came with a few others to scout out the Great Wall and Helm. We expect Myella won't be long in her effort to

173

reclaim Paravel. I was the forward man so to speak. Then we ran into that Hand of Keth. Chill. I swear it was him at Helm, dressed as a Hand of Keth."

"It was not your friend; at least not as you know him."

"What do you mean?" Tom waited expectantly for the other man to respond, but he seemed lost in thought. They had set camp some distance from the village, once more in the forest. The wolf that had spent most of the day with them was gone, but occasionally Tom would catch it at the edge of his vision. It acted as though it was keeping an eye on him.

Marad was now dressed in some clothing salvaged from the hostel, talking over the campfire. The remains of a rabbit sizzled above the flames.

"My knowledge of this type of sorcery is limited; my brother Adon would know more. I can tell you that what you saw may be his body, but anything that was him," he touched his head and his heart, "has long since fled."

Tom nodded, understanding the concept, but this just corrupted the memory of Chill. He felt sick in the pit of his stomach. "So, you seem to know a lot about these things. Why?"

"Myella is my sister."

Tom cleared the fire and had his knife at the man's throat before the other could blink. Marad was astonished at the speed with which Tom was capable. With a face as impassive as stone, Tom's whisper was deadly.

"Give me one reason why I should not kill you."

"Myella tried to kill me."

174

Breath hissed between Tom's teeth as he rolled off Marad and sat back. He pitched the blade into the ground between them. Marad stared at it a moment and sat up, rubbing at the nick from Tom's knife. He looked at the smear of blood on his finger.

"Tell me, and it better be good. I don't need the baggage. I've told you all about what we did to Myella. What I didn't tell you is that we were brought from another land, through, what my companion Mike calls a *Gate*."

"I had thought as much by the end of your story as well as your demeanor. Very well then, the whole story.

"I was sent by my father, the Conclavator, to Helm to do two things. The first was to investigate the disappearance of my brother, Adon. The second was to rein in my sister, Myella, and bring her back to Teshwa. I did not know she had so many supporters there or within my own Guard.

" I am Commander of the White Guard. My sergeant betrayed me to several Hands' on the journey from Teshwa to Helm. The Mage Guyle, my uncle, is in league with Myella. They want to usurp my father's Seat on the Clave, and hence rule the Conclaveum. It seems they are also delving into the *aether* for power, hence the Gate.

" I had been the target of previous assassination attempts; if she kills me, she has the Seat, she is Conclavatrix."

"And your brother?"

"He was one of the Sequestered, studying to be a priest of Tarn. He gave up all Claim to the Seat."

"So, you were betrayed. What happened?"

"I was taken to Helm, beaten, and brought before Guyle. There I saw Trevor Galfeon Crona, my uncle, who I had last seen only as a very little boy.

"He saved my life you know. He stopped a guard from giving me the death stroke and this gave me enough time to gather my wits. I leapt from the tower and by Tarn's grace, and what little sorcery I know, made it to the river in the Crevasse.

"I was lost for a time. I wandered. Then I came upon you. Here we are."

"What a mess."

"Aye."

"So what now? What do you plan to do?"

"The Guard of Oran would not be so brazen unless their activity was sanctioned. They were leaving a message that any who worship Tarn are not safe. Myella is behind that."

"So, do you go to Qwen to gain passage back to the Conclaveum?"

"I would like very much to see how Barish is faring with the White Guard . I would like very much to have my White Guard visit Helm and the Guard of Oran. I go to Qwen."

"As do I, but I will go no further than that. From there I will go to Paravel. I was to have been back already."

"Then to Qwen it is"

There was a darkness more absolute than just the absence of light; it was also the weight of thousands of tons of earthabove his head. The slab upon which he lay was cold; he shivered constantly for there was no blanket.

Darkness and the occasional drop of moisture as it fell from the mildew on the walls and ceiling. He let his hand trace the cut of the stone against his back, smooth and cold. Something multi-legged and long crawled over his hand. He flinched involuntarily and the thing stung him. It had happened before, there would be pain and it would swell, but it was not lethal.

He remembered the meeting in the room under the Tower of Pain; it played out before him in the blackness. Bej-et, leader of the Krim sat chained to a jade chair. She had an alien beauty that was disturbing; she spoke in a lilting tongue.

He smiled grimly as he drew his legs up to his chest. She had sworn against Guyle for his evil machinations and bringing her deep in the tower. In her lilting language, she had vowed vengeance, but she also feared Guyle was dealing in matters far beyond his ken. Guyle had been truly devious. By kidnapping Bej-et, he was fomenting the conflict with the Krim, bringing the Conclaveum ever closer to destruction.

Guyle had separated them after a while. He had sent Trevor away at the hands of Sir Chill to be locked in a chamber, deeper, darker and more foul than the one in which Guyle and Bej-et were. *What are you up to, Guyle?* Trevor Galfeon Crona asked himself. *Tarn, but I have not heard the familial name Crona in a long time. Not since the fight. He always conspired,* Trevor thought. He put a wedge between Ironeous and him by fabricating an affair; it led to his banishment, He was still scheming; scheming against the Conclaveum and against the Krim. He finally brought about the demise of their

177

brother Ironeas; poison. At the very least, he could expect the same, but where did Bej-et figure in?

I am thankful for you, Uriel; you gave me a beautiful girl. I just pray that Gabrielle is safe and out of harm's way. He sighed, the darkness sucking that into the vacuum. Twenty-two years ago his Uriel passed. She had been a commoner from the village of Yor. In the three years he had known her, he had loved her, and she had borne to him Gabrielle. Then the fever took her. *But, what bliss we had in those three years.*

It all seemed a lifetime ago.

There was a grinding noise from off to his right, and the iron door opened a crack, blinding him with torchlight from the other side. He heard footsteps and the soft jangle of mail, the rub of leather. Slowly his eyes adjusted to the light and he looked up to see Sir Chill.

"And what do you want?" Trevor asked in a voice that cracked with thirst. Chill did not answer; he just stood to the side and let the yellow light bathe his face, highlighting the scar on his forehead.

"You wish me to escape? So maybe you can strike me down with your kris-voulge. No, I will not give Guyle the pleasure of that, nor of him making me into what you have become. My spirit goes with Tarn."

A smile appeared on Chill's lips. The white hand on his tabard seemed to glow. Trevor looked out into the hall; there was no guard, only steps going up and up.

He dashed Chill back against the wall; Trevor knocked the kris-voulge from the young man's

178

hands with ease and placed his own hand over the other's throat.

"So easy, Sir Chill? Did Guyle rip your fleeing soul, bind it with the fire of Oran and put it back in this shell? Are you a true Hand of Keth, a tortured bound spirit, or are you just a resurrected automaton?" Trevor let go of the man, and Chill bent to pick up his Kris-voulge.

"In death there is no surcease for the damned," Trevor said as he sat back on his slab. Chill's eyes narrowed and he pointed outside the cell, to the floor. There was a wool blanket, a half loaf of dark bread, and a bucket of water.

Trevor sighed, got up and brought the things into his cell. Chill nodded and ducked as he stepped out through the portal. As he was about to close the iron door Trevor spoke once more. "Do the damned walk and live in your land? Or do they rest? I wonder. Sir Chill, did you protect my daughter as I charged?"

It looked as if the stout man was about to reply, his mouth opened slightly, then he slammed shut the iron door. Trevor sighed and wrapped the thin blanket about his shoulders. He broke off a piece of bread and found it was filled will meat. Why the Hand of Keth would give him something that would strengthen him, he did not know. He began to wonder on the nature of Sir Chill.

Far above, in the summit of the Tower of Iss, Guyle ripped the arras from its rails, exposing the summit to the sunlight. He scowled as the shadows fled and the city was revealed below him.

179

"Do you see that with your alien eyes, Bej-et? That is Teshwa, which is the Seat of the Conclaveum."

Bej-et walked along the edge of the portico, her hands still in shackles, locked with sorcery. The wind caught her multi-hued cape and spread it out behind her. Three hundred feet below was the paved courtyard and the canal that ran alongside the tower. She walked the ledge with ease.

"Why did you bring me here under guise of truce only to bind me?"

"All for a purpose."

"You are Oran's servant."

"I am not concerned with your thoughts on this matter."

"I understand the politics of the Clave. If a sympathetic member of the Clave were to see your half-brother here, he may displace Myella. He does take precedence over her."

"He will not live long enough."

"Oh, so Oran's power is mighty? The Krim are not an instrument of his will." She looked at him, her eyes like obsidian and her skin a dull bronze. The overcast sky only deepened the quicksilver of her hair. Guyle looked from where he sat on his throne-like chair, his staff across his knees.

The Daemon had said it was necessary to have her and the Krim for the communion to be complete. The Daemon had said it would be easier to gain the Power that the Outlanders possessed, but that seemed a distant thing.

Those damned Outlanders that he had brought through the *Gate*, through the *aether*, had almost ruined his plans. Luckily, they recovered from

180

Myella's ejection from Paravel. The Outlanders had the power to destroy his plans, but that was the risk he was willing to take to exact his revenge and obtain the Power Oran had promised; power to rule the Seven Spheres, and govern the sorcerous worlds that lie in the *aether*; power for Immortality, like the Krim.

"I have done the bidding of Oran." he cracked out. "For you, even bound I have a gift." She looked at him then with two quick steps she seemed to fly toward him.

"Have you, mortal? Even bound I could kill you." Her chitinous armor, glassine and bright, hissed and smoked where she crossed her thin arms. "Oran manipulates. Remember that."

Guyle frowned and parchment-like skin was drawn even tighter. His gnarled hand gripped the staff as he stared at this spirit-like creature.

"The gift is the *Home Gate*, Bej-et. Something your people have sought out for the past five hundred years."

Her eyes narrowed and she stepped back.

"Yes, I know your people were brought to this realm en-masse with the broaching of the Wall. Would it not be nice to see your alien sun once more? I can give that to you."

"At what price?"

"Not yet. Take this to your people. I know where the *Gate* is. I know how to open it and return you to your world. As I have the power to wrack a Hand, I have this gift," he said ever so softly.

There was a sound at his back; it was one of his Hand's, Sir Chill.

"This is one of them, one of the Outlander's from the *Gate*?" He nodded as she walked up to the stout man. Chill gazed at the Krim. "You wracked his dead body to produce this Hand and in doing so you lost the Power that was his. He has no aura, Guyle." She laughed; the sound was like crystal bells shattering on stone.

"There is the Power of him being a Hand. The Daemon said I must 'break the six.' They are broken and I wait."

She paused. Her face was unreadable, as alien as was possible. Her upturned eyes blinked once, twice.

"I will tell my people." She grinned then, her teeth black as onyx; the gesture was more feral than friendly.

Guyle's hands came together in a thunderous clap and she was gone. He looked over his shoulder at the Hand. He was as impassive as ever, having lost that one thing that made him special, that made him Chill.

Chapter 15

Snowflakes drifted down from the gray sky, obscuring most of the wall that lay before him. The summit lay in a thick layer of white, tilted at an odd angle outward to prevent an assault over the top. Before him, in the wall's surface was a dark maw, large enough for horses and wagons to travel through, but at an odd angle. It was deep and no doubt riddled with arrow slots.

This formidable wall bisected the peninsula on which Bastion Hold sat. Beyond that wall of stone lay a city with a population near thirty thousand. It was also the last large city of the west; the last one that Lord Duran, Regent of the Southern Seat and Commander of the Army of the Conclaveum, really cared about. If he took Bastion, Western Hold could rot as far as he was concerned.

His ships were pounding the coast with a barrage of catapult missiles. Still Bastion held, protected by a break-wall that didn't allow a ship to come within adequate range.

Through the snow, Duran looked hard at that damnable wall. It must have been ninety feet high and thirty feet deep at the base. Beyond that wall was a city with fresh water springs, gardens, orchards and even pastures for herds of horses, cattle and sheep. With food and water inside, and a break-wall protecting the peninsula, Bastion could hold indefinitely against a siege.

Duran's black cloak whipped out behind him, the snow was now coming down heavily. It was early for this type of weather, but they were in the far south. He wondered if the men stationed atop that wall would see his Guard. They carried the standard of the Black Guard horizontally, symbolic of a truce.

The four guards waited twenty paces from the gate. Duran peered through the flurries, conscious now that the pounding had stopped; even the assault from sea was proving useless. He watched as an emissary appeared on the open ground before the wall. He wore a conical shaped helm that curved forward at the very top, and he was dressed in armor covered with warm furs. His skin was dark brown, more like a northerner. He carried a blue and yellow banner horizontally.

Duran nodded. It was good that whoever ruled this city had the sense to send out a representative to the besieging army. At least they were not being ignored. Duran smiled cynically as Kiuf, his lieutenant, led a stallion to the Lord of Qwen.

"Well, Kiuf, do you think we shall take Bastion this day?"

Kiuf laughed and shook his head. "Only if we use treachery, and by the looks of that wall my lord, even that may not prove helpful."

"Treachery, indeed. I agree that not even that would work to our benefit here." He pulled himself up onto his horse, grunting as pain stabbed through his left arm. The damn thing still hurt, even after all these months. He pulled his cloak about his shoulders and let Kiuf lead the mount down the hill to the four Guardsmen and the emissary from Bastion.

The man looked up from beneath the fur-trimmed helm and nodded.

"You are the Lord Duran?" the man asked. His voice was distant and cold.

"I am."

"Why do you assault the city of Bastion? Why do your ships attack?"

"I am Regent of the Southern Seat and I claim all the land south of the Great Wall for the Conclaveum, by order of Conclavatrix Myella."

The man frowned and tilted his head to the side. "This land was never the Conclaveum's, Lord Duran. It was not even so in the days of Narn-toc."

"Be that as it may, I lay Claim now."

"Milord, as you can see, we are not going to surrender Bastion to anyone. It is a free city. We are protected and have the stores to withstand an indefinite siege. You may as well be on your way. If you fear attack from behind, do not worry; we had no quarrel with you to begin with. Your ships do us no damage and we will consider this as never having happened. You waste your time and possibly the lives of your men."

"Forgive me, but I wish to speak with your Lord, or council, or whatever ruling body you have. The Conclaveum has need of your port. And as you can see," he nodded his head in the direction of his, near twenty thousand, soldiers, "I have plenty of men to waste if need be."

The man shook his head, but nonetheless agreed to take Duran and one other within the wall to see the Lord of the City. Kiuf led Duran's steed, ever mindful of the defenses they passed when entering the tunnel. Above their heads were slits for bowman and drains for hot oil. This was not the way to gain entrance by force.

The tunnel narrowed, becoming almost claustrophobic, as they came to the inner doors. The emissary paused at the doors; they were oak, bound in iron. He tapped the wood twice with the butt of the banner and they swung outward to reveal a portcullis. Duran and Kiuf passed row upon row of men with crossbow and sword.

Kiuf looked to the Lord of Qwen, who just frowned.

Once past the wall they were in an open field, the snow a lace curtain in front of his vision. Now used as pasture, during a pitched battle this field would be open for a fight. In the distance, Duran could see a regimented line of cavalry.

Gods, but these people are prepared. The Duke of Albien must have sent word. But why did they not come to his aid?

The representative led their way through the ranks of the mounted and to the town of Bastion. A fortified wall surrounded even the town.

People paused in sweeping the snow from the sidewalks to watch as Duran moved down the street to the center of the city. The buildings were like those of any other town. Large and small, they held businesses and families, shops and restaurants. It reminded him very much of Paravel, though the buildings seemed more suited to colder nights and winters. The streets were paved with cobbles and there were many people about, seemingly ignorant of the army just outside the wall. He looked to the center of the town and saw three towers, joined by thin bridges. These towers were guarded by another stout wall, the Lord's Keep.

"Bastion. They named the city well. But, from what do you defend?" Duran asked of their guide.

"I said before, that even in the time of Narn-toc we were not part of the Conclaveum. The Founder built that tower before us. He was a member of the Clave, in Narn-toc, when Untheran went mad. He built the defenses of this city after the Great Wall was raised. The Founder guides us."

Duran looked askance at the man. To hold such a tradition for over five hundred years was astounding. There had been relative peace in the south until he came to reclaim it.

At their guides approach the gate to the Keep swung open. Two men dressed very similarly to the emissary ushered Duran and Kiuf in. They surrendered their standard and Duran's horse, but were allowed to keep their arms.

They have but to kill us. By the lesser god's of Carn we are but lucky this Lord has honor. The foremost tower stood before him. All three towers were octagonal in shape and could be separately defended; the bridges, several stories up, allowed movement from one tower to the other. Duran looked to their guide, who ushered them through a solid copper and brass door.

Duran shrugged off his cloak to the servant and Kiuf looked around warily. Duran trusted him; he was a good man to have at his back. Kiuf was short, a head shorter than Duran, and one of the best lieutenants he had. Kiuf; superb commander of men and better than most as a cavalryman. He had sharp dark eyes and a plain face, tight lines etching it out in relief. Now he stood, resting his hand on the pommel of his long sword. Snow dusted his shoulders and began to turn to fine droplets of moisture on the black tabard. That tabard had been green when Duran had served with the Jaggiers. In the service of Duran it had changed to that of the Guard of Oran; black field with a gold dagger encircled by a ring of fire.

Their guide methodically placed his helmet on bench, letting the golden light of the lamps outline his dark skin, his straight, jet-black hair and his gray eyes. He placed his gauntlets next to the helmet and then gestured for the two invaders to follow him.

The tower was decorated with strange artifacts, presumably from when the Founder left the Seat in Narn-toc and came here. Duran noticed a few kris-voulges mounted on the wall next to chitinous armor that looked like glass. *So these people know of the Krim.* He and Kiuf walked straight back into the tower, not up the opposing spiral staircases to their right and left. They passed two more sets of double barred doors and into a large audience chamber. There were no windows, chandeliers suspended by chains from the ceiling provided light. The floor shone, its marble polished smooth, the walls were covered with arras, and tapestries depicting scenes he was not familiar with. Fifty paces to the end of the hall was a desk. Behind the desk was an empty, high backed chair and off to the side was another chair. Here sat a young boy, perhaps nine, copying a manuscript; perhaps he was learning his letters. He looked up from the table as the two men in black approached. He smiled.

Duran noted the similarity to their guide in his physical features, though his skin was much lighter. His tunic was a bright redand had a blue ermine

188

hood and sleeves. It would definitely keep the lad warm this far from the huge fireplace another twenty paces away.

The emissary stopped and Kiuf looked at him expectantly. Duran looked to the youth and scowled, hoping what he was seeing was not what he thought it was.

"The Lord of Bastion?" he growled.

The emissary placed both palms on his forehead and bent low at the waist. "Lord of Bastion, Last of the Line of the Founder, Viren Holt."

The lad looked up and smiled warmly. He pushed the scroll away and stood, acting much older than his age.

"Welcome to Bastion."

Kiuf was speechless. He had heard of young lords before, but had never actually met one. Duran just took a deep breath and bowed.

"Lord Duran, Regent of the Summer Seat of the Conclaveum and Commander of the Guard."

"Lord Duran," began the lad, in a voice yet to mature, "Kole tells me that you have an army beyond the wall and that your ships are trying to assail us. Why?"

Duran cleared his throat; he would have to treat this lad just as if he were an adult lord, and with the same message with which he was charged.

"Myella, Conclavatrix of the Conclaveum, has charged me and my army to secure the new borders of the Conclaveum. It shall henceforth extend from Tasseem to Narn-toc and from Clef to past Western Hold. Bastion, falling within that boundary gives up

189

all Claims to sole sovereignty and is hereby claimed by the Conclaveum."

"I am sorry, Lord Duran, we are a free-city. You'll have to go home." Duran's face flushed at the lad's curt response.

"Lord Viren Holt. I have an army and a navy. If you will not surrender this city freely, then I will take it by force of arms if necessary. You can avoid a great loss of life if you capitulate, I do not want to repeat what happened in Albien."

"Albien?" asked the young lord. "What of Albien, Kole?"

"They fell to Duran's army, my lord," Kole, the emissary, replied. "The Duke was killed."

"Why was I not informed of this, Kole, I would have dispatched one of the regiments?" Kole seemed to be in a quandary.

"My lord, your advisers did not want to worry you. We felt that if Lord Duran attacked Bastion we would need all our forces to protect *you*, the last heir of the Founder. Your father would have wanted it that way."

Kiuf looked at Duran. There were several points during the battle for Albien at which a surprise attack on their flank may have devastated the Army of the North. Clearly, whoever gave the command not to help Albien had been a fool.

"Bring my advisers, Kole, they should be here."

"Yes, my lord." Kole motioned for two guards to stand with the young lord as he left by a side door. Duran and Kiuf stood patiently as Viren Holt tapped his little foot and crossed his arms. He looked as though he would throw a tantrum.

190

It was an awkward silence. Duran knew that he and Kiuf could probably take the two guards and kill the child, but they would never get out of this fortress alive. It would also prevent them from ever taking Bastion without significant losses and a very long siege. Finally, Kole returned with six older men, all bearded and in various colored robes. They were weathered, their dark skin wrinkled like dyed linen left to dry in the summer sun.

The foremost stepped forward and wrung his hands.

"Lord Duran, we implore you, leave this place, we will not hinder your activities in the South-"

"Silence!" roared the little child at the pleading man. "You will talk to me, not this usurper!" Duran raised his eyebrow at the rebuke. "Who thought it better that I not know of Albien?" Viren continued. The six looked at one another and then the one who had spoken out of turn cast his eyes to the floor.

"It was I, Lord Holt." The man was humbled when Viren spoke quickly.

"You are banished from the Keep of the Founder. I hope you have relatives in the city that can support you, clearly you are useless here." The man nodded and quickly left their presence. The remaining five advisers were all quite.

"Now," the lad went on, "Regent Duran is laying Claim to Bastion. I cannot allow that for the sake of my people. We are peaceful, but we have the means to defend ourselves. I do not fear your army and I do not fear your navy. You may as well go home." Young Lord Viren Holt was very solemn. He sat at the table once more and went on looking at the parchment. Duran had the distinct

191

feeling that he had been dismissed; he was even slightly amused at the rebuff.

"Myella needs your port, my lord. I fear that she may use sorcerous means that would render your defenses useless."

"Sorcery?" one of the advisers asked. He looked at another who whispered and the man nodded. Viren looked over his shoulder.

"Go on," he urged the adviser.

"What kind of sorcery?" the advisor asked. Duran smiled, thinking this may allay any siege at all. *If they would capitulate now...*

"Myella is a Priestess of Oran and a Sorceress of Iss. In Tarn Hold she commanded the Keth."

The adviser smiled and dismissed Duran's threat with a wave of his hand.

"Oran has no stake here, Duran, we worship Tarn," the adviser said. "The Keth would perish as they came over the wall."

"What mean you, wards? Tarn Hold was the seat of that religion and the Sequestiary failed to hold against the Keth." Duran directed his attention to the youth. "Clearly these men are fools, Lord Viren. Do not let them tell you the Keth will fail. They will not. If you capitulate I will grant you amnesty. You may be Myella's Regent in Bastion Hold. The only difference would be the garrison and the use of your port."

"Lord Duran," Viren Holt replied, "Though some of my counselors may be overprotective, they are hardly the cretins you make them out to be. They do know what they are talking about."

"There are wards that the Founder contained within the wall and in the tower," replied another

192

advisor. "They protect the city of Bastion and for that matter, the peninsula. Even if the Keth were to come, they too would perish, but only after a long and painful death."

Duran was speechless. He looked at Kiuf who only cocked his head to the side. It was a signal to Duran, it said *I am willing to die if you want me to kill the lad.* Duran shook his head.

"Lord Holt, if what your adviser says is true, then I do not have the patience to send my men at your wall and watch them die. However, I warn you lad, there will come a day when my mistress, Myella, will bring the might Oran upon you. That day will not be far off. If you are wise you will capitulate today."

"Regent Duran," the boy replied, "When that day comes, Tarn will protect us." And that was all he said. He looked back down and waved Duran, Kiuf, and the advisers away. Kole motioned for Duran and his lieutenant to follow. Duran just shook his head as he turned to go; Kiuf followed, silent. As they were upon the door, Duran stopped suddenly, gazing at a portrait that hung on the wall near the door. His face turned white as he stared at the person portrayed there.

"Who is that?" he asked his voice suddenly hoarse.

Kole looked at the portrait and back to the Lord of Qwen. "That is the Founder. That is Ghin-jo."

Duran looked at the rendition of an older man, but a man he knew, nonetheless. Even though the person portrayed had dark skin and hair, the mustache and build were the same. It was as if he were looking at an older Lord Michael: the White Knight's companion.

Shaken, he allowed Kiuf to take him by the arm and lead him out.

Much later, as he sat in his tent, warmed by a brazier filled with scented wood and coals, he contemplated what he had heard and seen.

"Surely you do not believe that the Keth can be defeated?" Kiuf asked of his commander.

"Do I, Kiuf? If you know your history you would know that Ghin-jo, the Founder, defeated the Keth at the Great Wall; the wall that he created. If this Founder is indeed the same Ghin-jo, then I fear that the sorcery of Iss will fail.

"As for our army breaching that wall...no, it would take many more men, and much more time than I have. I would have to construct siege engines at least ninety feet high, my engineers are capable, but not that capable."

"Are we just leaving Bastion Hold behind then, my Lord Regent?

Duran rubbed his eyes and took a deep drought of his mulled wine.

"Myella won't be pleased," Kiuf persisted.

"To Hell's frozen lake with Myella, Kiuf."

The lieutenant was silent for a moment. He looked to his commander who seemed very tired this instant. Duran was slumped in his field chair, his wine spilling on the table that held a map of the peninsula and the layout of the wall and city. His sword and armor lay discarded on a cot, waiting for the squire to polish. Nearly twenty thousand men waited for his order. They knew, as Kiuf did, that an attack against the wall at bastion Hold would be futile. Duran was not one to waste lives for a lost cause and this certainly looked lost.

"Did you see his face, Kiuf?" Duran asked in a haunted voice.

"Face? You mean the boy's?"

"Ghin-jo's, in the portrait."

"What of it."

"Never mind."

"What now, milord? We cannot camp here. Winter comes, and we attempt the city or we break and march. Where to?"

"Paravel, Kiuf. That city will be ours or my blood will be spilled in the attempt." He stood suddenly, a fire in his eyes that was not there a moment ago. "We march this eve."

Kiuf nodded and Duran followed him out of the tent and to the forefront of his army. He was eager to meet his destiny; eager to meet Sir John and the man with the face of Ghin-jo: Lord Michael.

The Breach, deep and dark, was the only point in the Great Wall where a large flottila could gain entrance to the Conclaveum. Helm spread out before the thousand-foot gap in the mountainous structure, the Tower of the Breach guarded the city and gave vantage to the river, the crevasse and points south.

Myella, was Conclavatrix, now proclaimed by her supporters in the Clave. She stood in the preceptor's office and stared hard over the Plains of Straw, thinking all the while of Narn-toc and her destiny.

Before Myella lay a dead man. Her insatiable sexual appetite had not wavered since she had become the supreme ruler of the Conclaveum, rather it had grown. She did not mourn for her father as he lay in State amid the Enclave; rather she exploredthe darker sides of her nature.

He is just one more soul for Oran, she thought. She caught her reflection in the silvered mirror above the secretary. She pulled her long hair from her khol laden eyes; her form was lithe and taut. Like a supple animal, ready to leap with the intensity of a cat she paced sround the body. *I have caused the fall of many a man and woman, even you Surik,* and the thought was followed by the brief image of Surik Shadowlord. She frowned and pulled her robe over her shoulders, suddenly chilled by the wind that flowed through the open balcony.

"Balq, nictu, apa Oran," she said and moved her hand away in a sweeping gesture. The body erupted in flames, leaving nothing more than a silhouette of ash on the polished floor. Soon the breeze blew away even that.

She felt *its* presence then, as if *it* were just out of sight. She bathed within *its* radiance with an unholy glee, allowing a new sensation to course through her again, this time in a communion that was warped and evil.

Oran relishes your sacrifice.

It was the sound of steel crunching bone, nails on slate. It was the sound of hell.

"I am pleased that Oran has found it fitting."

Many things he finds pleasing.

What is it you wish, daughter of Oran?

"The Power. My uncle has failed to understand the power within Sir Chill. He has yet to destroy that which makes the white knight powerfuland binds the power to them."

It will come. Events in motion, you have sent them flying along the aether.

This you must know.

To Narn-toc goes one of like and one of past.

Be watchful, lest that which was Iss's is lost, and the Gates shut.

"What does this mean?"

Mortal, thou are but a tool of Oran.

Remember that always.

The presence was gone, leaving the faint odor of sour-sweet death. No longer in the ecstasy of the sacrifice, she slumped to the floor and gazed out at the horizon. She knew that it was time for her to go to Narn-toc, to reclaim the Dead City.

Chapter 16

It seemed the Hand of Keth moved casually up the defile and into the quarry that was Crag Place. Five *Soulservants* flanked him, their black-fringed surcoats rustling as they followed. The kris-voulge that he bore trailed a wisp of black smoke as he swung it around; the tip of the sorcerous weapon began to glow a dull red, and then resonated with a low thump. Wherever it spit an agonizing death followed, the Hand of Keth choosing his victims with care and precision.

Tar'elah had to drag Bill away from the center of the guardsmen's attention and toward the sheer face of the quarry wall. Bill looked back as the fifty or so conspirator's fled in all directions; chaos reigned as few took up arms to defend themselves. Only twelve remained about Rhianne ar'Liayne, among them Torec el'Kirien, Tilva ar'Jimra and Sir Brunwurst. Her dogs, Ikn and Teg, barked wildly, but ar'Liayne whistled and the dogs held their tongues as they set up guard around her.

Bill followed Tar'elah as she struggled over shattered slabs of marble and toward one of the many mine openings that dotted the quarry wall. Sheathing her short sword, she helped the Bard over the last remaining rock and into the low entrance of the mine. Quarrels and crossbow bolts began to rain down from the lip of the quarry as the Guard of Oran began to descend the narrow trails, firing their bows and arbalests. Bill was thankful that the projectiles fell well beyond the face of the wall.

As he ducked into the mine, the sounds of the shouting and the clashing of steel dissolved.

Tar'elah hugged the wall of the shaft, her short sword once more in her hand. She was ready to make her last stand if necessary. Realizing that Torec was still out in the middle of the fray, the Bard turned to go to his aid, but a firm hand stopped him.

"Do not go out there, Bard," the bandit said. Her voice was flat and emotionless.

"They'll be slaughtered!"

"No. Maybe captured, but not killed. There were over two hundred guardsmen on the ridge, at least fifty more coming up the defile. There were only sixty of us at the most. No, I think that they intend to capture them, to make them examples to the people of Clef. That was what the Black Guard tried to do to my people at the Ghisik Pass and that is what they'll do here."

Bill twisted out of her grip, his hands shaking as they clenched at his walking stick.

"We have to do something." Bill's plea was full of frustration.

"Wait."

Bill sagged against the wall and felt Tar'elah crouch down next to him. Before them, the ambush unfolded. The Hand of Keth and his men were selectively killing the conspirators that were attempting to flee Crag Place through the defile. Many of the others who were spread out over the floor of the quarry were being pinned down by bow. Men in the livery of the Guard of Oran began to surround the small pockets of dissenters.

The party led by Torec and Brunwurst had spotted Bill and Tar'elah and moved in their general direction. Inexorably the Hand of Keth approached, his men coming around the small lake in a pincer movement designed to cut them off. The Hand no longer used his *kris-voulge*, instead he motioned to his men and they trotted forward, their morning stars swinging against even those who were on their knees surrendering.

The forward men of the Guard of Oran met Sir Brunwurst and Torec when they were no more than fifty yards from Bill's position. Brunwurst was a machine, his sword moving in a scythe-like manner. Those that got past him were taken out by Torec, or had to deal with Ikn and Teg. The two hounds would leap up to strike the man heavy in the chest. Their heads would dart forward, their sharp teeth doing considerable damage to the men's unprotected neck. They worked in tandem, two on one, and were quite effective in protecting the governor.

Bill was amazed that a man of Brunwurst's muscle mass could move with such agility. Muscles rippled, veins swelled and he moved with a speed and grace that belied his size.

Torec knew the mine was only a short distance away and was hurrying the group toward the quarry wall. There was an exchange between Torec and Rhianne's suitor, then six of the party peeled away from the group. Bill saw that they were attempting to divert the attention of the guardsmen away from the governor. They fled toward the other end of the quarry.

It did not divert one of the Hand's lieutenants from confronting Brunwurst. The Vassal of Oran smashed his spiked mace into the face of one of the remaining conspirators who tried to protect ar'Liayne. He was down in a minute, crying out at

200

his ruined face. The man kicked Ikn, who yelped and cringed back. Ar'Liayne's silver dagger flashed out, but not before Brunwurst was there.

Up came the morning star aimed for a bone-crushing blow to the man's thigh. Brunwurst's sword was there, meeting the haft of the other's weapon. The *Soulservant* spun, this time catching the hilt of Brunwurst's sword and sending it flying.

The lieutenant, having disarmed Brunwurst, brought his spiked mace back with both hands. The knight was too fast. Brunwurst smashed his foot into the man's mid-section and he doubled over, the morning star flailing out wildly. Brunwurst slammed his gauntlet into the back of the man's neck, causing the helmet to pop off like a cork from a wine bottle. He then pulled the head of the lieutenant into his knee and grabbed the man up with his hands. Holding him high over his head, he tossed him over the ledge of the quarry and into the small lake. The cold water swallowed up the man as his armor carried him swiftly to the bottom.

Torec, having dispatched his assailants, tossed Brunwurst his sword. The way was now clear for them to sprint to the mine entrance. The group of five stumbled over the rocks and into the mine, but one poorly shot arrow somehow found its way into the back of the last man. The conspirator from Icam fell forward, an arrow solid between his shoulder blades. Bill pulled him to cover, but he was dead before the Bard could lay him down. The outlander looked to Torec who was panting with exertion; he just shook his head. Brunwurst had barely broken a sweat and now positioned himself at the head of the shaft with Tar'elah and Rhianne's two guard dogs.

Rhianne gave Torec and Bill raking glares as she knelt to look at Tilva's arm; blood flowed freely from a cut that nearly circumscribed it. She tore away the cuff of her sleeve to fashion a tourniquet in an effort to staunch the bleeding. Tilva laughed nervously.

"I'm a chef, not a fighter." He laughed some more and sweat began to trickle down his forehead. He was on the verge of becoming hysterical, muttering, "Poor Bobel, poor Bobel." All the while, Rhianne was having a difficult time stopping the blood from flowing down his arm. The blood had turned her hands and his shirt crimson. She shook her head.

"He will bleed to death if I don't stop this."

Bill nodded. There was still the sound of fighting out in the quarry. He lifted the man's arm above his head and directed the former governor of Clef to apply direct pressure to the artery that ran along his humerus. The flow of blood eased a bit. Bill then took his belt and made a more restrictive tourniquet.

"Loosen it every ten minutes; otherwise he will lose the arm. We'll have to get him to a healer."

"We need to keep him warm." She nodded understanding, seeing Tilva's waxy pallor and shivering. She immediately took her long coat off and covered him with it.

Bill turned to Torec who was at the head of the mine with Tar'elah and Brunwurst. They were looking out into the bowl of the quarry. Apparently the fighting had stopped. Now there was only the echo of voices, bouncing off the rock face, as men

202

shouted orders. Bill peered between the two men as he absently wiped his bloody hands on his trousers.

"What's happening?"

"They are herding them like cattle," Brunwurst said. He had a surprisingly soft voice for the big man that he was.

"Then we are trapped in here?"

"Like rats," Torec replied. Brunwurst nodded.

Below them, the remaining Guard and the Hand of Keth were herding together the remaining thirty or so conspirators. None had escaped, the other men were lying lifeless, scattered amid the tumble of stone that was Crag Place.

Suddenly the Hand of Keth turned and it seemed to Bill that he looked directly at the outlander. The man motioned to a contingent of guardsmen and began to walk toward the mouth of the mine. They watched, expecting the guardsmen to charge the mine, but they stopped about fifty yards out where the one lieutenant had perished. The Hand of Keth stepped forward and took off his helmet.

Bill had expected to see a grizzled old warrior, but instead he saw the features of youth. The man must have been in his mid-twenties. Clean-shaven, he had his silky black hair pulled back in a cropped ponytail. Most women would consider him handsome. One of his guard's came up the jumble of rock to stand next to him; he was homely by comparison.

"Ectel," remarked Brunwurst. Immediately, Ikn and Teg began to growl low in their throats.

The Hand nodded to Ectel and he took a step forward. The pudgy man cleared his throat.

"Governor ar'Liayne, I see my suspicions were correct. My Regent would like to speak with you. You will surrender to him and give freely the one among you who is an outlander."

Brunwurst's gaze swung around and impaled Bill. The Bard just frowned and stepped between him and Torec to get a better view of what was going on.

"It would be best if you came down, Rhianne. I should not have to send men up to fetch you. They can be so brutish, you know. I-"

He stopped as a large piece of stone struck him on the temple. He staggered back, putting a hand to his bloody forehead. Bill gave a sidelong glance to the governor, who was brushing her hands off on her split skirt. She nodded at a job well done and went back to tend to Tilva.

Below them the Hand of Keth laughed and, using his kris-voulge as a staff, stepped forward to speak with the group.

"There is no way out. Come now, you can see that. We will not hurt you if you come out freely." His voice was musical and reassuring.

"What is he afraid of?" Brunwurst asked of no one in particular.

"What mean you?" queried Torec.

"He could easily dispatch thirty of his men to come up here and take us. Yet, he does not. What is staying his hand?"

Torec and Tar'elah immediately looked at Bill. He was incredulous, but Brunwurst was not paying attention and missed the whole exchange; he just peered over the tumble of rocks and at the group of guardsmen below. He shook his head.

"I know not. We are cornered like rats, as Torec says." He crossed his arms and looked like he was willing to stand there until he dropped of old age if necessary.

"Come, come," called the Hand of Keth. "I give you until the sun moves a span. Then I will personally come up." Moreover, to prove his point he leveled the Kris-voulge at the mine entrance; an explosion of rock and debris followed the low thump. They ducked away from the entrance as a ton of marble crashed down from the rock face just outside the entrance; it obscured half the shaft opening and almost crushed Brunwurst. He frowned as he picked himself up and brushed dust off his harness.

"There is no way out. We will just have to wait until they come in for us. We can make a stand," Tar'elah said as if she were awaiting the arrival of friends.

"Yes. It will be a fine way to die," commented Brunwurst sarcastically.

"No *way* is fine to die," retorted ar'Liayne from where she sat with Tilva. He had passed out now, his breathing shallow. "Besides, there is a way out."

"What?" asked Torec.

"When the marble is mined they cannot take it down through the defile; or did you think they just magicked it out?" She gave him a long hard stare. "These mines go clear through the Mount to the north shore of Clef. I played here as a child, with my friends. The quarry had been long quit, but there was many a cave to explore. My father told me they rolled the marble along tracks and then lowered them by ropes to waiting ships below." She raised her chin defiantly as Torec sheathed his sword.

"Why did you not tell us this before?"

"I wanted to learn what they wanted, or at the very least who betrayed us."

Torec shook his head. "There is no time for that, woman. We have but a quarter hour and you dally. *Id'hala!*"

"Let us go then," Tar'elah urged.

"We may get lost," Rhianne reminded them. "I do not know the way, only the story."

"It is better than waiting here and having that Hand shoot us," Bill retorted.

"Very well; Ikn, Teg, lead the way. Brunwurst, you shall carry Tilva. Torec, you and the outlander bring up the rear."

"Yes, your highness," Torec replied acidly.

"What about light?" Bill asked.

"Yes, what about it? Take your staff, you fool, wrap some linen about it and light it with a flint. It won't last long, but maybe we'll find something better along the way."

As the mineshaft sloped down, Bill could feel the ever-present weight of the Mount above him, pressing down. He knew that it was absurd to think that the mountain would crumble as they passed beneath it; the shaft had stood so long without collapsing, had it not? In the sputtering light of the makeshift torch, he could make out roughly shorn granite. The walls were no longer smooth as they widened. Stalactites stood silhouetted in the gloom and the ever-present drip of moisture made Bill's skin crawl. He realized that if they did not find some alternate light source soon the darkness would consume them.

There was also the pursuit. No doubt, the Hand and Ectel were already moving into the mineshaft with the guard at their beck. To Bill, the possibilities of escape were limited. What happened when they reached the end of this tunnel? If it were a dead-end then the torch would gutter and the Hand would find them cowering in the dark. If they came to the spot where the quarry stone was loaded on barges it was highly unlikely that a boat would be waiting and they could hardly swim away.

As Bill was lost in these thoughts, he did not notice that the mine opened into a relatively large chamber. Here, he could make out the remnants of tracks for the cars that had at one time hauled stone. Several cars were upended and rusting; others still sat on their tracks. Ropes and pulleys hung from the darkness of the cavernous roof, and in the flickering torchlight, Bill could make out a pile of detritus, among which were several broken oil lamps.

"We must hurry," Torec called from the rear. "Our friends will not be far behind." He moved quickly to the pile and began to sort through the junk. He indiscriminately tossed aside shards of glass and wood, until he found an unbroken glass shield for the lamp, which he then placed on a rusty, but otherwise undamaged lamp base. There was still the slick liquid in the bottom of the tiny well. He motioned for Bill to bring the torch near. Slowly, the oil took to the mildewed wick, almost guttered, but then flared brightly. Bill doused the makeshift torch with the oil from another lamp and then hitched the broken lamp to his belt.

Torec spotted a coil of cable lying undisturbed to the side. He slung it over his shoulder and looked to Rhianne and the Bard. Tar'elah and Brunwurst were still at the entrance to this chamber, watching for their pursuers. So far, there was no sign of them.

"Well, Governor, where to now?"

She looked thoughtfully to the darkness at the far end of the chamber. This was a main intersection and many of the tracks split off into the darkness. They could as quickly get lost as they could find themselves in the outstretched arms of the Hand of Keth. She nodded toward the far end, motioned for Ikn and Teg to precede her. The two hounds loped off into the darkness, not hindered by the absence of light.

Torec called to Tar'elah and Brunwurst and soon they were all trudging into the shaft, following the rail tracks into the heart of the mountain.

"We could have doubled back, up another shaft," Brunwurst called. He seemed unflagging as he carried Tilva on his shoulder.

"That Hand would sniff us out, and what if we eluded him? We would only find ourselves lost or back in the Crag Place, with two hundred Guards of Oran." Torec's breath hissed as he motioned the bandit from the Ghisik Pass ahead of him.

"So? We go to our death anyway. Rhianne knows not what lay at the end of this tunnel. The Mount is miles thick. I did hear that the people of Clef once mined the Mount, but I had no idea that they carted the rock through it to waiting boats."

"I had heard that many of the ships took the stone to the mainland, to Paravel and Qwen. Farok told me that."

208

"That blind fool?" Brunwurst growled from somewhere ahead. "Look where his tongue got him. He's lucky to be alive."

"Watch *your* tongue, Brunwurst, lest you find my steel replacing it. Farok has more sense and bravery than most men." Torec had to suppress his anger when he heard the big knight chuckle.

They soon bunched up behind Bill and Rhianne, who were watching the two dogs sniff out the base of a steel door. The track passed beneath this heavily rusted portal; there were lazy black characters scrawled across the door, and set to the side was a winch and a chain. There seemed to be a bench here and the jetsam of its one time tender.

Bill squinted at the writing on the door, trying to make it out. Torec shouldered his way to the front, pressing behind Rhianne. She did not seem to notice, but he did. He recognized her perfume mixed with sweat. He shook his head and she looked over her shoulder at him, a quizzical expression on her face.

"What do you make of it, Torec?" Bill asked.

"Halq al, it looks like *quyi.*"

"What's that?"

"A language the masons use, I have seen it before, but I cannot read it."

"The door is warm," Rhianne whispered as she rested her hand on its surface.

Bill looked at Torec, who looked at him and then to Brunwurst, who just shrugged and placed Tilva gingerly on the floor. The chef moaned as is damaged arm bumped against the stone. Ikn and Teg, both panting, looked up to Rhianne ar'Liayne.

"Well, let us open it, we certainly cannot go back," Rhianne said. "Who knows, beyond may be the north face of the Mount and the sea."

"Not the sea, we did not come nearly far enough to be there."

"We should rest, for Tilva's sake." Bill looked at the man who sat hunched against the stone. His breathing was labored and even in the yellow cast of the torch he looked ashen.

"Let him rest, Bard. We open the door." Brunwurst slung his sword and spit in his hands. He set himself low on the ground, like a power lifter, and heaved up. His muscles strained and veins popped along his arms and on his forehead. He gasped and stopped. "It is frozen with rust." Again, he leaned into the winch and a low squeal of metal pierced the gloom; it moved about a half an inch.

He straightened, his chest heaving from the effort. Hands on hips he shook his head. "It is no use."

"Wait," Bill called and pulled the spare lamp from his side. He poured oil liberally over the gears of the winch. Brunwurst frowned at the waste of the fluid, yet the winch began to move.

Slowly it turned, the first notch on the gear setting into a groove, but the door moved only a little. It was after Brunwurst worked at the winch, sweating and straining for another ten minutes, that the door lifted enough for a faint red glow spread from the crack at the bottom; warmth issued up.

Rhianne smiled winningly as she folded her arms and looked at the men in the group.

"The sun is low on the horizon, gentlemen. Behold."

210

"Rhianne, it cannot be." There was exasperation in Torec's voice. She only looked on with an arched eyebrow.

"Help me, Bard, use that back of yours," Brunwurst asked of the outlander. Bill nodded, and handed his torch and *ighuire* to the former merchant. He stretched his arms for a moment, the knight looked at him oddly, and then Bill put his weight into the lever on his side of the winch. His thickly corded muscles, not nearly as massive as Brunwurst's, strained at the lever, but he was satisfied to hear the steel door rising behind him. He felt warmth at his back and a dryness that was unusual for the island this time of year. *Was that the roar of the surf?*

Sweat dripped from his eyes and to his arms, he looked up as Brunwurst paused and saw the big man staring through the portal. His face aglow.

"Gods of the Dark!" the knight muttered as he stood straight. Bill turned and looked past the silhouettes of his friends.

"I have never seen such," Tar'elah said to no one in particular.

Bill looked into a great crater. Blackened rock was awash in a red glow. The heat that bounced off the walls and into the mineshaft did so in waves. Stalactites pierced downward from the dome of the cavern, mocking them with the jagged teeth of some hellish maw. As Torec and Rhianne leaned through the door, Bill saw that the track continued out over a trestle. Alongside the tracks were a railing and a walkway, but halfway across, the tracks fell away, destroyed, or just deteriorated. About ten feet beyond the wreck, the tracks continued to a similar

211

door on the other side. Bill guessed it was about fifty yards to the other side.

Below was another matter entirely. They gazed down into a churning mass of red and black, occasionally disrupted by a welling bubble of molten rock. The cavern spread out to the right and left and, fifty yards in either direction, they saw similar trestles and portals, some in disrepair some not. It was a huge vent in the island and possibly the Mount had many such chambers, none of them knew for sure.

"You didn't say the Mount was a volcano."

"I did not know. Did you, Rhianne?"

"No," she said curtly, her bravado of early now evaporated.

"We must go to the other side then," Tar'elah said from behind.

"Over that?" Torec asked.

"Of course. Obviously the miners used this bridge frequently."

"Why the doors?"

"Maybe it erupts often," Bill quipped.

"Are you as big a fool as you seem?" ar'Liayne asked of the tall outlander. "If it erupted would it have that roof? The doors are probably to keep fumes out of the mine. We must hurry."

She gestured to Ikn and Teg and they immediately took off down the walkway. When they approached the gap in the trestle their pace did not slacken, rather they leapt easily over the gap and to the other side. They continued down to the other steel door where they sat, panting.

"They made that look easy," Bill commented as Brunwurst hefted Tilva to his shoulder.

212

Slowly they made their way across the span. It seemed sturdy enough, considering its age; then again, it did have to support tons of rock that rode across the rail.

Tar'elah was bringing up the rear, directly behind Torec. Suddenly she stopped and cocked her head back toward the mineshaft.

"Quickly, I hear voices. They are not far behind!" Urgency filled her voice. All they could do for the moment was stop at the middle of the trestle where the rails had twisted and fallen into the molten crater below them. Out here, the heat was almost unbearable; it welled up from below in waves, and the fumes were noxious. Bill looked to Torec, who was busy untangling the coiled cable.

"Man, didn't that come in handy," said Bill as he helped. Rhianne looked tentatively at the twisted edge of the trestle. The gap was only eight or ten feet.

Torec quickly looped the end of the rigid cable into a noose. He sidestepped Brunwurst, noticing that sweat poured from the man's heat reddened face. He went to the edge of the trestle and tossed out the cable to the other side. It was true to its mark the first time, catching the post of the opposite guardrail. He pulled tightly and the noose constricted around the post. Torec secured it about the rail on his side. He snapped the cable; it looked like it could hold a man's weight.

"You do not expect me to walk that, like some traveling entertainer, do you?" the Governor asked the merchant. He just frowned and gathered their gear. Piling everything onto his cloak, including

Bill's *ighuire* and the dowsed lamps, he bound the bundle with his belt.

"Brunwurst, give me that harness you wear." The knight grunted and gently laid Tilva in Bill's arms. He began to unbuckle the sword belt and harness.

"Quickly," Tar'elah urged from near the door. Bill looked at her, expecting to see the Hand of Keth any moment. She seemed taut, ready to attack. The harsh light of the crater and the sheen of sweat cut her lithe form. Bill looked to Torec.

"You first, Bard, you can pull the rest of us across."

Bill nodded. This would be just like repelling. He pulled on the harness, tying a length of the cable to the main wire. Without thought, he turned on his back, the cable easily supporting him, and pulled himself hand over hand to the other side. He sighed as he reached the tracks and shoved the harness back to the awaiting group.

Torec came next, just as easily as Bill. Rhianne, though, took some coaching; she froze three quarters of the way across and Torec had to lean out precariously and snatched her golden tresses. He pulled the protesting governor across.

The unconscious Tilva followed, pulled across by the two men. Torec and Rhianne lifted Tilva to where Ikn and Teg relaxed on the ledge at the steel door. As Brunwurst began to fasten his harness, Torec found a lever similar to the one on the opposite portal and began to turn the winch. This one was much easier and soon he could feel the coolness from the shaft pass over his feet.

Brunwurst finally slid onto his back and began to pull himself across. When he was almost within Bill's reach Tar'elah gave a shout. He looked sharply down the length of the cable to the woman.

"They are upon us!" she shouted. She tilted to the side, almost losing her balance on the walkway, and Bill heard the low thump he had come to associate with a kris-voulge. Metal shivered where he sat, the guardrail glowed molten and rang with the sound of the impacting spike. The metal twisted and shivered and, as Bill fell back onto the walkway, Brunwurst grabbed the twisted track. The post fell away into the crater, the remaining cable recoiling from the shock of the hellish spike. It hissed through Brunwurst's harness and he almost lost his grip as a red weal appeared across his chest, clear through his tunic. He pulled himself onto the track and yanked the remaining cable from his harness.

"No!" Bill shouted, reaching out for the cable as it fell. Brunwurst just looked over his shoulder as he realized his mistake. The bundle of gear and Tar'elah were still on the other side of the trestle.

Tar'elah ran to the edge of the tracks and beheld her situation. She quickly tossed the bundle across; Brunwurst caught it deftly and was moving along the tracks to the ledge. Torec beckoned him on, needing his help with the winch.

Tar'elah looked back. Where the trestle began stood four black uniformed soldiers and the Hand of Keth, his kris-voulge now blocked by the portly Ectel. For a moment, Bill thought the bandit would draw her short sword and charge the black armored servants of Oran. To him it seemed as if time passed

215

in slow motion. The guards brandished their morning stars and began to step aside to make way for the Hand of Keth. Tar'elah turned to Bill, her fine, sandy hair fanning out behind her. Muscles taut, legs flexed, she sprang, her hands outstretched. Bill saw a shadow of something black pass where she had been standing; he heard the thump. She was falling forward and he too, his belly striking the walkway hard, sending his breath hissing between clenched teeth. Hands outstretched, he soon felt Tar'elah grasp his wrist. Then she fell down and time once more contracted to normal. She hung there in his grip; his hands white with strain. She did not struggle, only looked into his eyes expectantly.

He gaze shifted to the pony-tailed Hand of Keth as he approached along the walkway. There was a smile on his face when he looked at the Bard and the woman. Bill strained, trying to pull Tar'elah onto the trestle, but he could not catch his breath. The Hand of Keth raised his kris-voulge. Bill tugged at the bandit, all the while looking at the tip of that unearthly weapon as it began to glow a red more deep and hateful than all the magma below.

There was a flash of white and suddenly Teg was upon the throat of the Hand of Keth. The man's kris-voulge had fired up into the dome of the cavern, causing shards of rock to fall. Seeing this, Bill strained and pulled Tar'elah up onto the walkway. Quickly, she got to her feet and pulled Bill to his. It seemed as though his ribs would explode outward from the strain and from the noxious fumes all around them. He watched as the guardsmen went to the aid of the Hand of Keth. The man had been taken so suddenly by the attack of the hound that he was doing all he could to keep his throat from being ripped out. The dog looked to see the four guards approach and sprang back across the gap in the trestle. Bill and Tar'elah followed the hound to their waiting companions. Bill looked back, seeing the Hand wipe blood from a long gash on his face; he was not nearly as handsome as before.

The next shot from the kris-voulge was wide of its mark; it struck the wall of the chamber ten feet from the steel door. As the black armored men stood at the edge of the tracks, the Hand wiped blood from his eyes and raised the weapon once more.

Bill and Tar'elah were last as they rolled under the door. Brunwurst tripped the ratchet on the winch, and it fell just as the Hand let loose a volley with the hellish weapon. There were three loud clangs followed by the tips of three spikes, hissing and protruding a good inch through the thick steel door. Bill sighed and slouched against the coolness of the rock wall.

"I think I'll be sick," he mumbled. His lungs hurt from the effort and the fumes.

"No time for that, Bard. They will be quick in getting across. I fear Teg, there, earned himself the enmity of a Hand." Torec slammed his dagger between the gears of the winch. "That will hold him until he summons some dark sorcery, no doubt."

Bill nodded and gathered up his gear along with the others. He looked meaningfully at Tar'elah. Her eyes conveyed the thanks she had no time to express, but she smiled and clutched his hand.

217

Brunwurst, ever impassive, hefted a now mumbling Tilva once more to his shoulder and began to carry the man down the shaft lit only by Torec's oil lamp.

After about an hour of walking they rested, confident that their pursuers would be long in coming. Thirst and hunger were taking their toll. Bill's lips were dry and cracked; the furnace-like heat had dehydrated all of them. It was not critical at this point, but they would need water soon, especially Tilva, who had lost so much blood.

The Bard watched as Torec poured the last of the oil into the lamp. He looked to the Bard and shrugged.

"How much longer," Bill asked. He was parched.

"Who knows? We are heading deeper into the mountain; *that* I know for sure."

Rhianne looked up sharply, but did not comment on what the merchant said. Brunwurst surprised them as he knelt before Tar'elah and the Bard.

"I must ask your forgiveness."

"What?" Bill asked, incredulous.

"I thought only of myself when the cable snapped. I did not think of Tar'elah, or you Bard." Bill could tell it was hard for the man to say this. He cast his eyes to the floor and it seemed as though he awaited a sentence.

"There is nothing to forgive," Tar'elah said softly as she squeezed the Bard's hand.

"I owe you a debt of honor, thank you." He sat back, once more his stalwart self.

"We should be moving," Torec urged. Once more, they were on their weary feet. The hounds

218

trotted up ahead, and so it was that they once more came to a steel door, though this one was not warm like the former.

"Not again," Bill moaned. He was getting tired of this little adventure; all he wanted to do was lay down on a soft bed and sleep.

"I think not, Bard," Rhianne, echoed. "The script is different.

"What then?"

"Let us find out." Once more Brunwurst set to the task of levering the winch. Slowly the door raised, a cool breeze issuing from beyond, and the smell of salt air: the sea.

As they wearily trudged into the chamber beyond, the coolness of an evening shower met them. They stood at the threshold of a wide mouth cave, which must have been in the northern face of the Mount. Before them was a staging area, where the masons and quarrymen could load their ships, thirty feet below, with the stone liberated from the mountain. Two large wooden cranes, now derelict, stood hanging out over the cliff. Below, Bill could hear the crashing of the surf, and the call of sea birds. Rain splashed against the mouth of the cave and he soon found himself standing with mouth agape, letting the cleansing shower wash over him.

Behind, Brunwurst let the steel door fall and quickly wedged some scrap metal into the gear system.

"They will be hard put to clear two steel doors, whatever sorcery that bastard has up his sleeve," Brunwurst said with a slight sneer. He looked down the length of the chamber to similar portals and decided he would sabotage them in a similar manner. This escapade was wearing on him.

"We should figure a way down and get some rest. We need it," Rhianne said. She walked to the ledge and lay out a piece of cloth torn from her skirt; it would soak up some water for Tilva. She looked down to a rock jetty below; she would not have seen it if not for the occasional flash of lightening in the distance.

"We need a boat," Torec called to her. In addition, they needed a way to get it to the water; the stairs that had led to the jetty had been made of wood and had long since rotted away. There were a few railcars left and two wooden cranes, but nothing that looked like a raft.

"Well," Bill said as he looked over the open cave. "We have wood, we can build a raft. Those carts look fairly sturdy; we could use them, if they float."

"I am no seaman, Bard. I doubt if I would know what to do," Brunwurst said with frustrated honesty.

"Aye, but I have sailed often enough. From the charts I've seen, if we floated out a quarter league there is a current that will sweep us around the leeward side of the isle, north of Icam," Torec replied.

"Then let us get to it. Tilva will need a healer." Torec nodded at Bill's directive. They set about first to strip one of the cranes of its wooden superstructure. They picked the least sturdy of the two, knowing that they would have to rely on the other to lower their craft into the water.

After about four hours of labor they slept, confident the two hounds would alert them to any trespass. When they awoke the sky was a pearly iridescent of pre-morning light. Below, the sea was a calm steely gray and the sea birds rose and fell into the water, catching their breakfast with their sharp beaks. The stone jetty seethed with white birds, which waited their turn at a passing school of fish. It looked to be a fine clear morning, the crisp breeze refreshing. It refreshed all but Tilva.

Sometime during the nightTilva had died.

"To come all this way, old friend, I am sorry." Torec bent over the famous chef of Bobel's, his face was serene in the soft light of morning. Torec took his helm from his head, unbound the veil, and placed it over Tilva ar'Jimra's face.

"May your journey be a peaceful one," he whispered as the others looked on. Bill once more felt the hollowness that was death. He looked to Tar'elah, who now went with Brunwurst to fashion two oars and check the bindings on the heavy wood beams fastened with steel cable.

Rhianne took the merchant by the shoulder and led him away from Tilva's body. She put her arm about him, in an effort to console. Finally, he shook his head at her muted whisper and turned to those that remained.

"Shall we get on with this voyage?" His voice was choked, but stern.

Bill nodded. Soon they were fastening the cable from the crane to the guide-wires on the makeshift raft. Ikn and Teg, named after the gods of the sea, stood on the bulky vessel amid the bundle of gear and the oars. Brunwurst was straining at a large pulley and Bill joined him. Soon the two of them were using the pulley to guide a complex of others.

The craft swung out under the crane and above the jetty.

"Wait a minute. Once it's in the water, how do we get down there?" Bill asked of anyone who could answer.

"Ah, that is a good question, Bard William." Torec scratched at his head. He looked to the others. Their faces were as blank as his mind for the moment.

"We ride the raft down," Tar'elah suggested.

"But who shall lower the raft. Someone must stay up here," Rhianne said.

"I will stay, as payment of my debt," Sir Brunwurst said quite solemnly.

"Don't be a dolt. Either we all go or we find another way," the merchant retorted.

"Look," said Bill as he leaned over the massive gear that was the main winch for the crane. "This has a ratchet like the one on the steel doors. If we set it, then we can ride the raft down to the water. By the size of the spring, I don't think it will drop us too fast.

"I think you are right, Bard." Torec nodded and clapped the younger man on the back.

Brunwurst quickly tied a length of rope to the ratchet and they stepped onto the swaying raft. The wind whistled through the cave and the skeletal crane, causing the raft to sway. Brunwurst looked to his companions, smiled, and yanked on the rope.

The raft dropped about a foot and stopped. Torec shrugged and Rhianne laughed nervously. Her laugh turned to a yell as the gear wound out and the raft fell with a hiss.

Luckily, it fell at slow enough rate to do them no harm. Ikn and Teg crouched near the center of the raft with ar'Liayne. The others were on all fours. The raft stopped descending with a jolt about ten feet above the water.

"We've stopped," Tar'elah observed and peered over the side to the choppy water below.

"Not for long," Brunwurst said as he stood and drew his sword. It struck the cable, there was a twang, and the raft fell into the water with a great splash. It bobbed to the surface, soaking them all, but they seemed to be no worse for the wear. Torec chuckled and tossed the Bard one of the makeshift oars.

"It is a ways to Icam, Bard, best we get started."

Sometime later, the steel door crumpled inward and fell with a clang. Six figures stood at the edge of the cave, looking out over the vista: the Hand of Keth, his men, and Ectel. The raft was nearly around the curve of the island, all but a black dot on the shiny surface of the water.

Rage filled the Hands face and he slammed the kris-voulge into the ground. Black spikes began spewing into the ceiling of the cave. Ectel and the others had to back away for fear of falling rock. The Hand screamed in frustration, the tip of the sorcerous weapon growing deep red with heat. Blood ran anew down the side of his face.

"You shall be Oran's yet, outlander!" he shouted. Ectel, near the door, crouched down in terror and covered his ears.

Chapter 17

John looked up from where he sat, rubbing his thumbs against his aching temples. He leaned back in the chair, propped his feet up on the edge of the desk, and sipped at his cup of cold karo. The stuff tasted awful when it was not hot.

John and Joe had come up with what they thought at the time was an absurd notion, but with the blessings of Lord Kelvin, they had embarked upon the task of putting together a civilian militia.

Now the courtyard was full of recruits.

He sighed as Joe, who stood next to him, leaned on the table and made a note on a piece of parchment. These recruits were here because of the promise of food and shelter, moreso than their ability with arms. Surik looked thoughtful. He stood with left hand on the pommel of his sword, and the other scratching his beard. He was dressed in full costume; a black and purple tunic emblazoned with a black skull, black britches, boots, and his flowing black and burgundy cape. The nervous lad that stood before him was agape in awe of being so close to a *Lord*. John looked at the long line of refugees and derelicts that spread out on the other side of the table behind the lad. All dressed shabbily in peasants clothes of tattered wool and course cloth; many had a gaunt, expectant look on their face.

"I don't know," Joe muttered as he looked over the lad. What John thought was truly funny was that they had not turned anyone away yet. There were plenty of jobs in preparation for the impending siege.

224

The lad was sixteen at the most. Joe suddenly grabbed a wooden pole-arm from the bench and tossed it at him. He fumbled, jumping back like a scared rabbit and it clattered on the flagstones. John looked to the blue sky, wondering why he had come to this world in the first place. Suddenly there was a gruff voice from behind and a solid short man pushed his way through. Several of the waiting refugees gave him grief, but he just tossed them an evil stare and they shut up. John looked at the older man and sat forward.

"You can't wait your turn?" he asked sharply. The man frowned and picked up the pole arm, handing it to the lad.

"I kin wait when I ave to. Now is not the time." John looked him over. He must have been nearly sixty-five, with a fringe a white hair running around his head. He was just over five foot five, but built stoutly, with heavy arms and a barrel chest. He wore a tattered white tunic, the kind that field laborers wore, cinched about his waist with a hemp cord. He wore leather britches and functional sandals. A thick leather cord graced his wrists and his hands were big and calloused.

"What can we do for you?"

"No, what kin I do for you!" he said and pointed a thick forefinger at Joe's chest.

"What can you do for me?" Joe asked as a patronizing grin crossed his face.

The stout man grabbed the pole-arm from the boy, spun it, and the dull edge was at Joe's throat. Joe looked appreciably down the length of the pole.

"These lads dinna know the pole from a hoe. I do. I spent twenty of my years in the service of the

Black Guard of the Wall. Twenty years and a land grant for a parcel of rocky earth in gods-forsaken Chez. Too rough and hot there; tis for yearlings. So, found me way here, but the docks dinna want an old man. I kin train these lads in the use of the pole and other things, if ye want, milord's."

Joe and John looked at each other.

"Sign here," Joe said, handing the quill to the man.

"First, a commission."

"If you're going to do training you will be a sergeant," John replied. He folded his arms across his chest; the brightly polished vambrace glinted in the sunlight.

"I expect'll get more'n the room 'n board?"

"Ten silver a month," Joe countered. That was about the going rate for one of Kelvin's sergeants. The man's eyes widened and he nodded. He took the quill from Joe and scratched out an 'X' on the parchment.

"Reos is my name."

Joe nodded and printed the man's name next to the 'X'.

"Okay, Reos, stand over there, and get these men in shape when we send them over. You are going to have a hell of a job ahead of you," John remarked as he looked to the line that stretched out of the courtyard and into the busy city street; they had already gone over about twenty recruits ranging in age from fifteen to fifty. Reos was the oldest.

"Well, we have our first non-com," John said as he nodded to the man who now was snapping the twenty recruits into a line and looking them up and down like they were cattle.

226

"Good, we have to spend the money we don't have somehow."

The day wore on and by noon, when Reos had marched sixty recruits into the keep, it still seemed the line had no end. John stood and stretched and Joe was leaning on the table. The noise in the courtyard had grown from a murmur to a cacophony and John was hard put to hear anything that his companion said.

"What?"

"I said do you want lunch?"

"Anything would be nice," John replied.

"Okay." He motioned one of the guards over and stepped close to the man, giving his lunch order. The guard nodded and trotted off to the kitchen. It would probably be the usual, bread, goat's cheese, spicy sausage, and some fruit. The latter was hard to come by; most of the fruit had to was dried to last through the fall and winter.

After the order was given, it seemed there was no quieting the crowd in the courtyard. John tried shouting and pounding the pommel of the heavy headsman's sword onto the desk, yet the noise only grew. Finally, two young men stepped forward and one whistled loudly. Immediately the ruckus ceased and the recruits looked once more toward the two 'Noblemen.'

John nodded his thanks to the two young men and motioned them forward. Just a few years younger than Joe or John, one was dark and swarthy, the other fair. Unlike those that stood in the courtyard waiting their turn, these two dressed in well-tailored clothing, though slightly dirty. The

227

two smiled and held up their hands in a sort of salute.

"Polwin-"

"And Gaj. We come from Albien."

John perked up at this last remark. "Albien, it fell. Were you there for the battle?"

They looked at each other, uneasiness passed between them and then Polwin spoke. "We left a month before the siege."

"Looking for adventure," countered Gaj.

"Our father was a minor noble. He was killed while fighting at the Duke's side." There was much sorrow in Polwin's voice and his brother reflected that in his look.

"I am sorry. Why do you wish to join the militia? You're members of the nobility." Joe's question was more than curiosity.

"Nobility does little if you do not have a roof over your head of food on the table," Gaj answered.

"We ran out of gold some time ago and have been living in the streets and alleys. We would also like a chance to avenge our father. Eventually we will retake what was ours." Polwin suddenly stood straighter, a gleam of defiance in his eyes.

"Can you fight," Surik Shadowlord, Master of the Shades, asked.

"We sold our swords for food." Gaj looked ashamed.

"To answer your question, yes, we can fight. The sword and other weapons were taught to us by our father's men-at-arms."

"Good," John said as he stood. "Then you won't mind showing us how well."

228

The two lads looked at each other and nodded. As they were moving off to the side of the courtyard, the guard returned with their midday fare. He set it on the table and John motioned for the guard to sit and take names while they watched the two fence.

Joe motioned to the headsman's sword John sometime carried, but the lads just shook their heads.

"You can't be picky in a fight," Joe said. He was getting impatient with the two.

"We are best with the saber," Gaj replied.

"Fine." Joe shook his head and grabbed two standard length sabers off a rack to one side of the courtyard. They had brought them out of Kelvin's armory just for this purpose. He handed the two basket-hilted blades to the two and backed away. They nodded their thanks and squared off against one another. There was some feint and parry, a few nice counter moves, but what concerned John was what would happen when armored men came over the walls with broadsword and axes. *For that matter, how would I handle it?*

Back and forth the two lads fenced, until Joe called it to a halt. He slung his cape and unbuckled his sword belt. *This will be the test,* John thought. It was undeniable that Joe's skill, honed in collegiate competition and practiced daily in his own fencing school would prove interesting against these young men; combine that with his magic bastard sword and he was an incredible swordsman.

He took one of the sabers from the rack, tested its balance and then he took his position opposite Polwin and waited. Gaj stepped aside and Polwin advanced, his sword technique was cautious and restrained, quite the opposite of his brother's maneuvers a moment ago. The clash of steel pealed through the courtyard with a staccato rhythm. John grabbed a piece of the sausage and ate while he watched.

Polwin was good, very good. John guessed that was the result when you had the tutoring of an aristocrat. Polwin's thrusts and parries were lightning-quick and it took a while for Joe to move from the defensive to the offensive. He finally began to see a flaw in the lad's technique and began to exploit it. Technically the lad was an expert and that was fine and good for competition among nobles or an occasional duel. Battle was an entirely different animal.

Joe feinted to Polwin's shoulder and the lad drew back. Joe thrust at his stomach, the lad parried and Joe swept the saber around and caught the basket hilt. The saber swung out, carried by Joe's blade. Normally, Joe would then thrust in and his opponent would meet the thrust with a riposte or he would score. This time Joe did what Surik Shadowlord would do, he slammed his foot into the man's stomach. Polwin doubled over, gasping for breath.

"Unfair!" shouted Gaj as he placed himself in from of the Shadowlord. A sneer grew on Joe's face and he knocked the sword in Gaj's hand away with the flick of his blade.

"Fair!" Joe's voice grew to a shout and John almost choked on a crust of bread. "What in God's name is fair about a sword fight? You either win or you die, plain and simple."

The two looked at Joe for a moment, somewhat vexed by his outburst.

"I suppose you don't want us in your militia," Polwin said, crestfallen.

"On the contrary, I'm making you lieutenants."

They both brightened and John stared in disbelief.

"One thing," Joe continued as he pulled his sword belt on. "You must train under Reos, our Sergeant. When he feels you are ready, only then will you receive your commission. I don't want two fools leading men to their deaths."

They both cracked smiles and saluted with the sabers. Then they ran off in search of Reos. Joe walked to the desk and grabbed up a piece of fruit. He shoved the wedge into his mouth.

"You made them lieutenants?"

"Of course," Joe said around a mouthful. "Polwin almost beat me and Gaj is better than him. If I didn't make them lieutenants, then I would be wasting their talent." John just laughed, his headache forgotten.

That day they recruited four hundred and twelve refugees, peasants, mercenaries and whatnot, for the militia. Of those, thirty-seven were women who they felt could hold their own in a fight. Those women who could not fight went to the aid of Preceptor Javin and his healers.

John felt it was a good start, seeing how they closed the portcullis and there were still people standing well into the street who waited to talk to the 'young lords.' John told them to be back the next day.

231

"Four hundred and twelve," Joe muttered as he rubbed his eyes and looked at the scroll. "Who was that girl with the two stilettos, what was her name?"

"Hjil, I think."

"Right, Hjil. Now, I think we should have one lieutenant for every hundred."

"Okay," John said as he picked up the headsman's sword and began to walk with Joe to the inner keep.

"Here's an idea. Hjil can command all the women. We got some real potential there. I think we can use them for the cannons; firing and guarding."

"Right, we can get them trained on the cannon by the end of the week, Pelles said that he'll be done with the first one by then."

"Yeah, but I don't think sealing the Gate of Osso was the best way to deal with the Hand of Keth and his conspirators. They will just find another place to meet and plan their sabotage.

"Now we have to find two more lieutenants; preferably someone with experience, maybe a former member of the aristocracy. Usually they're better educated and have a greater understanding of tactics."

John nodded as they began their ascent up the stairs to their chambers. He was thinking of who would be a good candidate. Most were refugees from the war in the west, shop owners, merchants, some mercenaries, but none worthy of that position. Some of those mercenaries, though, would make good sergeants. He said as much to Joe.

"Yeah, but what worries me about that is our own medieval history saw many mercenaries going where the money was. We don't need them turning on us during a pitched battle."

"That's why we make them sergeants. The L.T.'s can rein them in."

"Good point." Joe pushed his door open. The hearth cast a flickering red glow inside, keeping the chambers warm. He placed the parchment on the table, weighing the curled edge with his sword. This side of the Keep was in shadow this late in the day, so he went about lighting some oil lamps. John sat on the bed and fell back, staring at the canopy of embroidered cloth.

"Oh, God what about Bill?"

"You don't think he is in good hands with Torec and Tar'elah ?."

"We don't know when or if they'll return. "

"And now Mike, and who knows about Tom. We don't know when they'll be back either," Joe echoed as he sat in a deep chair. He kicked off his boots and let the warmth of the fire caress his toes.

"If they get back."

"Chill could've been a captain." They were silent for a moment, melancholy at the recollection of their friend.

Joe cleared his throat and John rolled onto his side, pulling the armadillo-like vambrace off; there was a ridge of blisters from the leather strap. He would have to get used to that. "How many men and women do you think we will have in the militia by the time we're done?"

"A couple thousand maybe three if we are very lucky, but that includes even the least qualified." John shook his head as he replied. *He* was building an army. It was ludicrous.

"Everybody will have a job to do. Nathal knows a guy who used to be a general, or something, named Pithorn, who was with this group of landowners that fought the Jaggiers in the Conclaveum."

"Jaggiers, Duran used to be with them," John replied.

"Huh?"

"Yeah, he told me in one of his more tender moments."

"Nice."

"I take it this Pithorn lost?"

"Withdrew. He relocated to Paravel. Now he owns a shipyard down at the docks."

"Great. Is he going to help the lieutenants with tactics?"

"That's what Chair Nathal suggested."

"So, we'll have exactly one legion."

"The Legion of the Black Skull. Too bad we can't have a cavalry."

"Yeah, half of them would be as afraid of their horses as they would be of the enemy.

" Reos and Pelles will be in charge of the armory. Pelles will have to time-share with the furnaces to produce sword, spear and an assortment of other steel weapons that may not be available in the city. We were gonna settle for fewer cannons anyway, we may as well do it right."

"That takes care of our end, but only three thousand?"

"At the most. Maybe Torec and Bill will be able to bring aid from Clef."

"There's a lot of 'maybes' and 'ifs' going around. What else do we have?"

"About eight hundred city guard, spread throughout the city to keep the peace and defend it under the leadership of Castellan Kelvin."

"Thirty eight hundred."

"You should have been a math teacher," Joe quipped. "Then we have Chair Nathal's personal guard; another seventy-five; and maybe a total of five hundred personal guards for all the council members. That's four thousand three hundred."

"Forty three hundred men and women defending a city of this size? Do you think we can squeeze seven hundred more into the militia?" John wondered.

"Hopefully, as more refugees come into the city we can recruit more, but our advantage will be the cannons."

"It would be nice if Tom came back here with a report on troop movements. Really, he should have returned."

"You don't think he's-"

"No," John answered quickly. "He's too good for that. He's probably on his way back with Torec's men at this very moment."

Joe nodded, staring into the flames that danced in the wide hearth. Lost in thought, he imagined he saw Mike's face.

Hey, butt-head. No, you're not dreaming, it really is me.

Joe sat bolt upright, catching John's attention. He tried to focus on the wavering image in the yellow flames. He was sure it was Mike.

"What's up?" John asked as he looked at his shocked friend. Joe just pointed to the fire. John

235

peered at the flames a moment and finally his jaw dropped.

Oh, you're there too, Lord Knight of Scary, or was that Erie?

"Mike? Is that you?"

No, it's Federal Express. Of course, it's me. What's up?

"Uh, Mike," Joe began as he narrowed his gray eyes. All he could see was the head of the former physics major. "How are you doing this?"

Something I read. It's like astral projection. I've got a room at a hostel, the Red Tripe Inn. It's in a small fishing village, oh, a fortnight from Paravel. Nice digs for the size of the town. His voice faded for a moment, then returned. *I think this is a great way to keep in touch, though another sorcerer could listen in, I suppose.*

"*Another* sorcerer. I take it you consider yourself a sorcerer, Blotto?" Joe was skeptical.

Yes, oh, master of the left hand, at least a novice. Anyway, let's get down to business. How are things going?

After some fashion, Joe and John explained what happened at the foundry, their contact with the Temple of Tarn, and their recruiting of a militia. Finally, they were finished and Lord Michael, Alchemist and Swordsman, nodded in approval.

Sabotage, I knew it. A Hand of Keth you say. Hmmm. Well, you'll have to watch your backs. I'll be watching mine that is for sure. I'm a week from Narn-toc. I'll call on you the same way say every couple of days. Same Bat time...

"Same Bat channel," John finished.

Adios, amigos. The fire returned to normal and Mike's voice faded from their thoughts. The two looked at each other.

"Man," Joe finally said. "This is some weird shit."

John could only agree.

Kelvin walked up the narrow steps to the loft above the Guildmaster Merchant's warehouse. The wooden steps creaked and groaned under his weight and that of his fully armored officer. It was an open warehouse, stacked to the crossbeams with crates and wares ready to be sold and shipped. Alaric Dirkajian was a wealthy man by any means and this was just a testament to that wealth. What concerned Kelvin was that Dirkajian did not want to spend any of that money for the defense of Paravel. Every man had his selfish motivations, but the Guildmaster's could hurt the city.

He stopped in front of the finely wrought softwood door and rapped on the plate. Alaric's assistant, Bale, answered the door and motioned for the Lord Protector and his officer to enter.

The office was spacious, decorated in a nautical theme, with quite a bit of brass and ivory. Behind a polished dark wood desk sat the Guildmaster Merchant. He was looking out the casement doors to the balcony and the *felucca* docked near the warehouse. He turned as Kelvin entered; a smile lit the man's face that was not quite as predatory as what was in his eyes. He stood, straightened his tunic, and strode around the desk. Alaric offered a hand to the Lord Protector who accepted it readily.

"What brings you to the merchant's quarter? I thought we were keeping things quiet around here, what with my men enforcing the law." Kelvin just smiled and shrugged.

"I am glad there are no more fires, I wouldn't want the stores of the merchants to suffer. We will be in great need of them in the coming months."

"Yes, there will be many a rich merchant by the time this is over." He motioned for Kelvin to sit. His officer remained standing while Bale poured two glasses of port and handed them to the two men. Kelvin tasted it and smiled.

"Qwen Port, Year of the Bathe, I believe."

"Year of the Growen, actually," Alaric replied and Kelvin nodded. "Well now, Lord Protector, what brings you to the docks on a chilly night like this?"

"Ah, to business as usual." Kelvin put the port down and leaned back, reaching into his tunic. He withdrew a folded piece of parchment and carefully opened it. Dark ink scrawled across the document and the Seal of the City Council graced the left hand corner. Alaric frowned upon seeing it.

"No more taxes, I hope."

"No, that would be foolish. The people only suffer with high taxes, especially when there is little money to go around. No, the council voted on this just this morning."

"What is it?" Alaric was getting impatient. He cocked one brow over a hazel eye and ran a hand through his curly black hair.

"It's a Proclamation."

"A proclamation."

"For an Inception of Crisis."

238

"What?!" Alaric shouted as he knocked the glass of port over; it spilled on his authentic Chez rug.

"Well, it seems that in order to build an adequate militia we have had to seize some of the cargos that have been stored in the warehouses along the merchant district; including yours."

"This, this can't be. It's preposterous!"

"Oh, no, not really. It's all in the city charter. The Council has the power, in a state of emergency, to issue an edict proclaiming the inception of crisis, thereby allowing them to confiscate necessary equipment, property and stores required for the building and maintaining of a militia."

"And you intend to do this to the Guildmaster?" Alaric's hands clenched into tight fists and he was shaking with anger.

"Not just you and it will not break you. Not to worry. The City Council wants to spread it among the merchants, even Pithorn agreed to donate his shipyard and the men working there."

"Pithorn," Alaric said between clenched teeth.

"And so," Kelvin replied with a smile that would only aggravate the other man further, "I have found several lading bills for the stores of your warehouse on Hel Lane. You have a store of three hundred bolts of un-dyed Qwen wool?" The merchant did not reply so Kelvin continued. "Well Lord John and the Shadowlord are building a militia and they have need of clothing and armor, another matter entirely, but we will get to that. This Qwen wool is fine for the autumn winds, as they will be patrolling the wall and drilling in the fields around the city. You do not have to worry about it being dyed. I think it has a nice uniform gray to the sheer.

"Now, on to Glaidel's warehouse. I see he has a store of mail, ready to be sent to Qwen. What a shame, well, he will just have to make do. Benthen has a store of wheat and corn. We'll need that, but tell him to never mind the karo, there seems so much of that lately."

By the time Kelvin left, Alaric was apoplectic. As it was, he came away with woolen bolts for tunics, mail armor, grain, and half boots numbering eight hundred. Sir John and Surik would be pleased.

He chuckled as he jauntily stepped down the stairs. He had not felt this good in a long time.

***

"How dare he!" Alaric shouted and threw a paperweight at the door opposite him. Bale winced when it took a large chunk out of the softwood door. "That bastard and his council, giving into the whim of those outlanders?"

Bale just stepped back as Alaric pushed over his chair. He stepped around it and began to pace furiously.

"Damn them, damn them all. This will cut into our profit margin for the next two seasons. I should have turned those outlanders over to Myella when I had the chance. But, no."

"It isn't your fault." Bale replied. Alaric looked at her, took a step and backhanded her across the mouth. She fell back against the hutch, blood creasing over her lip.

"I know it isn't my fault!" he shouted. "It's their fault, them and their quarrel with Myella." Bale remained silent. Blood dripped from her mouth onto her pale green tunic, staining the silk. She pulled her black hair back with her hand, wincing as a strand caught in the corner of her mouth.

"Take a message to Kryall," he ordered as he took his saber from the wall and gazed at his reflection in the blade. "Tell him what Kelvin is doing. Tell him I am open to suggestions. Tell him I don't care if it means I have to kill the outlanders myself."

Gabrielle looked at the trader at the front of the shop. He certainly was a large man, not exactly fat, but built more like a barrel. He was the one that was doing trade throughout the south and well into the Conclaveum. It was rumored he even traded his silks too far off Teshwa, the Seat of the Conclaveum, where her father was being held prisoner.

She had followed him through the markets and the merchant's quarter, trailing along in nondescript clothing so as not to alert him to her presence. Now she stood, fingering a bolt of broadcloth in a tailors shop not far from the docks. She surreptitiously looked over the material and watched as the man attempted to sell the tailor his silk. She herself did not dare dress as a Lady, especially if she was wandering through the city without escort. Instead, Gabrielle had worn a simple brown dress of wool, and a heavy cloak to keep out the chill. Her hair pulled back atop her head; she was hard put to keep curly strands from meandering over her brow.

Nonetheless, she gave the appearance of perhaps a merchant's wife, or the servant of a noble.

Finally, the man laughed and the shopkeeper just shook his head. He exchanged a note with the man, more than likely payment for goods and told the man where his warehouse was located. She looked up as he left the shop and followed him out into the crowded street. These days all parts of Paravel teamed with the throngs of people. All throughout the city there was a mass of humanity and it seemed as though the walls would spill over with the crowds. The refugees from the west were even erecting tents in the fields outside the wall proper, much to the dismay of the landowners who had peasants working their parcels of land. Kelvin had sent his guard into the fields to expel the squatters, but it was little use. Ultimately, one of the property owners had acquiesced to allow use of several tracts that were lying fallow; wooden shanties were springing up all over.

The silk trader paused at a venders stand and took a greasy sausage stick in exchange for a few copper bits. Even the price of confections where growing outrageous.

He plodded on and she followed. What would she say to the man once she confronted him? She did not know. Since Sir John now spent most of his time arranging for the defenses of the city, she felt alone and isolated. The vacuum that Trianna's death had left was not easy to fill, even knowing that the outlander knight felt more for her than a protector should; she dare thought that she felt that way also. However, with his long absences, emptiness filled her. Her thoughts ever went to the plight of her father. She felt that he was still alive and Sir John had reassured her so, but the need to do something, to have a purpose, was gnawing at the very fiber of her being. Would this silk merchant have the means to give her information?

She found herself lost in these thoughts as she walked through the crowds, brushing past peasants and refugees. She realized she lost sight of the merchant. Frantically she pushed on ahead, afraid that if she lost him now she would not be able to find him again. The crowd was too thick; she could not find a shred of the flamboyant clothing that the man wore, amid the dull brown and tans of the throngs. She stopped and spun.

"Damn!" she swore, to no one but herself.

"Milady!" It was a shocked reply from her elbow. She spun to find the trader at her side, a look of dismay on his face. He patted his brow as he looked at Gabrielle; she was speechless.

"Forgive me," she finally sputtered. This was the moment.

"There is nothing to forgive, especially for one of such beauty. Obviously you lost your escort in the crowd; otherwise such language would not grace your lovely lips." She blushed at his audacity.

"You are too kind. You are also correct. I fear that I have lost my escort."

"Allow me, then. The streets of Paravel have become swollen with the detritus of humanity and it is a shame that a lady of your obvious acumen has to tolerate it." He extended his arm and she took it without hesitation. She smiled demurely at the trader and allowed him to guide her through the throng.

"So, milady, what brings you to the merchant district? Bolts of fine Baed silk? Acturen saffron for the evening meal? Or is it the fine shoes that the cobblers here make?"

She saw that if she were to progress in her endeavor she would have to be equally bold. "Information," she stated, matter-of-fact.

He looked down at her, his eyes narrowed to two slits. "Information? What information would a lady be in need of that her suitors, or her family for that matter, could not provide." He shook his head.

"I fear that like many of the people in Paravel, I am without many resources. Other than the remnants of my estate and the few retainers that I have, little remains that would provide me with the information I need."

He nodded understanding. He had guided her through the throng and to a less busy avenue. The streets were lined with ash trees and the cobbles were clean and level; it was one of the wealthier districts. A carriage passed them and the few people that milled about made way. The man motioned toward a karo shop, with benches and tables set out on the walk. This time of year, with the leaves turning and the wind carrying the chill of winter, few people sat on the veranda. She nodded her accent and allowed the trader to seat her amid some flowering thorn bush, carefully cultivated amid the trellis that covered the veranda. The sun was low in the sky and a servant was dutifully lighting oil lamps situated around the karo shop. The waiter finally found his way to their table. There was a weary cast to his eyes; he must have had a very busy day.

244

"Yes. We shall have a pot of your cinril karo and two of those delightful pastries with the cream filling. Is that suitable for the Lady...?"

"Gabrielle. Yes, that would be fine."

"Lady Gabrielle," the man rolled her name on his tongue when the servant went to fetch the order. "I have heard of you. You are very prominent in the ranks of those that guide this city."

"You flatter me. Really, I have very little to do with what goes on in Paravel. I leave that to Chair Nathal and Lord Kelvin."

The man chuckled. He smoothed back the tuft of hair that graced the very top of his head, and accepted the pot of karo from the waiter. The trader poured a steaming cup of the cinril-flavored karo for his guest and then plunged his two-tined fork into the pastry. Gabrielle watched as he dipped it in the karo, letting the cream dissolve into the liquid, and then put it to his mouth.

"Mmmm, one of the delights of Paravel is this little karo shop and the pastries they serve. In all my wanderings, I dare say I have not found a finer shop. Your beauty only adds to the splendor of my fare."

"Again, you flatter me."

"Ah, but you flatter me, Lady Gabrielle. By thinking that I could provide you with the information you seek."

"What do you mean?" she asked, trying to hide the consternation brought on by his comment.

"By following me all day." He laughed at the look of surprise on her face. "Three tailors, a seamstress and you were either in the window or across the street each time. Finally, you were so

245

bold as to come into the shop. Even the tailor commented on your presence, since he dealt exclusively in very large men." He laughed again as he patted his stomach.

"It was that obvious." She smiled with embarrassment.

"It was. But, as I said, I am flattered. Not since Clef have I, Master Talbot, been so honored, but you may call me Talbot."

"Thank you, Master Talbot."

"Now," he said, as he finished off the pastry. He motioned to Gabrielle's untouched confection. She shook her head and he pulled it in front of him. "What kind of information would a Lady want, that a trader in silks would have?"

"I was told that you travel often to the Conclaveum, to trade your silks. It is news of the Conclaveum that I seek."

"Hmmm. Well, I do go to Baed and Acturen, if that is what you mean. The worms there are the best for silk. But, as for information, I fear that I am somewhat limited to my trade."

Gabrielle sipped her karo. "Come now, Master Talbot. Obviously a man of your resources has the means to obtain some simple information."

"I suppose that depends on the information." He wiped some cream from his mouth with a napkin and then settled back in his chair.

"I need information about the Tower of Iss, about a man who may have been taken there."

Suddenly a shadow crossed the man's brow and it seemed as though the sun was left behind the clouds. A cold wind stirred the thorn bush at their

246

backs. He looked uncomfortably at the cup of karo, swirling the liquid with a spoon.

"Milady, there are many things that merchants in the Conclaveum discuss. But, there are other things that are avoided like the orphans plague." He looked at her, his eyes sparkling and the corner of his mouth twisting into a reluctant grin. "In my youth, Lady Gabrielle, your suitors would have had keen competition from me." He laughed and went on.

"Let me tell you, I have been to the Seat, to Teshwa, only twice. I have never had the need to go there more often. I dislike large cities and by all accounts, that is one of the largest cities in all of Carn. Like the city, the Tower you speak of is ancient and carries with it the harbinger of evil. Why, just speaking its name conjures a foul taste on the palate. The citizens of the Conclave rarely talk of things like the Tower, or of the Cult of Iss that spawned there. I am a learned man, but my father had me learn of the merchant trade, not the politics of the Conclaveum. When I go to Baed, or Acturen, it is not as a diplomat, it is as a silk trader."

"I understand, but-"

He silenced her with a wave of his hand and continued. "I do not think that you do. It would be unheard of for me, a Southern Trader, to inquire into the workings of the Conclave, especially the ones so guarded that it is often death to speak of them.

"There are dark things afoot in this world, young lady, things that you or I should never witness, let alone speak of. I am sorry that your father is held in the Tower of Pain-"

247

"How did you know it was my father?" She leaned over the table, her green eyes were intent on his but he looked away.

"You have my sympathy, Gabrielle. But, Preceptor Javin Skettes has already asked me these same questions."

"Preceptor Skettes?"

"Yes, your Lord Knight Protector has asked him to gather information of your father. I told Javin all I knew. Which is very little, I fear."

"Sir John?" she asked in a faint voice. The blossom on the thorn bush was pale white.

"Yes and I shall tell you what I told Skettes. The Tower is not discussed in the Conclaveum. The Clave ignores its workings. It is Guyle's domain and now that Ironeas is dead, and Myella Conclavatrix, your father has little hope of ever seeing the light of day." He stood and slapped a silver shenk on the table. "Again, I am sorry."

She looked up at him, her mind numbed by what he had said.

"If you need me, I will be in Paravel for another month. Then I leave for Chestra, on the coast of the Conclaveum. The silk trade takes me there. If you need anything, please do not hesitate to call on me. I am staying at the Blue Heron, in the warehouse district."

He strode away, leaving Gabrielle to think things over in the twilight. The oil lamps cast a hazy glow through the late blooming flowers of the thorn bush.

248

Chapter 18

Barish made fast a line to the bowsprit of the *felucca*, he was being careful to avoid slipping on the wet deck. His was the fourth and last fast felucca to leave the docks of Tasseem and with it barely two score of his men in this boat, hardly worth the effort.

He could ignore events no longer and that was what prompted his desertion. The orders had been explicit. The Seat belonged to that witch, Myella, and she was the supreme ruler of the Conclaveum. With that, new word came that Marad was dead and he was to stand down. Myella had sent Kel bearing the edict and with this, he brought his new rank as Commander of the Guard of Oran. The White Guard would stand down from its vigilance at Tasseem and the Guard of Oran would replace the Command unit. So now, instead of the insignia of the White Guard, a hawk and a sunburst on a white tunic, there would be the dagger and circle of fire.

Barish spat, a foul taste in his mouth, as he watched the sun bleached port become fuzzy with the haze and heat that rose off the surface of the bright water. *What am I doing?*

Desertion that is what I am doing. It had become obvious that was what he was supposed to do. All the more so when the Guard of Oran allowed a Krim envoy to pass unmolested down the Kipris.

There was a truce, Kel had argued. Kel, the man who had opposed the truce most vehemently when Marad had proposed it, had let a Krim pass to the Interior. He had also watched impassively as the

White Guard was stripped of its arms. Men were being reassigned; some were to go to the Black Guard, others to the Guard of the Wall, or to the new units being formed in Tasseem under the watchful eyes of the Guard of Oran.

For Barish, there was no place. Ordered back to Teshwa, his commission stripped for no apparent reason, except possibly for his relationship to Marad. Marad had tutored him and with no love lost between him and his sister, it was apparent the new Conclavatrix wanted no sympathizers for the dead Lord.

So it was, that at midday, when the sun was the hottest and the activity at the docks was negligible, he and almost two hundred men had stolen four of the White Guard's fastest *feluccas.* Built for speed and stealth in naval combat these ships were unequaled and Barish was a masterful pilot. Gathering about him his most loyal men, he had broken through the gatehouse at the dock and with very little bloodshed had stolen the swift vessels, now crowded with men and women loyal only to him or their former Commander, Marad. They had sped past the stone breakwall, the slightest of breezes swelling the sail and bringing the prow up off the water. The ship seemed to glide on the glassy surface. Barish laughed as he watched Kel shout from the end of the docks, his sword useless in his hand.

A smile still on his face he called to the tiller man and motioned for him to order the sail trimmed. Again, the ship leapt ahead dipping to starboard as she keeled over slightly. Now she rode the waves, the plume of white spray shooting over the deck, she soon joined the three other *feluccas* that where in the channel, making a bearing for the Gangli Straits. He bent his knees, feeling the rise and fall of the boat, the coolness of the water, even in the sweltering heat of midday. It had been weeks since he had been on one of these boats. Weeks since Kel had returned with the news of Marad,\ and the order confining him to barracks until he returned to Teshwa.

He was a young man, with a high forehead and hair a tangled mess that ran to his shoulders. He had dark eyes and a wide face that told most that he came from Baed. He moved with a grace bred from the sea, his wide shoulders easily allowing the grasp of ropes, his stout legs moving fluidly over the deck. He had a thick build,\ and even in this heat, he managed to keep that insulating layer of fat that was more common to the high altitude of Baed, with its winters as harsh as those of the Deep South. He laughed as he saw his accompanying feluccas fall slightly behind and a comely smile spread across his face.

"What now, captain?" asked the man at the tiller. He still wore the uniform of the White Guard, a white linen tunic with a pale blue stylized hawk and gold sunburst. The traditional dagger of the guard was on his hip, a silken wrapped grip and tempered Qwen steel.

"What now? I think we have to get past those Krim ships in the Gangli Straits first." His voice was a slow drawl, but he had a quick mind, one of the reasons that Marad had left him in charge. "Then we'll round the Archipelago of Bequa and head on south. After that, I know not. I will not serve the Guard of Oran, though."

Many of his men heard his last remark and muttered approval. Almost exclusively, the men of the White Guard followed Tarn, not the evil god of the underworld. Barish thought that might have been one of the key reasons that Myella had ordered the Guard disbanded. He had one hundred ninety eight men and women and four ships.He would hold true the White Guard and its tradition, formed over eight hundred years ago by the Clave to protect the Winter Seat.

About the deck men began to stow the gear. They made fast the hatches fore and aft, tied down the heavy arbalest that stood four on port and starboard and some began to scramble below deck to check on stores or relax until their watch. These were good loyal men, now exiled by the Conclavatrix and they would be welcome nowhere within the boundaries of the Conclaveum.

Soon the sky turned to bronze, the four *feluccas* entered the Gangli Straits just to the north of the Archipelago of Bequa. Looking over his shoulder Barish watched as the sun began its plummet into the ocean. Before them was the cobalt night, broken only by the reflection of scarlet on the choppy waves. The four feluccas raced over the water in a staggered line, his ship the foremost. There was something else too; large looming silhouettes on the horizon, just outside of the archipelago, the toll ships of the Krim.

"Kel might have warned them, you know," called the dulcet voice of a young female ensign. He shrugged and moved from the bowsprit, along the

252

midline. His loyal men and women had loaded all his ballista and arbalest, prepared if necessary to fight. Barish had other plans though.

Feluccas were notoriously fast ships, able to maneuver about in battle with such agility that, even though the ships of the Krim were heavily armed, they could do little harm to the sprite craft.

"Let them taste salt!" he shouted to the helmsman. The man smiled and nodded as he spun the wheel and called to one of the mates on the rigging. The mate let out the rope and the jib ballooned, catching the wind. The felucca leapt over the waves, the hull sliding over the water as if it was ice. Barish laughed aloud for that was the magic of the craft.

His curly hair whipped back, stinging at his sun and wind burned face. He watched as the three other ships matched speed. They were drawing fast on the Krim toll ships. Over the starboard side was the ridge of stone that rose out of the water like some monstrous sea creature, the Archipelago of Bequa. Further on would be the port of Bequa just on this side of the cape. Bequa, conceded to the Krim, its citizens given naught more than a fortnight to leave. Marad did it to forestall an escalation. In losing Bequa, they had saved Tasseemand prevented an invasion. That was, until Myella became Conclavatrix.

The two toll ships loomed before them. They could have lost them easily if they had just veered to the north, but then that would take them into Krim waters and danger. As it was, they had to hug the ridge of the archipelago and swing around the cape. Once done, they would outdistance the larger ships in a matter of moments. The Krim ships made stark silhouettes in the twilight. The masts brandished sails of an alien design, multi-colored and translucent. The ships were dangerous. Thick dark wood, intricately carved, protected the hull from all but the most powerful projectiles and it was dotted with many a port, which could accommodate kris-voulge.

It would have been much easier the whole way around had night fallen, as it was twilight left them in clear view of the strangely designed craft. Barish watched, his hands tightening on the line as the two ships closed the gap on them, pushing them closer to the rocky strip to starboard. He swore under his breath, realizing the tactic of the Krim. In the distance, muted white foam danced about the jagged rocks, and Barish could imagine his keel splintering if they sailed any closer.

Still, the ships were out of their arbalest range, as if those weapons would do much good against the ornately carved hull of the large ship. He could almost make out the prickly skin of kris-voulge and Krim moving about the multi-decked craft. The other *feluccas* were close, there hulls not separated by more than a few spans. Barish nodded to the lieutenant on the other boat, who shrugged back. They had done this many times before, but usually with the bulk of one of their warships backing them up.

A flapping filled the air, over the sound of the spray and wave. "Trim that, damn you!" called the helmsman. The noise ceased, only to be replaced by the steady deep drone of a drumbeat and the

254

rhythmic splash of oars. The Krim ships were drawing closer. One aimed in not a hundred spans to port, the other stood down off the bow, wedging them in toward the shoals.

Unfortunately, now the two ships were in such close proximity as to allow the *feluccas* to scrape between them. Barish heard the low thump of kris-voulge and knew that the furthest felucca out had been hit. She would be taking water. His own *felucca* lurched to the side as the ship closest to him touched alongside. As abrupt as that was, so was the possible solution to their dilemma. He grabbed up a flag and signaled to the *felucca* to his stern. Suddenly all four ships were now neck and neck, the hulls not more than half a span apart. On an ordinary day, he would commend his men for such control of their craft. As it was, he noticed the fourth out was slowing and indeed, it was taking water.

Again, he waved the signal flags in a complicated display. The commander of the damaged *felucca* nodded and barked out a harsh order. The arbalest on her port twanged, launching a volley at the closing vessel. Even as this was happening, the men who were aboard began to leap to the next *felucca*, abandoning their sinking vessel.

The hellish spikes from the kris-voulge tore into the feluccas deck and cockpit. The commander shouted in agony as her right arm was taken off at the shoulder. As the last man jumped to the adjoining craft, the commander gritted her teeth amid the mortal spray of blood and spun the helm to port. Barish, astonished, watched as the vessel, now heavy with water nigh to the deck, lurched to the left and cut across the path of the toll ship. The damaged *felucca*, already traveling at a great speed, dipped in the water, its steel reinforced prow aimed just below the water line of the Krim ship. Barish was faintly aware that the drumming from the ship had stopped to be followed by a tremendous crash as the *felucca* plunged through the ornate hull of the toll ship. Most of the *felucca* splintered and exploded away, like so much flotsam, however the prow and keel tore into the thick hull of the ship just below the churning blue. The toll ship came to a halt in the water and Barish was satisfied to hear the astonished cries of the Krim sailors.

Thanking Tarn for the brave sacrifice of the wounded commander, he signaled the other ships and they heeled over to port, sails growing slack, then the booms swinging out and once more billowing with wind. The three remaining feluccas passed between the toll ships, the whoosh of kris-voulge falling aft as they gained speed and outran the Krim ship to starboard. Soon they were naught more than dark blots against the sunset.

Barish looked into the relieved faces of the men and women under his command.

"Where to now?" asked the helmsman deep in the cockpit.

"We are truly forsaken. Mayhap we shall go along the coast. We can avoid the larger cities. I hear Paravel is nice this time of year."

"Aye," echoed the helm. "Free men to a free city. Better that, than under the yoke of Myella and Oran."

256

Barish nodded. The ship sped off into the night, the stars their lonely guide as they passed Bequa and headed south.

Marad and Smiling Wolf passed through several villages that had suffered similar fates as the first, pillaged by the Guard of Oran. In the latest, the villagers had fared somewhat better, having fled into the nearby wood. The Guard frustrated and angry by their quarry fleeing had burned most of the buildings to the ground. Now, as Marad and Tom Smiling Wolf, trailed by the wolf that had befriended him, walked into the husk of a village, they watched as men and women picked through the ruins, gazing at them with wary eyes, tear streaked and wide.

It would have been an odd sight indeed, to see these two men, one armed with only a staff, the other with just a knife, followed by a large wolf. However, these people were numb and had seen enough strange things. The harsh shouts of men, the wailing of women and the cries of hungry children drowned out the suspicious whispers. Marad shook his head at the frown of his companion.

"At least they live, Smiling Wolf," Marad spoke to his ears alone. "There is some comfort in that."

Tom said nothing as he walked up what had been the main road of this small village. He watched as peasants rifled for some former belonging, or turned over a charred beam, wincing as they touched a still hot brick. Their faces were soot covered and drawn, their eyes cast down. Shock had set in for many. Tom stopped and looked to a woman with nothing more about her shoulders than rags. She wept as she rocked back and forth, cradling a child in her arms.

"This is what my sister brings to the South and to the whole Conclaveum," Marad spat as he looked on.

Tom knelt at the woman's side and was shocked to see that his enhanced vision not only saw her, but a faint blue shimmer around her head, now tainted by the shock and the trauma brought on by the evil that was wrought here. It seemed as though her aura flickered with a sickly yellow, then back to healthy blue.

"What is it?" Marad asked and Tom looked to him. He too, carried a faint aura, though his was a healthy pale blue. He looked back to the woman. He brushed her hair from her eyes. She stopped rocking and looked at him as his hand caressed her forehead. It was strange, this new vision of his, being able to see the damaged spirit of another. His vision, now more keen than ever, saw the hurt and the pain and for a moment he imagined it healing, he visualized the aura mending, the emotional damage undone. He blinked and the aura was complete again, without the sickly taint.

She grasped his hand, closed her eyes and held it to her face. Slowly he withdrew and stood.

"What did you do?" asked Marad. He gazed at the woman, a look of transfiguration on her face. She slowly stood, looked to the Sioux, wrapped the blanket around her child and moved off to where several women were gathering supplies.

"I-I don't know," he stammered. He looked at his own hand, seeing a faint glimmer of silver aura about the edges of his fingers. He closed his eyes

258

and when he opened them, his vision had returned to normal

"Well, whatever it was, she is better off for it. Tarn is with you this day, my friend." He clapped the Sioux on his back and once more began walking up the road through the village. Tom followed, trying to figure out what had just happened. The wolf loped to his side, his tongue lolling as he rubbed his shoulder against the outlander's thigh. He looked down into the gray eyes of his new friend and there was that smile. He smiled back and ran his hand through the beast's hackles. The wolf trotted off ahead.

Marad had stopped and, bending over, picked up the remains of a signpost. He scratched out dirt, and examined the writing carved therein.

"Qwen," he said as he nodded down the well-worn road. "Another twenty leagues. It will not be long Smiling Wolf. You know, the closest garrison of the Guard of Oran is in Qwen. That is from where they sortie, to do this. It seems they have no wish for this to remain secret. They are brazen in their campaign against Tarn."

"It won't be safe there."

"Qwen never was, even before it was annexed by the Conclaveum. Beneath its serene exterior is a pit of vipers. Always be aware of that, outlander. Intrigue is an art in Qwen, only second to that of Chez. The most prominent family in Qwen, the family of Orr, has brought it to an art."

"Orr, I recognize that name."

"You should. Lord Duran is of the family Orr, as was Gelion." Marad frowned and nodded down the road. "We'll pass through Dorber, which is where the waters pass from the Doran range and through the Crevasse meet the sea. There we will have to find some decent clothing, and some weapons. Do you have any silver?"

"You have to be kidding." Tom laughed. "I lost everything back near Helm."

"Then I hope you don't mind stealing."

"As long as it is from the Guard of Oran."

Marad gave Tom an appraising glance and then smiled. "I think that can be arranged."

The walk to Dorber was a long one. Many times, they had to skirt off the road and duck into the wooded fringe to avoid the roaming patrols of the Guard of Oran. Marad was surprised to see that not one of the patrols was made of the Black Guard, strange indeed. Had Myella displaced them also?

Tom figured it would take them a week to get to Dorber. Already, as he looked through the thinning wood to the south, he could spy the Plains of Straw. He knew that many leagues to the south lay Paravel. He was tempted to take his leave of Marad and just head out across the plains. A sort of affinity that had grown between them allayed this thought, however. Marad, in a way, was like Tom; cast out of the world he knew, hunted and lost. In many respects, they shared the same cause.

When evening drew near, they set camp in the woods, careful not be spotted by anyone who passed by on the road. It was becoming evident that they were nearing a city, as the merchant traffic would pass back and forth with more frequency. At night, Tom would tell Marad of his friends and how they were brought to this world. Tom found it strange that Marad was not surprised at their origins.

"I do not find it strange, because such things are possible with strong sorcery. My brother has said as much, but I have never seen it. The sorcery I have seen has been limited to its use in battle, or healing, or when the Krim employ it. It sounds like my father's half-brother has been delving into things that are beyond the ken of mere mortal men; thus the employ of the Hands of Keth. Oran, an evil god, is generous with knowledge to those that serve him with the souls of the innocent.

"It doesn't sound too pleasant."

"It is not, Smiling Wolf. I believe that you saw as much on our way here. Not only were the people slaughtered because of their belief in Tarn, by killing the hawks and mounting the standard of Oran over the grave, they became a sacrifice. The more innocents that are sacrificed, the stronger Oran becomes and the easier his evil is manifested in this realm. There is nothing pleasant about the Cult of Oran at all." Silence fell between them and the wolf trotted up and lay down next to Tom. "Now *that* is strange. Does that happen often with wolves?"

"He is the first. This world seems to be a place of firsts."

"There is no magic where you come from?"

"Not in the sense you mean. We have something more devastating, called technology." When Marad looked confused, Tom elaborated. "We built machines to do things for us. Just as a windmill crushes grain, we built complex machines to do a host of other things, carriages without horses, ships that fly across the sky and at great speeds. Sea ships the size of cities that cross our

261

oceans and weapons of destruction capable of laying waste to whole countries."

"It sounds like a frightening place."

"It is." Tom sighed as he rubbed his hand through the wolf's coarse hair. "Funny thing is, you become used to it and after a while, it doesn't bother you anymore."

"It is like that in the Conclaveum. Its citizens became lax; they let their guard down and up sprang the Cult of Oran from the very bowels of hell itself. My sister wallowed in it. The people cared only for the moment and even those that sat on the Clave grew inured to the strife in the north with the Krim. There was hardly a whisper of dissent when we surrendered the Gangli Strait to our enemy. And if we hadn't done that they would not have known the Krim had invaded until their sheets were red with their own blood."

Tom had learned more about the Conclaveum in the past several nights than he had heard since he arrived in this realm. It was information that would prove useful once he reached Paravel. Marad paused, looking into the yellow flames that danced above the small fire. Tom settled back against the bole of a tree, catching the lupine gaze of his new friend.

"I can only hope that I may visit revenge on my sister and her minions. I am far from my Command."

"What will you do when we get to Dorber?"

"In Dorber it would be best if we stayed together. They do not have much there except for their fishing. There a causeway runs from Dorber to Qwen. You'll get your eyeful of the Great Wall."

262

"So I've heard."

"Oh?"

"A friend of mine, named Torec el'Kirien, mentioned that he was in Qwen once."

"Yes, well, in Qwen you can gain passage to Paravel and I to Chestra."

"First we have to overcome the obstacle of silver."

"Well, maybe in Dorber we can find a generous guardsman." Tom smiled as the other man bedded down. Soon he was dreaming of loping across the Plains of Straw, his brother wolves at his side, chasing the *deathwing* from the land of Carn.

***

Dorber was little more than a fishing village, which benefited from its proximity to the isle of Qwen. The road leveled out as it crossed the open expanse to the town. Low walls partitioned the fields and farmers were busy harvesting the autumn crop. In the distance, masts bobbed against the glistening water. The sights and sounds of habitation became all the more evident with children playing in the village and dogs barking at their feet. The wolf pricked up his ears at the far off barking, but did not otherwise respond. It would be interesting how the people in the village would react to the beast at his side. If they entered the town under the concealment of the night it would not bring them too much notice.

"Well, what do you think?" Tom asked of his traveling companion. Marad frowned and looked

263

out to the causeway that ran from the main street in Dorber to the isle of Qwen.

"There will be a toll to cross the causeway. It would be best if we found some clothing and arms in Dorber."

"How easy will that be? If it's a fishing village, I don't think you'll find any swords lying around."

"I know towns like Dorber, there will be a whore house or a tavern and there will be soldiers."

Nightfall came fast, with the farmers retreating to their homes, their carts full of grain. Along the coast the fishing boats were heading back to harbor, the net's straining with this days catch. Lanterns soon blinked on through the shuttered windows and people could be seen milling on the streets as soldiers caroused and the anglers came in for a nightcap. Tom and Marad made their way into Dorber. They passed small homes and finally, on the edge of town, moved through the narrow paths between the small buildings. They were careful not to be spotted.

Keeping to the shadows, they made their way to the eastern section of the village, near the docks and the causeway. It was here, Marad had said, that it would be likely they would find their quarry.

Tom wrinkled his nose; the stench of rotting fish was thick in the air. As he proceeded down the dark alley, his feet crunched on scales and discarded fish bones. The wolf snorted, and then emitted a low growl as he reached the corner of the building ahead of the Sioux. Tom cautioned Marad to stop and then he peered around the corner and into the dimly lit street.

Tom's enhanced vision easily picked out several men stumbling along the street. It looked as though they had just come from a tavern across the way. They were dressed in simple tunics and britches and wore bloody aprons; no doubt, they were fish-gutters or some such thing. Tom crouched down; these men were not their targets.

He felt Marad's hand on his shoulder and looked back. The man was pointing the other way up the street. Though most of the buildings were dark, the sounds of voices and laughing often broke through the shutters to pierce the night. At the establishment, which Marad was gesturing, several horses stood at a rail. The panniers were the Guard of Oran.

Sticking to the dark back alley, they made their way to the tavern. Filth piled up against the cracking brick wall and rats scurried away at the wolf's approach. Out in the street the steeds snorted nervously at the smell of the wolf. Tom motioned him to the back of the alley, where he waited patiently, his eyes glowing.

"Can we use the horses?" Tom asked as he crouched down next to Marad. He absently flipped his large Bowie knife, testing the balance.

"It wouldn't be wise. They are branded with the mark of the Temple of Oran. They are probably officer's steeds; I doubt that a regular Guardsman would ride such. It would be foolish to steal one. Besides, we had planned to catch a ship in Qwen. Going to the city openly on horses branded under the Temple would be asking for trouble."

Tom nodded and settled back to wait. The minutes passed slowly and the wolf finally settled down in the filthy alley, resting his head on his forepaws. Marad was about to nod off when loud laughter erupted from the front of the tavern. Four men spilled into the street and staggered toward the horses.

They were dressed in the livery of the Guard of Oran; gold thread stitched into the tunic denoting them as officers. Two carried short swords and the third had a long narrow sword with an ornate hilt. Their voices filled the empty street.

"Gods below, Krank, but me bladder is full!" shouted one of the lesser officers. The one with the ornate sword laughed loudly and dragged on the tether of his horse, almost falling to the dirt.

"Do tell, Prit. You alone drank more than the three of us."

"Aye," said a third, a definite slur in his voice. "You'll be pissin buckets."

"I may be pissin buckets, but I also won me silver back. Can you say as much?"

"Palmin the dice helped, eh," shouted another and the commanding officer shushed him loudly.

"Yi dinna want the scullies to hear yi, now!"

"Aye, all their gonna hear is the river of me piss." The Guardsman stumbled over to the entrance of the alley, fumbling with the tie on his tabard. Soon he had it pulled aside and unlaced the top of his hose. He was not more than three feet from Tom, standing with his shoulder against the wall to be steady.

"Ah," he groaned as he began to relieve himself.

"Need a hand, Prit?" echoed one of the others with a laugh.

266

"I think not," he growled and sighed. The steady stream continued and Tom was amazed at the capacity of the man. As the others tended to their steeds, Marad gestured to Tom. It was time.

"I'll tell yi what, Krank, I think I never pissed as much as this, I-"

He was cut off abruptly as Tom darted forward, slicing down inside the man's arm. Prit stared dumfounded at his missing hands. Where once had been a steady stream of urine was now a mixture of blood and flesh.

"Ah!" he shouted. "I've lost me arms!" He was silenced as Tom grabbed the back of his head and slammed his knife up under the man's chin and into his brain. He fell with a gurgle into the alley.

"Prit? What do yi mean? Have yi gotten so drunk yi kinnot find em?"

"He probably ruined a gid pair of hose, ti boot," commented another. "Come on, Prit, we have to be gettin back."

"Get im," ordered the officer with the long sword. He sat unsteadily in his saddle.

Swearing, the one named Krank entered the alleyway looking for his friend. "He passed out!" he shouted back over his shoulder

The officer laughed and gestured for the other to help Krank. "Go, carry im out and tie im to his saddle."

He followed Krank into the alley and they both struggled to turn their cohort over. When they finally managed, Krank let out a gasp at seeing the vicious wound and stepped back. That was his undoing. He fell into the arms of Marad, who snatched the short sword from the man's scabbard and drew it up and across Krank's neck. He slumped to the ground without further struggle, wide eyed and clutching at his throat.

Tom took the third in the back, his knife entering between the third and fourth rib. The man slumped forward, on top of Prit.

"Come on, you three, we haven't got all night." The commanding officer edged his steed toward the alley and leaned over in his saddle, squinting. Instantly he spun his horse around, his face white with what he had seen. He slammed his heels into the flanks of his horse and snapped the reins, but it was too late. The wolf streaked out of the alley, a blur in the night. It leapt over the steed and crashed into the side of the officer, knocking him to the dirt road. The horse bolted off down the road toward the causeway. The officer lay on his back with his hands over his neck and face, but the wolf just stood on him, pinning him to the road as he looked over to Tom. Tom was soon at the wolf's side, staring down at the man. The wolf stepped off, circled around and sat next to Tom. The Sioux looked down at the man.

"Mercy! I beg it of thee." He looked from the Sioux to the wolf and back again. Tom's eyes adjusted as he looked at the officer in the livery of the Guard of the Temple of Oran. He noticed the man's aura, dark, almost black, like a malignant cancer encircling his head.

"Mercy? Did you ask that of the villagers that you slaughtered from here to Helm?"

The man looked at him, his eyes growing wide.

"I thought not," echoed Tom as he flipped his knife expertly forward. It sank into the man's chest with a thud. The officer gasped a moment then was still.

Tom dragged him back into the alley where Marad was lifting the belt pouch from the corpse of Prit. It jangled heavily with silver coins.

"I never thought evil could manifest itself so. Now I know it can. Here," Tom called and tossed the other man the long sword. "You look like you would be more comfortable with this than that walking stick."

"You are right, but we must make haste. I fear that a horse cantering around the town may alert the Guard. Let's find ourselves an inn."

Marad stripped the officer of his belt pouch and tucked it in his cloak. They then ducked out of the alley and headed the opposite way up the street, to the west side of Dorber, were they would find lodging for the night.

Tom watched as the morning mist parted and the sun rose over the jutting rough-hewn isle that was Qwen. Sea birds cawed far above, circling over the stone causeway that ran from the sheltered bay of Dorber and eventually formed a bridge to the island state that was Qwen.

The thinning fog swallowed the echo of Marad's boots on the timbered planking of the causeway road. The slapping of waves against stone pilings soon replaced the tinny clap of boots. They had left Dorber and the dead guardsmen. Now they were equipped with new clothes and supplies. Behind, they had paid their toll, with only a glance by the guard in green tabard. Sometime in the night the wolf had left Tom and Marad, silently trotting to the South. Tom felt sure he would see the wolf again and maybe the beast knew too, so the parting was not with loss or misgiving.

Before the sun had risen, they had left the small inn and had proceeded down toward the wide causeway. Behind them and to the north rose the Great Wall The morning sun licked at its crest and the clouds cast a gold shimmer at the summit. Down to the rocky harbor of Dorber went the former commander of the White Guard, dressed as wealthy traveler and perhaps Tom was his guard or guide, though Marad carried the long sword at his side.

Here, where the causeway met the shore, an arch of natural stone formed the gateway to the distant isle. This natural arch easily rose one hundred feet, topped by tall pines perched precariously on the rocky summit. Inside the shadows of the arch was where the toll-man had stood his guard.

For the moment, they walked in silence. So far, there had been no alarm in the village. Marad had surmised that the people of the village would ignore the slain guardsmen for as long as possible, out of apathy or resentment for their overlords.

"There will be a garrison of the Guard in Qwen, Smiling Wolf," Marad's said.

"Then Qwen is a subject of the Conclaveum?" Tom asked as he watched several wagons on the causeway about a mile distant.

"Actually, no. Qwen has a special status. She was annexed, but remains a free state. She contributes heavily in trade goods, and most significantly in arms. Think of Qwen as the Paravel of the Conclaveum. The man in the green tabard, at the tollgate, is a guard of the family Orr. There were four prominent families in Qwen, the family Orr, from which Duran comes, the family Koss, the family Rhinn and the family Jaggiers. The Conclaveum exiled the Koss from the island several decades ago for opposing the annexation. A blood feud developed between Koss and two other families, Jaggier and Orr.

"Duran had mentioned that he fought with the Jaggiers when he was younger."

"The family Koss had been trying to gain support in the council, but all for naught. Orr holds the majority, followed by Jaggier and Rhinn, and the rest of the minor families. Rhinn is somewhat sympathetic to Koss, but their position is tenuous at best. The minor families are as vultures, awaiting word from Orr to depose Rhinn. Yet Rhinn holds on."

"These factions vie for control?"

"Orr controls Qwen, though the other families would deny it. Orr rations the power, but they all vie for it. It seems that Orr hid itself from open despotism by linking itself with the Jaggier's to fight its feud with Koss."

Tom looked out over the glistening water, the sun still a white disk in the mist that shrouded the promontories of Qwen. Tom could now barely make out the road that wound steeply up the sheer cliffs, among the buildings that dotted the cliff and summit. Tom had seen similar islands once, in the South China Sea. From this distance, the isle of Qwen had a far-eastern flavor.

"Much intrigue. The family Orr controls Qwen, why then the need for a garrison?"

271

"Why indeed. Up until last year, it was a small garrison of the Black Guard, here only to protect the interest of the Conclaveum, mostly trade. Family Rhinn produces the finest weapons in Carn. Their steel is exquisite. Mayhap we can visit one of their armories while there. We shall see."

For a while, there was silence between them, broken only by the whisper of waves and the occasional cry of a gull. Most of the mist burned off and the sun cast the west face of the isle in shadow. There should have been more traffic at this hour, but Marad had attributed the lack thereof to the war in the west. He explained that most trading was done via shipping, not merchant wains. Ships would travel from the port on the eastern side of the island and venture to Chestra in the Conclaveum. Wains, on the other hand, would have to travel by barge along the Wall River to Helm and then up the Kipris to Teshwa or Baed.

Before them the steep cliffs of Qwen rose, dotted with red roofed villas surrounded by lush gardens and winding roadways. Sunlight was just now peeking over the jagged summit and Tom could make out the rock beaches, strewn with angler's nets drying in the midday sun. The causeway sloped down to the base of the west face where the small villages of Qwen gathered on shelves of worn granite and limestone. Bridges linked the clusters of houses and buildings as walkways strung out over pools of eddying water tens of feet below. On this face of the isle were the poorer, working class people. Those more affluent, with higher social rank, lived higher on the western face. Only the most powerful families, Orr, Jaggier, and Rhinn, occupied the highest reaches. Weaving their way up the cliffs between the sheer and often jagged rocks were the villages and markets.

At the summit of the isle, located amid the estates, were the temples, forums and government buildings. On the far side of Qwen, the isle sloped gradually down to the sea. There lay the pastures and farmlands that fed the isle. There also was the main port of Qwen. That was where they would find passage, three days travel by foot.

Tom stirred a cinril stick into his hot karo and watched the cloud swirl like tsunami in the cup. Behind him, there was the murmur of voices in the open courtyard of the karo house. Cinril had a taste like cinnamon and it was the only thing that saved the taste of the bitter karo he was drinking. He looked out over the wall of the veranda and to the cobalt waters, several hundred feet below. White-capped waves mirrored the sky as a blustery wind rushed from the cotton-like clouds that touched the summit of the Great Wall, less than a league away. Nevertheless the day was beautiful, the sky a brilliant blue, the wind brisk. Gulls and rock birds darted in and out of the crevasses and crags, amid the stunted trees and foliage and out over the causeway that speared its way to Dorber.

The karo house was unique in that it sat out over a high promontory, suspended in open air and supported by timbers wedged into the rocks below. Merchants and minor nobility, all enjoying the view and sipping at mediocre drink, crowded its open balconies.

The voices of the patrons were soon lost to Tom, who looked inward rather than at the

273

panorama before him. He was changing, but whether or not it was due to the magic of this land or why he and his friends were brought to Carn he did not know. His vision was complete he noticed, as a gull swept low and plucked a silver fish from the cool water. Actually, it was more than complete. Now, when he really tried hard, he could make out the faint shimmer of an aura around the body of the person sitting at the next table. He remembered the woman in the village, her psyche torn. He had manipulated her aura to start the healing. Had he come full circle? Was he now a warrior/healer? *No, I know my limitations all too well. But what? Magic?* He was evolving into something more. This must have been the reason why Myella and Guyle had such keen interest in them. Nevertheless, how would Myella benefit from their newfound abilities?

He sipped at the karo, now tepid. Marad had gone to Upper Qwen, where the angler, peasant and commoner rarely went. Upper Qwen was where the merchants, guildsmen and families conducted their business, away from the steep inclines of the western face. Marad would take his time to gather any information he could, so not to draw any undue attention. Then, in two days, they would leave for the port. A pretty server, with skin almost as dark a brown as the karo she served, stood before him. She had strange features, slightly chiseled, her nose was long and straight, her eyes nascent like an Asian, yet her skin was the color of sepia. She smiled winningly and he nodded for her to refresh his cup. She turned to move on but paused as curiosity sparked her eye.

274

"You are not from here. You are a traveler?" She had a strangely lilting accent, but her words were clear. He smiled and nodded.

"I am a man-at-arms. The merchant I work for is in upper Qwen. He gave me the day off." It was the story he and Marad had concocted should anyone question him.

"You are at your leisure." She nodded and looked out over the water. Her smile returned. "You have not been to Qwen before? No, I thought not. May I be of assistance to you, show you Qwen?"

His eyes narrowed slightly at her request. He noticed the faint glow of a pale blue aura framing her face. Most people of this world had that blue aura. There was no taint of black-green malignancy, as did the guardsman's in Dorber, as did those who served Oran"I can leave the karo house until this evening. I can show you the gardens and where the best karo in Qwen is served. The view is not as good, but the karo is much sweeter." She ended with a whisper, a sly look on her face.

"I had not realized that Qwen women were so forward."

"Oh?!" she exclaimed, somewhat startled and her shocked expression was again replaced by that sly look. "Have I offended you?"

"Not in the least. It is quite refreshing as a matter of fact." He placed the karo cup and three copper shenk on the table and stood. He held up a silver shenk. "Dinner for us."

She ran to the back of the establishment and was soon back, sans her apron, and with hair freshly combed. She put an arm in his and was soon leading

275

him out onto the breezy walkway that spanned the jagged rocks of the western face.

Marad walked up the Pristine Way, the widely set slabs of marble steps that would bring him to the summit of the isle and to Upper Qwen. There were quite a few people on the Way this day: traveler, noble, merchant, all commingled. A cacophony of voices , only piercedby the occasional shout of a merchant greeted him as he watched wares brought up the west face by pulley and rope. A Guard of the House of Orr stood his watch at the head of the Way, and another, in blue and white, the House of Rhinn, cast a wary glance as he took his station on the opposite side of the stair. *So,* Marad thought, *the tension has become more evident in the passing years.* He threw his cloak back, being careful to keep the stolen long sword hidden by the drape of it. The sun was warm on his shoulders as he surmounted the last step and looked back down the Pristine Way toward the red tiled roofs, hidden gardens, and threads of waterfalls. This was the upper city of Qwen in which he now stood, with its teaming masses, busy with their business of the day and blissfully ignorant of the murdering Guard of Oran who lay in wait like rabid dogs on the stoop.

He became one with those who crowded the avenue, careful to cast a wary eye for any guardsman dressed in green. Chances were that the Guard of Oran had aligned itself with the family Orr. He would have to be careful, yet he doubted that any of the guardsmen would recognize him, if so it would be by name and he would not be so foolish as to use it in Qwen. Around him rose the buildings of State and the Temples of various lesser

276

gods. Upper Qwen sat in a vast bowl atop the mountainous isle. In the distance, he could see the jagged rock, topped by pines that ringed the upper city. This jagged lip of rock obscured the views to the north and south to all but the tallest towers or well-placed villas. The Pristine Way upon which he now walked eventually left the city and continued down the gently sloping pastures of the eastern side of the isle, then to the cluttered ports of Qwen.

He had been to Qwen several years ago and then only to re-supply his ship that was running from Chestra to Helm. Then, he had ignored the talk of intrigues and politics in the Free State and had listened only in passing about the dominant family Orr. Could it possibly be that by ignoring those intrigues he had placed himself in his current situation? Marad Vien Crona, once Commander of the White Guard, now a pariah, hunted...brought down by his own arrogance.

Before him, the sea of humanity was a brightly colored display of silks and jewelry. Moreover, among the dazzling colors was the floating island of black. A Guardsman of Oran, mixing casually, but ever wary of what lay about. For the moment he remained free of their scrutiny and so he made his way toward the Forum. If his memory served him well it would lay to the center of Upper Qwen. The talk would be best at the Forum, that was where many of the citizens bought and traded with the merchants and where the Families mingled under the guise of civility.

The Forum was in a large open square; mostly tents and open-air market, there were some permanent buildings and shops. During this time of

277

the year, it would be quite crowded. His last trip here had left him on the isle in the dead of winter, with rough seas, a constant overcast and the streets ankle deep in slush. Fortunately, this autumn had been much kinder to the people of Qwen.

Before him loomed the entrance to the Forum, a narrow avenue flanked by two towering statues, fifty spans tall. They were the brother and sister, Ikn and Teg, gods of the seafaring traders. One was a beautiful woman holding a sword and the other her stern faced brother with scales. At their feet was a mosaic of tile in the design of a ship. Like a tide rushing over the ship, the people thrust forward into the Forum.

The cacophony of the open market, the smells, all seemed to numb the senses in their competition for dominance. Merchants hawked wares beneath canopied stalls, while their plump wives sat in the back, polishing brass or mending a worn cloak. The throng thickened as it squeezed through the narrow aisles, sometimes coming to an abrupt stop as folks stood before a popular bench. This was the common market, and the site of daily trading and grocery shopping. Merchants and trader's plied their cargos at the guildhall, at the center of the Forum. Ultimately, that was Marad's destination.

He shouldered his way past some burly merchants, nodding his apologies when they cast him an evil eye. Always he kept one hand on the purse at his belt and the other on the pommel of his sword.

Through the throng, he would occasionally spy the gray stucco walls of the guildhall. He seemed to be getting no closer as he fought the crowd, the

278

building would disappear behind the colorful arras of silk and canvas. With some struggle, he found himself standing a stone's throw from the guildhall. It was a very utilitarian building, with narrow windows and little decoration. Meant strictly for the business of commerce, there was no gaudy waste.

Richly dressed nobles and merchants passed in and out of the wide doorway, which at the time House Rhinn oversaw. It was a good sign if Rhinn was in cycle to monitor the guild house. Rhinn was always fair and even if there were spies within the house, trade issues would be unaffected. Thus, he walked through the low portal and into the guild house, unaware of the look given him by the first guard.

Evenly spaced windows brought the late afternoon light into the hall casting motes of dust amid beams of gold. The guildhall was one large open room, its vast expanse only broken by the even spacing of tables where the merchants sat and conversed. All along the length of the hall, small islands of nobles and merchants bartered for cargos of no small value. Some chatted without commitment over cups of steaming karo. There were far too many to count and Marad could mingle amongst them with ease.

Moving through the packed hall, he would often pause to look at a ships manifest or a sample of a ware, always careful to move on before the merchant shifted his interest from another customer. Ever careful to listen for destination and ports of call, he was soon satisfied to learn of several ships bound for Chestra. In addition, even though talk of

279

Paravel was rare, he knew that passage there could be bought for the right price.

Snippets of information came and went from one noble's tongue, often gilt and full of half-truths, to light upon the ear of another. There was much talk of intrigue. He learned, to his shock and dismay of the disbanding of the White Guard and its replacement by the Guard of Oran. It was not good news; the travel to the Conclaveum had become all the more perilous. More evil news came to him, with talk of Myella becoming Conclavatrix by the Clave. Myella had more support than he thought if she had accomplished all this within the time he had been 'killed'.

He floated among these islands of gossip, being very careful not to intrude or listen too obviously. It was when he was standing unobtrusively near a window sipping his karo and reading a manifest that he listened to several nobles discuss a confiscated cargo of mail armor, when someone tapped him upon the shoulder. He looked up to see one of Rhinn's Guards smiling and gesturing with open palm toward the rear of the hall.

"Milord, can you come with me?" He had said 'milord', not the traditional 'master' that was the proper greeting for a merchant.

The others in the hall appeared not to notice as he moved to an antechamber. If he were to cause a scene here, it could prove disastrous, so he let the guardsman take his elbow and steer him through the crowd.

In the antechamber an older man, worn and weathered, sat behind a sun-bleached desk and looked at him.

280

"Sit down, Commander Marad." Surprise lit his face as he swiftly took a step back and with one fluid motion drew his sword. Immediately several of the guards surrounded him, their curved blades poised at several vital areas of his body. He carefully laid his saber upon the older man's desk and stood back with arms crossed.

"You are wanted for murder, you know, those dogs of Oran in Dorber? Ah, I see that strikes a chord. You might as well have shouted that it was you, displaying that sword as such."

The man gestured toward the basket hilt of the blade and Marad's eyes drifted down toward the intricate workmanship. He then realized what a fool he had been; a Family crest of Orr worked in silver on the guard.

"Family Orr."

"They do sometimes serve as officers for Oran," replied the older man. "Bad luck for you. Had a Jaggier, Orr, or Guardsman spotted that they would have called you out right there and then, not even having known who you are." He sat back, also folding his arms. They formed the bow wave for the stylized *felucca* embroidered on his tunic.

"But *you* recognized me," Marad countered.

"Yes, I and the lads in my employ. Do relax, or do you not know the history of Rhinn's Guard?"

"I dare say no."

"Exten Rhinn, Commander of the White Guard during the reign of Untheran, retired with his family to Qwen. His legacy is what you see here. The White Guard that he had brought as his retinue became Rhinn's Guard.

"You are safe here, Lord Marad. We do not hearken to the vipers of Oran. We will not turn you in for killing that officer; he was after all, the son of Orr's matriarch. However, I would not so brazenly display that trophy."

"I was careless."

"Yes, but also lucky. Who would suspect that Upper Qwen would be your destination? Tarn is with you. We will take you to the Family estate under cover of night, and there you will be made welcome."

"My friend-"

"Yes, the tracker. Already have I sent men."

"It is quite beautiful," he murmured as he looked out over the garden and to the sun sinking behind the cliffs across the channel. Dorber was lost in shadow.

She smiled at him and brushed back her chestnut hair. Tom was relaxed in this rock garden perched on the cliffs of Qwen. Below, the water had turned to gunmetal and the gulls, feathers molten in the fading sunlight, speared out over the water for the coast.

He sat there for a time, not moving, nor saying a word.

"I do not come here that often." She broke the silence with her strangely accented voice and for some reason this disturbed the Sioux. Pushing it aside, he smiled as he replied.

"You are a gracious host for showing me one of the loveliest spots of Qwen."

"Not so lovely if you knew its history. But, the citizens of Qwen take pride in their gardens."

"History?"

"Oh yes," she replied.

The tone of her voice caused the hair on the nape of his neck to stand on end. As the gloaming settled in around them the air seemed to still, the garden took on an almost sinister quality. *Shaj'il Cziffer* sat low on the horizon, horned and with the spear thrusting downward. Long shadows broken only by the faint moonlight chopped across the garden, so many hidden images. Slowly he turned to his host. Something was different about her. She smiled as she noticed his sudden distraction.

"Like all things Qwen, this garden is special. This was where the great patriarch of the Family Orr fought a duel and killed the aging Exten Rhinn. His blood was dedicated to Oran in this garden." She smiled and somehow it looked sickening. He refocused. Her aura had changed from the calm blue to a streaked malignant green.

"Who are you?" he hissed out between clenched teeth. His hand slid imperceptibly toward the cool hilt of his knife.

"Who or what I am is not important. I have known about the Wolf Walker since he arrived in Qwen. I knew you killed in Dorber; and I know who you are."

"You are a Hand of Keth?" He noticed that his vision brought clarity and brightness to what otherwise should have been a garden wrapped in the folds of night.

"Am I that obvious to the Outlander? I was tasked to follow you all the way from Helm; I arrived only yesterday in Qwen. You are quite engaging, but I do have to turn you over to my

283

Master...eventually. In the meantime your punishment shall be satisfactory to House Orr."

He was on his feet in a flash and making for the garden path that would take him from this evil place.

Too late, he saw the dark figures converge around him. Some distinct, some not, as if his vision were tricking him into thinking there were more assailants than there were. He would count on the many. Several wore the green of the Jaggier; one wore red and most wore the black tabard of the Guard of Oran.

The first was upon him, the man's sword going wide as he lunged inward and eviscerated the man. Another came by his side and he rolled, came up behind the man and stomp-kicked him in the side of the knee. A crunch and a scream told him he was successful. Two men came at him now, one with a halberd and the other with a short sword; not so easily dispatched as one of the men cut a gash along his left deltoid. He noticed fleetingly that as he saw the man's malignant green aura that he also saw the nexus points of energy along the man's body.

As if by instinct, he focused his own energy in an open palm strike to one of these areas just below the guardsman's solar plexus. It was not a hard strike, but he saw the energy-flow at the nexus flash and dissolve. The man screamed out in agony, twisted around in a strange display of pain and fell over the rock wall that surrounded the garden. His scream echoed as he fell the hundred or so feet to the rocks below.

The second man with the halberd was still there, but his look had changed from fierce

284

determination to one of fear after seeing his comrade die in such a way. He hesitated and Tom Smiling Wolf jumped up, grabbed the man's hand and pirouetted, snapping it quickly.

Forty or so feet to the walkway, that led from this *garden*. Shadows converged upon him. At least eight guardsmen surrounded him. Coming at once, he had no recourse but to charge the group. Suddenly there were menacing growls and darting figures low to the ground. It was the wolf and his pack, coming over the garden wall to attack the assailants. The guardsmen screamed and fell apart as the wolves struck their unprotected necks, ripping their throats. Seeing this surprise attack some fled, most died.

"Wolf Walker," he heard behind and turned. It was his host. She held her hands out in a strange manner. As he squinted to see what she was doing with them, he saw her malignant aura brighten, and surges of green energy passed from her center of mass along her arms and built up there. He suddenly realized that what he was seeing was the beginning of some kind of sorcery. Without thought, he dove to her and came up from a shoulder roll right next to her. There was shock in her eyes seeing the viciousness of his attack and when Tom would look back upon this, he too would wonder at the violence that he doled out in that brief instant. His right hand grasped the hilt of his knife and swung full around her back. The blade laid wide the musculature along the right side of her spine, and then came down in an arc of moon glow to wedge between the woman's second and third vertebrae. It silenced any hope of a scream, but somehow there was an unholy howl and green energy discharged into the night, stunning him and destroying his knife in a shower of metal splinters. The hilt hit him squarely in the forehead. As his vision blurred he looked to the pack; saw the fire dancing in the wolf's eyes. Smiling Wolf. Then oblivion took him and there was darkness once more.

286

Chapter 19

One ice-cold drop of water found its way past the fold of his hood and began a course down the crease of his back. As it crossed the curve of Mike's shoulder blade, it banished all hope of his remaining warm in the storm.

It had been two and a half weeks since leaving Paravel and his friends. These past several nights the weather had been miserable and the villages further and further apart. According to his tattered map, there was one more village before the ride through the Teeth of Narn to Narn-toc.

The sun had dipped beneath the tree line some time ago and no doubt the curve of this planet. Now it was only the occasional flash of sheet lightening that showed clearly the muddy road before him. His dappled roan snorted derisively, letting him know it would not tolerate another night like this.

Luckily, for his horse, he could make out the low walls of farmlands. The village would not be far off. Slumped over his saddle, his spear across the saddle horn and his hood allowing water to drip before his vision, he came out of the copse of trees and looked down into the secluded vale. Therein lay the stone houses, no doubt their rooms warmly lit by fireplaces, but hidden to him, only a tint of yellow through closed shutters.

"Thomas Kinkade, how nice," Mike muttered to himself as he prodded his horse. The dirt road wound its way down into the vale and the town; the last one before Narn-toc.

It seemed as though all the villages were the same. Same people, same Inns, same suspicious stares. The people who lived on this stretch of the coast between Paravel and Narn-toc did so amid forest and valley. The villages were isolated from much of what was happening farther north and in the Conclaveum, but in these days of the war in the west there were many refugees streaming into the countryside and burdening the small hamlets and villages with their needs. So far, the people of the coast were tolerant, but also wary.

Tonight was like any other night of the past week - cold and rainy. Plodding through the autumn cold his horse finally came to the town's signpost, Tamos, it read in the common tongue; just another village. In this secluded vale, in the midst of the towering trees at the edge of the Great Forest, the streets were not dirt but clearly laid cobble, now wet and strewn with the leaves of autumn. Torch posts lit the way into the town, hissing and sputtering, casting yellow light across the collecting puddles.

Clip clop went the hooves as they splashed water about his knees. He reined in the horse at the front of an Inn. He thought the hinges on the sign needed oil, as it swung noisily in the gusty wind. *Tamos Inn.* He smiled crookedly at the lack of creativity. After all, Tamos was a storybook village with its stone houses with low tile roofs, its shuttered windows and flower boxes, quaint to say the least.

He quickly swung off his horse and swaddled the spear into its sheathe. He absently patted the horse's neck as he flipped the reins about the post. Soon the steed would be in a stable...he hoped.

Steam rolled off his head and shoulders as he stepped into the warmth of the Inn's common room.

He casually shrugged out of his cloak, all the while peering into the dim, low chamber. He scowled, not being able to see much past the smoke and shadow. Dark beams crossed the ceiling and threatened his forehead. Beyond, on the far side of the common room, the hearth threw scattering shadows through chair legs and past support beams. Men and women, eating their evening fare, hunched over their bowls of stew, the light of a single candle placed on their table illuminated the whites of their eyes as they turned suspiciously toward him. It was here and in every other village and town he had passed through, all the way back to Galfeon Yor. Finally, they turned back to their own devices, their tankards, and their pipes. The murmur of conversation finally returned to normal; only now perhaps it was not the crops they discussed, but the stranger in their midst.

He moved amid the tables, careful his large frame did not disturb the patrons. Not good enough for a man and woman who cast him the evil eye, or the farmer in field clothes and a wide brimmed hat who spat as he passed. None carried a sword or any other weapon. Finally, to the bar, he scraped his head on one of the low crossbeams. *Didn't they ever consider someone of his height when they built these places? Probably not.*

At the bar, a man with eyebrows as thick as his beard nodded to him and began to polish a tankard.

And they all go to the same bartending school, he thought.

"Stranger." Was all the man said.

"A room and a meal, stable for my horse. The room must have a fireplace."

289

"Humph," the man said as he put the tankard down and wiped his hands on his apron. "Room and boarding for the horse will be four coppers, and another two for the meal, naught more, just the evening meal."

"Fine," replied Lord Michael, Alchemist, Swordsman, and Novice Sorcerer. He tossed a silver shenk onto the bar. "And some ale," he finished.

The man motioned to a table in the corner, near the hearth, and soon a boy was putting a platter of sausage, a half loaf of dark bread with cheese, and a bowl of stew before the stranger. The bartender finally brought over a tankard of the ale and turned away without comment.

He finished his meal after some time and left the common room. Up the narrow stair and to a room that was equally claustrophobic. He tossed his saddlebag onto the narrow bed and slammed the door shut behind him. This was not a bedroom, it was a steamer trunk; the fireplace was a matchbox, and the wall opposite the bed sloped inward, following the canter of the roof. If it were not for the dormer, the size of a mailbox, and the small window, he would have though he was in an old closet. He noted by the water that dripped around the sill of the window that the rain had not yet abated.

He sat on the lumpy bed and looked to the small fire that crackled in the hearth. It would have to do. The difficulty would not be in concentration; there was very little noise from the common room, and the susurration of rain on the wooden shingles offered a calm white noise. He stood and roughly shoved the bed against the door. Sitting cross-legged before the hearth he quickly, but thoroughly, drew a circle in white chalk, then another within. Between these concentric rings he scribbled runes; they were somewhere between Sanskrit and calculus. He then placed white candles in the four compass points. He relaxed and looked over his work, making sure there was no gap in his sphere. He checked to make sure that his flintlock was still in his belt, and to see if the *Book of Shadows* and the *Ih'dia Om* were within his ward. He put his hand on the *Book of Shadows* and gazed into the dancing flames.

He breathed deeply, letting his respiration slow. It was considerable what he had learned during his time in this world; sorcery was very much like complex mathematical formulae. That was not to say that math was magic, rather he could interpret it as such. Where magic was wrought by a series of incantations, the incantations were only one means by which to harness the energies of the *aether*. Math was his tool. For Michael, a former physics student, his understanding of quantum mechanics and chaos physics and his manipulation of the complex equations necessary to derive these theories, allowed him to actualize the *aether* just as if he muttered an incantation in the High Tongue of the Conclaveum. - Numbers and symbols would tumble through his mind, filling him with endless possibility. The crux was recognizing the right equation for the particular magic. The wrong derivation would lead him to an incorrect sequence and that could be devastating. He had to be specific, the more complex the magic he wanted to weave, the more difficult the calculations.

291

Luckily, a phone call to his friends in Paravel via the fireplace was not that complex at all.

As he thought the proper equation, he felt the *aether* dissolve his surroundings into the gray; he had a profound sense of floating, of being displaced. It was not transcendental, though, like the time he had journeyed to the Temple of Oran in Paravel out-of-body. Here, at what he called the edge of the *aether*, energy flitted around the shell of his ward, ready to be used. It was a profoundly powerful and lonely place to be. He felt dwarfed and insignificant by the powers that swirled about him. Still, directly before him was the hearth and the fire, but soon that slowly dissolved too, and he could make out the interior of Joe's quarters in Kelvin's Keep.

I wonder if I could step through? Came a fleeting thought, but he dismissed it for now and concentrated on the task. He could make out movement in the room.

"Hey, Shadowbutte, is that you? And is John there?"

"Same time, same channel," came the reply as if from a long distance, there was an echo. Mike supposed they did not have fiber optics in the *aether*. He saw the forms of his two compatriots, as if distorted through frosted glass. It was always this way that was why he would hesitate at trying to step through. He guessed it was some kind of dimensional film, and he could not hazard a guess what would happen to him if he tried to push through.

"Hey, dudes, how are things up the coast?"

John leaned in and spoke. "Good, we have a really nice militia going here. We have foot soldiers

292

and archers and some good commanders. Pithorn is even giving us a hand with strategy. We may be able to withstand a siege if it comes to that."

"*If* they don't use magic," replied Surik. "We have three cannons finished. We're testing tomorrow with heavy rounds. We also have our people digging trenches and placing some nice little surprises for our friends."

"What about you?" that was John.

"I'm less than a week from Narn-toc. The weather is turning nasty and the closer I get to my goal, the worse it gets. How very Tolkienesque."

"Tom hasn't returned yet and no word from Bill and Torec. I don't want to think grim thoughts, but-"

"Then don't. They're still alive."

"How do you know?"

"I know."

"Okay, but...Mike are you okay?"

There was a fluttering noise and then the sound of wings, the distant noise of thunder and then something closer. The image before him distorted and a shadow passed over the gray.

"Shit! Listen, every time I contact you I risk being tracked. I thought I could ward for it, but apparently, *they* have stronger magic, much stronger. I don't know when I'll be able to contact you again. Put out the fire! Adios!"

He broke the link and the gray *aether* swirled about him and coalesced into nothing as he phased back to the room at the Inn. The thunder was the sound of someone trying to beat the door down. He quickly stuffed his paraphernalia into his saddlebag and scrubbed out the ward with his moccasins. The pounding was getting more insistent and whatever

293

was on the other side would probably be through in a minute. He looked to the dormer; the window was too small. He grabbed his spear and watched blue energy dissipate over the shaft. *Interesting,* he thought. There must have been some bleed-over from the *aether*. If he could channel energy from the *aether* into this staff...

The door splintered inward and beyond stood a group of angry men, some with cudgels, some with old rusty swords and others with clubs and pitchforks. They crowded the hallway and shouted curses in a dialect that did not resemble the Common Tongue. He leveled his gift from Pelles at the group, energy slowly discharged over the surface of the shaft, settled on the weld mark were Pelles had forged the razor of a spearhead. It finally faded.

Silence fell over the group as they saw the sorcery on the weapon. Mike smiled at their nervousness.

"What is the meaning of this?" he whispered in the ensuing pause. Men mumbled and edged back into the hallway. Finally, the bartender, an angry look on his face, shoved through the group and aimed the point of a well-kept short sword at the big man.

"Yi know the very reason, sorcerer. Your kind is forbidden in Tamos. Yet yi ply your evil in this very room. Under MY roof!"

"I did not hurt you," Mike countered.

"Tis forbidden!" another shouted.

"Too close to the dead-city, or are ye one of the dead?!" asked the keeper in an escalating tone of voice.

294

"Aye! Are ye dead?"

"If he isn't, he will be soon!" Mike noticed that they were all getting bolder as they edged about the doorway to his room. The barkeep was doing a fair job of riling them up.

"STOP!" Mike shouted and they took a step back in unison. He slammed the heel of the spear on the floor and a spark of energy arced from the tip and caressed his hand. "Lest I call the powers of my art upon you."

"Ye cannot, else ye call the winged death upon us!" one of the men screamed and fled when his companion yelled this. They were getting very nervous and agitated now. Mike realized that by communicating with his friends, he might have drawn some unwanted attention to himself by the forces of Oran.

"Let me pass, or those very same creatures will visit you this night."

"Kill him, I say," came another.

Mike slammed the butt of the spear onto the floor and the blue energy sizzled across the surface, again settling on the weld mark. This time however there was a muffled pop, and the spearhead promptly popped off and clattered to the floor. Mike looked at it in wonderment and so did the others.

"Shit." Mike said under his breath.

"Now's the time, kill em!"

"Aye, an burn his body."

"You guys aren't going to make this easy are you?" Mike retorted, not sure what to do.

The first man, with the pitchfork lunged for him.

295

"Don't think so." Aikido, which teaches the use of the staff as well as the sword is a fluid and graceful martial exercise. Mike, being somewhat rusty at using the staff, was not very graceful.

He easily deflected the man's awkward lunge and brought the spear-shaft around in a wide arc. Unfortunately, the room was not wide enough and the tip of the magically charged shaft imbedded into the plaster wall...then blew it out; lightening arced against the shaft and thunder crashed about him. Everyone, including Mike, stared for a moment, dumfounded. The upper wall of the Inn was torn wide open from the lightening.

Did I do that? Mike wondered. He looked back toward his assailants. They were all gone, he could hear them fleeing down the narrow step. Smiling, he looked out the rent in the building and saw that the jump to the ground was not that far. He tossed his saddlebag out ahead of him, and carefully jumped to the muddy ground. Soon he was pulling his unwilling horse from the stable.

"So, I lied when I said we wouldn't spend another night in the rain." The horse whinnied. "Let's go find a hemlock grove to hide ourselves in, what do you say?" The horse almost threw him when he mounted, but he finally got her under control and was soon out of the strange village of Tamos, looking for a thick and sheltering pine to harbor them for the night.

***

Gythel Boern, Commander of the Black Guard, looked over the shades in the city of the dead: Narn-toc. His men, stationed about the wall that overlooked the Field of Blood, were nervous and jumpy from their extended tour in this forsaken city. It seemed as though only the Guard of Oran enjoyed their stay in this haunted place. He patted one of his men on the shoulder. Evening was close and soon their watch would be over, then they could go back to strained comradery as they billeted for the night. There, behind closed and barred doors, they could vent about their fears. They could not do that out here, in sight of towers that stretched like soot-darkened lace toward bleak storm clouds.

"I'm sorry, Captain, I swear I saw something down there in the field, along the road. It is not there anymore." Boern smiled at the look of confusion on the young man's face. He looked to the spot that the guard had pointed out and found nothing. Stress, stress of the watch and the stress of the city; his men were jumping at shadows.

"Not to worry, lad," he soothed. "In the shadows and growing dim, the eyes are played upon. Besides, who would cross that field while there is still light?"

The guard gave him a wan smile and turned back to his watch. Gythel Boern moved along the wall, monitoring the morale of his men. *Morale, what was that anyway?* One tends to lose their morale when their unit is about to be disbanded and that was the word coming down the line. Myella sends the guard on some wild chase to a sorcery-forsaken city, and then rumor has it that upon their return the Black Guard was to be disbanded and the men reassigned.

As the Conclave orders so goes the Guard. That was the old phrase. He supposed that Myella was now the Conclave and her will was his order. He shook his head. The Black Guard of the Wall had a noble and distinguished past. A past that only recently had been tarnished by forays and missions that were more the beck and whim of Myella and not the dictate of the Conclave. He sighed and watched as a courier beast swept down from the Teeth of Narn. *No doubt with more orders and more disturbing news from the North.*

He looked over his men. The chill of the autumn evening was settling in his bones. He was a man of late middle years and had risen to the rank of Commander through his skill and bravery. Most of his duties were administrative now, but he still knew the sword. He touched the basket hilt of his saber absently.

Now something foul was afoot. He would not openly say, especially with the knowledge that some of his own men were servants of Oran, but Myella was doing things that threatened the Conclaveum. He had almost reeled with shock when he had learned that Marad, Commander of all the White Guard had been killed and that Guard was being broken apart. Soon all that would remain would be their memory. Two Guards of a once noble purpose brought down by the Conclavatrix Myella. Would the Krim sweep down from the North? Alternatively, would the Guard of Oran, now having officially taken over the duties of the White be able to fend off any advance? He did not know. Myella flirted with disaster.

298

The courier beast swept low over the wall, he could see several of his men crouch low as the draft brought their cloaks swirling up. Soon the wind would race off the sea like that. He would not have the comfort of plush quarters in the Commanders Keep at Helm. He would have the haunted halls of the Dead-City.

The black serpentine courier beast, its leathern wings beating laboriously, billowing with powerful gusts and its eyes turning to him with a baleful yellow glow, soon was lost within the vine covered minarets and towers of Narn-toc. Even in the late afternoon overcast, the scales that covered the creature scintillated with a rainbow of colors. The creature and its rider sped on toward the quarter where the Guard of Oran was stationed, effectively ignoring him and his rank. His was becoming an honorary duty; he was becoming a relic of the past.

What was the Guard of Oran up to in Narn-toc? This had been an accursed place for ages, abandoned to all but the most foolish of looters. To be caught here after nightfall...a shudder passed down his back; several of his patrols had already disappeared because they were late in returning from their watch. The Captain of the Guard of Oran had just shrugged and advised Boern that his discipline should be tighter, or more of his men would be lost. Then the Captain had turned back to Boern to speak with another man. Man or thing? Hand of Keth would be the appropriate title he had supposed. He had arrived the night before, by courier beast. He had spoken to the Captain of the Guard of Oran in a hushed voice. Nevertheless, he was a Hand. Boern had recognized the black-fringed tabard over black mail and the telltale pale white palm facing outward embroidered upon it.

What they were looking for was beyond him. They had secreted themselves into the quarter of the Old Seat, while his guards billeted in Ythrinny's Keep, home of the founder of the Black Guard of the Wall. At least there, the shades that had haunted the rest of the city left them in peace, no doubt because of the wards that Ythrinny had placed hundreds of years ago before he fled to the north. Gythel Boern had argued for a defensible and practical billet and had picked Ythrinny's Keep, arguing that they could keep the Field of Blood and the approach from the Teeth of Narn under scrutiny.

Therefore, it was that he left the Guard of Oran up to their own devices and they left him to his duties. Now as he strode above the shield shaped Gate of Untheran, he was uneasy by the thought of what would become of him and his men when they outgrew their usefulness. Brought out of his reverie by the sounding of an iron bell, he saw his men begin to put their gear together; the day watch was over. He saw in them the face of relief. They would have an hour until it was dark, the sun only setting now. *Time enough to get to the Keep. Time enough to be sequestered behind the safety of those walls.*

May Tarn guide us, he thought as he made his way toward the tower and the streets. He wondered if Tarn would hear his prayer from this evil begotten place.

Adon looked to Mrick, and he to Barj, and so on down the line of men who hid in the shadow of the wall that wrapped around the city of Narn-toc, a seamless and smooth wall that rose forty feet to the summit. It was doubtful that they could scale it. Occasionally a man bearing a torch would pace along the parapet and call the watch.

Barj and Mrick had been reluctant with Adon's decision to venture across the so-called Field of Blood during the daylight hours. Much of the basin to the west of the Dead City was littered with the same shale and polished stone that graced the beaches around the Teeth of Narn. Indeed, this basin had been at one time covered with water, but the engineers of the Conclaveum had erected simple dikes to the north and the south. Narn-toc, one time situated on an island only reachable by causeway, now sat on an artificial peninsula that bridged the gap from Narn-toc to the Teeth. A causeway, several spans high, ran from the southern roadway to the Gate of Untheran. The engineers, prudent of the defensive needs of the city, created a series of towers and gates along the dike. If someone were ever foolish enough to attack the city, the gates would be opened and the waters of the sea could rush in to flood them, effectively immobilizing any army that would lay siege. The causeway would then remain above the water, giving very little room for the attacker to maneuver and leaving them vulnerable to attack.

Barj stumbled along the slippery shale, noticing an occasional petrified beam of wood; the wall was a dark smear before them. Adon moved cautiously ahead, almost lost in the drizzle. In the distance, they could hear the pounding of the surf against the dike.

"Adon," Barj began, his tone hushed. "Why do they call it the Field of Blood? Was there a battle here?"

Adon looked over his shoulder and then forward again, careful of where he stepped. "No battle, friend Barj. In the final days of Untheran's reign, he crucified most of the remaining members of the Clave. Friend or no, Iss counseled that no one be trusted. It is said that before the Daemon fell upon Untheran there were four thousand crosses in the Field."

"I am sorry I asked-"

"No. Do not be sorry, for it is a lesson worth remembering. Myella seeks similar counsel from Guyle. I fear that she too would repeat the mistakes that her predecessor had made."

Barj nodded and carefully moved over the loose wet stones. He was now careful to avoid the pieces of petrified wood.

In the half-light that exists just before the dark of night the troupe made their way along the city wall, south of the Gate of Untheran. The mist of rain and fog deepened the murk, making them naught more than shadows the men who carried sputtering torches along the summit of the wall.

"Do we know where we are going?" Kael asked of no one in particular.

"My father told me, years after his ingress to the Dead City, that the Gate of Untheran had been sealed. He and his men used a portal south of the gate, just outside the dike."

"*Outside* the dike!" Kael's voice though a harsh whisper caused everyone to pause in alarm, fearing they would be found out. "Yet, you take us into this field, right to the wall?" He looked around, wide-eyed, his stringy hair plastered across his brow. "Why did we not follow the dike?"

"Are you that much of a fool?" came Mrick's answer. "Walk atop the dike and we expose ourselves and picking our way among the boulders at its base would take more hours than we have. It would be fine to let their guard pick us off with a long bow, eh?"

"Everything is a lesson, Kael," remarked Adon dryly.

Darkness finally closed in around them as they came to the junction of the city wall and the dike. Above, for the second time that evening, came the tolling of an iron bell and the settling in of the new watch.

As if the tumble of rocks that made up the dike were not treacherous enough, they also had to pass a defense where the wall joined the dike. Twisting from the wall and the jumble of rocks were steel spikes of varying length and thickness. They would have effectively prevented a fast attack over the dike, but after two centuries of neglect, most were rusted, dull and blunted. However, in the dark, with only faint moon glow to guide their way the troupe was required to move with care among the rocks. To compound their crossing, waves now crashed up over the dike, drenching them and making for slippery footing.

Adon paused at the summit of the dike, against the cold city wall. Soon Mrick and Barj joined him to look along the city wall and the sea. The rocks fell away to the churning surf; whitecaps flecked the water among the Teeth of Narn, somehow reminding Mrick of a rabid dog's fangs. On the Rim of the World, a storm brewed; high thunderheads sat in a ghostly white moonlight.

Immediately before them, along the slight curve of the city wall, sat a ledge, just out of the water, running the curve of the set stone. About a span wide, waves would splash up onto it, depositing salty brine and an occasional fish, which would flop about until it found its way back to the deep.

"Here we must be careful," Adon cautioned. "Though we are out of sight of the guards, the ledge will be slippery with the sea grass and water. Be careful that you are not pulled in and be wary of other...things."

"Other things?" Barj asked.

"Night has fallen, but do not fear, I have warded us against the powers of Oran. Tarn will guide us." Barj watched him skeptically as he descended the rocks to the ledge. Mrick motioned his men in behind and soon followed.

It seemed to Barj that hours passed, most of the time spent avoiding slips into the surf. He noticed that Adon's footing was sure and never faltered, but he almost slid into the waters twice and he heard Kael cry out once, followed by a loud splash. When he looked back, he noticed two of the men pulling Kael out of the water, wet from the neck down.

Eventually they moved enough around the curvature of the wall that they lost sight of the Field of Blood. Adon finally paused in the long walk and bent over, motioning Mrick and Barj to come forward. Here along the ledge was a shallow gutter filled with moss. Set into the wall was a circular grate about waist high.

"We can gain entrance to the city here," Adon said as he looked to each man. "However, once we remove the grate we wait until morning."

"Morning!" Kael hissed as he stomped his feet. There was the hint of a shiver in his voice.

"Oh, shut your mouth!" that from one of the men that had pulled him out of the water.

"Enough!" and Mrick's bark subdued them all. Adon had already set to work upon the grate. The metal was not mortared in the stone, rather it was set into the stone by a heavy hinge and locked with a device that Mrick had never seen the like of. "There is no keyhole," he echoed.

"No, friend Mrick, it is a sorcerous thing." Adon manipulated the strange device; he worked mostly by touch, for the only light was that of the stars and waning *Shaj'il Cziffer*. Finally, there came a click and the grate swiveled out. To Mrick, a strange cold draft seemed to issue forth; he shivered and stepped back against the wall. The ledge remained dry for the sea had calmed, so he slumped to his haunches, as did the rest of the men, and pulled his cloak about himself.

Morning came slowly, with a thin slice of salmon against the steely clouds, perceived only in the east between the Teeth. Mrick came over to where Adon sat, legs drawn up and forehead resting on his knee. The nobleman suddenly looked up and Mrick saw a dangerous thing in his hawkish green eyes.

"The sun rises," whispered Mrick. Adon nodded and stood, carefully stretching the aches of the chilly night from his body. He addressed the men.

"Now we go into the city. I seek a book and that is all. Do not be fooled by the fact that because men guard these walls they are the only things for which you must worry.

"Mrick has told you to hearken to my every word and this you must do. Always stay with the group. If you see a coin or bauble leave it where it lies, do not let it tempt you. Listen not to the rumors of a hoard of gold. Listen instead to what I tell you. If you stray from what I say, you risk death, or worse."

All of the men looked to him with somber and in some cases, frightened expressions. He nodded and continued.

"This is a sewer tunnel. It should bring us up into the street or the buildings on the other side of the wall. This quarter of the city is the Old Seat, where Untheran ruled. The book I seek was thought to be in Old Seat. However, I believe that it was moved. It will take time to get there and we may have to stay the night, but do not fear for if that is the case I shall find us safe haven for the night.

"Now, follow me and stay close. Remember what I have said." He bent low and entered the tunnel, a faint blue glow illuminating the area just ahead of him. Mrick accepted the magic with his usual stoic calm and Barj with open wonder. This nobleman was a strange fellow indeed.

Mrick expected the usual stench that comes from entering a sewer, but there was none. The walls were worn smooth and there was a carpet of moss on the outer edge of the tunnel, but within there was only the wisp of a cool draft, nothing more.

It was not long before Adon stopped. What room there was allowed Mrick to gaze over Adon's shoulder, and he saw that another grate blocked the tunnel; this one bore strange designs. The device at the center was made of flat strips of woven metal and formed a contorted face with horns and fangs. Mrick watched as Adon held his hand a fraction from it and an angry red energy tangled across the device.

"I had thought that my father would have disabled this ward, but I am mistaken." He looked at Mrick. "I must think a moment."

"What is it?" called Barj from the rear.

"Another grate," Mrick called back. He did not want to alarm his men with mention of the sorcerous device.

"Father must have set the ward aside. So that it could be replaced when he left, yes? But how?" He squatted down, his head brushing the ceiling, his hands tracing just inches afore the grate. As he did so, the red energy spread over the surface of the wrought face.

"Ah, it must be done in such a way so that when we pass it will be as if we were never here." Mrick watched as he took a small green stone, flecked with red, from his pouch. He placed it carefully in the mouth of the face on the grate and then closed his eyes. It seemed that the air between Adon and the grate shimmered, like that of a hot day. Suddenly Adon reached over and pulled the grate open. Other than squeaky hinges, all seemed normal.

"What did you do?" Mrick asked, for the angry face was now dull and lusterless.

307

"I occupied *its* thoughts for a time."

"Its?"

"Yes. Come on." Soon they had all passed to the other side of the grate, Adon having to flatten himself against the wall so the others could pass by. It was odd, but as Mrick looked back, he saw the same iron face graced this side of the grate also and when Adon closed the grate he plucked the very same stone from the mouth on this side; a shimmer and angry red sparks followed.

They continued. The tunnels beneath Narn-toc were strangely designed. Low enough for an upright walk to be impossible and just narrow enough to make a crawl tedious and tiring. It seemed as though they had been in the tunnel for hours when it split into a vertical shaft. Adon decided it was here that they would climb.

The climb was hard, but hand and footholds were found in the crumbling courses of brick. At the top was a cistern cover that they quickly removed. They found themselves coming up in a dingy little room, the late afternoon light filtering between bars on what soon became apparent was a cellar window. They were in the basement of some building. Once Barj and Mrick had helped the other men up the shaft they replaced the cover and stood before Adon.

"We have been longer in the tunnel that I anticipated. Mrick and I will check this building and the street. I ask you to rest and eat; we will spend the night here. Be patient, for on the morrow we must move swiftly."

Some of the men just turned and set about preparing their bedrolls. Others, full of nervous energy, grumbled and moved about restlessly and as Adon and Mrick climbed the stone steps out of the cellar, they could hear the soothing words of Barj trying to calm them.

The house they were in had stood the test of time well. Five hundred years of inclement weather and looting had done little to the structure itself. Wooden window frames were rotted and shutters fallen away to let the late evening sun drift through to illuminate motes of dust, but the stone courses were true. Outside was a courtyard, now overgrown with ivy and weed that must nearly cover this building and the ones that sat beside it, even a huge oak almost blocked the door jam, having grown since the last foot stepped over the threshold.

Some artifacts remained. There were cracked vases amid the mulch piles and detritus on the floor that may have at one time been a table or hutch. The plaster that once covered the wall had long since crumbled to dust, but the floorboards were true even though they creaked loudly.

"I cannot believe that the floor has not given way, nor the walls fallen in," remarked Mrick as he stepped over debris and unconsciously loosened *Baxel's Bane* in its scabbard.

"Powerful sorcery was wrought here, Mrick. If you were versed in such you could still feel it." He shivered at what he said. "The magic has preserved the city and has prevented it from being engulfed by the sea many years ago; like the bones left from a carcass." He stepped to the door and looked through the rusty leaves of the oak as they danced on a whirlwind, golden light spearing through. He touched the bough as he stepped into the courtyard, the road obscured by the overgrowth. His feet crunched through leaves as he stepped into the courtyard.

Mrick watched as he stopped and lifted his head, almost as if to sniff the air. His nostrils flared and his green eyes darted toward the street and the ensuing gloom.

"Night comes. I must ward this place quickly." He turned to Mrick and tossed the man a piece of chalk. "You know the signs of the seasons?" Mrick nodded his affirmative. "Draw them on the gate post there, winter at top, then to spring, summer and fall. Be quick now."

He went to do so and as he crossed the courtyard, the shadows deepened and the wind picked up, the leaves and twigs spun on the wind, flashing toward his eyes. A low moaning filled the streets and wind rushed through the eaves.

"What is it?" Mrick yelled out as he began to chalk in the patterns of the seasons on the gatepost. When Adon did not answer, he looked over his shoulder to see the man, straight long sword drawn and thrust into the ground, shoulders hunched and wind whipping his hair about his head frenetically. A strange ephemeral blue glow danced over the blade and spread out into the ground. As Mrick finished he could see Adon muttering a low, strange verse in a tongue he had never heard before. When it seemed that the wind would pull him away Adon stopped, looked up and quickly sheathed his sword. The wind ceased, as if it had not blown at all, and the leaves drifted to the earth.

Mrick looked to Adon; that same question in his gaze.

"What was it? Keth or worse, friend Mrick, or worse, but our ward will hold this night. Come, for tomorrow we must be prepared to move swiftly."

The next day they awoke with the dawn and were moving through the streets of the dead city as fast as caution would allow. It was obvious to the group that this quarter of the city had been where the wealthier residents resided. Huge old mansions lined the streets, barely discernable through the overgrowth. Occasionally a small keep or tower marked just how old this part of the city was. They passed through quickly, not wanting to allow those in the party to be tempted to explore for riches.

The cobbles were slick with rain this day and the trees grew more bare with each passing hour. It was past noon when they came to a low wall and a small bridge spanning what at one time had been a wide channel. Once this had been a river but now it was nothing more than an overgrown ditch spanned by half a stone bridge. Trees lined the channel and shaded the area.

"At least we shall have cover," Mrick noted.

"Aye," echoed Barj. "To think, this would have been such a grand city in its day."

"Teshwa is much like Narn-toc was," Adon replied as he looked for a good way to get across. The two men-at-arms looked at him as if he had spoken ill.

"Well, I *was* raised there. I only spent the last ten years of my life in Tarn Hold." This did not ease the men, but he just smiled and lowered himself along the ridge. Soon he was jumping from rock to rock through the scrub and making his way up the other bank. Mrick and his men followed, somewhat skeptical of the noble.

He laughed as he saw the look on Barj's face and offered him his hand to pull him up. "We of the Conclaveum are not demons friend Mrick. Many are normal hardworking folk like you. Sometimes forces dictate we take sides." He smiled sadly as if remembering something, then motioned them to follow. Soon they were moving down an old cobble road, thick with weeds and small trees.

"How much farther?" Barj asked as he kept a wary eye out.

"We just crossed from the Old Seat to the Common quarter. Ythrinny's Keep is not far. I do not expect any Guard of Oran in this quarter. I believe they will be concentrating their efforts in the Old Seat. I do-"

He stopped he rounded a bend in the park and walked right into a patrol. Instantly, twenty guardsmen surrounded them. Caught so unaware they did not even have time to draw their weapons.

"You were saying?" Mrick asked. It had begun to rain.

"It is not here!" she shrieked as she tore a moldy arras from a rail. Gythel Boern frowned and looked away as the two Hands' stared on impassively. They stood in the rotunda of the Old Seat. Myella had come in several days ago and had sent for the Captain of the Black Guard to come to Untheran's palace in the Old Seat. According to the mutterings of one of the Guard of Oran she had been searching for something for two days, tearing through Untheran's private places; her two Hand's constantly at her side.

312

"I do not understand, your Highness," he said it after a moment. Her black eyes burned into his. He could tell she was shaking even beneath the mantle of her robe and armor; she seethed in rage.

"Of course you don't. Tell me, have any of your men been to this Seat?"

He looked around the rotunda; stones black with age, the frescos long ago covered with mildew or soot, pillars cracked and covered with vines. Even the floor was covered with the rubble of the ages. Above, water dripped through the rent in the capital of the rotunda. Myth had it that it was here that the Daemon descended upon Untheran.

"My men guard the walls and patrol the streets of the Common and Merchant Quarter by day, nothing more."

She looked at him, still her chest heaving with the rage she felt. "It is a little thing, Boern, that I want, a book, nothing more. But it is not where it is supposed to be."

"Your Highness, surely over time this book would have been destroyed by the elements."

"If it were a normal book yes. This book, however, was protected." She stepped down off the raised dais that ran the perimeter of the rotunda and came up to him.

"My men of the Guard will search this city and leave not a stone unturned in the search. Your presence here is no longer required. You may quit the city at your leisure."

He almost smiled to himself, but thought better. Instead, he saluted smartly and turned on his heel. Just outside his guard waited with his mount.

"Baed is nice this time of year Commander. I hear you have an estate there; for your retirement?"

He snapped around.

"You have no choice. The Black Guard of the Wall is being disbanded. You will be well compensated."

Stricken he stumbled down the steps of the Rotunda. Concerned, his lieutenant hesitated at giving him the reins. "Commander?"

Ashen faced, Gythel Boern mounted his steed. "Come, we quit the city."

A lone rider crested the Teeth and looked down over rocky peninsula and the sea beyond. The sun, hidden by a girdle of steely clouds, managed to cast the remainder of the sky and sea in a wash of lavender. He recognized this place from his vision of the Daemon.

A place of dread: Narn-toc.

He smiled, for it had been a long journey. Grey eyes almost hidden by his cloak's hood were weary, but glad. He leveled his spear across the saddle horn and kicked the horse in the flanks. He had begun his long descent into the Dead City.

Chapter 20

The black warhorse reared as the rider guided it through the crowded street. He did it expertly, as though he had ridden a horse for years. In the pale moonlight its eyes flashed, yet the armor it wore on the curve of its neck and on its shod hooves were dull black, and so they were as pitch.

The crowd of people jerked back in shock as the rider galloped down the street. Some thought the Hands of Keth were in the streets, others, Myella's personal guard. Then they recognized the ornately wrought dragon helm that curved around flashing gray eyes. Surik Shadowlord jumped the horse over a small fruit cart and nearly trampled a prostitute. He reined his horse before a rough looking establishment, leapt from the snorting mount and strode purposefully to the young man who stood near the door; whose hand was on the hilt of his rapier, and who looked somewhat dismayed. Polwin nodded to the Shadowlord and motioned over his shoulder.

"He's in there, but they won't let me in." Joe frowned and removed his helm, giving it to the young lieutenant. He looked at the very large man who stood at the door. He was fatter than most, but had an intimidating eye and fierce expression. With a quick kick to the man's groin, Joe was past him and through the door of the Kifu Bar. It was one of many smoking dens in the poor quarter of the city, frequented by those needing the stupor of the drug to escape from the reality of this world.

Another bouncer stood in his way as he made a move to the curtain at the rear of the common room.

Naked girls, lounging amid the languid forms of addicted patrons watched in anticipation of a fight.

Joe looked back over his shoulder to see Polwin drawing his rapier and motioning for the owner to stay put. The Shadowlord then turned back to the bouncer and quickly smashed his mailed fist into the man's face. He fell in a heap, his features now a bloody ruined pulp. The patrons and Kifu girls looked on.

"Back there?" asked Joe tersely of Polwin; the lieutenant nodded. He pulled aside the curtain and beheld Gaj, Polwin's brother, lying on his back. The young man was stripped to the waist, covered with sweat, and had a pipe stem dangling from his mouth. His eyes were hooded, covering a glaze. He looked past Joe, not seeing him at all. Had Joe expected some shocked reaction, he did not get it. The young man passed a hand through his jet-black hair and drooled into his van dyke-like beard.

A girl tried to intercede and Joe shoved her roughly aside. He grabbed Gaj by the arm and pulled him to his feet. When the master of the house tried to stop him, Joe's dirk was out and at the man's throat.

"I have no patience for you." It was all he said, but the man paled and scurried away. Joe motioned for Polwin to take his brothers other arm and they led him from the establishment.

Polwin was fair and lean, and with a bright eye and incredible talent with a sword. Gaj seemed his antithesis, dark haired and verging on swarthy, not quite his brother's equal with a blade, but good enough.

"What brought him here?"

316

"Escape, he was closest to father and took his death most hard." Joe nodded and stepped from the wooden porch of the establishment. He looked around and saw a watering trough for horses and with one smooth motion, he tossed Gaj into the icy water.

He stayed under a moment and Polwin moved to help him. Surik Shadowlord just held him back. "Not yet."

Suddenly Gaj came up sputtering and coughing, his arms and legs flailing about as if the water were more than a foot deep.

"Take him to the keep. Sober him up and when he's alert bring him to me." Polwin nodded and the Shadowlord pulled himself upon the war steed. The young lieutenant just shook his head as he looked at his brother, and then lifted him to his feet.

"Brother, you test the boundaries."

***

Day broke by the time Joe found himself at the West Gate of the city. He tethered his horse at the guard gate of the barbican and mounted the rampart to the cannon towers that stood on each side of the gate. The heavy cannons were now in place, mounted after a harrowing day of hoisting upon a complex pulley system. A signalman was there already, looking out over the fields where the Legion practiced.

Rcos drilled the men and women for most of the day. Their ranks had swelled with an unexpected rise in the refugee population and now the defenses of the city neared ten thousand; ten thousand very green soldiers, almost three legions. Reos had his sergeants training the troops for the balance of the morning, but now they marshaled for the day

Several companies practiced with various weapons; some with sword, some with poleaxe, and others with spears. Only a small company practiced upon horseback and they all wore the white and blue of the City Guard. The remainder on the field wore the uniform grey of the Legion of the Black Skull.

Joe watched as John spurred a dappled mare and charged up one rank of recruits and then down past another. Large numbers of men marched in orderly columns and others made mock charges at their opponents.

"We are fortunate more refugees came," the signalman said as he prepared the red flag.

"Humph." It was Joe's only reply. The flagman waved it and his counterpart on the field issued an order to Reos. Soon the men were moving back to the wall from the first redoubt and negotiated trenches lined with fire-hardened stakes. John waved as he galloped through the barbican and into the bailey.

The tests were to begin.

After what seemed forever most of the men were within the wall. He knew that John would be mounting the rampart to join him. He stuffed some cotton in his ears and gave the order to Hjil and the other women who commanded the cannonade.

She smiled and dropped the brand to the primer cord, then leapt down behind a stone abutment.

BOOM! The report was loud enough to set John's ears ringing even though his hands were over

318

them. Several hundred yards in the distance, a clump of dirt and smoke erupted into the air. Once the smoke cleared, they could make out a crater about fifteen feet across and five deep. A cheer went up among those stationed upon the wall.

BOOM! The second cannon fired around the city as the flagmen signaled.

"I guess they work," remarked John as Joe surveyed the damage with a spyglass. Joe said nothing. "Alaric should be happy," John prodded.

"He'd be happier if we left the city," Joe replied. "He would throw the gates wide for Myella rather than suffer through the council's martial law. Chair Nathal is giving him nightmares."

"That he is." They both turned as Lord Kelvin joined them upon the battlements. The man smiled a greeting as he removed his gauntlets and placed them on the crenellation.

"Congratulation is in order milords. It seems your weapons work.

"Pithorn reports that the testing of the harbor cannonade was flawless. The projectiles flew far beyond the break wall and will discourage any ship from entering the harbor proper."

"That's good news. My biggest fear was an attack through the harbor." John looked to Joe for comment but the man just shook his head.

"It's all academic. We may prevent a landing, but they'll just blockade. We may kill several thousand of Duran's army, but he has close to twenty thousand marching and since Tom hasn't returned we don't know if any sally forth from the Great Wall. The cannon will keep them at bay for a time, but if he brings in sorcery..." Joe trailed off.

"He will learn the range of the cannon. Then the siege will begin. He will be here much sooner than we expected. At least the fall harvest will be in," Kelvin commented as he looked out to the farmer's fields in the distance.

"There are a few surprises that we have for him," John said grimly. "Maybe we'll be able to draw him in and then let loose with the cannon. It would be nice if we could demoralize and route them."

"I fought beside the Guard of Oran. I was a young lieutenant, stationed with the Black Guard. They do not demoralize easily. The best swordsmen and mercenaries tend to come out of Chez; I've seen scores of the Guard of Oran fall before them, and still they fought, often until the last man."

"Why is it there is no Guard of Tarn?" John asked.

"There is; Tarn was always favored by the White Guard. Exten Rhinn, the most famous Commander of the White, felt that their Patron should be Tarn and so it has been for five hundred years."

"My problem is this," Joe interrupted. "What happens if Duran breaches the wall? What happens to the refugees and the citizens of Paravel?"

"Remember Shadowlord that Duran has been driving people east to Paravel throughout his conquest. His army has destroyed their homes and villages, burned their crops, and slaughtered their livestock to keep the army's belly full. These people came to Paravel seeking refuge behind these walls. They hope and pray we will hold Duran's army at bay. Here they will stand or die.

320

"Ultimately, though, Duran will realize that Paravel is the largest center of civilization south of the Great Wall. He would not raze Paravel. He will kill many if he succeeds, but life will go on."

"It's not very comforting," John replied as the silver haired Keeper of the City fell quiet.

"No, but I always expect the worst, that way I will be pleasantly surprised should things end otherwise."

Joe smiled sardonically and turned from the field to Kelvin. "Any words of wisdom from the former Preceptor of Helm?"

Kelvin laughed and appraised the two younger men. "When I was Preceptor there was peace. We dealt with occasional bandits near Tarn Hold, put down a revolt in the Barony of Karsh. Remember, I had the might and right of the Conclaveum at my back.

"You, my young friends, have the might of it against you; worse, a power hungry Regent and a demented Conclavatrix. You have your work cut out for you. Nevertheless, you have done well so far. Stay the course it will serve you best.

"Now, I must be off. I need to meet with the city council. Pithorn needs another warehouse." They nodded as he turned away. No longer did the distant report of cannon-fire fill the morning; Hjil and her crews were cleaning the barrels.

"And then there's the apathy and disillusionment of our troops," Joe muttered.

"What are you talking about?" John was somewhat taken aback by Joe's remark. The Shadowlord gestured down toward the catwalk;

Polwin and Gaj were walking their way. Gaj looked haggard and drawn.

"Polwin and I dragged Gaj out of a Kifu bar last night."

"A Kifu bar? Why?"

"I don't know why, but sometimes I wonder why not. It's a lot like opium, I guess. Polwin said he was very close to his dad."

"What are you going to do?"

"Wing it."

The two young lieutenants walked up to them. Polwin, face swept with apprehension, shoved his brother before the Shadowlord.

"Yes, one moment." He turned toward John and winked, then drew his sword and held it before Gaj, hilt first. Gaj looked at the pommel.

"My lord?" he asked in a whisper. His voice was hoarse and raspy.

"Take it."

"My lord?"

"Take it." Joe shoved it toward him but he refused to take the pommel.

"You might as well. Just take it and run me through."

"What?" Both Gaj and Polwin were incredulous.

"Look, if you're going to use Kifu and then try to defend this city, you might as run me through now. It will save time." There was a slight twist to his lips and it was not from humor.

"Milord mocks me," replied Gaj, his eyes downcast, sullen.

"Mock you?" Joe shouted as he slammed his sword into its scabbard. "You mock them!" He grabbed Gaj by the shoulder and spun him around to look out over the rooftops of the city. People milled throughout the streets below.

"I valued and trusted you as a lieutenant. Reos assured me that your skills were more than adequate. You mock *him!*

"I find you in a Kifu bar whacked out of your mind. What if we had been attacked last night, or set upon by a Hand of Keth? What if that girl had been an agent of the Conclaveum?"

"I-" He stammered but Joe silenced him with a chopping motion of his hand.

"Enough, there is no excuse. Reos said that you were ready. He was wrong." Joe turned to John and under his breath, just loud enough for Gaj to hear he said, "I'll have his head."

"My lord, no! It was not his fault it was mine. I sought to lose my misery with the smoke. I was wrong; do not punish him for my mistake."

"Should I spare him?" Joe theatrically looked over his shoulder to John. The white knight shrugged.

"Then what shall Gaj's punishment be?" asked John.

"Condemned to serve me as a shadow for all eternity?" He motioned to draw his sword and Gaj paled. They had all heard the rumors that Surik Shadowlord was a necromancer and a stealer of souls. Joe had started those very rumors. "No, I think that too harsh.

"You are, as of this moment, on probation. You shall report to Reos and begin digging trenches. When he feels you are fit to return to duty he will let me know.

"If I learn that you have returned to that or any other Kifu bar, I will personally condemn you to eternity as a wraith."

Gaj nodded and Polwin pulled him away;after they were away a look of satisfaction crossed Joe's face.

"Pop psychology," John remarked dryly.

"It worked, didn't it?"

"We'll see.

***

That evening found John standing in the inner bailey of Kelvin's Keep. His daily routine had not changed much and this hour usually found him here practicing his forms for several hours. Only tonight was somewhat different, for he had a pupil. A pupil who he was beginning to doubt needed any training at all.

The wooden sword lashed out and almost struck John in the temple. He dodged back and brought his sword to bear. He parried the next move, slid out of the ichi-mongii position and brought the sword around in a deadly arc. His opponent danced back gracefully and countered with something that resembled a riposte, striking him between his ribs.

"Easy!" he gasped and dropped to the flags of the courtyard. He tried to catch his breath. He looked up and shook his head. "You're toying with me." Gabrielle smiled ruefully back at him, and brushed some of her curly locks from her eyes.

"Was that good?"

"Good? It was great. Tell me the truth, Lord Trevor taught his daughter a bit about the sword?"

"A bit."

"I knew it. You suckered me." He moved to engage her once more, this time stepping up his attack. It was difficult for her to read his offense, kenjutsu was totally foreign to this land and he supposed that was what had given him an advantage in most instances. Yet, Gabrielle held her own and more. Being of noble birth had its advantages when it came to the best teachers. She lunged with her practice sword and almost took out his liver. He slapped the wooden blade aside and countered with a slash meant to cut the deltoid of an opponent. Gabrielle did the unexpected by dropping her shoulder and her guard, coming up with the point of her sword under his sternum. He fell back from the blow.

"Are you alright?" she asked with sudden concern. He smiled and finally laughed.

"Again, you have me at the disadvantage." She nodded with a grin.

"More?" she asked, daring him to fight her.

"Rest," he stated and crossed to the water barrel. He ladled out some water and offered it to her. As she stood next to him sipping from the ladle, he could feel the heat radiating off her body. She brushed him as she turned away.

He wiped his brow with a towel and sat down on the bench. He had found scant time to practice technique with Gabrielle, but it was becoming more apparent that she was familiar with the use of the sword. It would definitely come in handy, what with scouts telling them that Duran's army was

325

approaching the pass north of the Great Forest. It looked like his army was less than seven weeks away.

Leaning his head back against the cool stone of the wall, he gave the woman he had sworn to protect a long look. Here there was more than met the eye. In the past year, he had not realized that beneath the calm beauty of this young woman there was a reserve of steel. Tempered in the conflict brought on by her cousin Myella, she now stood before him a strong and skilled woman. She constantly amazed him.

"What?" she asked at his long stare at her.

"Hmmm." Caught by the moment he responded frankly. "You are the most incredible person that I have met. And the most beautiful."

She blushed and looked away.

"Who taught you to use a sword? Your father?"

"Baxel," she said and a smile lit upon her face as she remembered the captain of her father's men-at-arms. "As good a swordsman as any. He urged my father to let me learn the art. He said it was unsafe for the girl of a frontier noble not to learn to defend herself. Finally, my father acquiesced. Baxel taught me everything he knew."

He nodded and looked around. Usually the bailey was busy at this time of the night, what with his militia training there. This night however, Reos had the troops camped in the fields about the city; he was having the men dig trenches of varying depth and length outside the city wall. The old soldier had a few tricks left up his sleeve.

She sat down next to him.

"Your father would shudder to see you wear that."

"The tailor said my buckskins were quite unique. I fear that I've started a scandal."

"So Javin Skettes has told me."

She looked up sharply at the mention of that name. Obviously, John was hinting at her quest for information about her father.

"Javin tells me that you were inquiring of a Master Talbot, about your father?"

She looked off. A sigh escaped her lips and then she smoothed her tunic with her hands, more a nervous habit than necessary.

"Gabrielle," John almost whispered as he turned her to him. "Believe me, I know how you feel. I left my family behind. I miss them. At the very least, we know where your father is. I swear to you that we will do our best to free him from Guyle's tower. It is just that we have an obligation to this city, to its people. We cannot leave until our business here is finished."

"I know. It is frustrating being unable to do anything about it."

He took her hand in his and instinctively she tried to pull away.

"What is wrong?"

Now, no longer the fencer, but the young woman, she bit her lower lip and looked at him out of the corner of her eye. "I fear the coming siege. I fear losing you." His heart took a stutter step and he once more touched her hand, this time she held his.

"You fear losing me? I fear failing your father as your protector and losing you. It happened once; I cannot let it happen again."

327

"John, Sir John, Lord Knight of Erie. You are every bit my knight protector as you were that day I asked you to be. You are also more."

He smiled, leaned forward and kissed her. His pulse quickened and he felt her shudder at his touch. He moved closer to her and instead of her retreat, she held onto him as if her life depended upon it. She pressed her lips to his, her arms wrapping around his neck. She became almost frantic in her passion for him; her breath coming in quick gasps as tears streaked down her face. He held her tight, knowing that at this moment the coming siege was a thing far away.

"It seems I have waited all my life for you, Sir John." Slowly she pulled herself away and stood. Then holding his gaze she turned and moved back toward the inner-keep. He followed her as she made her way inside.

***

Kryall stood before Alaric. Hidden by the deep hood of a flowing cloak, Alaric could not see the man's face, but he certainly recognized the voice. Bale had brought him, after a roundabout search and now he stood in Alaric's office near the docks. The Guildmaster from Chez looked out the leaded glass window to his felucca, the topmast was almost eye level.

"What do you want, Guildmaster? You risk much to bring me here." Alaric stood and motioned for the man to sit. He just crossed his arms and waited. The Guildmaster shrugged and told Bale to leave the room.

"Not even your trusted aide? This must be important."

"Look around you; you see it throughout the city. We've become the refuge for the flotsam of the south. We've lost our cargoes to feed the masses, where is the profit in that? Beggars and commoners fill the streets and the walls of the city are ready to burst at the seams." He shook his head and straightened his tunic; his sword was at his side.

"Well, you will have that with war."

Alaric waved dismissively as if the war was a nuisance at best. "I did not want this war. It should have spread from east to west not the reverse. It's those meddling outlanders, stirring up trouble with Myella."

"So you have told me before. You forget," Kryall, pointed out, "Myella brought them here and you helped them."

"Do not remind me," the Guildmaster spat. His voice rose and his face turned livid. "I should have killed Lord Michael and let the others rot. I realize that Myella's rule would have been harsh, but at least a man could have made a living. Kelvin and his city council are bleeding me dry."

"Why do you tell me this? It is only temporary after all."

"As was our original arrangement. Things change." Alaric trailed off as he peered intently at his guest. "I think it is time you spoke to your masters."

"I have only one Master." Then: "There are the others. But if you expect Duran to stop in his tracks and spare this city the sack, then I fear that you have overestimated me."

329

"No, I am not a fool, Kryall. I do know, though, that a few chosen words in the right ear will spare me *my* interests."

The man chuckled and there was no humor in it. "Now you have piqued my interest. Go on."

"A proposal for the Regent."

"I'm listening." Kryall finally sat in the seat that Alaric had offered him earlier. Alaric Dirkajian, Guildmaster merchant of Paravel, flashed a brilliant white smile. Kryall was reminded of those big mountain cats that lived near Baed; the ones that would tear your throat out and devour you.

Chapter 21

Though the sun had set, casting the snow-capped peaks of the lower Tarn Range in a red glow, the sky ahead remained a crisp cobalt blue. Kiuf pulled off his armored gauntlets and supervised the men of the Guard of Oran as they pitched camp. Regent Duran's pavilion had been the first erected and now two guards stood impassively at the flap, wary of those who approached.

Kiuf sighed and looked to the dense northern spur of the Great Forest. Caught up in the colors of the harvest season, they too seemed set afire by the last light of the sun. Almost three seasons had turned and now they found themselves once more in the pass between the mountains and the forest that would eventually open to the Plains of Straw and Paravel. He stretched his legs as he began his circuitous walk through the camp; it sat on a defensible hill, with an easily protected perimeter.

The Guard had been on a forced march since the failed siege at Bastion Hold. A day, a night, another day, then they would set up camp. Almost thirty thousand men, chewing up the countryside, confiscating the harvest of local farmers and devouring their livestock now pitched tents. They were strung out almost a league without any fear from a harrying force. Cavalry stood at the point, followed by archers and footman, then the siege engines and supply train. The quartermaster would supplement their pillage with supplies brought through the Ghisik Pass from Helm. The men were tired from the march, so they would be spending the next several days here; they were less than a month from Paravel.

Duran's personal lieutenant nodded to the sentries as they took their watch. Squires checked the tether lines and the hobbled steeds; it was often difficult to keep track of so many men, yet they all had their rank and place. The company commanders would be reporting to Duran as soon as the soldiers had settled in.

Kiuf often used this time to mull over the thoughts that had built throughout the day, but could not tend to immediately because of other concerns. Several things played upon his mind lately. Foremost was Duran's obsession with Gabrielle and the Outlanders.

In all the years that Kiuf had been with his commander, he had never known him to be so possessed with the thoughts of a woman. Driven, yes, but never given to obsession. He knew that in the period that Duran was sent by Gelion to Galfeon Yor, he had spent many an hour with Trevor's daughter. He had heard talk that initially she had welcomed his courtship, but it soured, and especially so with the arrival of the Lord Knight from Erie, wherever that was. Duran had even confided that had Gabrielle acquiesced to his courting, much of the war in the west could have been avoided through the political marriage.

Kiuf moved to a large oak and unbuckled his britches to relieve himself; he thanked the gods he was not wearing battle armor. Duran was deluding himself if he thought he could have prevented the war; the girl had enamored him. He would almost be tempted to say that Duran, knowing she was a prize that had eluded him, made her even more for the wanting. He knew his Lord would never concede that though, primarily because below the surface Duran chafed at what had happened in Paravel all those months ago. First he chafed at Myella awarding the southern regency to the Shadowlord, then at the losing of Gabrielle, and finally to be scarred and ousted by the White Knight. All those things conspired to make Duran a man driven by revenge, a dangerous man indeed.

In light of his performance at Albien, Kiuf had been rather surprised that Duran had withdrawn from Bastion. Finally, the man he had known before the Paravel incident had emerged and his passion had been tempered. Myella had desperately wanted Bastion Hold, but in their estimation it could not be won without devastating losses and more resources than they had. Better to withdraw and lose the day, than persist and risk the loss at the wall and any hope of retaking Paravel, let alone holding the south.

Myella had been furious; her rage had even frightened him. She had railed against Duran, but he just calmly explained the defenses of the city. When she wanted to call the Keth, he had laughed and told her to do so, at her own peril. Thus began the march east to Paravel.

Kiuf wondered at Duran's reluctance to use the Keth, as he watched campfires spring up amid tents and knots of men. The persistent drone of voices did not betray the call of the crickets. Since Tarn Hold, Duran had been loath to use the creatures of Oran, and with good reason. Sorcery had always made Kiuf uncomfortable, even when the family in Qwen

333

had used it to their advantage. The black magick's that Myella employed were beyond his ken. It had turned Ord into a dark, forbidding place and Tarn Hold - well, no one dwelt there anymore.

It was understandable why Duran had shied away from Myella's offer of sorcerous aid. He understood Duran's reluctance to enforce Myella's command to destroy any village that harbored a shrine or temple to Tarn. However, they all knew that the commanders in the Guard of Oran enforced that order fanatically.

No, Duran had changed. Kiuf was still unsure how much, but he had changed, nonetheless. The Regent, now just past thirty cycles, was becoming more than just the dedicated agent of the Clave.

The guards outside of Duran's pavilion saluted smartly as he ducked through the flap. Duran sat at his field desk as seven of the ten company commanders stood about, no doubt giving their reports. The Regent looked up and smiled as Kiuf strode the distance to the desk.

"Ah, Kiuf, outriders report heavy rains and even snows threatening the Plains. We shall encamp here a week to rest and gather our strength." Kiuf nodded as Duran paused and ran a hand through the shock of white hair that had grown above the spot where the Lord Knight's sword had sliced away his ear. "They also tell me Kryall has some news. Therefore, I want you and ten of your best men to ride to the edge of the Plains. Kryall will meet you there. Find out what he wants. Also find out all he knows of the outlander, Michael the alchemist."

"Yes, milord."

"Dismissed." Duran resumed speaking to his commanders as Kiuf left the tent. He motioned for his squire and gave him detailed instructions. They would ride at first light, so much for a few days' rest.

335

Chapter 22

They had hugged the coast for two days. That was all they could manage without proper stores. On the evening of the third day, they had beached the makeshift raft north of Icam. It was a secluded cove, its rocky beach strewn with driftwood and dead fish.

Sir Brunwurst lifted the governor over the lapping water and onto dry land as her dogs leapt off the raft and sprinted amid the rocks to relieve themselves. The two heavily maned hounds seemed to be the most self-conscious of the group. Two days on a raft made the group painfully familiar with one another.

When Tar'elah came ashore, the men set about dismantling their craft and sending the timbers adrift. They hoped that if anyone spotted the timbers they would assume it was just more detritus brought on by an angry sea.

Tar'elah scouted into the woods at the edge of the cove looking for any sign of patrol. Rhianne looked on dejectedly as she sat upon a large, bleached carcass of a tree; her blonde hair was limp and her skin was red and peeling from exposure. She shivered quietly in the chill damp air as her two hounds sat beside her, trying to lend their warmth.

Torec and Bill set about to gather whatever dry driftwood there was. Because the nights were getting colder, they would have to risk a fire. Bill voiced his apprehension at this to the former merchant.

"Not much to worry about Bard," Torec said from the deepening twilight. "We are about six days from Icam and it is rough going at that. The *Ish-deme* will be hard put to find us here. The ground is too rocky and thickly forested to allow for horse and there is no village nearby to speak of."

"Then it will be just as difficult to make it to Icam." He threw some driftwood on a large rock and Torec took out his flint and striking stone to get the brush started. "The roads will be crawling with the Guard after that fiasco at Crag Place. Maybe we would be better hugging the shore."

"No, that would be fine if it were uninterrupted beach. These coves are few though; mostly you will find cliffs and caves. We will be better off sticking to game trails and what not. I have some gold secreted at Farok's hut; we'll go there and then to Icam to buy passage back to Paravel."

Bill nodded and crouched down, holding his hands toward the warmth of the fire. Soon Brunwurst and the governor joined them. The two hounds rested their heads on their forepaws and began to doze.

"Well," said Bill, finally breaking the silence. "So much for getting aid from Clef." His laugh was far from humorous, yet Rhianne ar'Liayne shot him an angry look. Perhaps she had lost the most of all. It seemed that Clef no longer needed a governor.

"It will just be a matter of time before Ectel disbands the merchant's council." Torec frowned as he prodded the wood, hoping it would catch quicker. "They will not even be able to govern under the pretext that Clef has been annexed. She will be considered a territory of the Conclaveum and a Seat will form within the Clave."

"It is a sad day indeed," replied Torec.

337

"I think they soundly thrashed any opposition to a takeover," Brunwurst said as he unbuckled his vambrace and set it aside. "Anyone who would form a resistance would have been rounded up by now."

Tar'elah sauntered up and handed a pair of fat hares to Torec, already cleaned and dressed. She unbound the leather garrote she had used to snare them and fashioned a spit with a long slender piece of branch. Brunwurst looked on, appreciating the former bandit more and more. For some reason this brought a pang of jealousy to Bill. Soon his taste for the roasting meat soured by what he felt.

"That Hand of Keth was a surprise," mumbled Torec. He remembered the youthful face of the man with the kris-voulge. He shook his head.

"These are dark times for Carn," ar'Liayne said. "Not just Clef. Ectel should have tipped me off. Pleas for annexation, my fine ass!" Torec laughed at her expletive. "With that damned fanatical Cult of Oran, and their damned Guard, I should have known better. My predecessors never should have allowed that black ship into the harbor at Icam. When I became governor I should have expelled them."

"You could have tried," replied Torec, evenly. "I dare say, though, that you would have found a dagger between the ribs or poison in your food. Any resistance to the *cavas* would have been futile."

When the rabbit was done, they ate in silence, sipping occasionally from the water skin. Later they huddled around the fire as the wind picked up and blew the flames low. On the beach, breakers had started to roll in, the white-capped waves rolling

338

closer to their camp than they would have liked. The temperature was beginning to drop and it would go lower without cloud cover. Bill tossed more wood into the fire hoping to stave off the cold. Brunwurst took the first watch and Bill knew it was going to be a long night as they all sat around the fire staring at each other in silence.

The next day found Tar'elah at the point, hacking through dense undergrowth with her short sword. Torec had been correct in that they would have little to fear from the Guard of Oran. The ground cover was thick vine and fern and dead leaves, moist from a recent rain made each step along the rock strewn a risk for a twisted ankle. It took most of the day for them to find a game trail, and even then, it was vaguely discernable. Only the dogs seemed unhindered as they scampered through the woods a stone throw ahead of Tar'elah.

Finally, at the end of the day, they came upon a narrow farm road; it appeared not to have been used in several seasons. Torec and Brunwurst looked along the length of it from the dense foliage alongside the road. The only sound that greeted them in the late afternoon was that of a dove.

"We should be safe for a while," Brunwurst said as he stretched his legs. The road was rutted and muddy.

"I am not that familiar with this part of Clef," Torec muttered. He looked back to ar'Liayne; she remained silent, lost in thought.

"Very few taxes come from this precinct," she finally said. "Too few people. No villages or towns, just a few homesteads. I would say we are maybe four days walk from Farok's stead. Then another day and a half to Icam

"My feet will hate me for a month."

***

Rather than four days, it took twice that to reach the open coast lined with the burnt-out ruins of merchant estates. It would be several more days to Icam, where they would seek passage. Torec felt that they should stop at Farok's to retrieve some gold that he had cached away.

Now as twilight settled over them, they emerged from the woodlands and looked down the uncluttered coastline. Torec sighed loudly, in the distance he could make out the boundaries of his own estates.

"Once more a curse upon the *Ish-deme*. I fear that I will never settle my eyes upon this fair island again." He shook his head. A glance by Bill to Rhianne ar'Liayne told him that she felt the same way. As long as the Conclaveum held sway in Clef, it was no home for them.

"We will reach Farok's hut before the night is too deep," Torec finally said. "If we take the coast road we should be there in several hours."

The coast road was an empty strip of cobblestones that connected the former estates. It was now deserted and overgrown with weeds, but still allowed them to remain a brisk pace and they came upon Farok's hut after a fashion. Now, late in the evening, light leaked around the shuttered windows and a thin tracing of smoke drifted from the chimney.

340

"Finally," said a somewhat exasperated ar'Liayne. "I am about to collapse from exhaustion." She made a motion with her hands and Ikn and Teg were off, no doubt to hunt.

"A rather dismal dwelling," Brunwurst observed as he cracked his knuckles. Torec glanced angrily at the big man, but continued his walk into the yard and past bleating sheep that were awakened by their presence.

Bill leaned back against the low wall. He was looking forward to seeing his friends back in Paravel. He looked up to notice Tar'elah shuffling through the dirt. In the dark, it was difficult to see what she was looking at, but he thought she had her toe in some dung.

"What are you doing?" he asked. She looked up, a somewhat vacuous expression on her face.

"Nothing...really." She shrugged and looked away.

Torec knocked lightly at the door. After a moment, it cracked open to reveal the wizened and eyeless face of Farok. The old man cocked his head to the side and Torec gently took his friends hand and put it to his face.

"It is I, old friend, back after the debacle at Crag Place."

"Ah, Torec, you have returned. I have heard what has happened. I am gladdened that you have survived, are there others with you?"

"Aye, the Bard, Tar'elah, Rhianne ar'Liayne and Sir Brunwurst."

"The governor? She was there? It is an ill day indeed.

"Come in, it is cold out."

341

Torec beckoned the others and they entered the small stead. The only light came from the hearth and two oil lamps sitting in the windowsill near a table. Farok motioned for them to sit and deftly placed the pot on the fire to boil tea.

"Tell me, what has happened."

"Betrayed, dear friend. Ectel and a Hand of Keth were there with several hundred Guards. They routed us easily and we barely escaped. Many died, including Bobel."

"Bobel?" Farok shook his head and put his tealeaves into a pot. He took a small bag from the shelf and opened it. "Cinril?" No one objected and he sprinkled it directly into the pot of water.

"What now for the isle of Clef?"

"I came for my things. We'll buy passage to Paravel. We want you to come with us."

"What?" Brunwurst barked. "He'll slow us down."

"Not if we lighten the baggage by your weight Brunwurst!" Torec replied and made a motion to the dirk he wore at his waist.

"Enough!" Rhianne snapped. "This bickering will get us nowhere."

"He is correct though," Farok said. "I am a blind fool."

"Nonsense, you will come."

"No, I cannot."

"Why?" asked Torec.

Farok smiled and poured their tea, carefully and methodically. "That is a good question," he said as he handed them their cups. "Drink, it will warm you."

342

When he was satisfied they had drunk he sat down and took a thoughtful pose. "You see I must stay to regain my sight."

"He is mad," Brunwurst said and yawned.

"Not mad, Sir Brunwurst. No, I made a bargain and I will not regret it."

Torec looked agitated, Bill saw that much, but the warm fuzziness that the tea had imparted also calmed him, made him feel detached.

"What do you mean Farok? To the point."

"To the point," said another voice from the back of the home. The curtains parted and out stepped the Hand of Keth and Ectel. In an instant Brunwurst stood, took two steps and fell flat on his face. Bill could not move from where he sat.

"Drugged," Rhianne slurred. Tar'elah was up in a flash. As Ectel moved forward, her sword was out and took him in the stomach. He screamed and fell to the dirt floor. Farok struck her in the head with his stool, a glancing blow that stunned her.

Torec slumped to the floor. "Why, Farok, why?"

"For his sight, merchant. We promised to return his sight if he told us about the meeting. It seems his hunger for the written word has gotten the best of him." The youthful features of the Hand of Keth split into a grin, marred only by the rough stitches of catgut that crossed his forehead. There was something powerful and deadly in his gaze.

"Yes, you did promise. I have no regrets. Now, I wish you to fulfill your end of the bargain."

The Hand smiled, broader this time, as if wholly amused by the notion. Bill was vaguely aware of what was going on in his drugged state. He

343

heard Rhianne sobbing and the sounds of horses in the yard. The Bard watched as the Hand of Keth walked up to Farok and placed his hands on the old man's shoulders.

"Put your left hand on the kris-voulge, Farok." The old man did so and instantly went rigid. Pain coursed up his arm from touching the dark metal. He began to moan deep in his throat.

"There, there, old man, just a little pain. Oran gives sight to those who give their souls!"

Suddenly Farok let out a piercing wail and the empty sockets of his eyes glowed a malignant green. Finally, his scream spent, he crumpled to the floor. Smoke curled up from Farok's eye sockets.

"Now," said the Hand, as he turned. His smile was gone, replaced by a look of unholy rapture. He smoothed his black tabard and looked at the drugged group around him.

"A pity Ectel had to die, but there are many more like him. Ah, Bard," he finally said as his gaze lit upon the outlander. "I have something planned for you. If you are lucky your companions will live long enough to witness it." He tilted his head to the side and Bill looked on, glassy eyed. "Then again, maybe not."

Tar'elah groaned at the dull pain that seeped into her very bones. Faint light cast by *Shaj'il Cziffer* trickled across the straw on the floor and revealed the sleeping form of Rhianne ar'Liayne. Coming fully awake Tar'elah tried to sit up and a stabbing pain to her temple almost caused her to faint. Carefully, she probed her temple with a tentative finger and found her hair matted with what

344

she took to be blood. Yet, her skull seemed to be intact, however comforting that was.

She slowly levered herself up against the wall and took account of herself. Aside from the wound to her head, she had a few bruises, but that was about the extent of the damage. Her clothes were intact, as were ar'Liayne's, but her weapons were gone. She nudged ar'Liayne with her foot and the other woman came alert in an instant. She took stock of her surroundings and let out a heavy sigh.

"We're in the prison...below the government building. They must have overthrown the council." She squinted up the length of the shaft that let star and moonlight into the chamber.

"What of the others?" Rhianne asked of the former bandit.

"I don't know. I was not drugged, for I did not drink his tea. I should have known better. I saw the signs of horse in his yard, but I did not think anything of it. The horses had Guard shoes. They have a mark on the back curve, for traction in battle. I have been away from Ghisik too long. I did know enough not to trust his tea, all the good that did."

"At the least you killed that bastard, Ectel."

Tar'elah smiled wanly and touched her head. "That I did. What became of your hounds?"

"I suppose that they are about. They are much too smart to risk their lives foolishly. They will wait and not risk my life in a foolish attack. They are far smarter than people give them credit for."

Tar'elah stood somewhat unsteadily. Dizziness threatened on the edge of her awareness. She had been wounded like this before and knew that it would pass with time and rest; she also knew that she did not have the luxury of either. Taking stock of the cell, she saw that it was a relatively clean affair with a low, iron-bound wood door, and the shaft to admit light. On the far side of the cell was a privy hole, but by the lack of odor it had not seen use in quite a while. Finally, she sat down and tried to relax. The waiting would be the worst part. As she sat in silence, Rhianne remained to herself, brooding and pensive. The passage of time seemed to be wearing her down. Finally, after several hours had passed in silence, with a scraping of a steel bolt the door opened..

Tar'elah crouched down low, as if ready to spring. Ar'Liayne on the other hand stood, smoothed her ragged and dirty riding dress and watched as the door opened. A young man, in the livery of the Guard of Oran motioned for them to step out.

"Come on, I'm to exercise you two. Come along." He stood back as Rhianne looked to Tar'elah, who only shrugged. Finally, they emerged from the cell and were greeted by two guards. One held a lamp and the other a sword. The one with the sword, a rough looking man who seemed capable of any violence, motioned for them to follow the other. They were led out of the cellblock and up a long stair to a simple courtyard. Squinting as the morning sun crested the white walls of the courtyard, Rhianne explained this was where public floggings took place. Cross-bowman in the black tabard of Oran stood watch on the wall. There was a service door on the far side of the yard and two men from the charnel house were loading bodies onto a wagon. Rhianne gasped at the sight of the corpses.

346

"The council...every one of them. Even those that supported the Conclaveum."

"It seems that the Hand of Keth is cleaning house."

"Are we next?"

"We shall see."

The guard motioned for them to walk around the yard and the other laughed and made a rude comment about ar'Liayne's legs; upon hearing the comment the former governor snarled and spat, eliciting an even louder cackle from the man. As she paced the yard, he followed and finally, near the whitewashed wall of the courtyard, he reached out to tug part of her dress away. It tore clear up to her hip. She let out a scream and kicked at him, but he just danced away.

"Come now, wench. Don't ya want a piece a real Conclaveum meat?" She snarled again and made to strike him, but he just grabbed her wrist and pulled her close. His hand reached for her bare hip, but suddenly Tar'elah was there.

"Hold. Why take someone who doesn't want you? You could have someone who is willing."

"You think that you can handle me?" he asked, puffing up like a peacock.

"You and your friend," she said, motioning to the guard who was supervising the yard.

"Huh?" he said, somewhat surprised.

Tar'elah pulled him off Rhianne and winked at her. She pulled his hips close to hers and wrapped her one leg around his. She put his hands on her chest and kissed him hard. When she pulled away, he seemed mesmerized.

"Call your young friend over here." The young man looked up, smiled and came forward.

"What's the matter, Tic? Kinna handle her?"

"I want you both," Tar'elah said with a gasp. She motioned for the younger one to approach her from behind. As he began to unlace his hose, she grabbed his hips and pulled him into her buttocks. She ground into him and tossed her hair into his face. He laughed nervously and began to fumble once again with his hose.

"Enjoying it?" Tic asked. Tar'elah laughed.

"Oh yes, and so will you." As the younger guard made a move to tug down her britches she deftly reached back and grabbed the hilt of his sword. She twisted her leg and Tic fell to the ground. Then she spun, drew the sword and dragged it up across the young man's throat. He looked stunned as his hose fell to his knees and blood cascaded from his wound. He fell over backward; Tar'elah turned and ran Tic through the chest.

"Come on!" called Tar'elah and grabbed the governor by the wrist. They headed to the portal where bodies were being loaded onto the charnel wagon. A guard on the wall shouted alarm and raised his crossbow, but not before Tar'elah launched the short sword at him. It spun end over end until it took him in the gut. He fell with a thud to the ground. They passed him quickly and were soon through the gate and into the street.

Chapter 23

Guyle looked out over the rooftops and towers of Teshwa, his perch on the summit of the Tower of Iss more secure as each day passed. The clouds raced low overhead, brushing the horned spires of his tower. Rain pattered along the balustrade in steady rhythm, making the stones slick and precarious. As the season turned for the Conclaveum Guyle felt as though an age were coming to a close and a new one was about to begin; he was sure that age was his.

Thunder rolled in the distance over the Lake Ionet. From his vantage, he could make out waterspouts on the leaden surface. He smiled grimly and turned to the creature that awaited him. Bej-et.

"I have spoken to my Council," her voice was singsong, unused to the harsh syllables of human language. She moved, or rather glided, over the smooth marble floor, her strange insect-like armor glinting even though no sunlight touched it.

"And the gift I promised?" Guyle asked in a weary voice.

"You have the impatience of the short-lived."

"And that is what I want to change. With the power that I was promised being short-lived would not be a threat. There is that and the *Gates*."

"The *Home Gate*," she said and her quicksilver eyes narrowed. A faint breeze set her fine hair fanning out.

"Yes, I promised you the location of the *Home Gate*. It was the Daemon who promised me the *Keys* to the *Gates*."

349

"First *Key* you had. Third *Key* you had. Lost them both."

"First *Key*? Third *Key*?"

"First *Key*: the Words of Iss."

"Yes, the volumes of the *Ih'dia Om*," he said and his knuckles went white as they tightened upon the rune covered surface of his blackened staff.

"Third *Key*, the *Saint's Soul.*"

"What?!" he yelled. "What does that mean?"

"Break asunder the Six."

"Yes, yes, the Outlanders. I have done that."

"Not the *Saint's Soul.*"

"What is the *Saint's Soul*?"

Bej-et smiled, her obsidian teeth making a predatory display. "That is the *Key*."

Guyle knew that the frustration he felt would do him no good. Her logic was alien and mystifying, and almost as much a riddle as the words of the Daemon.

"What is the second *Key*?"

"If we knew that we would not need you to give us the location of the *Home Gate*. We do not need the *First Key* for going home does not require it. We do not require the *Third Key*, for that is the binding placed upon Oran and his servants in this world and we are not touched by it. We can manifest the *Gate* once the location is known."

The old man shook his head. He would get the *Ih'dia Om* and then he would bring the remaining Outlanders to his tower and sunder them. Then the final *Key* to the *Gate* would be in play. No longer would he be dependent upon his frail body, or the help of others. He would be master of Carn *and* the Outworlds.

Bej-et looked at him, her head tilted to the side. She looked as though she had read his thoughts. "Where is the *Gate*?" she asked.

"Then it is set? You wish to know?"

"I have spoken to my Council. What is it you wish in kind?" Her armor scintillated in the low light, almost mesmerizing him.

"It is but a subtle thing. You must kill my half-brother." he smiled wickedly.

***

Trevor knew that he would die here, in the bowels of the Tower, if he did not win his freedom soon. It seemed that Guyle had forgotten about his half-brother. After he had been brought to the Krim, Guyle had ordered him back to his cell. His only contact with the outside world had been Sir Chill, who usually brought him the gruel and hard bread once a day. Monotonous fare, but the gruel was nutritious, and he was not wasting away as fast as he thought he would.

He sighed; he had lost weight, almost two stones he would say. He ran his hands along his ribs. They were not that obvious yet, but he had lost a fair amount of fat. Luckily, his boredom had been broken by exercise. And thank Tarn for his ability to exercise, it took the edge off the cold dampness; the exercise and the woolen blanket that Sir Chill had given him surely had kept a racking cough from taking him.

He counted time not by the passing of the sun, but by the drip of moisture and the patter of insects. The cell's tomb-like blackness was only broken by the faint torchlight that crept beneath the iron bound door. At times like this, his thoughts would take flight, always bringing him to a circle of faces: Gabrielle, Sir John, Sir Chill, Duran, and Guyle. Chill's face was the one that intrigued him the most.

By rights, the young man should have been dead. A lance through the chest was something that even the best healers of Tarn would have a hard time correcting. He remembered that night in Galfeon Yor when Chill fell. Baxel had tried to save the young man, but he had been disarmed by Duran's men and forced to watch helplessly as Sir Chill and Gabrielle were surrounded. It had been a glancing blow to the head that stunned the stout Outlander; long enough for one of Duran's men to ride him down with a lance, pinning him to the ground. He was there to die and by rights, he should have. Baxel had been drawn and quartered, but Chill had been left to his own fate.

Trevor heaved a sigh and adjusted his position on the stone slab. He was no mage; he had never had the knack like Ironeas or the skill of Guyle to practice the Arts. Nor had he any desire, as his skills were always best suited for the battlefield. However, on his trip back to Teshwa he had heard talk of how Guyle and several other Hands of Keth had resurrected Chill to be a Hand. That was what had struck him as odd.

He had a very limited knowledge of necromancy, but he was not ignorant of the written word. At Galfeon Yor he had amassed a significant library, comparable to the one in Albien. In all his reading of the Keth and the Hands of Keth, he had come to understand that the *wracking* could be

352

forced, but the victim had to be alive for the spirit to be corrupted. Chill had been dead, his spirit supposedly fled to a higher plane. Yet, Guyle had done more than animate a corpse.

No, if his spirit had fled this realm, even the vessel that was the body of Chill, the *wracking* would have been impossible. Keth were controlled by the *Daemon*, who was the will and arm of Oran. Oran indirectly controlled the victim through his Keth and by way of the corrupt spirit. The demonology of Oran was complicated, but the hierarchy began with minor creatures of Oran, followed by the more powerful Hands of Keth, and the Keth themselves, though only Oran governed the Hand's. The upper tier was comprised of the *Daemon* and his ilk, and ultimately the evil Oran.

It was evident that something was amiss with Sir Chill. When he brought food, he would only speak rarely, distantly. His eyes would look past Trevor blankly. It was strange indeed.

It was as if his spirit was trapped, residing elsewhere, tangled but not corrupted. *Now that was a thought*, he smiled. The creaking of rusted hinges brought him from his reverie. Light poured through the portal, blinding him. After his eyes adjusted, he saw the familiar figure of Sir Chill placing his daily meal on the floor.

"Ah, Sir Chill. I was just thinking about you." It had been almost two weeks since he had seen the man, another had been providing his food in the interim, but now the Hand was back. Trevor knew better than to approach the man. He had earned a sharp backhand some time ago. Now the hand of Keth looked up and gave Trevor a knowing smile.

353

He said nothing, but did not leave either. Chill sometimes did this, as if humoring an old man.

"I have come to the conclusion that you are no true Hand of Keth." Chill gazed back. Most of his face was lost in shadow, but Trevor could make out a slightly raised eyebrow. "You cannot be, for your soul was not *wracked*. You are not undead either."

"Maybe," Chill said in a hollow voice. "I am somewhere in between."

Trevor sat forward, truly shocked by Chill engaging in conversation. Again, the young man did not make a move to leave and Trevor saw this as a unique opportunity.

"So, Sir Chill, where would that be?"

The man smiled and it was almost as if his former self was back. It was a shy smile, one uncorrupted by the evilness of the Keth. "Somewhere..." he began, but then his eyes clouded over. He shook his head slowly. Trevor was unsure what to say fearing that if he said anything it would break this tenuous bond of communication between them.

"It fills me, this...and I am removed from the shell. It strains...the distance, I-" suddenly his mouth clamped shut and he looked to be in some amount of pain.

"Tell me Sir Chill, do you enjoy being the lackey for Guyle?"

"Lackey?" he mouthed. Again the confused look. "I am free, my shell is bound, but I am free." He almost doubled over with physical pain. Trevor could see it twist his features and the scar at his temple turned an angry red.

354

Trevor leaned forward; anxious to learn anything that might help him escape. "Where are you Sir Chill?"

A faraway look came to Chill, his face still marked by discomfort. "I am as steel, I will remain unstained. Keth's Hand does not use me for such. Keth fills the shell."

"Help me Sir Chill. Help me from this place." Chill began to nod accent to the older man. As if in a dream, Chill turned and motioned for Trevor to follow but as the older man made ready, Chill's back went rigid and he let out a low moan. Quite suddenly, Chill turned and his staff swung out. The Kris-voulge touched Trevor on the arm and blue fire leapt out, enveloping his side and causing him to arch back and scream in agony. He fell to the floor, unmarked, the pain still convulsing the muscles on his left side.

"Fool!" came a low, threatening growl. It was Chill's voice, but now tainted by the Keth; it twisted between them full of the promise of damnation. "*This* is my domain! I am the Hand; you are my charge, my prisoner. My liege is Oran!"

"You are Keth. But the one known as Chill is free. Does Guyle know this? Or have you fooled him this long also?"

Chill's eyes narrowed, but he answered again in the corrupted voice. "Guyle sought something else with his necromancy. The *wracking* was done, its purpose served."

"Chill lives," Trevor whispered.

"No. There is the servant, the Hand. What was left was silk upon the wind. It is gone."

"Is it?

The Hand of Keth looked at him, his eyes reflecting blue from the energized Kris-voulge. Then he turned and slammed the cell door shut, leaving Trevor to his thoughts and naught more.

356

Chapter 24

Barish made sure that any White Guard markings on the feluccas were long gone. Now the hulls of the boats were painted a deep blue to the water line. They had picked up the dye in a small fishing town along the coast and had spent several days in the shallows scrubbing and painting the hull. They had also made sure the ships were no longer as ship-shape as they had been upon leaving the harbor in Tasseem. The decks were cluttered with tackle and rope. Ballistae lined up at haphazard angle and no longer did the feluccas fly the colors of the white guard. It would be unusual for privateers to own feluccas, but it was not unheard of. Some of the wealthier families in the Conclaveum owned fleets of the swift vessels, though probably not as heavily armed as these two ships.

It would just have to do, he thought as he looked along the deck of the boat and over the shallows that now reflected the cerulean of the sky. The weather was much milder here near Chestra than in the hotter domains of the north. Chestra was in the throes of autumn. In the shallows, the water was calm and glassy, mirroring an occasional cloud, and the cliffs were dotted with trees crimson and gold. A faint breeze fluttered the pennant on the top of the mast and the sun was at a low angle in the sky, illuminating all in the glow of fading summer.

He sighed and scratched the new growth of beard that graced his face. The men and women under his command lounged around the decks of the two boats. Some prepared the late afternoon meal;

others mended nets or polished fittings. He sipped at some hot karo and watched as brown leaves drifted from the cliffs. It was a week of following seas to Qwen, but with the coming weather they would not be able leave the Chestra province for a fortnight. They would remain in the sheltered bays here until the weather passed and then they would continue on their way south.

He frowned and fingered the chart that lay strewn over the cabin house. *But what then?* He wondered. Maybe Paravel. It reputedly had thrown off the shackles that Myella had imposed. Tarn knew that they no longer had a place in the Conclaveum and laying into the port at Qwen could be dangerous. However, if the winter weather proved ill then it would necessitate Qwen be their next port of call.

He looked at the chart and lifted a thin piece of onion paper over it, which had the tracings of currents and weather patterns typical of this time of the year. He saw that when they passed the Surmount, that place where the buttresses of the Great Wall met the ocean, the weather would turn from the mild they now felt to the cold breath of winter. He knew it would be that quick, a matter of crossing the imaginary line and the cooler waters and weather of the south met the warmer waters of the north. There the seas would become rough and possibly dangerous and he had sailed them only twice before. Luckily, the pilots had more experience with these seas than he did, and they would take care of their charges. The roughest passage would be just to the north of the Surmount, where the weather churned up waterspouts over deceptively calm water. Nevertheless, that was expected this time of the year. After the very balmy weather of Tasseem it would be difficult indeed to adjust to the winter weather of the south.

He leaned back against the mast, feeling the rocking of the boat, the cool breath of autumn air, he almost dozed off. After a moment, his eyes closed and when he reopened them again it was nigh dusk. The men and the woman who crewed the three ships were now busying themselves with the task of making dinner. The yards slapped against the mast and the yellow lights of Chestra dotted the cliffs far to the south. He stood, being careful not to slip off the curved roof of the pilothouse. Out beyond the shelter of the cove, where the lapping of waves rocked the feluccas gently, the water was white capped and rough. A pale red wash spread across the western sky and the cliffs and out to sea the sky looked cold and dark. He nodded to the crew and one handed him a bowl. There would be a cold rain tonight.

He spoke to his people then, now pariah in the Conclaveum and talked about their families and their loyalties. When they finished with dinner and talkthey had a sip of liquor to warm them against the chill, Barish knew that they could never go back. They could only go on.

Well then, he thought. *Paravel it is. Three weeks and we will coast into their harbor.*

Chapter 25

He moved with the pack, now grey beard in the rear, submitting to the new alpha. He belonged. He followed his brothers and sisters over the rock outcropping just as the fire in the sky rose like a blister over the unending water. They had safely made it over the man-bridge that went to the rock amid the unending water. They could run free now. Free from those that walked with the shadow. However, the Smiling Wolf felt something tug and the hackles on the back of his neck rose. He looked over his shoulder, to the rock, and raised his nose to the air. There was something there, something he could not leave as of yet. He felt drawn.

Once more, he looked to the pack as it continued into the sparse forest. Then back to the rock. He felt the tug, and let...go...

He awakened with a shudder, the breath leaving him with enough force to rattle his teeth. He sat up, the late morning light casting it across sweat-drenched sheets. The room was open and neat, the bed comfortable but firm. Plain wood chairs sat in each corner of the whitewashed room and across from his bed was a fireplace, cleanly swept. To his side was a wide window, small leaded glass panes allowing him a fantastic view of the northeastern side of the isle of Qwen. The cobalt skies dotted with their racing clouds across reflected in the jewel like sea below.

Tossing his sheets aside, he noticed that he was naked, but Tom Smiling Wolf did not let this disturb him. What disturbed him more were the strange dreams he had and the fact that the last thing he remembered was the melee in the garden with the minions of Oran and Utha.

He looked over himself. Aside from some bruising, he was no worse for the wear, though when he stood he felt somewhat lightheaded. His clothing lay on a low table, neatly folded, and his knife was casually slung over a chair. He quickly slipped into his britches and tunic, and as he did the door swung open. He looked at the person who stood there with raised eyebrow. It was Marad.

"It is good to see you up. How do you feel, friend Tracker?"

"Rested, but my time sense is all screwed up. How long?"

"A day and another night." He shook his head. "Come, let us get you something to eat and I'll tell you what is happening."

Later, as they sat out on a patio at the edge of this estate not a stone's throw from the sea, they ate their breakfast. Marad informed Tom that this was Rhinn's Estate, or as he had put it, House of Rhinn. With the house behind them and the vista before them, servants brought them food and drink allowing them privacy on this warm autumn day.

Marad explained how the Captain of House Rhinn's guard, one LuVic du' Rhinn, discovered him. He was brought to the estate, but only after learning that Smiling Wolf had been in danger.

It was only luck that a member of House Rhinn had spotted Tom and had followed him to the karo house. Knowing that House Orr owned the establishment and that it was likely that House Orr knew about the death of the guardsmen in Dorber, they realized that Tom might have unwittingly fallen into the lap of Orr. Knowing this, LuVic sent a man to follow Tom on his tour through Middle Qwen, a tour that led him to that despised garden. The man had sent word to House Rhinn and Captain LuVic had dispatched his guard to aid in the Tracker's escape. The men had arrived just as Tom and the wolves were attacking Utha and her minions. The wolves had fled into the night and LuVic had brought Tom to the estate; leaving no evidence that Tom or they had been at that melee.

Tom nodded and looked at the tray of fresh fruit that lay before him. "I thought I felt the wolves leaving, in my sleep. I don't know, maybe we will meet again."

"Yes, mayhap. Nevertheless, what of Utha, how did you defeat her? She was a Hand, or so LuVic has said." Marad looked at Tom out of the corner of his eye as he bit into a tangy red fruit.

"The gift of sight," Tom said, some doubt evident in the way he said it. "She fooled me at first. Her aura was normal, just as yours. However, it changed. Then, as she started her sorcery, I saw the energy. I knew that I had to stop her before she finished or I would be a goner."

"You are strange, Tracker. I have heard of men who are schooled in the Arts having limited skill at *sight*, but not such as you. Even the little knowledge of sorcery and the Arts that I possess does not hint at such. You bring something to this realm that is unheard of."

"Great." Tom looked off; watching gulls dip toward the rocky shore, then rise up on the breeze. "So, when do we leave for the ports? I need to get back to Paravel."

362

"Ah, that may be the problem. It seems that your prowess at killing was not unnoticed. LuVic tells me that both House Orr and Jaggier have men watching this estate. You would be an open target, as would I, should we leave for the ports."

"What about an escort?"

"For Rhinn to come out publicly and show they are protecting one who has killed the matriarch of Orr's son would be political suicide. Their current position is tenuous at best, especially after their support of Koss. No, it must be done another way."

"How?"

"Let me show you." He stood and walked to the edge of the patio, and looked over the waist high wall to the water, some one hundred feet below. Tom followed his gaze down to a small dock in the shallows and the *felucca* moored there. "One fast ship. LuVic has put it at our disposal."

Tom frowned and attempted to read Marad's face. "One ship and two of us with different destinations."

"Aye. I wish to go to Chestra. You go to Paravel. A dilemma."

"Yes."

"I could turn the vessel over to you and you could go to Paravel. Then I could wait here for the return, several weeks, or go on by another boat or foot for that matter to Chestra. Alternatively, we could go first to Chestra and then the boat could head for Paravel. By then the winter seas would be upon you and it may be months before you arrive in that city.

"The last option I see is going to Paravel with you. This time of year, the seas are mild, but the return trip could be delayed. Yet, I may be able to assess the war that Myella and her lackey Duran are waging in the west. And, mayhap, I may learn what happened in Tarn Hold and if there was any word of my brother."

"Well," Tom said as he sat on the low wall. "It seems that you have thought this all out very thoroughly. What did you decide?"

"I know not. I have a burning desire to get to Chestra and possibly reunite with some of my guard. Several have retired in that region and that Seat has often supported the White Guard."

"Listen, I need to get to Paravel quickly, but there are bigger things going on here and I understand that. You can drop me off a few leagues south of here, then head to Chestra. It will take me a little longer than by boat, but then you can get on your way."

"Tempting, Smiling Wolf. But, I wonder about Paravel and Myella. What would a month or two bring? After all, I am dead to them." Tom nodded; this was a decision Marad had to make. As tempting as it was for Tom to say Paravel or bust, he knew that the man had to make up his own mind.

"Paravel." It was all that Marad said, but in the saying, it told volumes. Tom nodded.

"When?"

"The sooner the better. Come, we'll go to LuVic and see about sailing within the week."

Captain LuVic du' Rhinn was in his office located in the barracks on the other side of the estate, away from the main house. A minor House had come into cycle for the Watch of the Guilds and so he was tending to the needs of House Rhinn.

Marad and Tom found him in well-appointed chambers on the first floor of the barracks. He surrounded himself with fine books and scrolls, excellent taste in furnishings and walls lined with weapons made of fine Qwen steel. He was lounging on a leather divan and reading a manifest when the two approached him. He looked up and motioned for the two to sit on the bench opposite him.

"Wine?" he asked. They nodded and he motioned for a servant to pour a clear golden fluid into to crystal glasses. Setting the manifest aside, he leaned forward.

"Welcome tracker, Marad here tells me you are from another realm."

Tom almost choked upon the drink, but then swallowed. Before he could say anything, the captain spoke, humor in his voice.

"Do not fear. Tarn's creations are many. You are welcome here. It seems that many things are afoot and Myella delves into those better left alone. However, I understand your plight and make my office and the resources it possess', at your disposal."

"I thank you Captain, it is good to know that there are allies and friends in this world. Also thank the family Rhinn for me."

Captain LuVic frowned at that and straightened his tunic where he sat. "I wish I could, Tracker, but there is no family Rhinn. Thirty-four years ago the last daughter of Exten Rhinn's line perished of the Orphus plague. She begat one son, but he left the isle some sixteen years ago to travel known Carn. He wanted knowledge and experience and he wanted wisdom. He left me in charge. I guide this

House as best I can and serve as Regent for House Rhinn in the Councils. It may be that some day he will return and then I may thank him for you. If he does not, then I would say that you are welcome. Serving the White Guard and Commander Marad is a duty and a pleasure."

"Thank you, captain."

"Now, unto stores and ships men. I will give you a good crew; the only thing I ask is that you return them to me. One of the Bushi, our elite guard, will join you. I can supply you with weapons and gold, and some fine Qwen liquor. That should carry you to Paravel under the guise of a merchant. You may encounter patrols at sea, near the shipping lanes to Clef, but you will fly House Rhinn and Qwen colors, so problems will be few if any."

"Marad tells me that Qwen steel is formidable."

"Indeed, Tracker, it is." He stood and walked to the wall where he had examples of daggers and spearheads displayed. He took down a dagger and brought it to the Sioux.

Tom took the pommel and turned the blade over in his hand, catching the glint of the steel in the light, noticing the grain and texture. He gasped when he realized what he was seeing; it was something that paralleled his own world in terms of the development of forging. Something, which John had brought into this world with him; Japanese steel, *Nihonto*. He felt the sudden sense of vertigo as he looked at the blade, his vision tunneling in on the steel.

"This dagger, how was it made?"

"As all Qwen steel is. A smith folds the steel, many times, then wraps it around a core of softer

366

iron and then hardens it. If we had more time I would give you a demonstration, we have our own smith here at the estate. Most large Houses have their own smith, and hence own style. We tend to make long curved swords, other House's may make straighter, what not."

"Nihonto." Tom muttered.

"Pardon?" Marad said as he watched a man entranced by a wavy temper line, something Tom and John knew as a *hamon*.

"Where did this technique of forging originate?" Tom looked directly to LuVic. The man hesitated, Tom could see a hint of untruth in the flicker of his aura, but then it faded back to normal. LuVic turned and went to a carved bust; it faced out his window and over the sea. It was turned away from them. LuVic gestured to it.

"Exten Rhinn, Commander of the White Guard over five hundred years ago. After defeating Untheran and the Daemon at the Wall, came to Qwen. It is said he loved the sea, and always wanted to be near it. Truth to tell, he could have gone anywhere, but Qwen is positioned between Narn-toc and Teshwa, if not a little east, and here he could keep an eye on the Guard of the Wall, as well as any trouble that might erupt out of Narn-toc.

"He brought with him many ideas, Smiling Wolf. He would travel and after being away for months, he would return. He brought back the method of forging Qwen steel from one of his trips."

"He used *Gates,* didn't he?" LuVic shot him a look, as if this were a family secret long kept hidden until now.

367

"Yes, he learned that method of travel from Ghin-jo, his friend and ally."

"How did you know that, Smiling Wolf?" Marad was curious. He was Commander of the White Guard and this history was new to him. House Rhinn, it seemed, were also adept historians.

"This style of forging was prevalent in my realm five hundred years ago. My companion Sir John carries a similar weapon, called a katana, made of very similar steel. It is possibly the finest forging technique of our world. Now I see yours as well. The only answer could be *Gates,* what your sister and uncle want to open by bringing us here. If Exten Rhinn traveled freely through these *Gates* then it is possible that we can return home. That is if the knowledge still exists."

"That knowledge perished with Exten Rhinn, in that duel at the foul garden you were taken to. There is no written word on them that I am aware of."

"Michael, another companion, would know more about this than I. I wish he were here. This makes it all the more important for me to get to him as soon as possible."

"Aye, and to Paravel it is."

"I only wish I could talk to this Exten Rhinn," Tom said, frustration in his voice.

"Unfortunately all we have is this carved likeness, tracker, and naught more." He paused and turned the marble bust to face the inside of the room. It was time worn smooth, but Tom Smiling Wolf gaped upon seeing it and the likeness therein: the brow, the jaw line. Stern and bold, the likeness was unmistakable.

He was looking at a former graduate student of his acquaintance. John.

Sir John, Lord Knight of Erie.

Tom shivered and having gone pale, the two men wondered if Tom had taken a more serious wound two nights ago. He shook it off and just whispered, barely audible to Marad and LuVic.

"Just pawns in a larger game."

***

Before they were to leave LuVic graciously allowed Tom and Marad to visit the House forge. It was there Tom firmed his belief that Exten Rhinn had crossed to Earth through one of the *Gates* and visited ancient Japan. He watched in fascination as a smith performed a cleansing ceremony over the forge and proceeded to sort the ore. In another room, an apprentice was pounding and folding the steel and in yet another part of the estate a man was polishing the finished blades; again in the traditional Japanese style. Tom was perplexed, especially when the polisher looked up to reveal Asian features.

"Rhinn brought others through the *Gate*, didn't he?"

Again, the look from LuVic. "Hundreds, it is said, to bring the skill. He did not master it like the ancestors of these men." He picked up a medium length curved blade. The *hamon* was also straight, following the edge; it looked similar to a Hizen blade. Tom could make out the tight *itame* pattern of the forging and the activity in the blade that was usually indicative of a finely wrought piece. It still had to be fitted with guard and pommel.

369

"A gift for the Tracker. Qwen steel is known the width and breadth of Carn. I presented a dagger to the Commander of the White Guard, here, yesterday. It will serve you well."

Tom accepted it graciously. LuVic du'Rhinn continued. "We shall have the guard and grip fitted shortly. The fitter had to adjust the guard. Ah, here it is now."

Another man, obviously of direct Japanese lineage, bowed before LuVic and presented him a flat guard still wrapped in oilcloth. LuVic unfolded it carefully and looked at the black ovoid guard; what Tom would call a *tsuba*. In very simple lines there was a *tagane* carving on it that depicted a wolf

"It is beautiful," Tom said, as he wondered about the symbolism.

"Yes, it is. The sword will be ready for you tomorrow, plenty of time before you set sail."

"Thank you, LuVic." Tom bowed to the man.

"Yes, we are in your debt, Captain." Marad bowed also.

"The only debt is that owed to Exten Rhinn and House Rhinn. Restore the White Guard to what is was Commander and I shall forever be in *your* debt."

Marad nodded to the Captain, hoping he would someday be able to do just that.

Salt spray caught Tom in the face, he was not accustomed to sailing and it took him some time to find his sea legs. When he finally got used to the rolling of the deck, he joined Marad at the bow. The man stood there, in the fine clothing of a noble, his newly wrought dagger in his belt. Tom looked closely at the man, his aura burning a bright blue; for Tom to see all those men's auras turned night into day while it lasted. Marad's burned brightest, seemingly tested by his ordeal, purified by it. Tom *knew* he could trust this person. However, with what lay ahead, with Myella, and Duran's army, could he trust him that far? He wondered.

Marad nodded to him and made way at the forecastle. This was a larger *felucca* than most and boasted three full decks below. This only diminished its speed slightly, so it still sped out swiftly over the water.

"What do you think of our new friend?" Marad asked as he gestured to the solitary figure on the foredeck. Tom examined him closely, noting the one most distinct thing about the man. His aura was silver with just hints of blue. Five hundred years could not breed out that aura, the aura of Earth.

"First I would say that what Guyle seeks was right before his eyes to begin with." Other than that, he was just another member of a Family of Qwen, darker complexion, yet with the features of Japanese lineage. His brow was high and he wore his hair pulled back and tied. Tom remembered what LuVic had called him, a Bushi. Bushi meant warrior in Japanese, it meant also, though somewhat loosely, Samurai. He wore the blue coat of House Rhinn and wide bottom pants: *hakama*. He carried two swords, edge up, one long and one short: *Daisho*. The man looked stoically ahead of the ship.

"What do I think? I have a lot of questions and no answers. However, I am sure some will be answered on this voyage. Our friend there looks formidable."

"Yes he does," Marad replied.

"Paravel lay only a little more than a week to the south. The captain will not go to Clef first. Word has it that it is to become a Seat. There will be more than a few of the Guard of Oran there. It seems my sister has won that isle as well."

"Eight days at sea?"

"A fortnight at the best."

"Great." Tom smiled wanly as Marad laughed heartily and slapped the tracker on the back.

Chapter 26

Snow lashed through the dark, scoring the rider of the brown steed for his foolishness at being out on such a night. Head down against the gale, he rode over the Plains of Straw to the pinprick of orange light on the horizon. It was to that campfire he now journeyed, to the rendezvous with Duran's man. His message had gotten through to the Regent several nights ago; he knew that the man there was Kiuf, Duran's personal man-at-arms. Kryall smiled at the thought of Alaric Dirkajian making a gesture to the Regent. As his master Oran was wont to deign, *plans within plans*.

It took him some time before he reined his horse in at the campsite. Several of the Black Guard stood at his approach and others just warmed themselves at the fire. As he tethered the horse to a stake, a man threw the tent flap open and motioned for the rider to enter.

Kiuf had kept it warm within the tent with a brazier. He motioned Kryall to the steaming liquor drink and sat in the lone field chair.

"You are Kryall?" Kiuf knew already. The man nodded and ignored the drink, he shrugged off the cloak he wore and immediately a wave of power hit Duran's lieutenant. He took in this man, Kryall, and shuddered. He was immense and the power with which he carried himself was incredible. Kiuf had met a Hand of Keth before, but never one of such age and power. The presence of this man within the small confines of the tent was overwhelming. What surprised Kiuf was that Kryall carried no weapon;

he did not carry the Kris-voulge common to other Hands and that seemed terribly ominous to Kiuf.

"Milord Duran tells me you have information."

Kryall smiled and Kiuf shivered, this man was evil.

"Yes, a message for the Regent," Kryall rumbled, his voice resonated with power. "But Duran has told me that he wishes some information?"

"Yes; information on the Alchemist, Michael."

Kryall smiled knowingly. "He has quit the city, some weeks ago. He journeys to Narn-toc."

"Narn-toc?"

"Yes, but there is a garrison in the city. He may be captured."

"Any other information about him?"

"He is one of the Outlanders. He comes from through the *Gate*. My Master Oran has a design for his ilk. As to his repute as a sorcerer, well I doubt the veracity of that. I have never met him, but it is said his ilk have very little skills in the Arts if any and he would have no knowledge of how to tap that which he brings. His like tend toward the mundane. That is the extent of my knowledge of the man. The remaining four seem uncommon, but not greatly so."

"Very well. And what other news do you bring?"

"Word from the Guildmaster Merchant of Paravel. Alaric Dirkajian of Chez would strike a bargain."

"I'm listening."

Kryall smiled and spoke and watched Kiuf shiver as the fire in the brazier waned.

Mike, Lord Michael, Alchemist, Swordsman, Sorcerer, stole through the Gate of Untheran in broad daylight while the Black Guard were dumping trash in the field that was outside the wall. Backs turned to him; he nonchalantly walked through the gate and around a corner, carefully disappearing into a shadowed alley. It was early in the morning and he wanted to be out of the city by nightfall, so he had to move quickly. He was using his crystal as a compass and had charged it to seek out the *Ih'dia Om* and home in on it. He slipped surreptitiously away from the patrols and walked down one of the deserted cobble streets of the city. He pulled out the crystal, suspended now on a gold chain and dangled it; it twisted around for a moment and then pointed to the northeast. He turned left at the next intersection, ever wary of listening for the sound of hooves, or men on patrol.

He looked around for other things too, sorcerous things. Unfortunately, he really did not know what to look for. The villagers that cast him out for using magic had said that sorcery could be detected close to the dead-city. His crystal used a benign, non-active magic, so he was not worried about that. What worried him was if he had to defend himself for some reason and use active magic, or destructive magic, what would the repercussions be?

He sighed and strode briskly down the street. The weeds pushed up between the cobblestones and were as high as the tops of his boots; some trees had even grown in the middle of the streets. The shops though, were strangely preserved. All the signs and walls were devoid of color and the windows had long since shattered, it seemed that a grey pall had settled over everything like a film. Then there was that hideous noise. Mike determined it to be the wind howling through the empty towers, but on a deeper, instinctual level, he knew there was something evil and sorcerous about it. Occasionally, as he neared a building the tip of his staff would fluoresce. This made him somewhat uneasy so he tried to stay near the center of the streets.

Around noon, he wandered into an overgrown square and spied through trees that had grown there, a large keep in the distance. The crystal aimed toward that keep like an arrow. It was funny that even within Narn-toc there were smaller citadels. This one appeared to be in better shape than most of the structures he saw. The vines avoided it and there was color in the copper capitol of the dome that surmounted the central structure. Flying buttresses flanked it and flowed down to a protective wall. From what Mike could see from the square, the structure covered about three city blocks. He figured from the way the crystal was behaving the other volume of the *Ih'dia Om* must be within those walls.

Ever mindful of where he was, he skirted the edge of the square and began the trek toward the citadel. A brisk breeze tore leaves from the trees and swept down the lane where he walked. He tried to imagine this city full of people, teaming with life and activity, gay colors painted on signs and walls, but it eluded him. Maybe the magic had warped the place, or maybe his preoccupation with the *book*. He did thank God that the *Daemon* and his ilk were not present. Maybe those creatures just occupied the *aether* realm.

The sun had passed its zenith and now began its downward path. It had seemed to Michael that the citadel was just a few blocks ahead, but the brush conspired to slow him and several times, he had to turn down a side street to bypass a copse that had sprung up in the middle of the road. The shadows began to lengthen and Mike began to worry.

He looked again for the citadel, this time spying it down a narrow alley to his left. It was odd; he had thought for sure that it should be straight ahead. He pulled the crystal from his pocket and held it aloft. Sure enough, it spun lazily in that direction. He sighed and made to put it away when he saw *it* reflected in the crystal.

Carefully he dropped the crystal in his pocket and adjusted his staff in his hand. Silently he cursed himself for being led astray, it was almost too late that he realized the peril he was in. He had been led around as if by a nose ring, while the sun gradually sank toward the horizon. No, *it,* that thing he caught in the prism, was not *here* but the *aether* and *it* was leading him astray. Had he not used the passive magic just then he may not have broken the spell of the thing until it was dark and then it would have been too late. Carefully, silently, he warded himself and when he made to enter the alley, he spun hard and low, swinging out the staff.

Was it magic or was it his imagination? Had the staff actually glowed along the length when passing through the shade that followed closely behind him? Had runes flared up all along the shaft for the briefest of moments? He did not know, but when it was over there were the sounds of a sheet ripping and a cold blast of wind.

He looked down the length of the staff where the runes had appeared. Now all that seemed to be there was the dull black metal of the shaft. He smiled crookedly and spun back to the alleyway. On the other side, he spied the citadel.

Night was fast approaching, the sky was a crisp burnished umber laced with lavender clouds. It reminded him of how the city had appeared the night of the attack by the *Daemon,* in his chambers, when he travelled to the *aether* realm. As he pushed through the alley to the other side, he came upon a wide avenue to behold the citadel with the copper dome. He did not have time to study it before a host of bats startled him as they sprang from the eaves of the building and leapt skyward with a flurry of wings and screeches. He stumbled short, watching them wing their way toward the opal moon and it was then he spotted the sentinel on the distant tower, keeping a watchful eye on the citadel across the boulevard.

A *Keth*, it had to be, its lower body wrapped languidly around the crumbly slate tiles of the parapet. It had not noticed him and he gathered, from the shimmer around its body, that there was glamour. He should *not* have noticed it. It sat there, wings folded about its shoulders, scanning below even though it had no eyes with which to behold. *Nevertheless, why?* Mike wondered as he watched the thing. He followed its gaze down toward the main gate of the citadel and there in the shadows stood two guards, gazing unknowingly into the lengthening shadows. They appeared not to be

378

aware that they were watched. Why would the *Keth* watch them?

Whatever the case, he would have to make a move soon; with the sun setting and night swiftly approaching, he would not be safe out in the open. The evil was manifest here. However, the citadel across the way seemed like a sanctuary from the encroaching darkness. He just had to get past the *Keth* and the guards. Peering intently at the two guards, he saw that their livery denoted they were members of the Black Guard, not the Guard of Oran. He felt slightly better for that. Now if he could only distract them both at the same time.

He realized what he needed to do. He could not use overt active magic against the *Keth*. That would just alert the creature to his presence and probably the guards too. He had to remove the glamour from the creature, so the guards would be distracted by its presence.

He took a deep breath and grabbed the shaft of the spear in both hands. Normally he would channel his *workings* through an object, like his orb (which had been destroyed) or his crystal, which was currently charged with passive magic. He decided to channel this magic along the staff; after all, it had displayed a propensity to channel sorcery in the past. He would concentrate on moving the crumbling tiles on the parapet, hoping to dislodge the creature and thus disrupt the glamour, allowing the guards to see something and respond. Since the sorcery was not directed at the creature, it would most likely not have time to realize it was originating with the outlander.

In his mind, he formulated the complex mathematical formula. Probability theory merged with complex calculus, mixed here and there with the High Tongue of the Conclaveum, more singsong chant than language, but it helped with the flow of the formula and it was as if it came unbidden. It was easy to touch the *aether* and tap the power in that grayness. It would flow from the *between* and into him, through the staff, to the target, the shingles of the parapet. All he had to do was let go...

...It went wrong. It was a trickle of energy from the *aether,* intended to be just enough, but when he focused it through the staff it amplified the power that leapt outward; it was multiplied a thousand fold. He could feel it in the shiver of the shaft, saw the strange runes appear and glow, and saw the air at the tip coalesce into silver light. Even more so than this, the top of the tower where the *Keth* sat erupted into flame and the creature fell from its precarious position to the street far below. The charred remains fell with a dull thud on the flagstones.

It was more than enough of a disturbance that the two guards rushed into the street and to the smoldering twisted corpse that lay below the tower. Mike, startled from the shock of the event, saw his chance and quickly stole across the boulevard and slipped through the portal and into the citadel.

Once inside, as the guardsman shouted alarm about the strange occurrence, he walked swiftly into a corridor, away from the sounds of boots stomping toward the portal. He stole into a long abandoned closet and closed the heavy door. The hinges made no sound and once darkness enveloped him, he muttered a curse and looked at the faint blue glow that still played over the surface of the staff. It definitely was no ordinary spear shaft. Pelles had said a man had found it near Baed and, obviously, it was some sort of magical staff. Old and dormant, he must have activated the thing with his use of sorcery over the past several weeks. He tried to read the runes, but the language, the *tongue* was beyond him.

***

Gythel Boern looked at the *smoldering* pile of black ice that now lay at the foot of a tower just outside of Ythrinny's Keep. Night was fast approaching and he wanted to get his men inside, but what was left of the thing held him in rapt fascination. When he and a dozen of the guard were called, he had found the charred remains of some winged creature. He had watched it change slowly to the black ice that now seemed to burn all the grass and weeds around where it had landed. What the creature had been he did not know, but instinctively he was revolted by it.

Over his shoulder, he heard the last of the patrols returning and then came the tolling of the iron bell somewhere in the Conclavator's Quarter. The bell told him night was falling and his men should be inside. He took one last look at the thing and motioned his men back to the keep. He saw the sergeant of the patrol waiting for him as he walked inside and the door was shut and barred.

"You were informed we quit the city in the morning?" he asked the man.

"Aye sir, but there is something else."

381

"What?" he asked as he walked down the corridor to the common room where his men were preparing the evening meal.

"Our patrol found something that you should see. I have it in the antechamber."

"Oh?" The man nodded, but Boern could not read his expression. He followed the sergeant to the antechamber just off the hall. Two guards stood outside the door and Boern raised his eyebrow. The sergeant grimaced and motioned him forward.

The door swung open and inside sat three men, their wrists bound before them.

"There are more. I have them in the inner courtyard. I believe twenty all told. They were crossing from the Old Seat to the Common city. You know, where the river used to be."

"Looters?"

"No Milord. Look closely at the dark haired one."

The man met his gaze as he looked at him and instantly he realized who it was. "Untie them sergeant!"

"Yes sir!" Immediately the sergeant unbound the three men. Adon stood and rubbed his wrists, nodding to the Commander of the Black Guard of the Wall.

"Thank you, Commander. I fear that I have never had the pleasure of your acquaintance."

"Gythel Boern, Preceptor of Helm. That is until about two hours ago when I was forced into retirement. What brings Adon Vien Crona to the Dead City? Especially since word has it that you and your brother are dead?"

382

"Dead am I? Marad too? Myella has been busy. First I must know Boern, where do you stand?"

The Commander glanced askew for a second at his sergeant. The man just looked blankly back. He was a good man, with family in Chestra and a slightly noble lineage. He was a follower of Tarn, typical of the unit. "Aye. It has been coming to this has it not? There were rumors about Ironeas dead by poison and the war that Duran wages for Myella in the west. Sides are being drawn. Had you been dead, or your brother...

"Adon Vien Crona, I cannot follow those who worship Oran, who would destroy the Conclavator and who would bring such evil into the world. Myella does not deserve the allegiance of these men of the Black Guard. My loyalty is and always shall be to the Conclaveum."

"Good, then I will tell you what I am doing here, after some food. I am famished, as are my men I am sure."

"Good enough. I must tell the men what is afoot. We quit the city at dawn. You will have to come with us. To remain is unsafe."

"Then I must be quick. Do you have plans to this keep?"

"Some, though incomplete. I will have the lieutenant bring them."

***

"Stew nevcr tasted so good, eh Mrick?"

"Yes, Adon, and I hope that my men are faring just as well."

383

"Boern has assured me that they will be tended to and outfitted as Black Guard regulars to get them out of the city. Barj is seeing to it."

"Humph." It was all Mrick could say around a mouthful of bread.

They sat in the common hall that Gythel Boern and his men had taken for their own. The tone was light, almost ebullient throughout the hall, as men had finished their meals and took to getting their gear packed for the deployment in the morning. Adon listened to the men as they talked about Gythel Boern's announcement about quitting the city. Boern would wait until they were a day outside Narn-toc before he discussed Myella's plan to disband the Black Guard. That was a subject best broached far from these walls.

Boern and his lieutenant sat at the bench next to Adon and Mrick. The latter looked on suspiciously at the Commander. In the past, anyone associated with the Conclaveum had been someone not to trust but to despise. Now he was learning differently.

"The plans are vague at best. We did a cursory patrol of the keep, found it to be safe and billeted here. It was much better than the warehouse. The inner courtyard proved sufficient stable. However, the cartographer only detailed the rooms we were to use and the men were discouraged from wandering about, especially after we lost an entire patrol. There were catacombs beneath the keep, but I noticed they were long since sealed off... and warded."

"Yes, Ythrinny would have done that in the months before he was sent to meet Rhinn. He was a more than competent sorcerer. Is there a sanctuary,

384

or chapel to Tarn? It too may have been sealed off. But for other reasons."

"We can find out. The lieutenant and several others are adepts of Tarn. They may prove useful in locating what you seek, that is if you feel you can tell them."

"A book-"

"So? A book? Your sister looks also for a book. She called me to the Seat and there asked me about a book. My men have not come across such a thing; she searchers for it even now."

"Then she searches in vain, for the book is in this keep."

"What? And she knows this not?"

"Sometimes my sister tends to be short sighted. No, some records show that Ghin-jo, the apprentice to Iss, stole the book and brought it to Ythrinny for safekeeping. That is why I believe it to be here. We must find it this night."

"Then we shall. MERN!" he called to the sergeant and instantly the man was at his side. "Tell the men we are on a hunt and the object of that hunt is a book, or a room that doesn't exist. Send out four teams, each with an adept. And for Tarn's sake tell them not to get lost, this place is huge."

"Yes sir!" he spun sharply and went to his task.

"I will join you."

"Come with me then, and Mrick, you are welcome, the more eyes the better."

He nodded, swallowed the last bit of bread and swung Baxel's Bane over his shoulder. Adon did not pay him to like Boern, just work with him.

Mike could barely make out the corridor for the faint light that drifted from his staff and to the surrounding dark. Sometimes the crystal spun lazily to the right of left, sometimes it strained upwards, necessitating he find a stairway and start all over. It was tedious and he was getting very tired. Soon it became one hallway after another, one vast hall, or some servant's chambers, on and on. There were no furnishings except an occasional table or chair, and dust two inches thick on the floor. He felt that inevitably someone would find he tracks, but he could not think about that now.

He entered a large hall, noticed the tattered banners of ages past still hanging from crossbeams, and saw the moonlight streaming down through windows long bereft of glass. He felt immense sadness in this place. Looking toward where a shallow dais and chair sat, alone to the side, he felt loss and wondered how powerful those feelings must have been to linger this long. Maybe it was the staff, which now shuddered in his grasp, which magnified these feelings. *Or maybe it's just my imagination.*

He passed through the door at the other side of the chamber and moved down its length; darkness completely enveloped him and this time the glow of the staff did not help. He stopped and backed out of the hallway. The crystal was pinned to that direction. This time he conjured some passive magic into the crystal and light emanated from within the matrix. *Thomas Edison, eat your heart out.* He smiled wryly.

Once more in the darkened hallway, he watched as the crystal pinned to the wall on his right, not down the length of the corridor. Mike could find no door, or seam that would denote a

386

hidden door. He felt the stones on the wall and essentially the blocks were all the same, in size, shape, texture and temperature. If there were a room behind this wall, it would have been sealed centuries ago. He peered back out into the hall and saw that it lay directly behind the dais, the *source* of the feelings of sadness and loss.

He walked over to the old chair, scratching the Van Dyke that graced his chin. Tracing the brittle wood of the chair, he knew instinctively that it would not support his large frame. He looked carefully at the wall behind the dais. The crystal pointed at it, maybe through it. Nevertheless, there was no seam in the wall, no apparent door. He shuffled his feet, stirring up dust as he moved around the seat. Looking down he noticed that the marble tile around the dais was a different shade from that at the edge of the dais. He smiled to himself and suddenly realized that the hidden door was not in the wall, but in the floor. He figured out the lever mechanism was in the leg of the seat and tilted it back just as he heard voices echoing down the corridor that led into the hall.

Damn, he thought as the tiles slid back to reveal a shallow stairwell. He ducked into it and tugged the chair back above his head. Once more blackness engulfed him, but his crystal kicked in and he could make out a narrow corridor and stairs a few yards ahead. He quickly found himself walking down and then back up into a room that would have been directly behind the dais.

It was as a burial vault. From here, the feelings of sadness and remorse were strongest. He moved tentatively inside, brushing aside the cobwebs of several hundred years and breathed stale air just as old. Guarding this room was a burnished suit of armor, deep metallic red, with great helm, that would have made Surik Shadowlord drool. He stepped around it and found the ornate sepulcher; carved upon the lid was the form of a beautiful young woman, in quiet repose.

The room was full of the remains of dried roses, his sleeve touched one and it shivered into dust. There was so much sadness here. He looked at the writing carved into the marble and knew that whoever had laid this woman to rest had suffered a great loss. He avoided touching the reliquary, but moved around it to the doorway behind.

"I would not pass through there were I you," came a calm voice from behind.

Mike spun around and blue energy crackled around the tip of the staff. In the darkness of the tomb several men now stood. Above the one who had spoken floated a globe of blue light, illuminating the tomb. He had raven hair and forest eyes and a stately bearing. Mike did not recognize him or the older man that stood at his side; it was Mrick he recognized. The sound of steel drawn from a scabbard filled the chamber.

"Nice sword, Mrick. Used to be Chill's. Hope you're taking good care of it." He said it flippantly and Mrick just growled. The man would have advanced on him had not the dark haired man held his arm.

"You know this grave robber, Mrick?"

"Aye, Adon, he is one of the swine I told you of. Lord Michael, Alchemist and Swordsman. He is the Outlander."

388

"Ah, one of those that killed Gelion."

"And who might you be?" Mike asked, still conscious of the power that the man radiated. He was a sorcerer of no mean skill. Mike was no match for him.

"I am Adon Vien Crona, from Tarn Hold and this is Gythel Boern, Commander of the Black Guard of the Wall. You know Mrick."

"Yeah, I know him. How ya doing, Mrick. I see you're hanging with the Conclaveum guys now. Were you with them all along?"

Mrick's eyes narrowed as he looked from Mike to the man who was paying him. "I serve Adon now...not the Conclaveum.

"Mrick, we didn't betray Trevor. In fact we found Gabrielle in Paravel. Saved her from Duran and Myella." At this Adon motioned for Mrick to put his sword away.

"Well, Lord Michael, it seems we are not at a cross purpose then, that is if what you say is true. However, we do not have time to debate the issue. Come morning, about two hours hence, this garrison will quit the city per Myella's orders. Commander Boern here has been ordered to disband the Black Guard and turn the auspices of the office over to the Guard of Oran."

"And to be quite truthful young man that galls me to no end," Gythel Boern said, his deep baritone filling the small chamber. "The Black Guard has served the Conclaveum for five hundred years. Now the Conclavatrix wants to disband us, just as she did the White Guard. That is why I help Milord Adon and you would do well to listen to him."

"Yada yada yada. Since my friends and I have gotten to this land we have been running from the likes of you. Now I am supposed to throw my lot in with you. And Haldeman thought Nixon was his friend."

"See, Adon, he speaks in riddles, let us just kill him and get on with it," Mrick made to draw his sword and once more his hand was stayed by the brother of Myella.

"Great things are afoot in this world, Lord Michael, things that you and your kind do not understand. It took the Keth and their ilk centuries to be able to show themselves, now they do it with ease. The *aether* is being pushed and warped. *Gates* are opened where they should not be and it will be no time at all before the *Daemon* can transgress as easily as the Keth.

"We seek a *grimoire*, Lord Michael, the *Ih'dia Om.* I believe that it is in that room beyond the doorway. But that chamber will be protected."

"I know. I have sensed it. And it is the second volume. *I* have the first. For you these books may stop the evil, but for me it may be a way to get us home. If I should help, you must help me."

"I believe there to be three volumes, Lord Michael. So we may be at this awhile."

"Three? I didn't know about three-"

"See, I have helped you already. Come now, you must decide fast."

"I have decided. To lay down with lions," the big man sighed and set the butt of the staff on the floor. "I cannot possibly beat you by force." He smiled crookedly and motioned with his hand for them to precede him down through the doorway. "After you."

Adon smiled and walked around the sarcophagus to meet Michael at the entrance to the next chamber. He greeted the man with a firm handshake.

"Adon, I like this not. This man is trouble," Mrick spoke quickly, as if it were the only way to stop his patron from engaging with the outlander.

"Mrick, you threw your lot in with me. You knew me to be of the Conclaveum. You did it because you trusted me. From what you tell me, Trevor and Baxel trusted this man and his friends. I would ask you to trust me in trusting him, at least for the time being."

Mrick just shook his head and crossed his arms.

"Good. Guard at the door. If any *thing* manifests itself in this chamber call out. And use that blade as best you can in the while."

"And I?" Gythel Boern asked.

"Follow closely, and be prepared." The Commander of the Black Guard nodded and loosened his saber in its scabbard.

They stepped into the darkness of the next chamber, the faint glow of Mike's staff and the orb of light floating above Adon illuminating the way. The runes on the staff flared momentarily and Mike felt a tingling all along his skin, but it soon passed as they proceeded down the narrow hallway.

"I underestimated your skill, Lord Michael. That staff of yours has eliminated the first Ward. Well done."

"Thanks." He stared down at the staff in his hand and wondered what he was getting into. It started to glow again as they came to an iron door. They all stopped.

"This I must do, Lord Michael. You are not of this world." Mike looked at him sharply. "Yes, I knew. My sister, Myella is capable of many things. Her allegiance with Guyle may yet prove to be her undoing."

Myella's brother? Mike was truly out of his depth here. "What now?" Mike asked, not wanting Adon to know how confused he was.

"This is no ordinary door. The sorcery imbedded in it has the signature of Ythrinny, the former Master of this keep. He was as powerful as lesser sorcerer's of his day. This means that his skill is almost unequaled in this age.

"Watch." Adon closed his eyes and clenched his fist. He raised his hand before the door and suddenly opened it, palm outward. Suddenly the hallway was bright, illuminated by the runes and etchings in the iron door. Mike was in awe of the overlay of power on the portal. The depth of the iron door was just a shell containing the protective energy of the Ward. Mike could sense strings of energy trailing into the *aether*.

"I have never seen anything so elaborate. Can we get through it?" Mike noticed a frown on Adon's face and began to think this task was beyond them all.

"Oh, yes. However, it will take time. Time I am afraid we do not have."

Mike looked at the three-dimensional patterns that stood as if in relief from the surface of the door. Blue energy seemed to twine about like vines, interspersed with glowing runes and glyphs. There

392

was something about this that was familiar, the writing maybe. Then it hit him; it was the same as the runes upon his staff.

"What type of magic is this?"

"What do you mean?"

"In my world they say there is white magic for good, and black for bad, and grey for those who are confused and try to use both. In this world, there is what I know as high sorcery, maybe necromancy and something else. This is something else. What is it?"

"I see. Yes, in this realm there is the High Sorcery, that which utilizes more abstract and pure methods, the Sorcery of the Dead and this, the Sorcery of the Living or Spiritual Sorcery. It is most often linked with Tarn, but not necessarily so. Ythrinny was adept, though he too delved into the High and the Other. In the end his loyalty was to Tarn and the Conclaveum and so it was reflected in his magic: in this."

Mike hefted his staff. "Do you believe in serendipity, or fate, Adon?"

The man smiled. "Yes."

"Good, because maybe only an outlander can do this. You and the good captain there, step back." They did so, Gythel Boern looking strangely at the large man

Mike took his staff in both hands and concentrated. He could not read the language, but with the help of the staff, he could feel it. It lived, formed by the *aether*; it breathed a life of its own and a purpose. Here the purpose was to protect, to guard and to keep locked away. He and the staff had to be the key to unlock the Ward. It pulsed about

393

him and into the hall; it touched him and warned him with its presence. He felt the runes caress his mind with their symbolism and yes, with their complex mathematics. Was God was a mathematician? He could believe that now. This was not only complex and pure, like the magic he had learned to use; it was also spiritual, of a higher order. It touched the core of his being and he felt unworthy at attempting to breach the Ward.

Somewhere, deep within the Ward, he also felt the overwhelming sadness and to some extent, despair. It was Ythrinny, who had put some of himself into the warding of the door and in doing so had left his anguish within the iron, forever bound. He had touched it with the core of his energy, so Michael did not dare manipulate it with the *aether* he controlled, but rather just attempted to nudge aside some of the strands of the ward. Immediately the strands of energy that split off into the *aether* enveloped him, wrapped about him in some powerful embrace. If he failed now, he would be destroyed. Then he saw in the *pattern* what he had to do. He took the staff and positioned it like a key in front of the door. He perceived the runes aligned within the matrix of the Ward and felt he had to adjust those that glowed upon his staff in like manner. He concentrated, his formulae now enhanced by the mystic. Slowly the runes upon the staff slid and moved into the proper position. Still, he could not read them, but he felt them. This sorcery was as much by formula as by feel. Moreover, as the runes aligned the Ward just let go. That is how he would describe it to Adon later, that the Ward seemed to hesitate, then exhale and all the anguish and sadness, for the briefest of moments, turned to relief as the ward let go. It evaporated into nothingness, as if it was never there to begin with. His staff did not absorb or dispel the energy. It was just gone and all that remained was a simple iron door on rusty hinges.

"Lord Michael, I am truly impressed. I dare say I could not achieve that task as quickly or cleanly."

"Thank you, Adon. I credit it with the power in this staff. I felt as though I have wielded it a lifetime. The knowledge was pure and mystical. I don't know if I could do it again, but then maybe I could." He shrugged and turned. Boern and Adon saw awe upon his face. He seemed humbled by the experience and motioned for the other two to open the door.

Boern held Adon back as he pulled his sword free of the scabbard. Now the determined veteran came to the fore, his hard-set features lined, his hair a thin halo of white. Saber held to the ready, his left hand probed along the door, noted hinges and a latch. He pushed the door open.

They looked within to a circular chamber of bare stone. The room held only one thing. In the center of the chamber was a pedestal and upon it was a book. Above the book was an indirect light source, illuminating the *grimoire* in soft moon glow.

The three entered the room cautiously and spread out in a semicircle around the pedestal.

"Any other surprises?" Mike looked at Adon, unsure of the power he had used, unsure of himself for the moment.

"None that I can detect. Ythrinny must have felt that the ward on the door would be sufficient for anyone," he said then looked pointedly at Michael. "That is until you came along."

"Is this the book you seek?" Boern asked, not moving to approach the item.

"Yes and also the one Myella seeks for Guyle," Adon replied.

"It looks different from the one I have." Mike's hand touched the satchel that held the *Ih'dia Om* and other things.

"Remember what we discussed about the magic of this world? Three types of magic; High Sorcery, which is pure and logical; the Sorcery of the Dead and the Sorcery of the Living.

"Which book do you have, Lord Michael?"

Mike thought about the text that he had recovered from the Seat in Paravel. It was a simple looking book, now dog-eared and marked with colored feathers. However, the tome itself was bound in leather, the writing spidery and tricky, but there was a mathematical sense to it. That was the key.

"I have the book of High Sorcery?"

"Yes, it was the first volume of the *Ih'dia Om* that Korman Iss wrote, when he was of middle age and relatively sane. The second tome seemed to be of divine inspiration, and some scholars doubt that Korman Iss wrote it at all; most attribute it to his novice, Ghin-jo.

"Before you is the last tome that Korman Iss wrote and probably the darkest. You must truly be confident in your own ability and self to read it. It is the Book of the Dead."

Mike looked up sharply. According to his own history, The Book of the Dead was an Egyptian text. Mike peered closely at this book of Necromancy. The binding and covers were black, and looked like they were made from slate. The body of the pages appeared to be a grey parchment. On the center of the cover there was a raised symbol that he could barely make out, a hand, pale white and palm outward.

"That's the Hand of Keth?"

"Yes. This power, this magic, knows no boundaries. The layer between the worlds is very thin, and he knew that if certain *Gates* are opened the Keth could slip through. Korman Iss slowly went mad, maybe because of his alliance with the Oran, maybe because he lusted too much for power. This is his last writing, before he fled to the *Firelands* and the Daemon descended upon Narn-toc. His thoughts, and his dark sorcery, are in that tome. It is perilous."

"So...why don't you just get it and let's get out of here." Mike looked nervously around. Usually he had a macabre sense of things, but his tapping into the magic had unsettled him.

Adon's green eyes flashed and he ran his hand through his raven hair. "I guess it has to be done."

"If you go up in a puff of smoke," Mike said, regaining some of his sardonic humor, "I'll offer up a goat to your god."

"Tarn doesn't espouse such tributes."

"Too bad." Mike took a step back, expecting the worst, but as Adon walked up to the pedestal and touched the book, the pale light shining from above just winked out. It was replaced by Adon's own light source. The former Sequestered of Tarn then took the tome in both hands and looked at the heavy bound book.

"There is much darkness here." He frowned and tucked the book in his own satchel. The chamber was now silent and suddenly barren.

"I see you can feel the difference Lord Michael. My pack is warded." The man turned to Gythel Boern and nodded. "We quit the city now. Lord Michael, you may join us. We are not at cross-purposes. We have much to talk about, my sister Myella, Uncle Trevor, Gabrielle my cousin. Many things, including the path of the Black Guard.

"Will you walk that path with us for a time?"

"Paravel will soon fall under siege from Duran's army, that same armyhas been laying waste to the west. I'm going there. But, we are linked." He looked at the two men, his light blue eyes darkened under heavy brow. It was a brooding look that many would come to confuse as desolate. "We must go to Paravel first."

Adon looked to Boern, who shrugged. "Myella will dog us if she finds out about the book, milord," Gythel said to Adon. "Paravel will not be a good place to be, come the siege."

"Yes, but we must also find my brother, Marad. If I know him, he is in dire straits, but very alive. He will try to assemble the White Guard. We can at the very least obtain information in Paravel and then we can go about the business of preventing my sister from further madness."

"Then to Paravel it is, but will they welcome the Black Guard into the city?"

"They will if I take you there as my prisoners," Mike's tone was humorless, but he could tell they appreciated the irony.

Chapter 27

Kryall had changed. The boon was from Oran, whose powers were boundless. Kryall was the oldest, the first. He was the Hand that whispered into Iss's ear and who slowly drew him to madness. He was the Hand responsible for the fall of Exten Rhinn. Banished with the others to the *Firelands,* now to return at the beck of the Mage Guyle.

He and his brothers and sisters had waited long to take the western realm, not for the typical reasons. For him, it was always plans within plans. For Oran to walk this realm, it would take the release of enormous energies, energies that the Outworlders did not solely possess. For him it was the release of the *Third Key*, the binding of Oran.

He looked at the black armor that sat in the chest, the tabard with the telltale white palm. He smiled secretly to himself, knowing that not only was he the most powerful Hand; he was also the strongest sorcerer. He could feel his brothers and know their work, all connected by the intangible web of the *aether*, all but for one and he was no true Hand of Keth.

He had dispatched messengers to Alaric Dirkajian, making sure that the Regent Duran's conditions were explicit. Then he had sat to enjoy the pleasures of this flesh: food, drink. Duran and his army would be here soon. His brother Aziall in Clef had one of the Outworlders captured, just as he kept the Shadowlord and the White Knight under scrutiny. He could not let them foil his plans again. The molten steel from the foundry had cost him two servants. *Costly, but not debilitating*. Soon the plans of his master would come to fruition.

He would be ready.

***

Aziall looked upon the face of death and laughed. After all, he was already dead, and the fires of his damnation only sustained him. His reflection in the mirror was that of youth and vigor, handsome and rakish except for the scar, now healed, that ran across his brow. Hair smoothed back to a ponytail, he smiled sardonically when he glimpsed the outlander, Bard William's reflection. He turned back toward the man.

"Ah, Bard, such unfortunate circumstances that brings you here," said Aziall, the Hand of Keth. Sweat drenched Bill's face, now grimacing with the pain. "Your friends have abandoned you and Torec."

"I doubt that," he managed to say between clenched teeth. He had been stripped to the waist, and welts covered his torso: not from a flail, but from the Hand's *Kris-voulge*.

"Oh, you can believe me in that, friend Bard. I let them escape. They are of no consequence to me. They are insignificant to the plan.

"I keep Torec el'Kirien only because I wish him to understand that the Conclaveum will not tolerate rebels. It is you, whom I have interest in Bard. Not because you are one of Gelion's killers, or have caused great dismay to my benefactor Myella. No, none of those things, I am afraid.

401

"You are special to Guyle and my Master. You come across the *Gates* from the *Outworlds*. So, unto this realm, that which you possess is very powerful."

"I have no magic. You tried this before with Sir John and it didn't work, what makes you think I'm special?"

"Because Myella tried to wrack the White Knight. I will not wrack you. I will use you, until you are naught more than a shell, a carcass." He laughed and sat across from the Bard on a stone chair. He leaned forward and a menacing green light seemed to catch fire in his eyes.

"I brought no sorcery!"

"You do not even realize it, Bard. You see, in order for Oran to walk this world, a certain *Gate* must be opened. But it is no ordinary *Gate*. The Krim thought this *Gate* to be in the western lands, far west, beyond the even Bastion Hold. However, Ghin-jo knew better. He built Bastion to keep an eye upon the west, but it was Rhinn who settled in Qwen to keep an eye not only upon Narn-toc, but also upon the Breach, where my Master's *Home Gate* is. There are many lesser *gates* in this world, but only the One does my Master want.

"The Krim seek this *Gate* because they wish to return to their long lost home. If sacrificing them to open a *Gate* is necessary, so be it."

"Why us? Why were we brought here?"

"You belong here, Bard."

"What-"

"Enough of this banter. We must get down to business. Certain energies need released. Prophecies need fulfilled. *The Saint's Soul must die*. When you

402

pushed through the *Gate* from your world, you brought the power. Let me show you." He passed his *kris-voulge* across the window, and immediately what light was gone, as if a shade fell. The simple chamber was now left in darkness.

"You do not have the skill to detect the aura. Look into the mirror Bard look at yourself. What do you see?"

Bill looked into the mirror, saw himself bound in chains and ever so faintly saw the silver aura about him; like little fingers of flame dancing around the periphery of his body. Then he caught sight of the Hand. He recoiled in fear and disgust.

Aziall appeared as a hideously deformed creature. A demon, Bill would say, caught in a malignant black-green aura. He gagged on bile while Aziall laughed and covered the mirror.

"The mirror's magic allows us to see our spirit. It seems that yours is not as mature as mine, yet."

"It never will be," Bill said with venom. He glared at the Hand of Keth, straining at his bonds.

Suddenly the Hand's visage changed to one of hate and he jabbed the *kris-voulge* into Bill's mid-section. The bard screamed as blue-green light discharged over his stomach. A black bruise slowly welled up to a blister and burst. Blood flowed down over the black-barreled weapon. Bill watched through tear-filled eyes as the blood covered the tip of the weapon. It sizzled and boiled as it traveled over the surface, finally disappearing to leave only silver energy dancing around likc little bolts of electricity.

"Your power, Bard William. Your essence, your life," he hissed as he watched it become as quicksilver on the surface of the *Kris-voulge*. He dared not to touch it he just watched it warily. Then he found a silver vial and let the essence drip into it. He carefully sealed it shut and set it on the table beside them.

"I will drain you of it, Bard. Your life essence, that silver light, that power which will break the *Gate* open, will be sucked from you. Until that is, you are an empty shell to be filled by the Keth. To be filled just as your friend Sir Chill."

Duran took the point with Kiuf, laughing at what he had to say about his meeting with Kryall. The stout lieutenant looked hard at his Regent, but continued on, detailing Alaric Dirkajian's message.

"So, Dirkajian would bargain?"

"It would seem so."

Duran nodded and looked ahead through the lazily drifting snow. Even through the flakes, the sun dazzled his eyes with its brilliance. The horse shied a bit, but he nudged it with his knees and it moved along through the inch thick blanket of white. They were moving through a large grove of birch trees and along the road meandered a gurgling and yet unfrozen stream. It was hard for Duran to believe that in a fortnight he would probably be knee deep in mud and blood.

"He does this without the knowledge of the city council, without the knowledge of Kelvin. He is a brave man to place himself so high considering what I did to the governor."

Kiuf nodded and looked over his shoulder to the column of soldiers that followed. The ranks were tight and they appeared well rested. The time in camp had done them well. With this news, Kiuf hoped the siege would be short. He said as much.

"Do not count on it my friend. Dirkajian is only interested in one thing: himself. He is very duplicitous." The Regent adjusted the collar of his fur cloak and looked through the snow, through the grove, to the Plains of Straw. "We will accommodate Dirkajian as long as it suits us. Then we will kill him."

Kiuf nodded grimly.

Trevor had not seen Sir Chill in weeks and realized that if this continued he would soon die. His fare had steadily declined and water was infrequent. He was losing his strength and there was the edge of a cough in his throat. He only maintained what he had from the food he had squirreled away. It was when he had eaten the last piece of stale bread that he heard the footsteps outside of his cell door, and the faint glow of light from the crack at the floor.

The door swung open and the light momentarily blinded him. When his eyes adjusted, he stared at the Krim, Bej-et. The light did not come from a torch, rather it emanated from her chitinous armor. She stared at him with quicksilver eyes and when she spoke, her voice was musical and soft.

"Greetings, brother of the *Iron Hand*, how fare you this night?"

"Well enough, Krim, well enough. However, I will probably perish in this state. I believe my half-brother has forgotten I am down here."

She nodded and moved into the chamber, graceful as a dancer, as deadly as a Keth.

"He has forgotten not." She stared at him a long moment. Even in the stillness of the cell, her ephemeral hair seemed to move with a breeze.

"And what are your designs for me? You move freely now, though last time we spoke you were bound." Trevor said.

"Designs many. Once we served the Tel. A bargain we have struck. By brief alliance, we may go to what we have lost. Only at our *Home Gate* does the knowledge exist. Only by releasing the antithesis of our magic will the *Gate* be opened."

"You Krim always did speak in riddles."

"That mortal coil you carry, it is important. Not so for us. We are almost ageless. Displaced to this realm and lost to ours. Nevertheless, for that immortality, Guyle struggles and it is as elusive as the air he breathes.

"I tell you this not to enjoin you. I tell you because you are part of the *Key*. We have waited too long, we watched. You, though unknown to Guyle, we will hold in Ransom for what he has promised."

"And only the magic that the outlanders bring can open it?"

"The antithesis of our magic. For this *Gate* is of our magic. Oran and his minions wish to walk this world. That is not our matter. When the *Gate* is opened, we may pass. Unsure we are of his design yet."

"So you would sacrifice this world to Oran, so that you may journey to that realm? The suffering you would cause." Trevor shook his head as he looked at the wondrous creature.

"We have suffered since we were exiled to this realm!" As she spoke, her armor sparked and flared,

406

a living thing emoting with her words. "Imagine an eternity suffering in this bleak lifeless world. For the Krim it has been so. Away from our realm, yet feeling it, knowing it is there. That is the agony of our race. And you forbid us from the western lands."

"The war, it is to prevent your kind from taking our land."

"We want nothing of your land. We want only to find the *Home Gate*. The Outworlders hold the *Keys*. Your half-brother will aid us."

She reached out and touched his forehead and a blinding light took his consciousness.

"Now brother of the *Iron Hand*, sleep."

When he awoke she was gone, he was hale and in another place. It was most disconcerting that he did not know how he had gotten to this other place. A gentle rocking brought him to wakefulness.

Alien carvings surrounded him. The wall was a living thing and it depicted the history of this ship, ten thousand years old. He knew where he was immediately upon seeing the carving and the coloring of the wood. There was an ovoid porthole, through which issued golden sunlight and the smell of water. He was on a Krim ship.

He struggled from the pallet upon which he lay, through the ephemeral gauze of warmth that was the Krim blanket. Weak still, he walked to the porthole and looked out.

It was Lake Ionet and in the distance was Teshwa. The ship anchored in the middle of the lake, a huge behemoth silent and aware.

"You wake," came the soft dulcet sound in the chamber. Bej-et had entered and stood in the cabin that had no visible door.

"Yes, it seems my half-brother has new designs for me."

"No. To him you are missing."

"What?" Trevor turned and looked into those black, enigmatic eyes.

"The *Daemon* did not wish you to live. Guyle perceived a threat to Myella should you be discovered. He ordered your death."

"I do not feel dead."

She smiled and he had to remind himself she was alien. "Oran wished you dead. Guyle wished you dead. The Krim did not. You are a minor part of the *Second Key*. We care not for Guyle's success. The *keys* need only be revealed to us, in time."

"Then why?"

"For now, you are removed here for the *skein*. Our Ransom will be what Guyle promised"

"I do not understand."

"No, you do not. But, you shall."

She turned and passed through the cabin door that was not there. Left alone, his cell improved, he realized he was in a prison, nonetheless.

The boat rocked to and the boat rocked fro. Barish gazed over the deck at the restless sea. Locked in the cove north of Qwen during an autumn storm the sea roiled around them. Stormy seas lay outside the sheltered cove and the protective hull of the *felucca,* but within he was calm and secure.

He scratched at his beard and wiped away the moisture from the sill of the port. Even through the twilight, he knew the weather would not get better this night. He turned back to his hammock and swung up into it, knowing the sway of the ship would soon lull him to sleep, regardless of the severity of the storm. Tucking the wool blanket about his chin, he folded his arms across his chest and closed his eyes. The sea, the wind, it beckoned him with its freedom, calling him to the unknown. It was then that he almost forsook his command and wondered if he could venture to the unknown. Nevertheless, he could not because of his duty.

Tomorrow they would sail. Not to Qwen, for in Chestra there had been rumors that the Guard of Oran had a heavy presence there. No they would go further down the coast, to Paravel. He sighed and settled back, the sway in the hammock bringing sleep.

Chapter 28

It was a cold and blustery day in Paravel; the rain had turned to ice and most found the warmth and security of the home and hearth preferable to being out of doors. Master Talbot had forsaken the karo house with its fine pastries for the inn of the Blue Heron and its mediocre fare.

He sat at the table and speared a leg of lamb, a rare luxury in these refugee-ridden days, and brought the two-tined fork to his mouth, being careful to wipe away drippings with the corner of a napkin. Gabrielle looked across the table in wonderment at the man's appetite.

"You seem positively radiant, my dear, a welcome change since last we spoke. That is good." She blushed, but she doubted he would notice as he looked down toward his plate assessing which vegetable to attack.

"Thank you, it seems Sir John has a way of keeping despair at bay."

The big man smiled, almost knowinglyand sat his fork down.

"Well I suppose you are wondering why I asked you to meet me. Yes."

"I was curious, we have heard very little from Preceptor Skettes. Did you hear any news of my father?"

"Not about your father, something else. What goes on in the Tower and who resides therein is not made known to the public. What I have to say is about this war. Duran is nigh, maybe a fortnight away. A friend who was traveling from the east passed his van and made haste to Paravel. You are in peril if you stay, my dear, and I could not bear to know that someone whom I think of as the daughter I never had could perish in the coming conflict."

"We know, outriders have informed us. I cannot leave, my Protector is here."

"Ah, the young knight you are so fond of." He motioned for a cup of mead and the stout server brought it quickly and curtly, unlike her treatment of other patrons. This behavior went mostly unnoticed to Talbot. "It is my fear Lady Gabrielle, that he may not be able to stop Duran's army. I fear he will be unable to afford you the protection you deserve. That is why I have asked you here. Come with me to Chestra. Bring your friends as my ship has the room. I can drop you in Qwen, along the coast, or in any friendly port. It is safe passage that I offer you."

"Master Talbot," she began, smiling sadly and shaking her head. "I appreciate the offer, truly. However, at this time I cannot accept. My place is here, with this city, with Sir John."

"I fear that you are being foolish, but I know better than to argue with a woman. My ship *is* at your disposal up until the point when the siege threatens, then I sail. Take it for what it is worth, milady."

"Thank you, I will."

"Now," he said as he moved the plate aside. "The pastries here are not as good as our favorite spot, but they have this pie..." She smiled again as his eyes lit up and he called the server over once more.

Gaj looked good, John thought, as he snapped the horse around and trotted past the swordsman. He

411

smiled as he realized he was not becoming too shabby of an equestrian either. Gaj had cleaned himself up rather well after that incident at the Kifu den. Still with a hint of melancholy, Gaj had for the moment straightened out. He had been sober several weeks now and others within the Legions of the Black Skull (as they had named themselves) had advised Joe and John that Gaj stayed away from even the weakest ale.

John sighed as his gaze swept out over the field and to the sky. It was cold and brisk, like those autumn days when winter is just around the corner. He loved this exposure to the elements when they were raw like this. He felt a patter of rain, covered the tsuba on his katana with a leather guard, and watched the recruits march in tight lines to the order of their commanders and Reos, Sergeant at Arms of the Legions of the Black Skull. They were ten thousand soldiers strong, just over three legions, with a modest cavalry, archers, cannonade, and infantry. Almost all were dressed in gray uniforms made from the bolts of cloth garnered through Kelvin and Chair Nathal's Edict. Many of the mounted soldiers were battle-hardened guardsmen of the council. Others were refugees who were practiced men-at-arms in such cities as Ord, Tarn Hold and Albien and who had fled shortly after those cities fell.

His cloak flared our behind him. The low clouds raced across fleeting blue, briskly bringing on winter, invigorating him as he sat upon horse with sword across knees like some ancient samurai. Reos saluted him from across the field and he nodded back. This was an army now, however

412

green, and it was up to them, Kelvin, and the city guard to get them through the oncoming siege.

Hjil and her command flitted across the battlements, tending to the score of cannons that sat upon the new ramparts; potentially they could ring the city with fire and protect the mouth of the harbor from blockade. John spied her stout form upon the gate wall, hand on hip and hilt of stiletto, other holding the ramrod for the cannon like it was a halberd. John knew her as a proud woman from the northern climes near Tarn Hold who had taken to the command of the cannonade with fervor and dedication.

The outriders had brought news of Duran's army, now less than a fortnight away chewing up the Plains of Straw, gathering strength and reinforcements from Dorber, Helm and, rumor from the south had it, a legion of the Guard of Oran from Narn-toc. Rich merchants, fat on the spoils of an exploited refugee population had set sail long ago to Qwen and points north, forsaking the city to Myella and the Conclaveum. Only Alaric and core group of the guild merchants remained, seemingly to weather the storm.

Still there was no word from Tom Smiling Wolf and this began to worry him. The scout should have returned long ago. He had not returned, nor had any of Torec's men. He felt that Tom was alive, but what else he did not know.

Above the din of the marching men and jingle of horses tack, came the sound of distant thunder, a darker cloud began to slide across the horizon to the northeast; it signaled the end of the temperate weather. With the sound of hooves, he looked over

413

his shoulder and watched as Surik Shadowlord and Lord Kelvin rode through the gate and toward him. Joe looked as morose as ever, Kelvin dignified and stolid. The Lord Protector of the city wore the burnished silver breastplate of his station; a gray and red cloak flung casually over his shoulder and carried his plumed helm upon his saddle horn. Surik wore black armor, fraught with spikes at the joints, which at times looked too dangerous to wear. His ensorcelled bastard sword was ever near his hand. He did not wear his helm and so his eyes echoed the clouds that raced above in both color and ferocity.

They reined in next to the self-proclaimed Lord Knight. Joe scowled and Kelvin nodded.

"Well, I think that the militia is maxed out for recruits," Joe said as he fixed his gaze in the distance. "I was at the Keep earlier and there were some young boys there. They can run messages and what not, but cannot fight. They were the only ones there, so I think that well has run dry."

"Probably," replied John. He smoothed his wavy brown hair back. "We train now, and train hard. When Duran's army is three days away, we rest them. Reos thinks that is best. Then we fight them in two shifts."

"We shall still be hard pressed," Kelvin stated. John noted he looked tired and the lines about his face deeper. He had aged over these past few months. "Duran will have three, maybe four times as many troops if the rumors of reinforcements are true. We have stores enough for winter, if we ration thinly." He frowned as his horse fidgeted; a steady hand on the beast's neck calmed her. "Chair Nathal has assured me that the Council will not sue for

414

peace with Duran. They value their heads and Duran does not. Pithorn has converted several *feluccas* to warships, he does expect attack from sea, and the harbor mouth cannot be blocked, so your cannon will have to do. So we wait."

"And if Duran brings sorcery?"

"We probably fail in protecting this city. Mark my word, Myella will bring sorcery, and Javin Skettes has said that his wards will hold for a time. But I know Myella and her warped sorcery so it will not be for the duration."

"So then," John interrupted, "it is just a matter of time before Duran has the city."

"We knew that from the start," Joe growled.

"Let us hope for a miracle," Kelvin replied.

"Well if there is a miracle it is them," John said as he pointed to the drilling militia.

"Great," Joe muttered and flexed his steel gauntleted hands. He was getting used to the new armor, getting used to what he would have to wear for the duration of the siege.

"The trenches are dug, the stockades and barricades set; it's just a matter of training at this point." John shrugged.

"You know," Joe replied. "We only have a finite amount of gun powder."

"Mike assured me it would go a long way. He said to use half charges at the beginning to draw them in and then full charges."

"This had better work."

"If it doesn't?"

"This city is doomed," Kelvin said flatly.

Chapter 29

The heavy wooden door swung open slowly. Torec looked up through eyes almost swollen shut and watched as Bard William's limp form was shoved into the cell and the door was shut behind him. He did not speak, his mouth swollen; he had lost a tooth. Bill did not stir for some time. Torec, considering the brutal hands of their captors, knew this was the norm now. They had been in the cell several weeks. Every night Bill was taken away to see the one named Aziall; he came back weaker in the morning. He was wasting away much faster than he should and he looked several years older now than he did when he had first set foot on the island.

He took stock. The cell was empty save he, the Bard and Brunwurst; normally it could accommodate maybe ten comfortably. He chuckled. It had been awhile since he had known comfort; this hidden laughter brought pain, his ribs were cracked his first night of imprisonment.

"Look you big oaf, the outlander stirs," Brunwurst's head lifted slightly, then sagged again; his movements were sluggish. They kept him drugged because of his great strength. Torec was slowly working at flushing the narcotic from the big man's system with his ration of water, but it was slow going.

The morning sun now pierced through the heavy bars above, chasing the cold when it lit upon his shoulder. He moved his shackles aside and touched Bill on the arm. The man groaned and began to stir. Finally, many long moments later his eyes opened and he looked at Torec.

"You look like shit," Bill mumbled.

"Aye, and I see the *Ishe deme* are treating you well?"

"Heh," he croaked and rolled over. There was a red welt along his stomach that looked irritated. Otherwise, there was no mark upon him except for cuts at his wrists and ankles where he had been bound. "Oh man, but do I feel awful."

"They did it again, the draining of your essence."

"Yeah, not so much this time. He says I'm too weak. Nice guy, this Aziall."

"What is he doing with this *essence*?"

"He has this chamber, there are these two short obelisks with a receptacle at the top of each. They face each other. There are runes upon them. Upon each obelisk, there are about twenty runes in all. When he pours the *essence* into it, the runes glow silver light. He shies away from the light, but it doesn't stop him from his incantations or whatever. Two runes are done.

"Wow, it took two weeks to do two runes. I'll be dead long before it's finished."

"And it's purpose?"

"He said they were *keys* for a *Gate*." And with that Bard William D'Asturien passed-out. Torec el'Kirien looked on in numb silence.

Rhianne ar'Liayne and Tar'elah crouched down behind a stack of barrels in the dock district of Avard Clef. Before them was the mercenary ship that the Hand Aziall had spoken of. It was a large troop transport from Chez flying a yellow flag. To the fore of it was a black *felucca* with the standard of the Conclaveum flying from its central mast.

417

"That ship from Chez could be a way off this rock," ar'Liayne said. She looked somewhat less disheveled than she did a fortnight previous on her flight from the stockade. She and Tar'elah had managed to secrete themselves in the abandoned estates along the coastline and in various warehouses in this district of the capital, trying to figure out their options. The only opportunity to leave the island lay before them and in three nights that too would be gone. Word on the docks had it that the ship from Chez was leaving; Aziall was to send payment to the captain, much to the dismay of the people of Clef.

In the past two weeks, more ships from the Conclaveum had arrived. Some bore soldiers, others civilians and Rhianne surmised that the annexation of Clef had begun. It was a sad time indeed.

"We must find a plan then, one that will allow us to rescue the Bard, Torec and your protector." Rhianne looked at the bandit long and hard. If it was not for her, the former governor would probably dead, or worse. *How far we have fallen these past weeks*, she thought. Both were dressed in loose fitting robes of fishermen's wives. Shawls were drawn over their heads to hide their faces, which surprisingly did not grace any wanted posters.

"How, do you propose we get them out, my back-country friend? Walk into the prison and ask for their release?"

"That is a choice."

"You are as bad as Torec." Tar'elah smiled at that and looked once more toward the ship from Chez.

"They say they are the best swordsmen alive, you know."

"The Chez?" Rhianne nodded. "Unfortunately they can be bought. I've seen swordsmen from Qwen who are better, but they are the exception I'm sure. These Chez take the duel to a high art."

It was night and the ship held steady against the dock in the calm waters. There were two, guards at the gangway, but they were so intent on the dock before them that they did not see the figure at the bow.

Slowly, Tar'elah pulled herself from the water. The bowline dipped to the water before it anchored on the docks mooring. She lifted herself quietly from the cold water, and hand over hand began to pull up the heavy rope. Soon she was twenty feet up at the top of the forecastle. She pulled herself over the rail and grew silent.

The only sound was the creaking of the boat, the slap of the waves and her own breathing. She moved into a crouch and peered down the long deck. There were at least fifty paces to the rear deck and the captain's quarters. It was too much space to cover without attracting the attention of the man who stood atop the rear deck at the helm. She would have to go below deck.

Masir Kasarian, Guildliege Mercenary of the ship looked at the Sea Master and fire burned across his amber eyes.

"Not yet? What is Aziall's excuse this time? He entered the contract; he signed the agreement before the governor could! Now he refuses to pay us!"

"My liege, three times he advised us that the gold was on the way. He is toying with us."

419

"But why, does he invite a fight? He has the gold."

"He tests us. Mayhap he wishes to keep us in port until the winter storms, I know not."

"Put an extra squad on deck. Send message to Aziall that we want payment on the contract he bought out."

"Aye, and-"

"He will betray you." Masir and the Sea Master looked up sharply. Tar'elah stood in the doorway dripping wet, but confident.

"Well, Sea Master seems we have a stow-away."

"No stow-away, but someone who seeks to enter into a contract."

Masir frowned and looked to the Sea Master. "How I wish we were in Chez."

Rhianne ar'Liayne and Tar'elah sat in the spacious quarters of the Guildliege Mercenary, the Chez equivalent of a General. He commanded the mercenaries on the ship and answered to no one save the Sea Master while at sea. He was an imposing man, and commanded attention, much like Alaric Dirkajian. Tall and dark haired, exceedingly handsome, his movements were more panther-like than Alaric's. He carried a slim long sword at his hip and a shorter, thinner blade opposite. Tar'elah was sure that he knew how to use them with exceptional skill. Yet his strong hands now served them tea.

"And what brings the former governor of Clef and her...er...friend to visit my ship?"

"For one, you had a bargain with the people of this island-"

420

"Who now for the most part are dead," he finished for her. "The gold was not delivered, nullifying the contract. I entered a new contract with this Aziall to sail away. The papers were signed and now I look for payment. He has one more chance."

"He is not an agent of the Conclaveum, Guildliege, he is a servant to Oran and Myella," Rhianne replied.

"Myella is Conclavatrix; he is her agent by proxy." He sat for a moment, sipping his tea. "Do not think I am unsympathetic, Governor. However, I have the contract to attend to and he has signed and promised."

Rhianne leaned forward to emphasize her point. "You haven't been paid one shenk yet Guildliege. Nor should you expect it. This *Ishe deme* will let you stew, and then they will fall upon you in the night. Aziall is not to be trusted."

"Compelling, Governor. However, they must be given the opportunity to pay. I will go myself to speak with this Aziall."

"Be warned, he is a treacherous man."

Masir Kasarian smiled.

The Hand, Aziall, had word that the mercenaries from Chez were coming. One of the patrols had broken early to report that they were on their way. He sat in the chair normally reserved for the governor of Clef, Rhianne ar'Liayne. He smiled as he toyed with the barrel of his *kris-voulge*. The scars from the dog had healed nicely and were now gone, after all, his liege to Oran had its benefits.

Two rows of guards flanked him, swords drawn. There were forty of them, all hardened

421

veterans, Aziall's personal entourage. The odds would be three to one if there were a problem.

Brunwurst was finally acting his old self, insulting everything that Torec did, and trying hard to feign lethargy from the drugs whenever the guards were present. Bard William on the other hand was not doing so well. The Hand had let him be for the past two nights because he had been so weak, and now a strip of gray hair had sprung up on his head where before there had been only dirty blond.

Torec had managed to regain some of his strength and most of the pain had become naught more than a manageable throb. He helped the Bard as best he could, but it was becoming apparent that the man needed the help of a healer. Bill had muttered to him that now more than half of the vessels were full. The obelisks that made a receptacle for his essence showed four of ten runes glowing on the surface. Torec feared that by the time the last was filled, the minstrel would be dead.

It was time for them to make their move, regardless of their weakened state. The next time the guard brought the food they would have to try to escape. Otherwise, the Bard would certainly perish.

Masir Kasarian knew that should the contract spoil with Aziall, it would be a hard fight back to the ship, however the Hand of Keth had signed the contract as proxy for the Conclaveum and Masir intended not to release them from it. His ten men strode resolutely next to him, the streets of Avard Clef were barren this time of day and as they approached the governor's hall, they noticed a squad of the Guard of Oran coming up the side street to their right. Instinctively he knew he was betrayed, but the Code said he must confront Aziall.

The doors to the great hall swung open and motes of dust swirled before them. Across the long hall, Masir saw Aziall sitting in the Governor's chair, holding his *kris-voulge* at his side like a scepter of power. Flanking him on the right and left were forty hardened veterans of the Guard; all were armored and all held bare blades at their side.

"Aziall, I have come for the contracted payment, overdue I might add."

"To the point, the mercenaries of Chez are always so succinct."

"The time for conversation is long past. You greet us with armed guards and no war chest. Well, what is the answer?"

"Ah, unfortunately Kasarian, I never had any intention of paying you. I would have allowed you to quit port, but you would never have done that would you?"

Kasarian sighed and closed his eyes a moment. The odds were not very bad. It was the *kris-voulge* they he worried about. "So you have chosen to break the contract? I thought as much."

"You and your men lay down your arms. Otherwise it will be bloody Kasarian and you should probably know I like a good slaughter now and then."

"You would kill us unarmed, no doubt." Aziall smiled, and did not notice the imperceptible shrug of Kasarian's left shoulder. It was a signal to the man on his immediate left. A bow came up from beneath a long cloak, arrow already nocked. The string vibrated and the arrow sped away, passing so close to Kasarian's head that the hair swept forward. Aziall had not expected a bowman among the Chez. Nobody really did, but Chez archers trained for this type of Contractual Contingency. Aziall noticed the arrow was speeding slightly off to the left. Too late, he felt the impact in his left arm, which was outstretched. The barbed shaft of the arrow easily pierced the mail sleeve, slicing through tendon and muscled. The *kris-voulge* fell to the marble flags with a clang. Immediately the guards rushed at the mercenaries and with a shout were on them. Aziall could not join the fray: his arm was skewered to the wooden frame of his chair.

It was a brief and bloody fight. The forty guardsmen were no match whatsoever for the skill of the Chez Swordmasters. Only the archer was injured slightly with a sword cut to the forearm. For a moment, he had to fight furiously with bow in one hand fending off sword thrusts and with Qwen dagger in the other, killing his three attackers.

Before Aziall could pull the arrow from his arm, Masir Kasarian's sword was pressed against his throat. Aziall spat, as he looked first to all his Guardsmen, dead, and then to Kasarian.

"Well, it seems I have the upper hand on the Hand." Kasarian smiled and pressed the tip of his sword ever so slightly into the man's neck. I weal of blood appeared.

"If you kill me Kasarian, you will have the might of Oran and the Conclaveum hunting you down."

"Oh, I do not plan to kill you, Aziall. What lesson would that teach to those who would break a contract with the Chez?"

424

"What can you do to hurt me? I am of the Keth, I am of Oran!"

Kasarian smiled and his sword flashed. Aziall screamed in agony as his nose was sliced off to the bone; blood gushed from the new wound choking him.

"That is for breaking your contract. This is for trying to kill us." His sword swept down and neatly sliced through Aziall's arm at the elbow, just above the arrow shaft. Aziall fell forward in a tremendous amount of pain. He desperately tried to staunch the flow of blood, muttering a curse in a strange tongue all the while. *Some type of healing magic, no doubt,* thought Kasarian and he was correct.

Masir Kasarian smiled grimly and pulled a leather cloth from his belt. He carefully picked up the *kris-voulge* and handed it to one of his men.

"This and the men you hold will be our payment. You may tell your *superiors* that we were ill pleased." He motioned to his men and they turned to leave. Aziall writhed on the ground as the flow of blood from the wounds ebbed to a trickle. He lay there unconscious, his chest heaving with exhaustion.

Masir looked to the archer, "Go ahead and warn the Pilot. We will find the three prisoners ar'Liayne spoke of." The man nodded and walked briskly toward the exit.

"Gentlemen, make haste, for soon he will rouse and so alarm."

Torec was alerted the clash of steel in the hallway and before Sir Brunwurst could get in position by the door is splintered inward like so

425

much kindling. It was not the Guard of Oran, but rather men in the livery of Mercenaries of Chez.

"Quickly!" The man in the fore said and motioned with his bloody sword for them to exit. Immediately Brunwurst hauled Bill over his shoulder. It was Torec though, who called them back.

"Wait. There is something in Aziall's chambers we need."

"We have no time for this. There is more than a Garrison in Avard Clef, and even though I have enough men in ship, we make to depart not tally." Kasarian was urgent in his speech.

"The Bard may die without it!" Torec replied.

"Then we must hasten," Brunwurst replied. Kasarian shook his head and motioned for his men to cover their escape.

It took them longer than expected to find the chamber where Bill had been taken. Nevertheless, finally they found the chamber of horrors and the two waist high obelisks with the runes. Brunwurst carefully lay Bill down in the chair in the center of the chamber. Kasarian and his men stood in the hall, awaiting Torec to be done with whatever task he had.

"What now, el'Kirien? We know no magic for this." Brunwurst looked at the obelisks hoping that by force of will something would happen. Nothing did.

"Put his palm on the top of the obelisk."

"What will that do?"

"I know not."

"If this fails... " Brunwurst trailed off, but did as the merchant said. He placed the Bard's right hand,

426

palm down on the rounded top of the obelisk. For a moment, nothing did happen. Finally, as the merchant of Clef was about to give up a low keening began to emanate from the stone and the runes began to glow. Bill took a deep shuddering breath and obelisk cracked down the center. Instead of the quicksilver liquid spilling outward, it flowed up into his palm, once more becoming part of him.

"Good call, Torec. I-"

"Fools!" came a harsh gurgling cry from the rear of the room. There stood a wrecked Aziall, Hand of Keth. Once handsome, now permanently disfigured. A red gash replaced his nose and blood dripped slowly from where his forearm had once hung. In his right hand, he carried long sword.

Bill looked up, his strength suddenly returning.

"Looks like you're showing your true form, Aziall." He said and slowly stood. It was amazing that though he still felt weak, he was not as close to death as he was moments ago. Bill began to stretch his hand out to the other obelisk.

"Do not!"

"Or what, you pathetic bastard?" His hand caressed the smooth stone surface of the second obelisk.

"No!" He shouted and raised his sword, but he would never reach the Bard in time. The keening sound, sweet to Bill, came harsh to the Hand and he staggered, dropping the sword. As the obelisk split the Hand surged forward, Bill was just a fraction quicker and stepped aside, interrupting the flow of the last of his essence. Instead, the Hand stumbled against the remnant of the stone pillar. The upward spray of quicksilver caught Aziall in the chest and face. It was like dousing flesh with acid. He howled in unbearable agony, writhing about striking himself with his remaining fist, trying to take his pain away. The marks left by the silver liquid pitted and burned his flesh; it began to peel away like the bark of a river birch, leaving only scarred muscle behind.

"That was worth five years off the end of my life," Bill muttered.

"Let us go from this evil place," Brunwurst called, anxious to quit the isle of Clef.

Torec pulled Bill from the room while Aziall was still seizing on the floor. Kasarian and his men waited in the hall, not knowing what had transpired within other than the Bard coming from the chamber haler than when he went in.

"Now, quickly," called the mercenary commander. They ran from the building and into the street. It was deserted in the mid-morning.

"A quiet alarm has been sounded no doubt. We must hurry to the docks." Along the way, they ran into three squads. It was an amazing sight for Torec and Brunwurst to witness the Chez at work. Each time they were outnumbered two to one; each time the mercenaries quickly dispatched their opponents with ease; clean kills, not messy slaughter, as was usually the case with such odds.

It was when they reached the end of the avenue and rounded the corner on the last leg of their flight to the ship that they encountered fifty men in the livery of the Guard of Oran. This fray was not as neat as the last. The Guard crashed into Kasarian's ten men. Fifteen sacrificed themselves in killing three of the Chez. Immediately Torec and Bill grabbed swords from the fallen men; deftly they wielded the blades and it was all they could do to fend off their assailants. Brunwurst took up a sword and an axe, weaving a pattern of death that equaled the Chez in its ferocity if not style. Soon they were through the fray and running toward the docks with the twenty Guardsmen on their heels. More shouting erupted from the rear as their pursuers grew to sixty men in armor.

"This goes ill," called one of the Chez to Kasarian.

"Our archers will cut them down."

"If we get to the ship," replied the man.

"Aye, if." Kasarian smiled and looked over his shoulder. "Dwerst and Gerer take the rear; do not worry, you will be remembered and your families will suffer naught."

"Aye, my Captain," called Dwerst and Gerer nodded assent.

"You send them to their death," Brunwurst called.

"It is their job, Sir Knight. Would you not do the same for the Governor?"

"Yes I would." The ship was in sight now, still out of range of the fifteen or so archers that lined the port side with bows set. All the lines were in and oars were in place. The sail was ready to be hoisted and his other three ships were already in the river heading out to sea. Dwerst and Gerer were twenty paces behind; they turned and faced seventy Guardsmen of Oran and they tore into the armored men with a ferocity heretofore not seen. The Guard slowed a bit, not enough as the two men were soon overwhelmed and the pursuers sprang forward with renewed vigor realizing that their quarry was reduced to eight.

"Torec," Sir Brunwurst called. "Tell Rhianne I loved her, after a fashion. And those damned dogs."

He grinned and halted in the street. Torec made to stop, but Brunwurst shook his head. "She loves you still. That I know. Here, I am her protector. That charge now falls on you. Go!"

Torec nodded and motioned Bill to the ship, only two blocks left, then the quay and the gangway, and the protection of long bows.

Brunwurst spun around and hefted the two weapons. He had picked a good spot, where the street narrowed enough to prevent passage of a large force. Bill heard Brunwurst laughing loudly over the footfall of many feet, then the clash of steel.

However he fought, Brunwurst must have taken many of the Guardsmen down. For the footfalls had ceased for the moment and soon Kasarian, the Bard, Torec and four of the mercenaries were within bowshot of the ship and then on the gangway before the archers released the arrows in shallow arcs over their heads. The plank soon dropped and the ship shoved off.

Gasping on the deck, Torec and Bill watched as the Guard of Oran was cut down in successive waves by the highly accurate Chez. Soon the sails were raised and Avard Clef was left behind. Distantly Bill heard the Sea Master tell Kasarian that their other ships would deal with any opposition ahead. He sagged against the deck, eyes closed and exhausted and then he felt her touch.

Warmth flooded through him as he looked up into the eyes of Tar'elah. She flashed him a winning smile and knelt next to him. "It seems Bard William, you are rescued." She kissed him and looked with wonder at the shock of white hair that graced his head.

"Long story, time enough later."

Torec leaned on the rail, looking back toward Avard Clef and Brunwurst. The bank sped by swiftly and soon they would be away from his isle, his home.

"He is gone isn't he?" came a quiet voice from behind. He bowed his head.

Rhianne ar'Liaiyne put her hand on his shoulder and he turned to see tears streaming down her face. Her stern countenance now replaced by sorrow.

"I am sorry, Rhianne. He loved you, you know."

"I know."

He took her in his arms and held her as heavy shudders passed through her. He looked sadly at the Bard and then turned away.

Masir Kasarian joined the Sea Master at the pilothouse. "Five is a heavy toll, Masir, especially without a war chest."

"I will pay it from my own, as the contract specifies."

"Where to? Qwen? Bequa? Chez?"

"Paravel, Sea Master." The older man raised his brow but did not question the Guildliege Mercenary. He just nodded, charted the course and informed his signalman to alert the other ships once at sea.

Chapter 30

Toshii du'Rhinn looked aft of the *felucca* and watched as storm clouds were made stark with lightening. The storm was still in the distant north and did not look as though it would threaten them.

"It is as you say; my family and many others were brought from the Land of the Rising Sun many years ago. The scrolls of our fathers and grandfathers tell it so. It is said that Exten Rhinn came in a Black Ship, like the Portuguese, but unlike. In Mishina and Horikawa he studied. He explained to the masters of the family from whence he came. He convinced them to come back to Carn, the Land of the New Sun, with him.

"It is said that with the warring states, and the *gaijin* coming, that they were willing to embark on this adventure. So it was that some of the greatest smiths of their *kei,* as well as many skilled Bushi came."

"But how can that be hidden? How many came?" asked Tom.

"There was an earthquake in my ancestor's province. Many came, but the Shogun did not notice it. We keep our traditions intact, but our peoples have mixed with those of Qwen. They have partaken of us and us of them."

"I believe that there may be some historical evidence. There is the problem of the Ainu, the people of the northern island of Japan; a swarthier people, almost Caucasian. The Japanese creation myth says they came from a 'high plane', and many scholars have spent their whole lives trying to determine where this 'high plane' was. No doubt, there was much embellishment and the facts are shrouded in the mists of time. So I would not doubt that this 'high plane' was reached through some portal or *gate* and Exten Rhinn employed them also."

"You know much of *Nippon*." Toshii replied.

"I studied in Japan for a while. You would find it was much changed from what you know from your oral history."

"You must tell me some time, but now we must tell Marad and the Captain that we may have problem."

"What is that?"

"Ships to the North, bearing down on us."

Tom looked to where the Bushi pointed and indeed, there were three small ships cresting the horizon.

Barish saw the lone ship far on the southern horizon and frowned. This chance meeting with another ship could prove disastrous, but it was too late to change direction. If he could see the lone ship then without a doubt they could see his three. In addition, they were overtaking it slowly but steadily.

"Lieutenant, let out the jib. We need to catch them ere nightfall. I want to make sure they are harmless and if not, scuttled!"

The ship of House Rhinn had reefed its sails and now drifted in the four-foot swells. The three *feluccas* had approached quickly and as pennants of House Rhinn were raised, two of the vessels tacked around the calmed ship while the other came alongside, its heavy arbalest ready to fire.

Marad, Tom and Toshii du'Rhinn stood in the low pilot's house, watching the three ships. "They are warships, *feluccas* of the Iremes class. They are very fast, faster than this ship, have steel keels for ramming below the water line, and several heavy bow blocks on deck. These have been dressed down. Privateers maybe, scoundrels in the least. He flies no colors."

"We talk first, then fight if need be, eh?" the Captain asked. Marad looked at him and nodded. Toshii took his swords from his obi and handed them to Tom.

"Stay in the pilot house. I will speak with them."

Toshii stepped out onto the deck and walked to the rail as the other ship came along side and cast lines to the deck hands.

The man who stood on the deck of the sleeker craft was stout, had longish, curly brown hair and expressionless face.

"Permission to board your ship, merchant of Qwen?"

"For what purpose?" Toshii du'Rhinn asked and stood with arms on hips.

"A ship at sea could sink and no one would be the wiser to the cause, eh?" Barish asked with a lopsided grin. "Come now, a social call that is all."

Toshii's eyes narrowed, he was about to speak when Marad came to his side; cloak-hood pulled over his head to avoid the pattering of rain that had begun to fall.

"Who would interfere with the business of House Rhinn of Qwen?"

"Just another merchant, wishing for news of the South."

"Aye," replied Marad. "And your other ships, if the news is not good news, will they sink us?"

"Let us hope for good tidings." Barish replied to the hooded man. It was his turn to frown, he thought he recognized the man's voice, but could not place it.

"Did you steal those ships of the Conclaveum, are you pirates?" Marad asked the last harshly, almost a shout. Barish, taken aback, motioned for his men to stand ready.

"Who are *you* to question us?"

Marad stepped forward and flung back his hood. Barish's jaw dropped agape and several of the White Guard on the opposite deck stopped what they were doing and dropped to their knees.

"I am Marad Vien Crona, Commander of the White Guard, your liege and Captain, Barish. Or have you forsaken that for pirating? Was Kel right all along by your not being ready for command of the guard in my absence?"

Barish leapt the short distance between the two ships, stumbling as he landed on the pitching deck. "Forgive me my lord, they said you were dead."

Marad allowed himself a small smile, which soon spread to a grin as he took Barish by the shoulders and looked at his sunburned face and tear filled eyes.

"I am sure they wish it were so, my friend," Marad replied. "Welcome aboard."

"Well met, Smiling Wolf," Barish shook hands with the tracker. They stood in the Captain's quarters of *Rhinn's Pride*. Marad, Barish, Toshii,

435

Tom and the two captains of the *feluccas* of the White Guard were in the ships well-appointed and comfortable cabin. Soon they were seated and sipping a rich Qwen wine. Tom sat in the aft window bay of the cabin, relaxed by the rocking motion of the vessel.

"Kel was led to betrayal by Myella and Guyle, no doubt for a princely sum. However, I escaped with Tarn's grace and met up with Smiling Wolf there. We ventured to Qwen and formed no small alliance with House Rhinn." He nodded to Toshii du'Rhinn, who curtly nodded back.

"Word came that the White Guard was to be disbanded. Kel brought it. Some of us refused transfer to the Guard of Oran. We are almost two hundred strong; milord, our swords are at your beck. The rest of the White Guard waits to be called up."

"How many men is that, Barish?" Tom asked as he examined a piece of carved stone that sat on the desk in the cabin.

"Twelve Legions, almost sixty thousand men."

Tom looked up sharply; he had not realized that the White Guard was so large. He expected ten thousand at the most. Obviously, the Conclaveum measured a Legion as five thousand strong.

"Do not be surprised, Smiling Wolf. The Black Guard of the Wall was forty thousand strong, until Myella started dismantling it. I am sure Gythel Boern had a fit when she told him of her plans to disband." Marad shook his head and sipped at the sweet wine.

"You mean to tell me there are one hundred thousand men floating around out there ready to take up arms and for you?"

"Yes, but remember they are scattered. Some will have joined with my sister, others retired and others I am sure were killed. The Guard of Oran was secretive, but my spies thought that they numbered twenty five thousand two years ago. Figure that it has almost tripled in number since. The baser side of man is measured by membership in that Guard. My sister would have recruited cruel and heartless men."

"Milord, what now?" Barish asked. "To Tasseem to teach Kel a lesson, then south to Teshwa?"

Marad smiled and looked at the young man. "No, first we go to Paravel to see how Myella's war goes." Marad saluted Smiling Wolf with his glass.

"Marad, I would understand if you wished to go with Barish. Toshii can take me to Paravel."

"Thank you Smiling Wolf. But I would not miss Paravel for all of Carn, especially if my sister brings war there."

"Well then, the Bushi of House Rhinn are at your service." Toshii du'Rhinn bowed to Marad. "I will inform the Pilot that we resume our course at first light."

Chapter 31

John and Joe sat in a little used guard tower in Kelvin's Keep. A fire burned in a small hearth and between them sat a dusty bottle of red wine, now open. The two glasses were empty and a wedge of cheese and dark bread lay on a large plate. They awaited a call from Michael through the *aether*. Through the thick arrow slit in the chamber, they could see the heavy snow falling and wrapping the city in twilight.

"It's good wine at least," remarked Joe as he played with the cork.

"Reminds me more of a meritage than a Cab," John tasted it again, savoring the flavor that had hints of pepper and raspberry. After a long pause and much staring outside, John finally broke the silence.

"Will we ever get home?"

"I think the question is: will we want to go home?"

"I'm sick of pissing in a slop pot, shaving with a knife. My jeans are faded to almost white from the soap they use in the laundry. The milk is awful, last time I had it I was sick for four days. Nobody knows how to make a good omelet. Most of the common folk smell, most of the aristocrats use too much perfume."

Joe chuckled. "Ever think you would kill someone?" He asked, barely a whisper.

"No."

"Fall in love?"

"No."

"Chill would die?"

"No."

"Piss off a lot of people?"

"I've been doing that for a long time, only this time they want to kill me, or suck the *'Force'* or whatever from my body."

"Are you falling for Gabrielle?" Joe asked with a sidelong glance.

"Fallen. Hard."

"Great."

John gave his friend a lopsided grin and took a sip of the wine. "Don't hold back, what do you think?"

"You can't take her home if we ever find a way."

"I know."

"We may get killed in this war. She may be killed in this war. But, one thing is for sure, I have never really *lived* until I came to this land."

"It is both intoxicating and depressing," John replied. The snow began to fall even harder and now his view was naught more than a sheet of white. "Are we that frightening to them? That powerful?"

Joe pondered the question for a moment, tossed another log on the fire and sat back. "There is something greater than us happening here. I don't know if we're some kind of catalyst or what, but we are important to Myella's plan."

John shook his head. "I want to get to the bottom of this. When this thing with Duran is over, if it's over, I'm going to find out just what the hell is going on."

Joe smiled and pulled his cloak tight about him. "I'm with you there, brother."

John sighed and sat back. "I don't think Mike is calling tonight."

Chapter 32

Gaj pulled his cloak tightly about him as he stood on the gate wall of Paravel looking east into the darkening wood. The snow had passed some time earlier, spinning out over the ocean, a curtain of lace over steel, but more would come soon. Watch fires lined the wall, lit the crenellated towers where the cannons sat and dimly illuminated the guards that huddled against the coal braziers. Gaj rubbed his palms together, gleaning what warmth he could from the friction. Reos had placed him on the midnight watch, no doubt in part for his past transgressions. How he longed for the taste of the *Kifu*, but with each day the desire was less. It still did not take the pain and the hurt of his loss away; the *Kifu* only numbed that. The Shadowlord had given him a second chance however slim and he would make the best of it. He heard footsteps to his left and turned to see who was approaching.

"Polwin, what brings you out on this hellishly cold night? You have a long day on the morrow."

"Well my brother, I thought I would bring some hot karo to warm you. Why do you stand out of the fire light?"

He looked at his light haired and fair brother, most like their mother, killed at Albien. "Well, dear brother, how can one see to watch if one has the glare of flame in his eyes?"

"To the point," Polwin replied. He smiled sardonically and tilted his own steaming mug in toast. He took a sip and grimaced. "Reos may be an excellent soldier, but he brews terrible karo."

"Aye, but it will keep you awake no doubt." Gaj laughed and looked outward from the wall, past the field fortifications to the edge of the forest some distance away. It was then that he spotted some movement in the edge of the wood. Dark fleeting shadows seemed to move amongst the lighter birch trees. The moonlight was faint but he could see the difference in the shade.

"Wolves?" Polwin asked. He noticed his brother's intense stare. Gaj always did have the sharper vision.

"I think... not. You had better wake Reos. There are great numbers in the wood. No scouting party this."

Polwin frowned but did as his brother said. He raced down the rampart to the stone stair at the gate, careful not to slip on ice. He gave a harsh shout to the guardsman there, relaying what Gaj had seen. Immediately the word spread along the wall and all the fires were doused. Still Polwin ran, to the barracks a short distance from the north gate.

The commotion, the dousing of the fires, all sufficed to send word ahead of him like a cresting wave. By the time he got to the barrack Reos was up and dressing.

"So, they are finally here, eh?" The older man smiled grimly at the young aristocrat. He buckled bracers on him forearms and a leather vest about his chest. Polwin had never seen him like this; he had always trained the troops in weathered wool clothing. Finally, he grabbed a falchion from a dark corner of his quarters. In the dim lamplight, it looked well used, well made and painfully sharp. "Tis time, my young lord. Now we fight the best of

442

the Conclaveum. We will see how well this army the Shadowlord and Lord Knight have put together can fight."

Faint light filtered down through the wood that surrounded the city. The thick flakes curled about the gnarled branches; the tops of the towering trees were lost in the increasing snowfall. Duran would occasionally catch glimpses of the wall that surrounded the city of Paravel. His horse sat stock still as Kiuf reined his in.

"Are the men in place, Kiuf?"

"Aye, they await the order. They stay within the boundary of the wood."

"And did you have the defenses examined?"

"Several of the scouts approached the wall last night. The defenses are formidable but not insurmountable. Trenches are placed strategically throughout the fields; they have the usual mantraps and cavalry blockades. There are some reinforcements along the wall itself, which are new since last we resided here. Strange equipment governs the summit of the gate towers-" Suddenly their horses shied apart. Duran looked down quickly to see that abomination, that Hand of Keth, Sir Chill, walk up the low rise.

"What do you want?" He barked harshly. He did not even try to hide the venom in his voice.

Chill stood before them and did not bother to remove his helm. "Myella has instructed me to stay here during the retaking Paravel."

Duran laughed abruptly. "Has she now, Hand? I am truly surprised she did not stay."

"She has other matters in the Conclaveum."

"All the better. I'll take this city without her help or yours."

"You may have need of the Keth... " Chill trailed off.

"Not here. I will not need your help or that of foul sorcery."

"I am not here to help you, Lord Regent Duran; I am here for the Outlanders."

Duran smiled wickedly and leaned over the neck of his horse.

"Then you shall not have long to wait."

John awoke to the sound of the alarm bell ringing throughout the keep. It was *the* bell, that which signaled the inevitable. He was up and dressed in a matter of moments. He buckled on his mail hauberk and strapped the vambrace on his shoulder. The headsman's sword found its place in the scabbard on his back. Finally, he grabbed his katana and moved into the hallway. He knocked heavily on the door to Joe's chamber. The door swung open to reveal one of the prettier serving girls of the keep; blanket wrapped about her shoulders and sleepy eyed. Joe sat on the edge of his bed pulling his boots on.

"Once more unto the breach, dear friend?" He quoted. John nodded and stepped inside, ignoring the naked girl. He pulled Joe's armor from the armoire and thought as he did how aptly named that piece of furniture was. Joe had the plate armor specially made by one of Pelles' men at the foundry. Light, the tempered plate was fluted at strategic points to carry a weapon away from vital areas. The forearm plates had a row of razor spikes along the side and could be used as a secondary weapon in

444

battle. The helm, designed by Joe, was the depiction of a dragon with unfolding wings. He *was* Surik Shadowlord, Master of Shades and Rider of the Black Dragon.

They walked quickly from the keep and as they did, Joe and John picked up an entourage of young men ready to defend the city. The keep was buzzing with new activity as Kelvin's men-at-arms raced to gather weapons and supplies for the defense of the walls. Polwin greeted them at the keep's sally port with their horses; he was having a much more difficult time with Joe's black warhorse than John's gray mare.

"Polwin," Surik nodded as he pulled on his gauntlets and adjusted his sword. "I take it we have company."

The young man nodded, out of breath from the running. "Gaj spotted them in the woods. It looks like Lord Duran has finally returned."

"Get your horse Polwin and meet us at the main gate," John said as he pulled himself onto the saddle. The horse whinnied and he kicked its flanks, urging it down the thoroughfare. People began to emerge from their homes and mill in the street. Their voices rose in a clamor as Surik and John rode their horses down the avenue. "I hope they don't riot," Joe shouted over the din. John just nodded and pushed through the mass of people. Soon they were at the gate, arriving just as Reos and several dozen of the Legion began to bring small arms and stores to the postern. They handed the reins over to a pair of young squires and mounted the steps to the rampart.

Snow had begun to fall in the early morning hours. Still dark, John could make out the salmon crease of dawn out over the city and the sea. Nevertheless, as he came to the summit of the wall his gaze swept over the crenellations, across the fields and to the wood beyond, now blurred by the flurry.

"Can't see shit," Surik muttered. John nodded and took the spyglass that Gaj offered him.

"Large force, Gaj?"

"Aye, I think so, and not a scout or patrol, much bigger." He sounded unsure, probably because of the strain in trust he had caused. However, Sir John, Lord Knight of Erie knew how to lead. He smiled grimly and gazed out at the tree line.

"Well, that's why you were on the wall at night Gaj. You had the best sense for it." He could see nothing now, for the movement had ceased and the light snow obscured anything over a kilometer away.

"Where's Reos?" Surik asked, he carefully placed his helm on the battlement and watched as Hjil and her cannoniers surmount the tower and ready the casks of gunpowder and shot.

"Walking the wall," Polwin answered breathlessly as he ran to the top of the wall. There was a commotion below; Kelvin had arrived with Pithorn and a force of men. They soon joined the *outlanders*.

"So it begins," Pithorn said as he adjusted his belt over his paunch. He was sharp-eyed and good-natured, he would be the one man responsible for ensuring their retreat from the harbor should it be necessary.

Kelvin took the spyglass from John and looked to the wood. He frowned at his inability to see anything, but then heaved a sigh and shrugged his red cloak about his shoulders.

"The morning will tell, if they will attack or sue for our surrender." He nodded to Hjil when she approached and finally Reos joined them.

"So do we have a tactical discussion right here on the wall?" Surik Shadowlord asked somewhat facetiously.

"You will learn it is as good a place as any. Keeps and castles often have ears." Kelvin leaned against the stone wall. "My men will issue an order of Marshal Law. It will keep the citizen's in their homes. They will ensure the wall at all the gates and strategic points. Reos, the Legion will support them and what cavalry we do have will provide the offensive should that ever become possible."

"Hjil," John interjected. "Once they attack, and they will, use the short loads and shot. This will draw them in. Let them get comfortable with that and we let loose with the long rounds."

"Pithorn will prevent any blockade with his long cannon," replied Kelvin. "We will have ships outside the harbor by the morning no doubt. Expect trouble from the Merchant Guild. Alaric has been quiet of late. I am surprised he hasn't fled."

"He won't," Surik countered. "He has too much invested in the city. It's his in a way, built in part with his money."

"He thinks he can ride it out, regardless of the politics he will weather the storm and go on." John

447

pulled his gloves on wishing there was a brazier to warm them.

"Then he will find some disappointment in that," Kelvin barked with some mirth. Of all of them, he knew the Conclaveum and Duran best. "Come, let's go to the gatehouse and warm up. There are still two long hours till full dawn."

Gabrielle had been charged with getting the city maps and having them brought to the gatehouse. As she was walking from Kelvin's administrative office with scrolls in hand she ran into an unlikely duo: Alaric Dirkajian and Master Talbot.

"Ah, Lady Gabrielle, I was looking for you," Talbot started before Alaric could get a word in. "Word has spread that the army of the Conclaveum has arrived. They have come sooner than expected, no?"

"Does it matter Master Talbot?" She asked, she was in a hurry get the maps to the main gate. "I must get to the gate."

"Of course milady," replied Alaric. "Master Talbot?"

"I go to ready my ships. Gabrielle, the offer still stands; you and that young knight may have passage on my vessel. Kelvin can handle the situation. With you and your friends gone I am sure the transition of power will not result in any loss of life."

"I do not believe that Master Talbot. I will not abandon this city to sack by Duran."

"Master Talbot may be right. Duran does not care one wit for what happens to the city. He does care about Sir John and Surik Shadowlord." Once in the courtyard Talbot motioned them both toward the carriage, he had waiting there.

448

Alaric helped Gabrielle into the carriage and Talbot followed her. However, Alaric stood outside and latched the door shut.

"Are you not coming, Guildmaster?"

"I have my horse, milady." His smile was imperceptible. He nodded to the driver and the coach lurched forward across the cobbles and into the street.

"How many?" John asked.

"Thirty thousand strong," replied Kelvin.

"Oh my God," John hissed between clenched teeth as he stared across the fields in the early morning light. The snowfall had abated for the moment and the defenders of Paravel stood on the battlements and gazed at their foe.

"Look at the siege engines," said Joe in a weak voice. He gazed at the monstrous towers, bristling with hooks and spikes.

"You will have to fire the trenches when they cross, otherwise we are doomed," echoed Kelvin. "This city will not stand facing this number. It will just be a matter of time."

"They will know pain and death fore we are done," Reos called, defiance in his voice, and then he cracked a crooked smile. Joe slowly turned and after seeing the look on the sergeant-at-arms face, he laughed. It was Surik Shadowlord, Master of the Shades and Rider of the Black Dragon, who spoke.

"You are right in that. The black sword will drink many souls this coming battle." He grinned even harder upon seeing the shocked looks on Polwin and Gaj's face.

"Oh brother," John cringed at his bravado. It was talk like that, which would get them killed.

Before them was a mass of soldiers, dark armor and black tabards silhouetted against the leafless wood. Between them, once verdant fields now were lined with trenches and dotted with cavalry and mantraps. Pavilions were being raised behind the line as the army of the Conclaveum stood in regimented columns.

John, Joe and the others just stood, mesmerized by the precision and order of their enemy.

"They are formidable," Gaj remarked. The others remained silent as they watched a central column separate and several horsemen ride forward with the banner of the Guard of Oran hung horizontally in momentary truce.

Kelvin looked to his lieutenant. "Prepare my horse," he smiled. "Polwin and Gaj will be my banner men." The man nodded and Kelvin turned to the two brothers, so unlike in appearance. "Have either of you held the Banner of Truce?" The two young men shook their heads. "You Polwin will carry the banner of Paravel. Should it at any time move beyond horizontal we are subject to attack. Gaj, you will carry my sword. You will be on my right, with the sword across your knees, the pommel toward me." He smiled wryly. "Should your brother raise the banner I will need to draw my sword rather quickly."

Kelvin saluted Joe and John and stepped quickly down to the courtyard, the brothers following behind.

"If he is so concerned about their performance why does he take them?" Hjil asked.

"Because they are expendable and he dare not risk his own experienced men," Reos echoed.

450

"On-cannon," said John to Hjil. She stared at him a moment and then turned to mount the steps to the tower where the cannon sat. They watched as the portcullis opened and Kelvin and his entourage rode through the gate. Their horses meandered through the field, avoiding the trenches and obstacle that were laid down. All the while Polwin was very careful to carry the banner appropriately.

John heard steps behind him, looking over his shoulder he saw Dirkajian, Master Talbot and Gabrielle emerge from the tower stair. He smiled at Gabrielle carrying not only the map of the city, but a long sword on her hip. Alaric mistook the smile and glared at the *Outlander*.

"So, you have what you wish and you find it amusing?" Alaric strode forward with fists clenched.

"I find none of this amusing, Guildmaster." He watched the progression of Kelvin out of the corner of his eye. He noticed a similar party approaching from Duran's forces. He expected it would be Duran himself in the lead.

"Look at the army he brings, Sir Knight. You cannot possibly defeat him. Sue for peace and quit the city. Master Talbot has offered his ship. You can be spirited away in the night."

John looked hard from Dirkajian to Talbot. Then to Joe who was leaning nonchalantly on the battlement watching Kelvin's progress. Joe just shrugged, but did not say a word.

"And what of the other cities in the South, Guildmaster? The ones all these refugees spilled out of, the ones that were sacked and pillaged by

451

Duran's army? You think he will just let Paravel be?"

"Oh, I am sure there will be payment for your transgressions."

"Payment for transgressions? Guildmaster you astound me," this came from Gabrielle. She gave the dark haired man a withering look and strolled over to the low table, throwing the map down and standing next to John with her hands on her hips.

"Let me remind you Alaric, you and the men under you helped depose Myella's Seat from this city, nay I would say you were fairly instrumental in purging the city of her loyalists."

Alaric scowled and looked to the army that lay before the gates of his city. "Heed my words, Sir Knight, ere this is over it shall not be my city that falls."

"Alaric," Surik finally spoke. "I was unaware it was *your* city." He looked hard at the Shadowlord and spun away, back down the steps and no doubt to his horse below.

"My offer stands gentlemen," Talbot said softly. "If you wish to go, my ship is available. But it will not always be so." He nodded to Gabrielle and followed Alaric's retreat.

"I love positive reinforcement," muttered Surik.

John sighed and smiled wanly at Gabrielle who took his hand in hers. "You are doing the right thing, my Protector."

"I hope so." They walked over to the wall and stood next to Joe who was intent on Kelvin and the entourage. Fine flakes of snow had begun to fall, casting a curtain before them. The figures had now met on the field and were conversing.

452

"I hate this," John said to no one in particular.

"It is the Great Game, John," Gabrielle replied. "My father calls is a dance of sorts."

"Yeah, well where we come from it's the same bullshit," Surik opined.

They waited for what seemed an eternally long time. Finally, they saw three horsemen coming through the thickening snow. The portcullis raised and the gate was opened. Joe, John and Gabrielle met them at street level.

"We must seek council," Kelvin said. Gaj and Polwin were ashen.

"They are white as ghosts," Gabrielle remarked. "And I do not think it is the cold.

***

Chair Nathal motioned them to enter, Pithorn, Dirkajian, Javin Skettes and four council members where already there. It was as quiet as a tomb in the council chamber. Kelvin cleared his throat and looked around the room.

"Duran has given us a choice," he stated levelly. "Turn over the outlanders and the city will be spared-"

"There you have it," Alaric interjected. "This course will spare-"

"I am not through, Guildmaster. Duran had other conditions... Turn over Chair Nathal and the Council and the city will be spared. Turn over Preceptor Skettes and the city will be spared. Surrender my office, disband the city guard and any armed militia and the city will be spared. Omit any of these things and Paravel will be razed."

He paused as this sunk in. "And finally, all who surrender will be given a quick death, with the exception of the outlanders."

"And if we flee, take a ship out of here?"

"He knows you are here Sir John. It is unconditional, his offer. If we do not meet any of the requirements, then I dare say he will not be staid."

"He has no desire other than to kill us and sack the city," Javin Skettes said softly. "His intention was never to make this easy."

"It is because of the Outlanders that it has come to this."

"I think not," Chair Nathal replied. "The Conclaveum under Myella has been waging this war in the south for one purpose: total domination. These young men were just pawns, pawns that became something she did not count on. Now Duran is meting out his twisted form of justice."

"Do not forget, Guildmaster, what happened to all the cities in the West that Duran has taken and what they are said to have become," this from Preceptor Skettes.

"What then, oh wise council?" Alaric Dirkajian asked. "Do we not at least offer up these insurgents and pray for the mercy of Myella?"

"I am not that eager to lose my head," replied Chair Nathal.

"You are all fools," Dirkajian shook his head. He walked out quietly.

"His arrogance will be his undoing I think," Javin Skettes remarked. He smoothed his vestment and smiled wanly. "Pray to Tarn gentlemen, and lady, that we can hold. For I fear Duran's design is

454

far more malevolent than he lets on. I fear that he is driven by vengeance and that I can understand. But, Myella, she is driven by her allegiance to Oran and whatever evil designs that creature may have."

Pithorn leaned his heavy frame on the table. He suddenly looked much older, and worn. "Then we must fight and in doing so make them rue the day they lay siege."

"Kelvin," John looked to the older veteran. "What is our course from here?"

"Normally, we would raise our war banner and wait."

"I want to talk to Duran," John said.

"I do not think that would be a good idea," Kelvin replied. Gabrielle just looked shocked.

"I do not intend on surrendering. I intend on unnerving him. And I want Surik to accompany me." He looked levelly at the other men in the room. "If he wants a fight then we'll give it to him."

"John, no-" Gabrielle began, but she stopped at the look in his eyes. Then he smiled wickedly and looked to Joe. "A great game, I've played a few of those in the past."

Joe smiled back and stood a little more proudly. "Aye Sir John, Lord Knight of Erie, let the games begin."

Alaric sat in his office contemplating what mess things had become. He knew he was partly to blame. After all, he had wanted Myella out of Paravel just as badly as the others had. However, he could not have foreseen the costs the Outlanders would bring to his city. He leaned back in his chair and looked out toward the bay. A brisk breeze blew in off the sea, fluttering the curtains on his open-air veranda. He did not mind. He was expecting Kryall.

Bale padded softly into the room. She looked at her employer and lover. He looked tired, strained and ready to strike out. She knew this was not to his liking or his way and it was not the Chez way, that of duel and vendetta.

"Kryall is here, Alaric." He looked up and his eyes narrowed.

"So soon. Send him in." Alaric smoothed his tunic and looked to the door as the large man stepped through. "So, they are going to fight." It was a statement of fact.

"It was inevitable. However, I believe I can mitigate it. For a price."

"And what would that be?"

"The girl of course, because whether I or Myella get the Outlanders, the outcome for them is the same."

"And my task?"

"What Duran asked for and one more thing...."

"What else?"

"Kill Sir John in front of Gabrielle."

Alaric smiled. He knew it would not be a simple task, but it was doable. "I thought the Outlanders were to be turned over to Duran."

"Not him, he can die, he is the *third key*."

Alaric did not know what he meant by that and he also really did not care. "And what of Paravel and me?"

"Oh, you will be taken care of. There must be some sacking, but nothing you cannot overcome. You will be there to pick up the pieces, a reassuring face to a troubled citizenry."

456

Alaric smiled and steepled his fingers; Kryall was enigmatic as usual. Nevertheless, this would ensure his survival.

"Then consider the bargain struck."

***

John disliked wearing armor. He wore it during society events and it was heavy, cumbersome and hot. Yet, the armor that had been made for him was like a second skin, light, comfortable and he was sure it would do the job or at least he hoped so. It amounted to a breastplate, or cuirass, very much like Kelvin's. He wore the vambrace that ran from shoulder to forearm. Underneath this was a light chain hauberk. He wore leather britches and boots. A white cloak was slung over his shoulder and he wore his katana, *Mountain Pine* on his hip. The headsman's sword he had taken to doing forms with sat in a scabbard on the table. He would speak to the Legion of the Black Skullfirst, just as Kelvin would be speaking to the city guard.

It was cold and brisk in the late afternoon as he walked into the courtyard of the keep. Filled with their militia; they spilled out into the streets waiting for word as to what was happening. Most knew already from rumor and idle chatter.

John moved to the third step from the portal. Joe lounged against the stone balustrade, and Gabrielle stood next to him. They had decided he was the better speaker, though Joe had offered to give the St. Crispin Day speech from "Henry V". John thought it a bit much.

A quiet descended upon the crowd. John handed the long sword over to Joe. He looked at it, then to John as if to say *What the hell am I supposed to do with this?* John cleared his throat.

"The day you knew was coming is at hand. Duran and the Armies of the Conclaveum stand before Paravel, with no truce offered, no parlay given.

"You could have fled, but where would you have gone? You chose to stay and defend this city and the citizens who welcomed you here. The evil that Myella has brought to the South has spread like a disease. Well, the line is now drawn; it stops here and you will defend it, for you represent all that is good and right and just."

He took a step up, looked out over the heads of the Grey Cloaks, the Swords of the Legion of the Black Skull and smiled.

"I am Sir John, Lord Knight of Erie. This is Surik Shadowlord, Master of the Shades and rider of the Black Dragon. We will stand by your side and fight with you to defend this city. What say you?"

A deafening hurrah filled the square and men and women, young and old made for their stations along the city wall. Sending many to death and an uncertain fate suddenly saddened John. Gabrielle touched his hand and he looked at her, brightening.

"That was very nicely done, milord."

"You didn't say anything to me about fighting," Surik cracked a grin and tossed the flat tipped sword to John who deftly caught it. "Now, the face-off with Duran."

Kelvin looked up to John who sat on his white mare in front of the city gate. Joe sat next to him on his black war-horse. Joe held a lantern and John held the banner across his knees. It was time to talk, but Kelvin was not happy about it.

"Are you sure you wish to do this milord? Duran may not honor the Truce, he is known for greater treachery. He may seize the opportunity."

"Oh, be assured Lord Kelvin, we will be cautious," Surik said as he motioned for the portcullis to be raised and the heavy oak doors opened. He kicked the flanks of his steed and it reared up and jumped as though from a starting gate. John followed quickly behind until they were at a pace. It was late afternoon, overcast and threatening more snow, hence the lantern. The two *Outworlders* wove their way through a thicket of horse and mantraps until they reined in their steeds in the open fallow fields where Duran's army awaited.

There was some commotion on the sentry line, but shortly thereafter, three horsemen were making their way across the field to meet them.

John could make out Duran and his aide carrying the banner. The third horseman, armored all in black, with helm and what looked like a lance in his right hand, rode behind. On his surcoat was emblazoned a white hand.

The men stopped about ten yards apart.

"Well, the Lord Knight himself comes to parlay? I suppose you would have me spare all the insurgents in that fair city yonder?" He asked it with a certain amount of irony.

"Oh no, Duran, not at all. I come to offer you your life and the life of your men. Lay down your arms and go back to the Conclaveum now. Do this and your life will be spared. If not, you and all your men will perish." John watched out of the corner of his eye as the Hand of Keth trotted his horse forward a few paces. The figure that sat there leaned forward as if peering at him intently.

Duran laughed aloud, he seemed truly humored by what John had said. "Oh? You think that rag tag militia of yours will defeat the Guard of Oran? You managed to expel us out of the city, but fortune was on your side that day. This is not a garrison, this is thirty thousand."

"Thirty thousand damned souls for the slaughter," echoed Surik Shadowlord. His horse snorted eager to be on its way.

"Enough of this idle banter and cheap bravado. You carry the Banner of Truce, yet are not of this land. I should take you now, but that would spoil the fun of taking the city. Why are you here? What is your answer to our demands?"

"My answer is this. You people brought us to this land and now you will face the consequences. By God we will unleash a force terrible in its making!"

With that, John took up the Banner of Truce and broke it across his knee. He tossed it to the ground, in the same motion drew the headsman's sword, and spurred his horse forward. Duran, slightly stunned by the display jerked back on the reins and spun his horse to the right, into the Hand's steed. Kiuf fumbled with the banner, finally raising it and swinging it forward. With a rush, the entire

460

front line of Duran's army was on its feet or on horseback surging forward. John was upon Duran before the man could draw his own sword and was about to take him across the temple when he heard a low thump and his horse was knocked back. John caught a glance of the Hand's lance, no kris-voulge, lowered and was left smoking. His horse fell hard and so did he, but luckily, he rolled away from the dying beast. Surik drew his own blade, which hissed silver flame in the early evening.

Kiuf bore down on John, his sword raised. Yet, John crouched low and swung the heavy blade laterally, cutting clean through the horse's front legs and spilling its rider forward onto the ground. Just as the man stood, Surik's horse came up from behind and the mystical blade flashed forward slicing through the man's bald head, capping him from the eyebrows up. Kiuf fell to his knees with a stunned look, and then face first into the muck. Surik slid past John and leaned down with his left arm out. John swung up and the horse wheeled about to make a mad dash to the city walls.

Amid the sound of charging soldiers behind them, John could make out the screaming of a horse and the bellowing of Duran who leapt from his steed to the fallen body of his aide. Mud churned up on the right and left as arrows fell far and short of them. Surik's horse was strong and it was not fazed a bit by carrying two riders. It danced between the trenches, weaving its way back to the safety of the walls, all the while John looked back, marking the progress of the charging line. "Not yet," he muttered under his breath.

He looked back, noticing the Hand trotting his horse in circles around the man that Surik had killed. Duran appeared to be cradling him in his arms. *What wreckage you have caused, Duran,* John thought.

"Now?" Surik asked as he passed the last entrapment and headed for the bridge that spanned the moat. He sheathed his sword and reached to his belt.

"Now!" echoed John and Surik tossed up a weighted red flag high in the air. The result was the deafening report of four cannon firing simultaneously into the ranks of the soldiers who had been pursuing them.

Well within the range of the cannon, John had planned to lure them in as far as they could. Great gouts of dirt and steel erupted into the air as the shot tore through the flesh of men and horse before furrowing the ground. Before they could see the result, they were through the gate and the bridge rose. The doors shut solidly and were barred, the portcullis slammed downward. John leapt from the saddle, almost fell on the slippery flags and ran to the battlement, wanting to see the damage they had done. He heard Joe follow.

Breathless, John raced along the crenellations to where Kelvin, Reos and Gabrielle awaited. He looked out over the fields as the cannons reported again and again, creating chaos for the advancing line. Finally, in disarray the Guard of Oran fell back to where they thought they were safe. John looked up to Hjil and gave her the cut off sign. They would not increase the range... yet.

"If they get under the range, then we have to worry," Surik muttered. However, for now the fantastic new weapon was doing its job.

"Now we wait," Kelvin said. "And we see what they throw at us."

Wait they did, for Duran did not come at them the next morning, or the next. He waited and in the distance, one could hear the hacking and cutting of trees, the pounding and sawing of wood. Through the occasional break in snow, one could make out the silhouette of dark towers erected for the scaling of walls or the spanning of the trenches. Duran was busy with his war machine.

At sunset on the third day, they came. It started with the slow trundling of the siege towers and the march of pikemen. Reos and Kelvin stood on the battlement as the sun dipped below the horizon and everything faded to a dismal grey.

"These lads we've trained, kin they handle hardened soldiers. The Guard of Oran is brutal."

"They will have to. Many of them will die in the trying." Kelvin shook his head sadly. Surik and John soon joined them on the battlement.

"I see it has begun," Surik remarked.

Kelvin rested his arms on the low wall. "They will be on the wall nigh midnight."

"We can't stop them from scaling the wall?"

"Oh, no," the Lord Protector of Paravel replied. "Even with your cannon they will not be repelled. There are too many of them. I would suggest you have Hjil aim on the siege towers."

"Done," John broke from the group and made for the battlement where the gate wall cannon sat. He found Hjil and her cannoniers smoking pipes

463

and playing at dice. He wrapped his cloak about himself as he stood before the younger woman. She looked up at his approach and smiled, smoke billowing from her nostrils.

"Is it time?" She asked eager to use the powerful weapons once more.

"Yes, Hjil, but not til they are at the third trench. I don't want them to know the range. Have all the cannons on the West, North and South walls target the siege engines. Bring them down. Gaj and Polwin are covering the North wall. I don't think the main force will pursue any other gate aside from the West. Pithorn has men on the South. Duran comes this way, so we meet him here. Otherwise they are spread too thin."

"We will bring down the towers," she grinned and adjusted her leather cuirass.

"Good." He turned and made his way back to the others. Out of the corner of his eye, he thought he caught something and it gave him pause. He surreptitiously scanned the base of the wall, near the frozen moat. That was when he saw six men carefully scaling the wall, they were almost at the top. It appeared their target was the cannon.

Along the wall, the defenders of the city had cached arms. Bows and arrows, crossbows, sword, spears, rocks, whatever could be used should a defender lose his weapon. John now carried only his katana, *Mountain Pine*, so he grabbed a spear and hefted it. Just as the first man was pulling himself over the crenellation, John chucked the spear from ten feet squarely into the man's chest. The man fell back, knocking the climber immediately behind him from the wall. They screamed as they fell, hopefully

464

alerting the guard of the city's peril. The remaining men spread out, surmounted the wall quickly and drew weapons. John could hear a distant alarm, but none near him; he drew his blade and confronted them.

They were big, dangerous looking men dressed in black leather who drew their swords and knives. The remaining four were taller and more powerful of build than John .

John tilted his katana back and they rushed him silently. He stood still as they came and when the first was upon him he dropped to one knee, his sword slicing out and kneecapping the man. The intruder dropped to the left off the wall and onto the roof of a stable below. The second man's blade came at John's head, but the White Knight rolled forward, came up on the third man and shoved his katana though his midsection. He withdrew it, turned 180 degrees and swung the sword down and through the second man's shoulder in mid turn. The assailant fell to his knees and John kicked him onto his back.

The last man, however, was too fast, but fortunately, he was stopped mid stride with one of Hjil's stilettos in his neck. He collapsed forward with a thud.

"Alarm!" shouted one of Hjil's cannoniers, as a sharp bell began to ring signaling their peril the cannon on the north side of the gate exploded; someone had set fire to the gunpowder. John watched as the cannon tilted to the side and slipped off the parapet, taking the remains of the powder and shot with it. As it crushed the out-building

465

below, there was a loud thump and the building went up in flames and black smoke.

John staggered back as a large piece of the wall slammed into the crenel next to him, sending pieces of rock and stone flying into the air. He moved behind the curve of the tower and watched in the gloom as several more catapults snapped forward, sending the missiles over the wall and crashing through the roofs of the building below. One large stone caromed down the street slamming into several of the militia and killing them.

His guard suddenly surmounted the wall and surrounded him in a protective shield. All along its length, torches and braziers caught fire. Archers strung their bows and cannoniers prepped their cannon; except for the north tower, where now was a smoldering hole at summit.

Surik rushed to John's side, giving him a quick once over to make sure he was all right and then he smiled wickedly and drew his sword.

"Bet you never thought being part of a 'Society' event would ever lead to the real thing."

John just shook his head and watched as the advancing men and towers came within range of the remaining cannon. The first report was deafening and the shot fell short of the siege tower. Chunks of dirt sailed into the air, propelling the soldiers along with it. Moments later a timber bridge fell across the first trench and the tower ambled across, pushed by a squad of burly men. The cannon reported again and this time the mark was true as the first tower splintered apart in the middle and collapsed in upon it, crushing those within. Then snow began to fall heavily, impairing visibility.

466

"Dammit!" John swore, realizing the cannon would be useless if the snowfall became worse; they would not be able to see the target. "Reos! Order the cannon to lay down a suppressing fire inside the first trench. All we can do is randomly fire. Hopefully we'll hit something." Reos nodded and ran along the wall, issuing orders to the runners. The wind had picked up and the torches sputtered. The walkway was icing up. John watched as the archers threw ash and salt at their feet.

"It will slow them down also," Surik said. "They won't know where the trenches are til they are upon them."

"Duran's cleverer than that. He has it scouted and paced off. They know where everything is. I-" He was cut off as a gust of wind tore a rent in the snow and a dark tower appeared not twenty feet from the wall. "What the... "

The archers saw it too and immediately sent a volley into the night. Men screamed below but the tower still trundled forward at a fast clip; it was under the range of the cannon.

John grabbed his heavy broad sword and motioned his men to guard Hjil and the cannon, which still fired at regular intervals into the dense night. He wondered if they were being effective at all.

Then the tower was just across the moat and a long bridge dropped down from the crown, metal spikes jamming into the parapet. The archers knew their job for as soon as the maw opened up a score or arrows struck deep, felling the men inside. However, their shields came up and men advanced across the narrow bridge. Not waiting for the enemy to reach the walkway Surik Shadowlord jumped forward and slammed his ensorcelled sword into the spikes holding the bridge to the stone. It sliced through the iron as if it were butter. The weight of the men twisted the frame of the bridge and suddenly they were gone, falling the thirty feet and slamming into the ice that covered the moat. Flaming arrows were sent into the siege tower, but for some reason had little effect upon it.

Ladders soon appeared all along wall. John spun; it was all happening so fast he did not know where to start. In the darkness, he was aware of figures emerging over the wall and men dispatching them with bow and spear and then closing with their swords. However, they were coming too quickly and soon arrows were arcing over the wall from below. Several arrows came jarringly close to him and Surik and he ducked back, realizing the difficulty in defending the wall against the aggressors.

John swung the heavy blade; months of practice ingrained in muscle memory. He leapt forward letting his momentum carry the blade into the first man coming over the ladder. The sword crunched into the man's armor, not cutting through it, hit with enough force to send the man falling back into the pike man below. John tried to push the ladder away, but the weight of it with the men on it was too much. He would have to do his best to fend them off as they came over the wall.

Someone bumped into him and he turned to the left. Surik slipped on the pavers and thrust his glimmering blade into another man, but right behind him on the ladder was another and soon they were

468

both fighting in their own microcosm of battle. Archers tried to cover their flanks by firing into the side of those coming up but there were more than even they could handle. Slowly men atop the wall began falling back as arrows cut them down. John looked down to see a few had even pierced his cloak only to be stopped by the cuirass. Two men came over the wall with axes; both fell to his blade before they could get their balance. Surik Shadowlord was a whirling dervish, cutting back in forth, his blade easily slicing through armor, flesh and bone. John soon realized most of the men he fought fell because of the blunt force trauma of his broadsword impacting their armor. Only when he went for a joint in the armor, the piercing in the helm or the neck did his sword cut into them; it was then he was rewarded with a sickening crunch and a spray of blood.

The falling snow turned to crimson slush on the stone battlement. The Guard of Oran who were past the defenders dropped to the street level but were struck down by the cavalry stationed there. The shouting and clanging of steel on steel, the twang of bows and the screaming of the wounded and dying was deafening. Every few minutes the cannon would fire into the thickening snow and a muted thud in the night would tell them it hit something. On the other side of the gate, John caught a glimpse of Reos pouring oil on the ladders and tipping a brazier into it. It sent both the ladder and those climbing aflame. John shouted for the men on his side of the gate to do the same; several managed to do so, though one of their men caught himself aflame and fell to the street and his death.

Most of the ladders fell back burning; the few that remained were repulsed and destroyed. The men that remained fought hard, but where killed after an interminable time.

The sun was cresting the East wall and harbor when the sally abated. The torches were guttering. John leaned over behind the turret and looked to Surik who sagged back. There were two arrows sticking out of his back, but they hung loosely; they had not pierced his armor. John was spent; his arm was so sore he could barely lift it. He set the sword down and had to chop through two inches of ice in the water barrel to get the ladle in. He started shivering as the adrenaline wore off. How long. Surik answered as if reading his thoughts.

"Off and on all night. I wouldn't think it possible." The snow suddenly ceased with the dawn and they both looked down the length of the gate wall, aghast. John gasped at the carnage, not believing his eyes. Hundreds of men lay dead and dismembered on the street behind them, and on the frozen moat below. What was truly grisly were the men who, warm when they hit the ice, had melted partly through, and were suspended, limbs twisted covered in a quarter inch of fresh blown snow.

Militiamen moved along the wall, helping the injured to their feet. Several of the Preceptor's clerics moved with them, murmuring prayers for the dead or healing those not too badly wounded. Ash and straw was placed wherever there was blood and that was everywhere. Fresh defenders appeared along the wall with pikes and halberds, finally he and Joe stepped from the cover of the turret as the remaining snowfall cleared and looked out over the field.

Some portions of the trenches were gone, now gaping scars where cannon balls cratered the earth. Siege engines lay in wreckage, creating a new barrier the attackers would have to surmount. At least four more siege tower stood aflame on the north side of the gate and to the north of the city John could make out black smoke rising in the grey morning.

Gaj and Polwin's siege of the north wall and the small postern that allowed traffic from up the coast began in the early morning hours. They had charge of a ten-inch cannon, which spat mercilessly into the night, into the snow. Yet Duran brought no siege towers to this wall, rather there were a large number of men with ladders and one felled oak tree turned battering ram. The postern was twenty-feet deep ending in a heavy steel bound door secured with heavy posts. Murder holes looked down on any who would enter and in this case, the outside of the postern was littered with the dead bodies of the Guard of Oran.

The ram stood fifteen feet from the wall on an earthen bridge that had replaced the wooden bridge Gaj had burned in the first hours of the assault. In the heavy snow, the ten-inch gun could not be brought around quick enough to damage the ram but it had done considerable damage to those infantrymen in the sloping field to the north. Polwin, the fairer of the two brothers smiled as the ram rolled forward. He gave the command and archers popped over the crenel, arrows arcing down and slamming into the shields above the battering ram. The ram made it into the postern and that was when Gaj motioned for help. He and three others moved to a large cauldron of oil that had been sitting above a brazier. Below their feet, through the murder holes they could see the bulk of the ram moving toward the barred gate. Then they heaved the boiling oil over and it poured steadily into the slots. Steam, the shouts and the screams flooded upward

Alaric ran up the winding stairs, sometime taking two at a time, Bale close behind. The tallest tower in the city was in Kelvin's Keep. The second tallest was on the grounds of the Temple of Oran. This was the tower that the merchant of Chez now ascended. Finally, he emerged in the topmost room and tore open the shutters to gaze upon the city.

Snowfall came and went in sheets thrown on the wind. Between the gusts, he could see in all directions. To the North a battalion of Duran's army assailed the gate and to the West the largest amassing attempted to break through the defenses.

At the various small gates to the south, the defenders staved off the assault of Duran's army. Two cannon that had sunk three ships outside the harbor break wall. Mounted on opposite peninsula, Pithorn was finding them much more effective than a catapult. If Alaric could find a way to disable those weapons, then the assault would shift radically with a wide-open port. Yet, Pithorn had effectively kept what few ships Duran had, at bay.

"Master, what is your plan?" Bale asked as she noticed the frown on his face.

"Other than killing the Outlanders myself? I know not. Kryall talks in riddles half the time. The

472

longer we are besieged the worse the outcome." He leaned against the rail and looked down into the courtyard of the abandoned temple. "Unless... "

She followed his gaze not sure exactly what he was looking at.

"Perhaps there is a way? The tunnels underneath the temple, I wonder if any near the north wall. If they cannot go over the perhaps they can go underneath?"

"What do you mean?"

"Send my men into the tunnels beneath the Temple. A passage there leads outside the wall. Long sealed, but they can break through with enough sweat. Tell them to send priests to destroy the cannons. They prove much more effective than brute force. Then at noon on the marrow, I will signal Duran to storm the gate."

She nodded, looked at him for a moment and sped down the stairs to alert his men.

He looked again over the city, clenching the rail tightly. "Soon you will be mine again. Soon."

Chapter 33

John wiped blood from his face. Sickened by the constant fight, the wave after wave of men that had come at the city wall; he wondered when it would end. Unceasing, the cannons spat their fire into the fields that surrounded the cityand still Duran sent his men at the walls. Reos at the south gate had poured oil onto men of the Guard of Oran then set it afire; still they came. Gaj and Polwin at the north gate, were almost breached twice, but held as their men were slaughtered like lambs. In addition, Pithorn, who sat with two of their mightiest cannons in the harbor, had kept the blockade at bay to save their back.

Three weeks and the ground, once pristine white with the first fall of snow, was now a muddy morass stained with the blood of many. Their men, garbed in scarlet splashed gray, lay dead at the base of the wall. Some, by a small miracle still groaned in agony, amid the limbs and bodies of the Guard of Oran. John was too numb to hearken to their strangled cries. He had seen his own good men fall. He had watched as Kelvin repelled assault after assault. Watched as the proud soldier, who had forsaken his loyalty to the Conclaveum for that of the city, was reduced by exhaustion.

It would be wrong to say that the fighting was a constant thing. There were lulls of days at a time, when Duran's trebuchet pounded the walls to the point of driving them mad. It was fortunate that the cannon had more range than these sling based catapults, otherwise all the buildings on the inside perimeter would be rubble or aflame. During the lulls, John and Surik would patrol the north and south walls checking on the status of the men there. They walked the peninsula with Pithorn, and watch the small flotilla anchored off shore; just waiting for the moment when they could sail into the harbor. They would sleep then, deathlike in their exhaustion. John would remember vaguely, tromping into Kelvin's keep, and Gabrielle was there with several servants to strip him of his gear. When he tried to protest, Gabrielle would hush him.

"This is what we do, Sir John, take care of our embattled."

He remembered being taken to his quarters as one lad took away his swords to be cleaned. Gabrielle dismissed the servants who brought steaming water, stripped him of his gore-covered clothing, and bathed him before the warm hearth fire. It was all he could do to stay awake as he watched her. Then she helped him to the bed and as he lay there, she slipped in next to him, kissing him lightly on the chest as she did so.

Then the next day it would repeat, sometimes with no fighting at the wall, other times with so much he would have to be pulled from the gate by Reos and taken back to the keep to rest.

Twice he had a wound severe enough to an arm or leg that it required the intervention of one of Preceptor Skettes men. Bleeding quite steadily from a slash to the shoulder, he watched as a young priest cleaned it and then applied a clay like substance to it. When the substance was removed, his wound was healed. It would be stiff and sore, but otherwise it was as if he had been untouched.

Of course, this did not work with more severe wounds, ones to the head, or those that were too damaging; no, there was fatality in this land.

Fatigue was taking its toll. He leaned back, the weight of the broadsword dragging his arm down. He looked across the parapet to Surik, more haggard and grim than he had ever seen him. His cloak was torn, and his battle armor dented and bloody, some of it was his own. He gazed to his friend and a haunted look stared back. His tunic was ripped to reveal the black mail, rent open to reveal an under tunic. Far too close had the axe come, by the grace of God he had been spared.

He snapped around as the huge report of the cannon sounded, louder than ever before. Smoke billowed up from the tower and shards of steel embedded in the surrounding wall, all those that manned that gun were thrown to their death and the summit of the tower was blown away. The men below cheered and rallied once more to the postern. John looked but outside the wall there was nothing and no one that could have done that. Then he felt a tingling on his chest, the medallion. He turned and looked to the streets behind him and saw the man under the eaves of a nearby building, a priest of Oran. He cursed and took the crossbow from the hands of a dead man, knocked a bolt and let fly.

The priest never knew death was coming, but John knew the projectile was true, he dropped the crossbow to the stone flags even before it struck. The priest stumbled back; the bolt pinning right to the wall of the building.

John sank against the wall, his knees buckling.

After some time the report of the cannons faded and the world had turned gray, threatening snow. John felt a warm touch upon his neck and looked up to see concern in the eyes of Gabrielle. He looked to her face and the worry therein. Her dark hair framing that lovely face, the lips parted, as if about to say something.

He jerked himself up, swaying as the armor fought inertia. He twisted her around and away from the open crenel and cleared his throat.

"You shouldn't be here," he said it, his voice cracked from thirst and smoke.

"Where else could I be, *my* lord, but at your side?"

"I can't afford to lose you," his face reflected his resolve as he looked into her eyes. "You must go to the keep. Preceptor Skettes is there."

"Master Talbot brought me, he said we could use his ship if need be..."

He looked over her shoulder to the fat merchant, tucked into the portal of the tower, waiting for her.

"Not yet."

She tilted her head to the side, her eyes pleading with his. "And when can you? I love you, my Lord Knight. You serve no one by dying here. Aren't you afraid to die?"

"Afraid to die with so many questions unanswered. Those that have died deserve more." He looked up to Talbot; saw the merchant, Alaric, behind him with his second, Bale.

"Talbot, take Gabrielle. I charge you to get her to your ship and to safety if need be. Understand?"

The man nodded and smiled, holding out his hand as John placed hers in his. He touched her cheek, carefully, as if she was a vision that would fade; tears streamed down. He turned back to the wall as Talbot led her down the stone stairs of the gate tower. He caught Surik looking at him out of the corner of his eye. Then as his friend nodded to the field, he too saw what the Shadowlord was looking at.

Where Duran's pavilion sat, he could make out the Regent himself. He sat astride a warhorse and next to him stood a Hand of Keth and four priests of Oran. As the Hand of Keth removed his helm all time stood still, Joe gasped and the two *outworlders* beheld the Hand. Chill.

As if out of the distance, John could hear Surik drop his sword against the flags. He also heard a woman scream, as if far away, but he was rooted to the spot. Chill looked to them, John could almost see the pain in his eyes. Then that was an illusion, for the man raised his *kris-voulge* and the tip glowed red. They did not hear the report, but like a tracer of fire, in slow motion John watched, as the deadly projectile sped toward them, no, toward Surik.

Time contracted as John felt his St. Christopher medallion burn at his chest. He moved then, faster than he thought would be humanly possible. Surik was rooted where he stood, but John leapt in front of him, pushing his left arm, covered by the vambrace, in front of his friend's forehead. He heard and then felt the missile tear into the armor. His forearm slammed Joe back onto the flags; the force of the blow sheared the vambrace in two, and

478

deflected the projectile out over the city. John screamed in agony as the molten metal of the sheared vambrace burned into his arm. He frantically pulled at the leather strap and watched as the ruined piece of armor fell to the streets. He thrust his arm into the snow and tears of pain coursed down his face.

"I guess we're even now," Surik groaned as he sat up, rubbing at his temple. "I think that-" he could not finish, nor would John be able to hear, as the remaining cannons along the North and South walls erupted in shrapnel filled fireballs. The gate-walls shuddered and some collapsed inward. "We're done," Surik shouted. Then the shout of thousands as soldiers in Duran's infantry followed in the wake of their cavalry, storming the holes in the walls.

John was on his feet in an instant, motioning to the foot soldiers in gray livery and of Kelvin's remaining guard. "The gate!"

He saw that most followed his order, but some broke ranks and fled. He watched as Reos urged them on, short sword flailing about.

"You fool!" came a shout from behind. John spun. "You are finished!" spat Alaric. He gripped Gabrielle's arm tightly in his left hand. His other held his saber, now John knew who had screamed. "At least she may be spared."

It was then that John recognized the viper in their midst, it was Alaric and all his machinations, the sabotage of the foundry, the fires in the wharf district. It was as if they were under the Temple of Oran, witnessing the Hand of Keth delivering the conspiracy, and in the flickering torch light Alaric stood with him, hand poised on saber.

479

"Let her go."

"Surrender. Lower your banner and I let her go."

Exhausted from countless hours of fighting John threw down his heavy blade. Alaric smiled and loosened his hold on Gabrielle, long enough for her to twist away. In one fluid motion, John drew his katana. Alaric sneered and advanced. Amazingly fast, he parried John's sword and was inside his guard.

"NO!" Gabrielle screamed and John wondered why. Then the pain followed, searing his left side. He looked down to the see the blade nearly to its hilt in the side of his cuirass. He stepped back, the only thing that saved him and the blade exited straight away. He looked at the wound, his sword still in his right hand, his left touching the blood that was spreading down his left thigh. He frowned and fell to his knees, pain finally registering.

"Cut the banner, Bale." She swiftly carried out her master's order, and John could hear the flutter of the fabric as it caught on the wind and was carried over the parapet and field. A shout of victory from the other side of the wall went up and the sound of steel clashing grew louder.

"Now white knight, it is your time." John looked at the tip of the saber; his own blood stained it. Then a shadow fell between them and he fell onto his back; flakes of snow drifted down and blurred his vision.

Surik Shadowlord, Master of the Shades, stepped in front of his fallen friend and brandished his sorcerous blade. Alaric scoffed and lunged. Back and forth, they dueled, neither gaining the advantage. The sounds of the battle grew distant, and Surik could feel perspiration build in the chill air.

"You don't think you can beat me, do you Alaric?" he asked as he parried a blow to the side and lunged. The blade narrowly missed the Merchant of Chez.

"I am a Blade Master as well, Surik, I have fought many." He stepped forward, dancing over a piece of toppled battlement. He managed to get slightly behind Surik, but only caught the man's cloak with the tip of his saber. Surik smiled and spun, cleaving through the air where Dirkajian had stood. Surik sidestepped and lunged again, pushing his opponent back to where John was laying, his blood pooling out around him, freezing to the granite in the icy air. In character, Surik spat with contempt.

"Blade Master, what's that? You learned to fight in some school so you could duel better. You are nothing Alaric. Soon my sword will drink your blood and send your soul to hell."

"Such bravado, Shadowlord, it will not stay the inevitable." Alaric's sword glanced off the shoulder spike of Surik's armor.

"You don't expect Duran to just let you live?" he asked. He jerked back as Alaric's blade nicked his armor again.

"I am under contract; he will oblige what was struck between me and Kryall, and for this city."

"Kryall, what snake is this?"

"Not to worry Shadowlord, soon you will be too dead to care." Alaric leapt forward the blade coming straight away, but instead of Joe parrying

481

the saber he let it slide between his left arm and torso. It brought the Chez face to face with Joe, who smiled.

"I don't think so."

Alaric realized his mistake and tried to pull back, but he overstepped his withdrawal and slipped on the blood-soaked stones. He jerked himself upright and watched Surik's descending sword. He tried to bring his own blade up to parry, but only managed to twist the hilt up. Too late he beheld the flash of sparks as Surik's blade cleaved through his, then through his arm, then into his shoulder and down through his chest and across to his hip, and then into the free air again. Blood sprayed everywhere for a moment, then the Shadowlord turned to his fallen friend.

"That was easy," he muttered. "Reos, to me! Gaj, Polwin, to me!" he shouted as he knelt next to John. Gabrielle was there, staunching the blood with her cloak.

"No!" a shout from behind and Joe turned in time to see Bale running at him with a sword drawn. Her assault was stopped in mid-stride as Reos casually shoved her from the wall into the pike men who stood below.

John gasped in pain and forced his eyes open. He grasped Gabrielle's hand tightly.

"Hold on buddy," Surik sheathed his blade. "Reos, fetch some horses. Talbot!" He looked to the tower and the fat merchant emerged, wide eyed. "Take Gabrielle to your ship, Gaj and Polwin will guard you; with their lives if need be." They saluted and Gabrielle began to protest.

"Don't start. Reos and I will take John to Skettes. Then we'll be to the ship." There was a boom, an explosion as more of the wall caught, and the gunpowder went up.

"Reos, order the retreat from the wall. Take the fight to the streets. The Legion knows to fall back to the ships." Soon the city would be aflame and Duran's army would be looting and killing in the very streets below.

He forced Gabrielle to stand. He handed her Alaric's sword. "You know how to use this? Good."

"Talbot! Take her, now!" The man nodded and took her from them. "Gaj, don't wait too long. If your chance to flee is lost then we have failed. Get the boat out of the harbor if you have to."

Gaj nodded and he and his brother were soon gone. Surik tossed John's broadsword to Reos and soon had the Lord Knight of Erie over his shoulder in a firefighter's carry. "Blow the reserves, then to the keep." Reos nodded, he twisted the handle on the special box Pelles had made and was satisfied to feel the ground rumble then hear the explosion as the hidden reserves of gunpowder blew. Cached beneath the fields, right under the encampment of Duran, they sent tons of dirt and shrapnel flying into the air. It was not a decisive blow to Duran and his army, but it would definitely cost them and slow them down. Surik smiled grimly as they made their way down to the streets.

Kelvin led a charge into the breach, only to fall back under the onslaught. His armor, once burnished to a shine was covered with gore, tarnished beyond hope. He saw Surik carrying John over his shoulder and signaled for his lieutenant to

483

bring up their horses. Men shouted and the clash of steel was deafening. Gaj and Polwin led Gabrielle and Talbot hurriedly down the avenue before the full onslaught of Duran's soldiers.

"Surik!" shouted Kelvin, "The Lord Knight, how bad?"

"I need to get him to Skettes!"

"Aye, we'll fight through if we have to." He gave a signal to his second and the men fell back and formed a wedge. Immediately Duran's troops filled the gap in the gate, and it seemed they would overwhelm the defenders. With a deafening crash, the remainder of the gate and wall fell inward, crushing the Guard of Oran. Silence took over as a cloud of dust filled the air.

"They will regroup soon. Our chance comes now." Kelvin pulled himself atop his steed, and Surik and Reos threw John over the saddle of another. Reos was up behind him, and Surik reined in his black war-horse. The men, about sixty all told, began to run quickly ahead, making sure the path to the Temple of Tarn was clear. Joe noted grimly that the wounded and dying stayed at the gate to cover their retreat.

The streets were clear. The people having long since boarded their shops and stores, had fled to the inner city days ago.

***

Duran's horse carefully maneuvered through the rubble of the front gate. The dead or dying littered the cobbled street, and several Guards of Oran picked over the bodies, checking for anything

484

they deemed of value. Finally, one found what was left of Alaric amid the fallen stones of the gate tower. Duran looked down from his mount with some contempt at the upper torso of the Guildmaster Merchant; there was a look of surprise frozen on his face.

"Well, Dirkajian, it seems our contract is void." He reined his horse around sharply. "Gorwin!"

"Milord?" The Captain of the Guard pulled off his helmet and wiped sweat from his brow. Steam rose from his head. He had a hard grim look about him.

"The city is yours, be judicious."

"Of course milord," he smiled darkly.

"To duty then!" He shouted to the Captain of this phalanx of the Guard of Oran. The large man nodded and snapped blood from his long sword as he did so; blood and mud covered his armor and now the snow that had begun to fall.

"Tell your men they may do as they want with those that remain. For all I care we can repopulate with the loyal citizens of the Conclaveum or maybe it will be a port for the ghosts that remain." His fist tightened on the reins as he watched as the Hand of Keth, Sir Chill, walk among the bodies; he used his *kris-voulge* as a walking stick, occasionally pushing aside a cloak or a shield to expose a face or a body.

"They have fled, Hand, you will not find their bodies here."

He looked at Duran though the eye slits of his hclm. His head throbbed where the scar was. "Then you must find them," he said distantly, "I must inform Myella." He turned and strode onto the flurry, back to where his courier beast waited in the wood.

Guardsmen had cleared the gate of rubble so soldiers could begin to file in. Those that had fought the hardest at the gate would rest. These men were relatively fresh, having not fought since the afternoon before. They marched in sharply, their pikes held aloft. Gorwin sheathed his sword and pulled out a map of the city.

He barked to his men. "You men, take the Temple of Tarn and bring it to the ground. Then secure the Temple of Oran, we will station there. Sergeant, order the rest of your men to go house by house, street by street, and bring all the men and boys of this city to the field north of the city. Take them there, have them dig their own graves and then kill them. Are we clear?"

"Aye." The men marched off.

A squad of old men guarded the doors to the Temple of Tarn. When they saw a contingent of soldiers running their way they grabbed their swords and prepared to fight. Then they saw Kelvin and the others and they stood down. The temple doors swung wide and Joe and Reos carried the Lord Knight inside. Kelvin dismounted more slowly.

"This city is lost," he called out. He looked to the small contingent of city guard and militia. He knew men were falling back to the docks and boarding ships that would take them to a point of rendezvous up the coast. He knew the number would barely fall into the thousands.

Inside the Temple, silence struck Surik as he lowered John to a pallet. They lay empty on the

486

floor, there were no wounded or dying, and the Preceptor, Javin Skettes, sat slumped on step of the dais.

"Preceptor," Surik said, somewhat out of breath. "John's been hurt."

Skettes looked up and struggled to his feet. He was exhausted by the healing he had been doing over the past several weeks.

"Where is everybody?" Surik asked.

"I had the clerics take them to the ships. I remained with the dying. Now, what happened to Sir John?"

"He took a saber through the side. He's exhausted and he's lost blood," Reos answered.

Skettes bent over him and removed the cuirass. He examined the wound in John's side. A two-inch entrance wound and one-inch exit wound. "Was the blade dirty?"

"No, Dirkajian hadn't been fighting."

"No vital organ seems to have suffered from the blow. He is most likely unconscious from fatigue." His brow creased and he pulled a blue clay-like substance from a pouch. He pressed some into each palm then pressed his palms to each open wound. John groaned out in pain, and to Surik it seemed static energy leapt over Skettes hands. When he pulled them away, John's wound was no longer open, but rather a red weal, like that of one healed for weeks.

"He lost much blood, for that I do not have the time or the strength. He will be weak for some time," said the Preceptor as he sat back and wiped his hands on a towel.

"We do not have time," Reos said as he looked over his shoulder.

"We lost the gate wall. I am sure the Guard of Oran is on its way. We must leave."

"Yes, we must. I feared they would destroy this Temple. I have already prepared it, when we leave the doors will be sealed, much like Ythrinny sealed the tomb of his beloved." The last was a whisper, yet Surik still wondered at it, unsure of what the cleric meant.

Their reverie was cut short as a shout from the vestibule interrupted them. Kelvin ducked his head through the door.

"Duran's men, not two blocks away, we must retreat to the docks, and quickly." Surik nodded and he and Reos lifted John between them. Skettes grabbed his staff and a bag and followed them. Once outside he turned to the Temple. As the men pulled John upon his horse, Preceptor Javin Skettes called something out in the High Tongue and slammed his staff into the marble flags. Suddenly all the crystal windows turned opaque and the massive wooden doors turned into white stone, forever sealed to the Guard of Oran."Preceptor," Reos motioned him to take his horse. He would make it on foot with the rest of his men.

They moved quickly down the street toward the docks. Now the snow had begun to fall more heavily, and seeing beyond two blocks was impossible, hindering their pursuit by Duran's soldiers. The streets were deserted; an eerie silence followed them, the snow muting the horse's hooves and the jangle of harness.

They were fortunate that most of them wore gray or white, for they saw the column of black clad soldiers ahead and had time to duck down a side street without notice. In the distance, they began to hear the screams of people.

Joe and Kelvin looked down the street. It was, for them, the only way to the docks and the ships.

"Now what?"

"Ah, this has us in a predicament, Shadowlord. I fear that by going to the Temple we have allowed the Guard to cut us off from the docks."

"The ships will leave, soon. The moment they see the Guard of Oran in the Wharf district they will sail, and we're stuck here."

"We are closest to the Northern Postern. But by now-"

"Wait a minute, the last time...Bill, er the Bard told me that when he and Tar'elah had to flee the city there was a culvert that exited under the wall. It was just east of the North gate."

"I know which one you speak of, we had it sealed with brick and mortar after he fled. The outside wall was camouflaged so we just posted a sentry during the siege."

"Well, if we can get to that, I can get the brick wall down," Joe smiled wryly as he hefted a sack of Mike's gunpowder.

Gaj and Polwin helped Gabrielle across the gangway and watched as Master Talbot walked expertly over and to the pilot's cabin. The merchant seemed at case on the boat, his ebullient demeanor on the land had disappeared the moment they boarded the ship. He barked an order and his men began pulling in lines and preparing for the sails to be let out as they pushed from the dock.

Gaj pushed his way past a sailor and went to the pilothouse where Talbot stood.

"We were to wait for the Shadowlord, or til the city was lost."

"It is lost," the merchant replied flatly. "I suggest you take Gabrielle below deck, to my cabin and wait there until we break from the harbor."

"But-" Gaj was cut off.

"Now, young lord."

Gaj backed out and turned to Polwin, shaking his head.

"We are to take Gabrielle below decks, to safety. His cabin is aft."

As they walked aft, the ship pushed away from the dock and the foresail let out, catching a slight breeze, it pulled the ship out into the channel and the crew let out quarter sail to speed their progress. Gabrielle, numb, looked out over the rooftops of Paravel. Black smoke drifted up from sources too numerous to count.

"Sir John will get out, milady, be assured," Gaj said as he guided her to the quarterdeck where there was access to Talbot's cabin.

"Talbot wants us below, milady, no doubt in case it gets dangerous," Polwin opined. "He must get us through the blockade."

The merchant's master-at-arms opened the hatchway for them and as the ship yawed a bit, they stepped down into the cool darkness of the below deck. The master escorted them to the aft cabin. Ushered inside, Gabrielle turned to ask the master a question, but he door shut.

A bolt was thrown, hard, and a key turned.

Immediately Gaj threw himself at the thick door.

"He locked us in!" Polwin added his weight in with his brothers, but the door was too solid. It did not budge.

"It is of no avail," a mellifluous voice penetrated from the darkness of the cabin. A wick caught in a lamp and dimly illuminated a large figure who sat in the dark.

Gabrielle gasped and slid back between Gaj and Polwin. They instinctively drew their swords.

"Tsk, tsk, lads. I would not, were I you." The man stood, brushing the beams with his massive frame. He wore a black tabard with a gold threaded hand embroidered on it.

"I am Kryall," he moved forward and into the halo of dim light, illuminating his head.

Gabrielle screamed.

Chapter 34

The black ships of Masir Kasarian approached the port of Paravel, the bows striking flotsam soon told them a grim story that the snowstorm was hiding. Bill stood at the bow with Torec and Kasarian, watching as a mast would slide by followed by a body or two. Occasionally the thick snowfall would clear to reveal pillars of black smoke rising from the shore. The ship master ordered the sails reefed and that was when a shout arose from the lookout high atop the mainsail.

"Aft, Master! Three ships astern!"

"Damn!" Masir raced aft, Bill and Torec following. There, about two hundred your due East were three *felucca*. A quick look identified them as armed and rigged.

"We seem to be caught, Bard William."

Chapter 35

Dawn found the Black Guard of the Wall preparing to quit Narn-toc in the Inner Courtyard of Ythrinny's Keep. Men milled about, gathering the tack and saddles of their horses, footman lumbered under the weight of their packs and others made sure their stores were enough and proper to get them back to Helm in the encroaching winter weather.

Engulfed in a sea of black tunic and armor, Mike stood out like a sore thumb. He was not only apprehensive about allying himself with these men, but he wondered if Mrick would find time to stab him in the back in the middle of the night.

Then there was Adon.

He had calmly stated that he indeed was Myella's brother. In the brief time they had spoken, after they had obtained the *Book of the Dead*, Mike had learned that it was not the Conclaveum that was the enemy, but rather Myella, who was in league with Oran. Those were the forces, which brought the outlanders to this world. Adon had assured him that if Myella did not have the greed and lust for power that she did, the Conclaveum would have been happy to leave the south be and deal with the problems on its northern border. Adon had said that Myella, in the belief that she was uniting all the lands, was slowly destroying that which she sought to rule; she was tearing it down the middle. Not only had she betrayed the Conclaveum by her act of patricide, but also she had betrayed her humanity by giving herself to Oran.

493

Adon broke from his reverie as Commander Boern approached with the clothing they were to wear.

"We lost a patrol of twelve in the first week of our garrison here. We have their clothes and their horses. I can put Lord Michael, you Lord Adon, Mrick and some of your men on horse. The others will have to be within the ranks of the foot soldiers. They will blend in more easily."

"That is as it must be then," Adon said, taking the clothing from the veteran. Mike looked at the livery of the guardsman. It carried the symbol of the Wall: a sunburst over a crenellated tower.

"I hope this fits," he said as he shook his head. What he truly longed for at this moment was the hot drag of a cigarette.

As Mike began to pull the tunic over his own clothing, Mrick walked up to Adon. He addressed his patron, pointedly ignoring the outlander.

"Kale and two other men are missing. The guard at the gate said they stepped out for fresh air not ten minutes ago, when next he looked they were gone!"

"Fools," Adon hissed as he looked toward the gate. There were at least two hundred men in the courtyard, some mounting up, others falling into columns. They would be moving out in the next few minutes. Barj came running up; he was out of breath from searching the grounds of the keep.

"Jasdi says they were talking last night about Mrick throwing in with Lord Michael and the Black Guard; said some things about him betraying the memory of Trevor and got some of the men spooked." He looked at Michael who just raised his eyebrow. "My guess is that they snuck out of the Keep and are just trying to get out of the city on their own."

"Aye, I agree," Mrick said, but his expression was sour.

"Those fools will be luckily if they find their way out of the city before nightfall." Adon looked around and then just sighed.

"Do you wish to go after them, Mrick?"

"No, Adon, I do not. Kale has always been trouble. Let him find his own way."

Adon nodded and then motioned for them to move along. The gates to the inner courtyard were opening and the Black Guard was exiting the keep. "Then mount up."

Soon they were upon their steeds, trying to blend in behind the other mounted cavalry. Adon rode alongside Michael, which was well behind Gythel Boern at the front of the column. Somewhere behind rode Mrick, Barj and the few others. Further back the column of footman, the wagoniers and the supply wains followed. Boern thought it ironic that they had arrived by ship left in this manner. The column was wending its way down a curved avenue long before the last man closed the gates to Ythrinny's Keep. For Commander Boern the long dark siege in this city had ended, but he was uncertain of what lay ahead.

It took them a full two hours before they came to the gate wall. There, atop the postern on the right and left of the gate stood men of the Guard of Oran. Like silent sentinels in the gray of the early morning, they watched the procession of departing troops, steam rising off their shoulders in the cold, watchful eyes hidden by dark helms. The sky was turning the color of salmon behind them; the sun would not break through the clouds this day.

Michael peered over the braided mane of his steed, the dark grey gatewall the only thing between them and the ascent to the Great Forest. Men in black armor, with crossbows aimed off hips skyward, seemed to watch them mockingly. Mike involuntarily shuddered. Soon the entire procession was through the circular gate and the heavy stone portal rolled shut.

Before them lay the raised causeway, flanked on either side by the low flat expanse of the Field of Blood and the levees that sheltered it from the sea's waters. The column of soldiers stretched out on the causeway, the Teeth of Narn rising in the distance through the mist. The men moved on in silence. Mike imagined it was like the dead walking off to judgment. The only sound was that of the horse's hooves and feet on gravel. Men's eyes were mostly downcast; it seemed that the spirit of Narn-toc was moving along with them. Perhaps that was the reason why none noticed the three crosses that stood atop the causeway.

Gythel Boern reined in sharply and the rest of his Guard halted almost instantly in their tracks. Immediately Adon saw the 'X' shaped crosses and three spread-eagle forms upon them. He spurred his horse to the front of the column, edging aside the other riders; Mike trailed behind wondering just what was going on. As Adon neared the front, he caught sight of the crucified men and frowned. He recognized the three men as Kale and his two friends.

496

Boern looked hard at Adon and then to Mike as his horse trotted up.

"Mrick's men, I presume. I think we are now in a poor position."

"What's up?" Mike asked as he looked at the three dead men. Ravens had already plucked out Kale's eyes and the other two men had been disemboweled so the carrion could feast more easily. It was a disgusting and frightening sight.

"I think that Myella knows that something is afoot." Mike nodded and pulled the visor down on the helm. It made him feel claustrophobic, but as long as it kept Myella from recognizing him, he would tolerate it.

"Well, if it's meant to be an ambush, where are they?" Adon asked. His horse danced nervously and its nostrils flared.

"There they are, My Lord." Boern pointed to the ascent and the Teeth of Narn that fringed the western edge of the Field of Blood. They moved out of the mist and into the depressed plain strewn with fossilized wood and smooth gravel; dark silhouettes in armor, with sword, spear and bow. Myella walked slowly down the causeway from the ascent, two guards trailing her and behind, having just alighted from a courier beast came a figure in black tabard and great helm; the ensign of the Hand of Keth upon his breast.

"Great, just great," Mike said as he watched men swarm down into the flood plain. Soon the west quarter of the Field of Blood was full of men looking up at the column of soldiers on the causeway. Myella walked to within a stone's throw of Gythel Boern, her dark minions right behind. The Hand remained in the rear.

"Commander, it seems we have a problem. These young men," she gestured to those crucified, "told me that my brother Adon is among you, that you harbor him and that he has my book." She shook her head, but smiled. "That is treason my lord and if so, there shall be a new sacrifice to Oran upon this field."

Adon trotted forward, his horse whinnying. "Dear sister, you are a fool to have aligned yourself with Oran. You must think us fools even more to believe that you ascended the throne of the Conclavator by wholly honest means. You have disbanded the White Guard; you seek to disband the Black. What *you* do betrays the Conclaveum!"

"Your reasoning has always been impeccable, brother. Yet, I think history will side with the victor and that will be me." She smoothed back her long brown hair, a very innocuous gesture and immediately her men snapped to a defensive position, arms ready.

"I want the book. I know you have it. The *Book of the Dead.*"

"Ah, and to think I would give it to you *before* you slaughter us? At the very least I should make you search through the bodies like the carrion you are."

"If need be I shall do that. Yet, if you give me the book Boern's men may take their leave; only you, he and the ones from Galfeon Yor will be required to stay."

"That is very kind of you, but unnecessary. We will be leaving with them and with the book."

"My brother, ever the optimist. I do miss your special touch. You have one minute to surrender yourself to me with the *Id'hia Om*."

"That's all we need," he muttered under his breath. He back-pedaled his horse into Boern's vicinity. He looked over his shoulder to Michael. "You see those flood gates along the dike? Four in all? Can you break open the southern while I work on the northern?" Mike nodded and pulled his staff from its sheath. He felt the invisible runes upon it, felt them change with his thoughts.

"Commander, when I give the word, your men will have to fight through. They must stay on the causeway." Boern nodded and motioned to his second, Mern. The man understood. Instantly he began to move back through the ranks, whispering to the men all the way.

Mike pictured the floodgates in his mind's eye, imagined the mechanism that controlled them. Yet, somehow it was all wrong, he did not know what technology controlled the gates, was it gears? Was it levers? Or magic? It was frustrating, but then the power within the staff gave him some insight into his predicament. He could not possibly know the mechanism of the floodgates and neither did Adon. They only knew that the floodgates must be removed. He would concentrate on that.

Blue power began to surge off the staff and immediately it began to whine and vibrate. Something was amiss. He looked up sharply to see Myella dancing to the right, the sword on her hip vibrating and whining, but also glowing the antithetical red.

"Damn!" He heard Adon say. "She has a *Kris-blade!*" He wheeled his horse around and drew his own blade, blue *aether* bled off it and melded with the early morning mist. "NOW!" he shouted to Boern and instantly his men surged forward.

Mike concentrated. He did not have the luxury of time to formulate a complex pattern, what he did have time for was to visualize the water coming in and then channel the energy into the staff. What he got was not what he intended; rather it was as if the staff spun the spell on its own, as with the Keth atop the tower near Ythrinny's Keep.

To the north, the floodgates opened and water began to pour in ever so slowly.

The dike wall to the south, the entire levee that held the seawater at bay, was gone. Vanished. Water rushed inward like a tidal wave, sweeping toward the causeway. Men heard the rumbling, horses bolted and an eight-foot wall of water spread across the Field of Blood.

Myella's troops were in disarray. The water was upon them from the south before they could react. The horses toppled, sweeping men off their feet, pulling them under with the weight of their armor. The Guard of Oran that were on the north flood plain panicked and immediately began to try to scramble up the banks of the causeway. The swords and spears of the Black Guard of the Wall met them, where they were slaughtered.

Gythel Boern charged ahead and was upon Myella and her guards before they could draw their weapons. He drove his sword through the visor of the first and the man spun off the causeway and into the churning, debris filled water. Myella grabbed at

500

her sword, only to be pushed over by a charging horse. Instantly the other guard struck and killed one of Boern's, but another in turn killed him. Immediately a fray broke out on the wide causeway as Black Guard mixed with the Guard of Oran. Mrick charged forward and drew his sword, *Baxel's Bane*.

The Hand of Keth looked up sharply.

Adon shouted for them to move forward. Soon the circular gate would roll back and more men stationed within the walls would sally forth. They needed to move up the ascent and disappear into the Great Forest.

Michael struck out with his staff, catching a man in the chin and spinning him around. It looked as though three quarters of Myella's Guard were lost in the onrush of water, which now lapped across the causeway. Men splashed forward, slowed by the water and mud and the mounted Black Guard easily struck them down. Myella climbed to her feet, dazed. The Hand of Keth raised his *Kris-voulge* to deflect a blow and then fired off a spike into the crowd. That one blow felled four men, but soon he would be overwhelmed. He pulled Myella back toward the courier beast.

Mrick rushed on, hacking back and forth. Finally, he was upon Myella and the Hand. He swung his sword around hard and it was partially blocked. It glanced upon the Hand's great helm, striking a bell tone. The sword shivered in his hand and the Helm split in two.

Mrick looked at a dead man and almost fell from the mount.

Chill stared up at him, momentary confusion in his eyes.

Mike looked across the causeway, disbelieving.

Mrick's horse reared, almost throwing him and the Hand, Chill, grabbed Myella and threw her over the horned saddle of the courier beast. With a smooth leap he was in the saddle and with two long strides, powerful backswept wings, the courier beast was aloft and gliding over the water to the north.

The remaining Guard of Oran broke off the attack, some even fleeing toward the city. Their ambush turned back upon them. Boern quickly ordered his men forward at a fast trot; the ascent lay before them.

Some hours later, as the ascent lay behind and the Great Forest engulfed them with its nearly bare trees and loamy earth, they tended their wounds. Guards carefully watched the coast road from all directions, ever mindful of the Teeth of Narn and Narn-toc that lay to the east. Midday brought the white disk of the sun low to the north and what little warmth there was would not last. Mike sat on a log, his staff across his knees, a pipe hanging from his mouth. His eyes were haunted, as if he had seen a ghost.

I have seen a ghost, he mused. Chill was dead, or should be. Now he was fighting on the other side. Nothing seemed to make sense anymore.

"Your skills are more than I thought. You saved us by teleporting the dike. Tell me, where did you teleport the stones, to the sea?"

"I don't know. I just visualized them gone and they were."

502

Adon frowned, but left the big man alone. There would be time enough for questions later.

Mike stared out over the cliffs and among the Teeth of Narn, the great stones that sat in the sea and pushed their way skyward. It was so much like the time in Paravel, when he came to this place in the aether *world* and met the *Daemon*. Things were spinning out of control.

Myella watched from a great height, the courier beast circling high above the debacle at Narn-toc's Field of Blood.

She clung tightly to the Hand of Keth as the serpentine beast wove and dipped with the air currents. Sir Chill the Cold looked over his shoulder at the Conclavatrix, smiled bitterly at the look on her face, and then prodded the courier beast to swing around, back to Narn-toc.

"What are you doing!" she snapped. The Black Guard had made it up the ascent and was dispersing into the Great Forest. At this height and distance and on the courier, they could follow the Guard at a discreet distance and report on their movements. Then she could have Duran intercept and destroy them. Now this *Hand* would not listen to her.

He just nodded and kicked the flanks of the beast, urging it onward. As they neared the walls of the city, a hideous howling filled her senses, penetrating the deafening flow of air. She shook his shoulders, but he just ignored her as they speared toward the city. Ahead was Untheran's Palace. It was then she caught sight of the rubble from the dike-wall falling from the heavens into the rent open capitol of the Seat. She was stunned at the power that would move so much earth and cast it

503

that far into the sky. Chill pointed to it, mute, but the smirk still on his face. She was sure Adon did not have the skill or the knowledge, yet somehow he or *someone else* had achieved the feat.

Chill circled the rent dome of the Seat and they watched as the stream of rubble cascaded down. It seemed endless, but then the last pieces of rock finally fell to the earth; the unholy screaming, however, did not end. It persisted. It was then that Myella did the casting, to see what type of magic was used.

She gasped at the vision of the *aether* that she beheld. Pure Spiritual Sorcery, that which is of Tarn, cascaded about the grey; a prismatic rainbow. Moreover, there, within the superimposed reality, was the signature of the wizard that had worked the magic. It was not the brilliant blue of her brother Adon, or even the malignant green of a subject of Oran. It was an alien hue, like the golden hue of the Krim. It was the silver aura of the outlander's, or more accurately the *Outworlders*.

Fury etched her features as she spun around in the wide saddle, looking back through the Teeth of Narn to the Great Forest. One of the outlanders was among them.

"Follow them, damn you, follow them!"

"I am already damned, my liege." His dull brown hair whipped back revealing the livid scar on his forehead. It throbbed and a weal of blood coursed down his face where Mrick's sword had grazed him after striking his helm. He prodded the courier beast once more, this time directing it toward a tower at the edge of the break-wall, overlooking the harbor.

504

There, atop the beacon tower sat the *Daemon*, its snake-like torso wrapped around the pinnacle. Wings folded down around double shoulders, four arms crossed, it looked up to her from the blackness of its being, feral red eyes aglow.

I have awaited you, it hissed, screeched into her mind; that same agonized scream that accompanied the burying of Untheran's Seat.

The courier beast shied away from the tower, but the Hand wrested it back, slowly circling the evil minion of Oran. Myella looked to the powerful creature, her long hair flowing in the wind, *its* voice screaming in her head.

You have seen? Yes, upon the wind, the aether breathes silver light. It is that you seek, that you fail to find. Look upon the insurgents work. It has not been so since the raising of the Wall.

"Who, who did this?" She screamed over the wind. She held onto Chill with one hand while the other pressed against her stomach, trying to suppress the upwelling vomit.

Not the bearer of the Saints Soul, or he who walks among the Shadows. The mage among them, though he knows it not.

"The alchemist," she hissed. A harsh, grating laugh filled the twilight and the *Daemon* spread all four taloned arms, encompassing the city and the approaching night.

This was Oran's, now tainted. You are the one. For Oran to walk, for your eternal life, for all this, Home Gate must be opened. Sunder the Six, render the Saints Soul. You have been charged.

Fail Oran this, and Untheran's fate you shall suffer.

The *Daemon* sprang from the tower, its powerful lower body shearing the stonework away. It seemed to be springing directly toward her and the mount, but before it reached her, the air shimmered, phased, and it was gone.

Sir Chill the Damned smiled no more. Now pain crossed his features and he reined in the courier, its scales shimmering in the failing light. The primal creature banked and swept on toward the Great Forest. The Hand looked back at his liege for direction.

"Take me to Duran's army. Take me to Paravel. The key is the Lord Knight. I will not be as gentle as I was the last time!"

Epilogue

In the Old City of Narn-toc, in Untheran's once beloved Seat, with capitol long since sundered by the *Daemon*, stones and rubble rained down through the rent in the dome. The long stream of rock seemed to be falling from the heavens, the tons of stone beginning to fill the vast chamber. Ere night would fall, the Seat of Untheran would be buried and the chamber forever sealed to the outside world and the Gate beneath no longer accessible. Now a *Dead Gate*.

The *Daemon* screamed and it was the sound of hell.

Also by J.J. Eliyas

From Fiction4All / Double Dragon
www.doubledragonbooks.com

The Perilous Gate

Just beyond your fingertips is another world. It's in the whisper of the wind, the sigh of the trees. It's the shadow in the mirror or the fleeting glance of something out of the corner of your eye.